PRAISE FOR *CH*

"A perceptive and gripping tale of race and family... While Woodstone profoundly addresses modern African American struggles, the tale is equally dynamic in the supernatural and historical genres."

— *Kirkus Reviews*

"An exceptional story that will place you in the heart and mind of each of the amazing characters...Prepare to be moved by a unique story that delves deep into the historical abuse of a people but has dynamic pockets of excitement, heartbreak, and the paranormal. Highly recommended."

— *Lesley Jones, International best-selling author*

"★★★★★ The beauty of Woodstone's prose evokes the intensity and allegorical journey that is usually reserved for literary fiction. The writing is simultaneously gorgeous, terrifying, and hopeful. Amara and Van Owen may be fictional, but the subjugation of race still screams in the face of civil liberties even today, making Woodstone's work more poignant than ever."

— *Readers' Favorite*

"R.B. Woodstone has crafted a thoughtful, time-spanning novel that touches on family, oppression, and otherness in *Chains of Time*... the dramatic blend of history, tragedy, and magic pulls a reader in from the very start."

— *Self-Publishing Review*

"With captivating characters on a fulfilling magical journey, *Chains of Time* is a strong novel that does not disappoint."

— *IndependentBookReview.com*

"Though the work is rooted in fantasy and magical realism, there's a highly realistic quality to the historical content and the experience of Africans in the tragedy of the slave trade. Young adult and adult readers alike can appreciate the sophistication of ideas, which are layered into a powerful storyline that blends present and past exceedingly well."

— *K.C. Finn, USA Today best-selling author & Chanticleer Book Award winner*

"A poignant tale of a people betrayed by themselves and the inhumanity of the white slavers in African lands. The author does an impeccable job in exploring themes of family, African tradition, and slavery... *Chains of Time* is filled with emotionally rich scenes... An engrossing story that will keep the reader awake throughout the night. ★★★★★"

— *Readers' Favorite*

CHAINS OF TIME

R.B. WOODSTONE

888888829b1f3f7cbc0fabd3bdae0441a5f88c9dcdb3f5d75c81bcf3cf28dd14bdab31c8888888

For MD

And now the storm-blast came, and he
Was tyrannous and strong:
He struck with his o'ertaking wings,
And chased us south along.

— Samuel Taylor Coleridge

PART I

The Waking

ONE

I know what's going to happen.

I can see the ship though it has not yet arrived. It cuts through our waters so savagely, white cloth suspended from ropes, enslaving the wind and forcing it to push the vessel toward our shores. I can see Van Owen on the deck. He is taller than the others. Tall and gaunt, ghostly white. All sinew and vein. The others are bearded and filthy and rank, yet he is clean, his face hairless, his garments bright and unblemished. He is holding something to his eye—a long black pipe with a piece of curved glass at the end. He points it toward our land and gazes through it as if he can see everything though he is still so far away. As if he can see me staring back at him. I almost turn away, but he is not here. Not yet. This is only a vision—my first one. He is not even near.

He is the first one off the ship. The others follow him—twenty of them, thirty, maybe more—into tiny boats that are lowered from the side of the large one. The men carry weapons. Nets, sabers, whips. The tools for hunting animals. Strange, angry objects hang from their hips. Somehow, I know what these things are for—to put holes in human flesh. They are called guns. Van Owen puts his hand to his hip and holds his gun steady as he steps from one of the smaller boats into the ocean. The water rises almost to his knees, much higher than he had expected. He turns back, berating his men silently with a scowl. They cower in apology. They treat him as our people treat my father. Like a king.

Soon there will be other kings here—other kings and their followers—for today is the day of my wedding ceremony. I lie awake at sunrise, waiting for my cousins to bring me libation and face paints and jewelry, for my mother to come with the blessing, for my father to tell me again of the importance of the day—how this marriage will unite two warring peoples, bringing peace where there has been only conflict for generations, how the child of my betrothed and me will be blessed, the firstborn of a new family. My father always speaks with such certainty of my child's future, though the child has not yet been conceived and though my husband and I have not even met.

My betrothed is Kwame—son of Berantu, the leader of the Merlante people. Three days ago, father and son came here for the making of the contract. They were not what I had imagined. My father is such a large man, taller and stronger than any man in our village. I assumed that all kings must be like him, but Berantu and Kwame were barely taller than I. Yet they walked with such confidence. They came alone, without guards or weapons. My father met them by the adansonia tree that marks the entrance to our village and then led them to the spirit cave. Kwame waited outside while the two kings ventured within, neither one looking back. My father and Berantu remained in there for so long. Or maybe it only seemed long to all of us who watched and waited from afar. Then there was a flash of fire from the mouth of the cave and stout voices and the sound of laughter, and the two kings exited the cave, all smiles and mirth. Kwame turned toward me, and, for a moment, our eyes met. My mother tugged on my arm and told me not to look upon him—that he and I were not yet joined and must observe custom. Berantu scolded Kwame too, pulling him away so fast, warning of curses brought upon those who loved before their ceremonies.

I remember my father's hand on my shoulder as we walked the silt path back to our home. "Now our peoples will be one," he told me. "Now we can face the might of Glele, who picks away at both of our clans. Now we will stand strong."

But he was wrong. There will be no unified clan to face the tyrant Glele. There will be no child. And there will be no marriage. For the slavers have come. Van Owen has come.

If I were to stare out at the ocean now, past even the sun, I might see it—the faint shadow of a ship on the horizon, and the silhouette of a man who will haunt my family forever.

I know what's going to happen.

TWO

Terry stopped at the foot of the staircase when he heard the commotion above.

"She's *my* daughter," shouted his father. "She's *my* daughter, and I say she shouldn't spend all her time hiding away in some dark room with her grandmother. Now open this damn door, Willa!"

Without a thought, Terry bounded up the stairs and planted himself between his father and the closed door. "Pop," he barely mustered, "leave them alone. They're just..."

"Move out of the way," said his father through a clenched jaw. Carl Kelly was looking older. His hair had turned gray years ago—shortly after Terry's mother died—but now the beard was graying, and even his deep brown skin had taken on a gray tint. His eyes were puffy. He looked haggard. Angry, too. He always looked angry. And his anger made Terry angry.

"No," said Terry. At fifteen, he still needed to fill out, but he stood an inch taller than his father. It didn't matter.

With a shot of his elbow, Carl sent his son sprawling across the landing. Then he turned back to the door and raised both arms as if he might break it down. But the door slid open, and Regina leaned out and stared up at her father. She was small for an eleven year-old and rail-thin. Her hair was parted down the middle into two short braids that swung almost in unison when she moved her head, making her appear only eight or nine.

Her father's anger seemed to fade when he met Regina's gaze. Her eyes were huge, almost too large for her face, giving her an ethereal quality. And her skin tone, light brown and flawless, mimicked her mother's. Sighing, he put his hand on the top of her head and told her in a softer tone, "Go on now. Get yourself ready for school."

Regina reached down to help Terry up, but he nodded her off and rose on his own. His shoulder hurt but not as much as his pride. He glanced back toward his father, eager for some sign of remorse, but the man was focused again on the door to his mother-in-law's room. "You know, Willa, it's just not right..." he started, but the door slammed before he could finish.

"Carl," came the old woman's voice, robust but serene through the closed door, "the child doesn't have a mother. What isn't *right* is you trying to keep her away from her grandmother."

Terry almost smiled at his grandmother's knack for winning an argument without even raising her voice. She then capped her victory by playing a bouncy ragtime piano melody that spilled through the slender door, taunting Carl. His jaw clenched, and his mustache and beard closed in around his mouth. "How is it," asked Carl, "that you can get yourself out of bed to play that piano and slam a door on me, but you're too frail to come out of that room and speak with me face to face?"

"Don't you have to get those kids to school, Carl?" she asked with a bored weariness. "Today's the first day."

He checked his watch and seemed to get only more infuriated. He put his hand on the doorknob and started to turn it as if he might enter her room, but the lock clicked in place from inside, even as the piano music continued. His shoulders tensed, and he grunted, "Damn it, Willa. I wasn't going to come in."

"Oh, I know that, Carl. I just wanted you to know that you

couldn't—even if you wanted to."

"Wasting my time on you," he muttered under his breath as he stomped down the stairs. "Time for school," he added in Terry's direction.

"I'm ready," said Terry as he sat down on the living room sofa and ran a pick through his short afro.

"You're ready?" his father barked from the archway into the living room. He looked down at his gangly son as if sickened by the sight of him. "Good. Then you can make your sister's lunch."

"I already did," said Terry, pointing at two brown paper bags at his feet.

His father's response was unintelligible, more an acknowledgement that he had heard his son speak than recognition of what Terry had said.

"You're welcome," Terry added, just loud enough for his father to hear.

"You don't need me to thank you for doing what you ought to be doing."

"Maybe I don't *need* it, but it might be nice if I *got* it sometime anyway."

But his father was already heading down the hall to collect his jacket. His blue overalls and Stilson Stable cap disappeared behind the closet door, the wad of keys jingling from his belt.

"Whatever," Terry groaned more loudly as he pulled a book from his bag and flipped to the chapter where he'd left off.

"That's right—*whatever*," his father called back. "Whatever I say goes. So don't talk back to me." He craned his neck far enough into the hallway to glare at his son, daring a response. Terry just moved his head from side to side, fixing his eyes on the page. "That's right," said his father. "You just keep your nose in that book. You don't want any of this."

Terry closed his eyes for a moment and breathed in. *Don't be like him,* he thought to himself, and he began to calm down. But then he remembered the dream that had come to him again, the same dream he'd had so many times for the last two years: the slave ship closing in on Africa; the girl watching from the shore; the pale captain on the deck.

"Did Jerome take the pickup?" his father interrupted with a gruffness as if he'd asked the question several times.

"Yes. And when was the last time *Jerome* ever made anybody's lunch?"

"Your brother's got his own responsibilities."

"Football's not a responsibility. It's a game. I don't know why...." But Regina appeared at Terry's side, tugging on his arm, her expression pleading him to stop arguing. He paused, eager to continue, but he knew Regina was right. He sighed and told her, "Okay, I'll stop."

Their father was still rambling on, though. He was back in the living room, flicking off the lights and looking around for anything else he might need. "School hasn't even started, but Jerome's been up for practice at 5:00 AM six days a week for the last three weeks. You work a few hours a day at that market, and you think you get to complain about making a goddamned lunch for your sister...?"

"Hey, I stopped already, okay?" Terry snapped. "And I wasn't complaining about making lunch. Just about not ever being noticed for anything I..."

"Just get out to the car." Their father's tone signified that his was the final word, so Terry and Regina headed for the door.

The early morning Harlem streets were full of children for the first time since June, and Terry marveled at how all of them seemed so calm on the first day of school. He wanted to feel that calm too. He wondered if things would be different this year. Would the other kids treat him any better? Even more important—would they treat Regina better? Terry was always worried about Regina.

As if in response, Regina tapped his arm and offered a half-smile. She didn't speak—she hadn't spoken in two years—but Terry could hear her question in his mind, her voice as full as if she were speaking aloud. He wished he had the ability to answer her telepathically, but his only special gift seemed to be the ability to hear her.

"I doubt it," he answered her as she eased into the front passenger seat of the faded Ford Mustang. The car was almost fifty years old and looked its age.

"You doubt what?" asked their father, suddenly just a step behind them.

"Nothing." Terry climbed into the seat behind Regina and slammed the door hard.

In the driver's seat, Carl Kelly spun his head until his brown eyes caught up with Terry's green ones. The same color as his mother's. "You doubt what?" he repeated.

Terry enunciated each syllable as he spoke. "I doubt you'll let me drive either of the cars next year."

"What's next year?"

"When I'm sixteen."

His father started the engine. "I gave Jerome the pickup when he turned sixteen because he'd earned it. When you start earning your place around here, then we can talk about what you get."

"See," Terry said, tapping one of his sister's braids. "Like I told you, I don't even exist—just like..." But Regina spun her head and glared, and Terry knew better than to finish that sentence.

The ride to school was quick and quiet. Their father pulled the car in front of the main entrance to Harlem Community School, where students milled about on the sidewalk, sat on the steps, reclined against parked cars and school buses. Most of the kids were clustered in groups of three or more—talking, joking, laughing.

There were police, too. HCS was one of the more respected public schools in Harlem, but Harlem was still Harlem. One squad car sat sentry across the street; another circled the neighborhood throughout the day. "You'll be safe here," their father had told them when they moved from Saratoga to New York City. "You'll all be together," for HCS was both a high school and a middle school.

But Terry and Regina were alone together. The other students all seemed to have someone to greet them—handshake rituals, hugs, shouts. Nobody greeted Terry and Regina. They walked through the throngs of teens and preteens as if invisible.

"Be careful," their father called out after them.

Regina turned and waved. Terry didn't.

After a quick stop in the middle school to drop off Regina, Terry raced out the athletic exit to get to the football field before practice was over. The security guard almost stopped him before recognizing him as "Jerome Kelly's little brother." Terry wondered if anyone would ever know him just for being Terry Kelly.

The football field was really just twelve cones in a rectangular formation across a frayed baseball diamond. The players were filthy, but that was to be expected; they were practicing on a dirt field on the morning after a rainstorm. Their practice outfits—uniforms culled together from disparate team sports—were stained brown with mud and age. Jerome was easy to spot, though; he was the tallest boy on the field and the only one who wasn't out of breath. His offensive line squad moved into a huddle, most of them weary as they bent forward. But Jerome stood upright, a tower leaning in only at the last instant to hear the play.

The boys jerked from the huddle at the sound of Coach Dodge's whistle, and Jerome moved into position at center, just a few feet in front of the quarterback, Nate Percy. Jerome's gait was graceful, particularly for such a large boy. Even as he crouched into formation, he remained composed, almost too refined for football.

At Nate's command, Jerome snapped the ball to him and then backed up, shadowing the quarterback, protecting him. When both defensive tackles broke through the line, Jerome was prepared. He leaned forward, his arms outstretched, and caught the rushing defenders, one in each arm. The three boys seemed almost frozen in time.

Don't hug them, Jerome, Terry wanted to shout from his vantage point beneath a tree. *Take them down.*

Jerome was bigger and stronger than both rushers. He needed only to fall forward and envelope them, and the quarterback would have an open field for running or passing. But Jerome hesitated, as if just stopping them were enough. One of the rushers seemed to sense Jerome's hesitancy; he wriggled under Jerome's arm and glided away. Within seconds, the boy had sacked the quarterback and the play was over. Coach Dodge shrugged as he blew the whistle, ending practice.

Jerome was helping with the cleanup—scooping up the rubber cones and dropping them into the coach's cart—when Terry called out to him. When Jerome's head turned, Terry pointed to his watch and Jerome nodded.

He waved to his teammates and trotted away into the bushes.

"Where are you off to, Jerome?" asked Coach Dodge.

"Taking a piss," Jerome answered quickly. Then he slipped behind the foliage and joined Terry at the fence that ran parallel to the field. "You see him yet," he asked.

"No," Terry answered. He looked at his watch again. They would need to get back to school soon for first period.

They waited in silence until Jerome asked, "How was Pop this morning?"

"What do you think?" Terry sighed. "Snapping at Willa. Snapping at me. Same as ever."

Jerome nodded. "Sorry."

After another minute, a ragged figure ambled through the trees and approached the fence. His build suggested he was in his early twenties, but his unshaven face and inset eyes told another story. He wore a torn black jean jacket and blue jeans that hung almost around his thighs. Sitting atop his matted afro was a New York Yankees cap that cast a shadow over his eyes. Terry was glad that Warren's eyes were hidden. He had trouble looking his oldest brother in the eye these days.

"Hey, little bros," said Warren in a gravelly voice. I caught your act there on the field, J."

"You had those two rushers," he smiled, "until you didn't."

Jerome removed his helmet. His hair was buzzed short, silhouetting his forehead in a square pattern that made him look simple, which he wasn't.

"Good thing Dad didn't see that play," Warren continued as if trying to fill the air. He scrunched his mouth into a scowl and mimicked Carl's voice. "You can't be weak! This is no game."

Jerome nodded and sighed. "Dad is...what he is."

Jerome and Terry stood less than a foot apart from Warren with the chain-link fence between them, yet their eyes never met his. Finally, Jerome broke the silence. "Do you have to dress like that, Warren? Especially around here. You look like..." He stopped.

"You can finish," said Warren. "I know I look like a thug."

Jerome seemed to cringe at the word and hung his head. "I...I'm..."

Warren saved him from having to apologize. "So, do you have...anything...?" Jerome spoke in a low, defeated tone.

"Yeah, We've got something." He knelt to the ground and unrolled one of his socks, revealing several bills wrapped around his ankle. He counted fifty dollars. Then he stood and passed the bills through the fence.

Warren's face sagged as he took the money and rushed it into his pants pocket. He breathed in deeply through his nose and coughed as if suffering from a bad cold. "All right. I...uh... I...you know...Thanks..."

"Whatever," said Jerome, already walking away. "Come on, Terry."

"It'll be okay," Warren called after them. "You'll see. I'm getting it together. It's all gonna be better."

"No, it won't," Jerome said, loud enough for only Terry to hear. "No, it won't."

THREE

As I am dressing for the wedding, I tell my mother of the vision. I tell her of the flood of images—the ship, the men who speak the strange language that I can understand, the boys on the field, the scenes that play before me almost as clear to me as she is. She listens, smiling, nodding, stroking my face while she paints it with the mixture of fruit nectars and ocean water. A stream of salt water and sweetness trickles down my cheek and onto my lips. I taste the paint and close my eyes, trying to lose myself in this moment with my mother, in these moments of preparation for the ritual. I promise myself that I will always remember the taste of the fruit paint and the touch of my mother's finger as she draws our family emblem on my cheek.

I try to believe her—that I am stricken with waking dreams brought upon me by the gods, who are testing my resolve to see if I am worthy of a princess's nuptials. Worthy of marrying the next king.

My cousins arrive. They are young and as giddy as I was only yesterday. I fight to focus on them and on my mother—to force the visions away. My mother takes my face in her palms and tells me, "Do not scare these girls. Keep those dreams to yourself."

"Maybe Father should know..."

"Amara, your father is readying our village for the ceremony. He does not have time for children's stories."

She will not believe me. I could tell her every detail, and it would not matter. Van Owen will still come, and nothing will stop him.

My cousins bear garments and libation. They embrace me, laughing. The youngest one, Daquimé, whispers in my ear: "Kwame is beautiful. All of the girls are envious."

I smile and try to see only what is tangible. I try to bury the apparitions that dance before me: the images of the strange gray city, of the young girl who does not speak, of her father whose anger is like armor, his sons—so different and so damaged, of ropes around me, of chains on my legs, of my face ravaged by age and loss, of places so unfamiliar, and yet I know them. Boston and Atlanta and Harlem.

"There has never been a ceremony such as this," Daquimé tells me. "With our peoples united, even Glele would not dream of sending his spirits here to steal away more of our people."

She is speaking of the disappearances. Many of our people have vanished in the last year—but never while they were in our village. They were off fishing or hunting or collecting herbs. But they did not return, and no one heard anything of them again. The legends have spread of our enemy Glele and his hold on the sprits that he has summoned demons to do his will, to weaken his foes, dragging our people off to be servants to his clan. But these were all myth. I had thought so before, but now I know it for certain. There is only one dark spirit allied with Glele: Van Owen.

He is there in almost every vision. Even when he is not there, he is there. I see myself older and different. I see other faces that age and change—Dara's, Rolanda's, Willa's. Yet Van Owen always remains the same. He does not age. He never grows old. He never changes.

My cousins finish dressing me and stare at me suddenly as if I am no longer the girl they have known all of their lives. Or maybe it is *they* who look different now to *me*. When my mother returns, they hurry away, turning back to wave before they run off to describe my garments to the other girls in our village. They are so proud. I am to become a woman, to fulfill my destiny as princess of my people. I try to cling to their excitement, to use it as an anchor to keep me from slipping into one of the myriad scenes that play in my mind, but everything is happening at once, and I can see all of it.

As my mother leads me by the hand from my hut and toward the village center, Van Owen and his men are lowering themselves into the smaller boat. On the coastline, a bluish light flashes. He glances at the strand but sees nothing. Perhaps it is the sun reflecting off our azure ocean, trying to blind him. They row shoreward and then wade through the knee-high waters and step onto our sands. My sands. My father's sands. My people's sands.

Then I see Glele. He is fat and pampered, decked in odd garments that are not of our land—more like those worn by Van Owen and his band. Glele smiles, his mouth extending broadly across his face. The smile of a tyrant and a traitor, betraying his kind, selling them into servitude. How can he do these things? Are we not one race? Are we not all Africans? Should we not stand together against those who would enslave us?

Glele wears the red headdress of his clan, but around his neck are jewels so shiny that they are ugly. He greets Van Owen as if they have known each other for years. They clasp hands. Van Owen forces a smile and then lets go and turns to clean his hands on a cloth. He wipes away Glele's touch before dropping the cloth in the surf. Then he sends two pale men back onto the rowboat for a wooden chest. They stumble through the water, hefting the heavy box onto the sand. Van Owen kneels and opens the lock and lifts the lid. The chest is full of jewels and coins. And tobacco.

"Glele is a fool," Van Owen whispers to one of his men. "The coins are worthless. Lustrous but valueless. Copper and tin. The jewels are mostly glass. And the tobacco is the lowest grade. I couldn't sell it anywhere."

How do I understand his language? How do I hear him at all? I am not there on the shore with them.

My mother is speaking to me still, but her face changes. Suddenly, she is Willa, scolding her own daughter—pleading with her not to run off with "that man." Then, just as quickly, she is my mother again. We are alone in the hut, but she is drowned out by visions of Glele, who is barking orders to his men. They scoop the jewel chest onto a latticework rope platform and begin the trek back to their village. Glele is jabbering on with another dark-skinned man—one dressed like Van Owen's men. His face is scarred. His head is hung low. Why is this man with Van Owen? He is brown like us. Why does he conspire with these white men? Why is he translating between Glele and Van Owen? Why is he helping them?

Glele points toward our village. He is speaking of the ceremony, of our two peoples—the Merlante and the Mkembro—which will soon be together. Unprepared. Vulnerable.

"He knows," I tell my mother, "about the wedding."

"Of course he knows. He has planned it."

"No, not Father," I say, but my words are meaningless to her. I wonder whether I am still speaking my language or whether I have lapsed into the other one—English.

"Your father will speak to you now." I already know what my father will say. His words will mix with Carl's and Jerome's and Willa's and Terry's, and I will have to fight to distinguish who is speaking and which time and place are mine. My father enters wearing the green headdress that has been passed down from chieftain to chieftain. He looms over me, and I stare upward, feeling like a child. His eyes, so deep-set and dark, have always made him seem special—powerful—able to keep our people safe. For our leader is the fiercest warrior of all, the most commanding of men. In my vision, though, my father is bleeding and bleeding. The blood won't stop.

"Now, there will be no more war," he tells me. "Because you, my daughter, will share your life with Kwame, and our clans will become one. We will build villages and shrines together, and we will fight together against Glele."

"No!" I scream. "Glele comes now with white men!"

"Glele?" my father says, confused, looking behind him.

"Yes, Father. Glele makes trade with white men, and he brings them here to slaughter us... to take us away..."

My father stares at me with a puzzled expression. "What are these words you speak? What language is this?"

No! I am speaking English! I try to force the words from my throat in my own language, but Van Owen slaps me in another time. I cannot feel the pain, but, instinctively, I touch my cheek. My hand is wet and red, but it is not blood. It is only fruit paint.

"Amara, why do you behave this way?" asks my father. His hands seem almost to glow as he reaches them toward my head. He takes my face in his hands, and, instantly, I feel safe. The visions stop, and I can feel only my father's strength. I wonder if it has all been a fantasy, simply the irrational daydreams of a girl who is about to marry, about to become a woman.

My father takes my hand and leads me from the hut. We walk through the village, past rows and rows of our people, smiling and stretching their hands toward us, overjoyed. The singing starts, followed soon by the drumming. I open my mouth, wondering if English will come out, but it is the song of my people that pours from my lips:

Mai Wa kmaro
Mai Wa kmaro
Dji mi sarro ti kee la ti na-arro

The dream language is gone. There is no ship with light-colored men and weapons. Glele is not on the outskirts of our village, leading evil to our gates. I am singing in the language of my people and walking with my father—toward the village center, toward my wedding. I smile and sing louder. I am at peace again. The day is joyous. As my father said, there will be no more war.

In the distance, I see Berantu and the Merlante people approaching, a parade of colors stretched across the yellow horizon. Kwame walks beside his father. He wears a purple sash, the color of royalty. He sees me but turns to his father, and I turn to mine.

"You can look now," my father tells me, squeezing my hand harder. "You may look upon your betrothed." Berantu must have told Kwame the same. He turns toward me as well. Our eyes meet. My cousin was right. Kwame *is* beautiful. His skin glows in the sunlight. His eyes are bright, and his smile is so lovely and peaceful. He is beaming at me. We will be happy. I know we will be happy.

The singing grows louder. Berantu's people form into seven lines, and they begin to sing. The tune is new to me, but the words are familiar. The melody mixes with the Mkembro song, the two meshing into one. I think about all the ways that our peoples will change and grow from the joining. We will be a new, stronger people. We will create our own customs and songs and stories and legends.

Ja dee tna-arrai
Tee rah see la-awai
Kai ma jee ha-anai
Sai-Ree tna-arrai

The two clans close in circles around us as we approach the elders. I recognize Sai-Ree, who is oldest of all of my Mkembro people. His headdress rises high above all others. Beside him is a Merlante elder. He is old as well but not as old as Sai-Ree. In unison, Sai-Ree and the Merlante elder each raise a hand high, and the singing stops.

The Merlante elder begins chanting, and Sai-Ree joins him. Sai-Ree is reciting the nuptial words of the Mkembro. I have been to many ceremonies, and his words are always the same. The Merlante elder's words are similar—almost identical—but chanted in a different order. I realize then that the Merlante were singing the same song that my people were—*Dji mi sarro ti kee la ti na-arro*—but the tune was different. Can it be that we share the same lineage? Generations ago, were we one people? If so, then this ceremony is fate—we are meant to be one. Kwame and I are meant to unite our clans.

As the chanting grows more intense, the Merlante elder turns to Berantu and nods. Berantu steps back, leaving Kwame alone. My father, still holding my hand, bends and kisses my forehead. He squeezes both my hands. My heart quickens, and I shut my eyes to push away the tears of joy that come rushing forth.

"To Kwame of the Merlante," my father announces, "I give my daughter, Amara of the Mkembro." He lets go of my hand, and the world turns dark.

For a moment, I am nowhere. Everything is black, as if I am floating in nighttime without land or sea or anything solid at all. There is no sound, no scent, no touch, no warm, no cold, no earth on which to stand. Then the visions start again. In an instant, I am in so many different times at once. The Merlante elder is taking Kwame's hand to bring it toward mine. Willa is shouting with her eyes closed. Terry is arguing with his father; Akins is pushing him to the floor. Van Owen is hacking at trees with a saber. Glele is celebrating over his chest of worthless gems. And Regina, like me, is opening her mouth to scream, but nothing is coming out.

My people—the Merlante and the Mkembro—start singing again. Sai-Ree takes my wrist to bring my hand toward Kwame's. I can almost feel Kwame's smile. He stares into my eyes, and I feel I have known him forever. But then his lips curl downward and his eyes flare in fear, fixed on something behind me. I hear the sound of sabers slashing through leaves, the sound of angry, foreign footsteps, and I know what Kwame has seen: the white men have arrived.

The visions swirl in my mind, and I fight to control them—to place them in in the correct sequence so that I can read them like a story. I try to focus on Kwame's eyes, to root myself in what is happening now. I try not to hear Willa playing the piano. I try not to see Terry and Jerome across the fence from Warren. I look up at Sai-Ree, who is about to join my hand with Kwame's, but then I hear the explosion from the pistol. The bullet flies. I hear myself scream as the Merlante elder topples backward and falls to the earth.

The sound of the gun echoes. For a moment, it is the only sound. Then, all at once, the screaming starts. Our people scatter in terror. The Merlante and Mkembro have come in peace; they have not brought weapons to a wedding. We cannot defend ourselves.

My father turns unarmed to face the invaders. I turn with him and see Van Owen for the first time.

FOUR

Terry was reading in the school library when the bell rang, jolting him from his only break in the day. He rechecked Regina's schedule. Her math class had just ended, and he'd promised to meet her outside the classroom so that they could go to lunch together. He was standing up when Regina's voice echoed in his mind.

"*Terry,*" she said, "*watch.*"

She called it *broadcasting*—using their telepathic link not just for communicating but for showing him what she was seeing. He was looking out through her eyes, experiencing the world as she did. If they were in the same room, Regina would sometimes try to offer a helpful broadcast. One time in the previous school year, Regina entered the gym while Terry was playing basketball in PE class. He was dribbling down the court for a layup, and Regina wanted to help by showing him that a defender was closing in on him from behind. She reached into his mind and sent him the view from her angle, but the 360-degree image—the combination of what Terry could see and what Regina was showing him—was so disorienting that Terry ran right past the basket and into a wall.

Today, Regina's broadcast stream wasn't so disorienting, but it was jarring. Terry could still see the library around him—the shelves of books, the broken grandfather clock against the wall, the door that led to the corridor—but superimposed over it was an almost transparent view of Regina's eighth grade math classroom.

Mr. Dodge was at the front of the room. "Regina," he was saying, "would you stay for a minute?"

"Ooooooh," came the response from the other students as they scooped up their books and dashed for the door.

Regina remained in her seat. She stacked her algebra textbook on top of her three-ring binder and grammar workbook. She reached down for her backpack, lifting it just in time to avoid Leticia March's foot, which stomped toward it. Leticia stumbled a bit but kept moving forward to catch up with her friends. The bell was still ringing, and the classroom was still noisy enough that only Regina— and Terry—could hear Leticia whisper "Mute bitch" as she passed and exited the room.

"Regina," said Mr. Dodge, his back to her while he erased the blackboard, "would you come up here, please?"

Regina loaded the books into her backpack and walked to his desk. She watched the chalk dust clouds dissipate in the fluorescent light, animal shapes shimmering in the dust.

"Regina," he said, "your brother Jerome told me that you'd be in my class. You know I'm his football coach, right?"

Regina nodded slowly, meeting his eyes with hers. He was an uneven man, his head a bit small for his bulky football coach body.

"He also told me you probably wouldn't speak in class." He said it with an easy grin, tossing it off as if her silence were commonplace.

Regina lowered her head.

"And that's okay," he went on. "As long as you show up and do your assignments, you're going to do fine. And I hear you're as strong a student as Jerome." He was speaking rapidly, trying to conceal his discomfort. "I've seen your test scores. I know you skipped a grade at your old school upstate. It can't be easy being the youngest kid in the grade."

"What's he getting at?" Terry asked her silently. Regina shrugged and looked up again at Mr. Dodge. Terry could feel her shoulders rise and fall as if they were his.

"I heard the way the other kids laugh when I called your name during attendance," said Mr. Dodge. "I just want you to know that I'm not going to tolerate anyone being made fun of in my class." Regina offered a slight nod to show her appreciation, but then he went on. "Jerome and I also talked about your speech problem."

Her eyes fell to the floor. And Terry bolted from his seat in the library. Regina and he had made a pact to avoid all discussions about her *speech problem*. Her ability to connect to other people's minds was strange—and maybe they should have asked for help when it first emerged—but they'd learned to deal with it on their own. Besides, no one else would understand it. And they certainly wouldn't understand why Regina wouldn't speak anymore. Only Terry and she knew why.

Terry was moving quickly now, out of the library, down the stairs, through the corridor that led to the middle school—all while trying to distinguish between what Regina was showing him and what was right in front of him.

"Jerome told me," Dodge went on, "that you don't have a physical problem—that you're not...that you're *able* to speak. So if you're embarrassed about your voice—if it's a stutter or something...and if you want help—there are people who can help you. My wife is a speech therapist. She's worked with other kids who've had trouble fitting in at school and just stopped talking for whatever reason. She's here twice a week after school. Perhaps I could give your father a call and..."

Regina was shaking her head no and moving toward the door before Dodge could even react. She was already out of the room when she turned back and waved—just to say thanks. Dodge held up his hand to wave back, but Regina was gone. As she exited the room, she almost collided with Terry. Instinctively, she shut off the broadcast. *"He wants to call Pop!"* she shouted in his mind. The words resounded in Terry's head as his sister's eyes shot and back and forth. He could feel her agitation. Terry almost flinched at the thought of Dodge calling home—the less their father knew, the better—but Terry responded gently and aloud, "He's just trying to help." He leaned toward the doorway, trying to get a look at Jason Dodge. Terry had heard Jerome speak highly of the man, a Black man who had graduated from HCS and gone on to an Ivy League university but returned to teach in Harlem.

Regina looked up at her brother with a pleading expression. *"Jerome has to stop. I'm fine!"*

"I know," said Terry, "I'll talk to him. I'll convince him that you're just shy and you don't need any help." Regina nodded. "Now we'd better get into lunch while we can get a seat."

As they made their way down the hallway of lockers and open classroom doors, Terry tried to tell himself that the others—the ones propped against the walls, the ones passing them in the corridor, the ones seated on the floor—were not staring at his sister and him. He tried to imagine that nobody noticed him—that they didn't recognize him as the weakling brother of Jerome Kelly, that they didn't know his sister as the little mute girl. But he felt certain that they *were* staring at him, that they *were* thinking those things.

Terry had always been an easy target. He was skinny, and he had a gentle manner, and both attributes seemed to invite bullying. He'd kept up on the hip-hop fashions and the latest rap songs. He'd tried wearing baggy pants, headscarves, chains, sunglasses. He'd learned the street slang. None of it made a difference. He still seemed out of place and out of touch. Worst of all, he looked self-conscious; his self-consciousness hung like a target across his chest.

As expected, the lunchroom was full. Stepping through the

doorway was like passing through a wall of sound. The administration had begun testing a new theory the previous year, scheduling lunchtime for all grades in the same timeslot, attempting to make students intermingle more, and in a place where they could all be watched. The cacophony of nearly eight hundred voices—talking, yelling, laughing, singing—was an assault on Terry's ears. He kept his head down as they entered, pulling his sister with him to the counter to grab two orange juices. The counter was an escape, a few moments of solace with his back to the masses. No one could see his face, and no one could see him emptying his brownbag lunch onto his tray.

"Your bag," he told Regina, "empty it. I don't want them to know we brought lunch from home. It just gives them another thing to laugh at." *They*, he knew, were always finding some reason to single out Terry and belittle him.

She did as he asked. Her sandwich and apple slumped onto her tray, looking as nondescript as the cafeteria food. Terry crumpled their empty bags and tossed them in the trash, and then the siblings turned toward the neat rows of tables that lined the massive room. The athletes sat nearest to the food counter, always ready to return for seconds and thirds. Jerome would have welcomed them there, of course, and no one at his table would complain—he was Jerome Kelly after all—but Terry always felt worthless when he hid behind Jerome's notoriety.

After the athletes, the students ordered themselves by grade, beginning with the seniors and working backward, so that Terry's sophomore classmates were, more or less, in the middle of the room, and Regina's eighth graders were next to last. Terry had already decided, though, that Regina shouldn't sit with her class. She was too small, too fragile. She couldn't be left alone. She would sit with him.

The students sat segregated almost entirely by gender. Here and there, a girl or two sat at a boys' table, or a boy at a girls'. Nearly all of the students were Black. The rest, a smattering of Hispanic, white, and Asian, were relegated to two tables at the very edge of the room—after even the seventh graders. Those were the tables that Terry was steering toward. He and Regina had eaten most of their meals at those tables for their first year at HCS. Sitting there again would ensure their continued outcast status, but it would also keep them out of the fray, safe among a pool of fellow misfits.

They had barely passed the sophomore section when a gruff male voice sounded behind them. "Yo, faggot..."

Terry walked on. He recognized the voice and knew that the words were intended for him, but he kept his eyes focused on the far tables, checking peripherally that Regina was still with him.

"Yo, Terry Kelly," Stephon Akins's voice rang out again, "I'm talking to you."

"Hey, you," a girl's voice joined in, "you with the mute bitch." It was Leticia March, Akins's girlfriend.

At this, Terry turned, though he hadn't meant to. He knew he had no good comeback to offer and no strength to support it, but his instinct to protect his sister was innate.

"Yeah, faggot," said Stephon Akins as he stood up, "we're talking to you."

Akins was actually slightly shorter than Terry, but he outweighed Terry by at least thirty pounds. Though they were both fifteen, Terry looked his age while Akins looked like a small adult. He'd been shaving since seventh grade, and he puffed his chest constantly, his t-shirt outlining dense biceps that dwarfed Terry's. Beside him, still sitting, was Leticia. Her middle finger went up as soon as Regina glanced her way. Regina didn't react. She just stared back expressionless.

"You got something to say, mute bitch?" Leticia asked. "I ain't heard you talk since you came here. What's your problem anyway?

You only talk to kids who ain't Black? Maybe you ain't noticed you're as black as I am. Or if you really can't talk, maybe you shouldn't be at a school with *normal* people..."

Terry had been in only a few fights ever, and he'd lost them all. Most of the time, he walked away from altercations. He never understood what could be gained through violence. But when he heard his sister being abused, he found a reason to take a stand.

"Leave her alone," said Terry.

"What?" said Stephon Akins as he climbed out from his bench and walked toward the siblings. "Who said you could talk to my girl? You got something to say to her, you say it to me, faggot."

All of the talking at Akins's table stopped. As the students at each adjacent table noticed the ensuing silence, their attention was grabbed as well, and they became silent too. By the time Terry spoke, Akins was only a foot away from him, and much of the sophomore class could hear Terry's stammered response, which came out much louder than intended.

"T-t-tell your girlfriend not to talk to my sister that way."

"What?" shouted Akins as he threw his chest against Terry's, forcing him backward. "*Tell* my girlfriend? Who the hell are you to *tell me* what to do?" His face was inches from Terry's now. Several more tables had quieted down. Some of the students had even stood. A fight was brewing, the first of the young school year.

Terry was about to answer, but Regina reached for his sleeve, and he turned his head to her. *"Don't,"* she told him in their private-speak, but his pupils were enlarged as he met her gaze. He could feel his heart pounding, feel everyone's eyes on him.

"Is that it?" asked Akins. "You ain't got nothing to say to me, faggot?" He shoved Terry, who stumbled but didn't fall.

Then Terry noticed that Regina was glancing back toward the athlete table. "No," he told her, though he had not meant to say it aloud. "I know what you're..."

"You don't know shit," Akins responded. You spent all last year sitting with the trash at the end of the room, and now you come and tell me to shut my girlfriend up!" The crowd noise was dying all around them. The conflict was the center of attention, and Akins seemed to love it. "Come on!" he yelled as he grabbed Terry by the shoulders and flung him to the floor on his back.

Terry's head struck the linoleum, bouncing up just in time for him to see Akins leap on top of him, pinning Terry down. Akins laughed as he pressed his hands against Terry's shoulders, holding him tight to the floor in a wrestling pin. Terry struggled, flailing his fists and managing to connect once to Akins's jaw before the stronger boy caught the swinging hands and pressed them over Terry's mouth.

"You fight like a girl," laughed Akins. "Look at you with your stupid green eyes. Are those colored contacts, or are you actually white?" He laughed, and his friends howled.

Snapping his head up and down, Terry freed his mouth and shouted, "Get the hell off me!" His voice sounded fuller, deeper than he'd expected, but he wasn't sure why. Instantly, Akins's grip loosened, and his arms fell to his sides. He stood and backed away, his eyes fixed straight ahead—straight into the massive form of the approaching Jerome Kelly.

"Yeah!" shouted Terry. He rose to his knees, shaking his fist. "You'd better..." And then he noticed his brother's colossal presence behind him.

"You," said Jerome calmly as he pointed at Akins, "if you come near my brother or sister again, I'll..." He paused as if searching for the right threat. "I'll end you."

Akins didn't answer. He simply stared into Jerome's hulking chest. He didn't seem scared as much as transfixed.

The two security guards at the ends of the room finally noticed that something was happening, but they were too late. The silence was breaking. Students were returning to their food and chatter. Everybody knew who Jerome Kelly was—the biggest and strongest boy in the school. He'd never actually been in a fight, but that was only because no one had ever dared to challenge him. The sight of Jerome towering over Akins meant that the conflict was over.

Akins looked smaller as he receded to his bench, oddly befuddled, but his friends welcomed him back to the table. There was no shame, after all, in yielding to Jerome Kelly. But, even seated, Akins's eyes were still focused on the Kelly brothers.

"You all right?" Jerome asked Terry, feigning nonchalance. He straightened his shirt collar though it needed no straightening.

"I'm fine," said Terry in a rushed tone, as if he had somewhere else to be. He gathered his lunch and books from the floor and stood again. "I'm fine. You didn't need to come over. I didn't need your help."

"Yeah," said Jerome, nodding. "Yeah, I know." He turned away, speaking softly, trying not to shame Terry. "I really just came over to make sure Regina was okay." He started toward the athlete tables, his large frame moving gracefully through the packed room.

Terry moved to Regina. "Did you see that—the way I shoved Akins off me? I didn't think I even pushed him that hard."

Regina stared up at him and tilted her head sidewise. *"Akins saw Jerome,"* Regina told him. *"That's why he got up."*

"What—no way! Akins didn't see Jerome! He was looking at me. I think he was so surprised that I stood up to him that he just jumped off of me ..."

She lowered her eyes to the floor, embarrassed. For him.

Terry replayed the scene in his mind, trying to remember exactly how the altercation had played out. Akins pinned him down. Terry hit him. Akins covered his mouth. Terry yelled at him. Then Akins got up because... Terry nodded reluctantly through a steely pout. Regina had convinced him: Akins must have backed off because he'd seen Jerome approaching.

Terry gathered his pride and called, "Hey, Jerome." Jerome swiveled his head, and Terry gave him a thank-you nod of the head. In response, Jerome waved his hand as if to say *it was nothing* and kept on walking. Then Terry turned back to Regina and told her to wait there for him. He caught up to his brother. "Hey, Jerome," he repeated. "I don't want Regina to hear. That thing you said about Warren this morning—do you really think he's not going to get better?"

Jerome sighed. "I don't know. We have to stop giving him money—that much I know. I just don't know how we stop." He opened his mouth as if he had more to say, but then he simply patted Terry's shoulder. "We'll figure it out," he said as he headed back to his table. Terry's eyes were on Jerome, so he didn't notice that Regina had approached him until her voice resounded in his mind. "*What was that about?*"

"Nothing," he told her. "I just wanted to thank Jerome."

Regina nodded, but Terry saw the doubt in her eyes: she knew that her brothers were keeping something from her. And she didn't like it.

FIVE

Van Owen is just as I saw him in my visions. Tall, lean, with skin so pale—so white—it is almost transparent, almost blue. His eyes are that color too—they are lifeless eyes like those of a fish pulled from the water and left to drown in the open air. He does not notice me yet. I am a woman after all, an African woman. He looks through me as if I am not even there, as if only the men could pose a challenge for him.

He strides toward us, reloading his pistol as if he has nothing to fear from any of us. He comes closer, closer, and then Kwame steps in front of me, protecting me and yet impeding my view of Van Owen at the same time. I have seen this in my visions. It was out of order then, but I recognize all of it. And so I struggle to find some way to do something different—to make things end differently, but the visions are still coming, and I cannot even tell what is happening now and what is to come another day. So I act out of instinct.

"Kwame," I shout, "we must run! We all must run."

"*You* must run!" he tells me. His first words to me. He does not turn to look at me. He stands strong, blocking Van Owen from seeing me. "Run!" he repeats, turning back this time.

Then, in front of Kwame, I see my father's arms rise, extend out to his sides as if he is reaching for something. I wonder if he is trying to surrender, offering himself in supplication.

Then the dirt at my father's feet begins to rise in a twisting pattern around his legs, as if blown by a whirlwind in a storm. But there is no storm. The sky is clear and cloudless. I hear a faint hum, a buzzing in my ears as my father's hands ball into fists.

Van Owen's eyebrows arch, and he grits his teeth as the wind grows stronger, but he is not afraid. He struggles against it, throwing one hand up in front of his face as he tries to comprehend what is happening. The hand with the gun remains down at his side. Then the humming sound grows louder. My father moves one arm in a sideways motion, and Van Owen is lifted off the ground as if carried by an ocean wave. His body rocks in the air, and he looks down in disbelief, his feet kicking at imperceptible waters. He looks for strings, for hands, for some plausible reason why he has left the earth. Then my father raises his palm and Van Own sails backward on the air, careening into his men. They tumble to the ground, rolling over one another as if struggling not to drown.

The wind grows fiercer, louder. More white men arrive, pushing through the trees into the clearing. My father lowers his arms again, and the wind withers. Whatever force he has called on to make the wind blow has taken a great effort from him. He struggles to catch his breath. "Berantu," he shouts to Kwame's father. He turns to see that Berantu is already there beside him.

"Stop," Berantu calls to the approaching white men. His voice is deep and rich as thunder. It fills the air, echoing in our ears. He does not speak their English, but the men stop as if entranced. "Turn and leave this place now! Turn and leave Mkembro and return to your own land!"

Like tamed beasts, the men pivot, expressionless, and begin walking back toward the trees. Their arms hang limp at their sides. Their eyes do not blink. They shuffle across the dirt, bumping into one another. One trips over a vine, stumbles, but then rights himself and continues on, spellbound.

Suddenly a vision consumes me. I am in a cage, looking out, watching the ocean rush by me. I look out through the bars and see Berantu—here, now—falling. Even before the gun is fired, I see him falling. I scream and close my eyes. When I open them, the bars and the cage are gone, but Berantu is still there. The gun has not been fired yet, but I can see Berantu falling.

I turn to Van Owen. With the wind gone, he has clambered back to his feet. He is perplexed but still unafraid. Where there should be fear, his eyes show only resolve. He is curious, pleased somehow to have found a challenge. He raises the gun to shoulder level and fires. The gunpowder sound pierces my mind like an axe splitting an ancient tree.

Berantu gasps as the bullet enters his chest, and he drops to his knees. He touches the wound with both hands and then examines them. They are crimson and dripping with his blood and his life, both of which are ebbing away. His breathing is labored. He groans with pain even as he struggles against it. He struggles to one knee and points at Van Owen. In our language, he shouts, "Burn!"

Van Owen's eyes suddenly enlarge and focus on his gun. His hand begins to shake. Smoke rises from the handle of the pistol, and Van Owen bellows. He drops his gun and clutches his hand. He turns it over and examines his reddened palm.

"Black witches," Van Owen curses. He reaches beneath his jacket for a second pistol. "Don't be frightened. These savages will fall like any other animals." He trains the pistol at the weakened Berantu. "Bleed," he says softly as he fires again, again striking Berantu in the chest.

Van Owen's men—the ones who had obeyed Berantu's command and fled—stop and turn back toward us, bewildered. "After them," he commands, pointing at my people. "Go after the ones who ran. We're taking all of them. All of them!"

Kwame has just begun to understand what has happened, that

Van Owen's weapon has penetrated his father's skin. He kneels beside Berantu and sees the blood rushing from the wounds. The chieftain trembles. Finally he topples into Kwame's arms. He stares up at the sky, whispering something that I cannot hear. He breathes in deeply to make one final plea to his son: "Run...take Amara and run..." Then his spirit leaves him and he lies there in Kwame's arms, motionless, dead.

"Go," my father orders me. "I cannot protect you here. Go—both of you!" At his feet, the dirt begins to rise again. It seems to hover in the air like a wall of dust all around him, and then it spreads outward. It is far stronger than the first time and not directed solely at Van Owen. It is a maelstrom of dust churning around all of us. The air hums. The wind makes a deep, crying sound, so loud that it drowns out even the humming. It is the song of the sky when it is angry and threatening and wreaking vengeance upon the land. Leaves rip from their branches, which crack against the wind. Van Owen grabs on to a thick tree trunk to secure his stance. He tries to raise the pistol again. Nearby, I can hear guns firing; Van Owen's men are herding our people together as if we are animals. The whips are striking, the nets are being thrown, the women—my mother among them—are being led toward the water.

Sand swirls, blowing everything, blinding everyone except my father, who stands rigid, the eye of the storm. Around him, the air is tranquil. Van Owen hides behind the tree, shielding his eyes, still fighting to raise the pistol. I can already hear my screams echoing across five generations.

"Kwame," my father shouts, "your father is dead. Go now. Take Amara and go!"

Kwame turns to me. I am on the ground, struggling to stand, but the sandstorm has forced me down. I can barely see. Through a wrathful ocean of wind, I will myself to my hands and knees, but instead of moving toward Kwame, I crawl toward my father, waiting for that sound, waiting to catch him. I watch him commanding the air currents, sending them sweeping out over the trees, tearing asunder the earth at his feet. He is so powerful, and yet I know he is still only a man. Kwame is moving toward me when we hear Van Owen speak again. "Bleed," he cries into the storm. Then his gun fires again. And the wind stops.

"No, no...," I am screaming as I shake my father's lifeless body. I can see the hole through his forehead, the blood streaming from it, his eyes open and pained and yet hollow somehow. I have seen the scene before, lived it already—I should know what comes next—yet I am unable to move. Kwame appears at my side. I don't see him, though; I feel him there beside me. I long to reach out to him, to take his hand, for I know I will never have this chance again.

"You see," Van Owen calls to his men, his gun still smoking, "their barbarian voodoo is nothing. These black witch-doctors bleed and die. They were both too old to fetch a good price anyway." He is reloading his gun, coming toward us. "But this wench," he says as he approaches me, "will make a good whore for some lonely master." I lift my head, and for the first of many times to come, Van Owen and I gaze into each other's eyes. His mouth seems to drop open slightly, as if he has seen something wondrous. He tilts his hand to one side and smiles. When he finally speaks again, his tone is lecherous. "Or maybe," he says softly, "I'll keep her for myself."

Kwame does not understand Van Owen's words, but he senses the evil man's intentions. He rises, his body tense, and I notice his hands. They are glowing like wood that has burned so hot that it has turned to ember. Light seems to emanate from them, yet his hands do not burn. He is not in pain; he is empowered.

Until now, everything that has happened today—my cousins, the ceremony, Van Owen's arrival, my father's death—I had seen it all in my visions. This thing that Kwame is doing, though, is new. I know what will come later—the plantation, the war, so much death and pain—but I do not know this moment. Why can't I see it?

"More witchcraft?" cries Van Owen as he points the pistol toward Kwame.

Kwame advances toward him, fire crackling from his hands in tiny branches of light. In his eyes, I can see it—Kwame is as surprised as I am. Just as I had never had the visions before today, he has never known this ability of his either. Even as he moves forward, he stares at his hands as if he does not know what to do with them.

Van Owen fires his gun at Kwame but misses. The gunpowder billows, clouding Van Owen's eyes. While he is occupied with reloading, I rise and come at him from behind. Kwame runs directly at him, placing his hands on Van Owen's chest at the same instant that I grasp the slaver's neck from behind. I squeeze with all of my strength, trying to wring the life from his pale throat. Van Owen's flesh burns from Kwame's touch. He tries to scream but my grip keeps his words trapped inside. I focus all of my rage at him—rage for everything he has done already and for everything he will do in all the years to come. I twist my hands tighter around his throat, drawing all the hatred in my heart and directing it at him. His milky, blue skin is cold. Veins on his neck bloat; I can almost feel the blood slowing.

And then I feel a jolt.

For a moment, everything is dark again. I am blind, hurtling downward through a tunnel. No, not a tunnel—a cavern, silent, vacant, closing in on me as I traverse its depths. Then a light: two slits closing and opening. I push onward until I can see again— through the two openings—but something is different. The trees, the sand, my father's body—they are all still there, but the world is dimmer; the horizon is etched with clouds that should not be there. And the world lacks color. Everything is gray or black or white.

Van Owen moans, but I hear his voice not through my ears but inside my head as if his voice is mine. I feel my hands coiling around his throat, but at the same time I feel the pain of their clenching. I see the smoke emanating from Van Owen's chest where Kwame is scalding him. I can smell the blistering skin. And I feel the pain of the burns.

I know what is happening—I am seeing through Van Owen's eyes as if I am he, as if my thoughts, my senses, my will are all lost inside him. I can hear his thoughts, rancid and warped. I can still feel my own body quivering as I maintain my grip on him, but I am more aware of his body than I am of my own. I can feel his hand still clutching the pistol that he used to murder my father. I focus on that hand, on that pistol, and I force the hand to raise and turn the pistol back toward him. I can sense his awareness of what is happening. He knows I am inside him, inside his mind, taking control of his body. Through his eyes, I look out and see the barrel of his own gun veering back toward his face. I can feel him fighting me, trying to push me out. His hatred of women is almost as palpable as his hatred of dark-skinned people. The images in his mind—I could never have imagined anything so foul. He wants to whip me, to rend my flesh even as he wants to thrust his body against mine.

I am drowning in blood; it flows over me, heaving and thick, so thick I can barely wade through it. But I focus on the hand, the hand with the gun. I feel his eyes—mine now—grow wide with fear as I will his finger against the trigger, tighter, ever tighter.

Kwame is still holding on, too. He curses Van Owen for murdering our fathers. He screams, and lightning crackles from his glowing fingers and pours into Van Owen's body. The slaver wails, his head snapping back, but so does mine. As one, Van Owen and I cry out. For what seems an interminable moment, the three of us stand there, locked in our embrace—me clutching on from behind, draped around his neck and draped inside his mind, Kwame attacking from the front, driving lightning currents through Van Owen's body, while gun smoke and sand hover in the air around us.

I feel Van Owen's fear. He shrieks, and I feel his hatred for us. I feel his shame at being hurt by two savages. I feel him fighting to wrest control from me, to keep the trigger from pressing all the way down. Then I sense his mind working—forming an idea: to let go, to stop struggling and allow our attacks—mine and Kwame's—to be used against each other. I try to break away—to pull my mind loose, to relax my grip on his neck—but I am too late. All at once, Van Owen stops struggling and allows me to take complete control of him, and as soon as he does, Kwame's lightning attack passes through Van Owen and flows into me. And my attack on Van Owen's mind slips through Van Owen and into Kwame.

For a moment, Kwame and I are connected as my consciousness is propelled into his. Time hangs suspended as my betrothed and I share an entire world unto ourselves. There is no air, no land, no water surrounding us, no death, no Van Owen. There is only Kwame and Amara. I sense his gentle soul, forced into violence by the most tragic of events. Fury and grief are one in him. I can feel his lack of control over his hands as the lighting spews from them. So I was right then: like me, he did not know that he had this power. Like me, he had heard tales that our fathers possessed strange abilities—abilities that they had used in battle. But unlike me, Kwame knew that they were *not merely tales*, that the powers were *not* just myth. His father had told him the origin of the power. I must know it as well, but I cannot explore it now. There is no time. I need to fight. I need to break free. But this joining with Kwame overwhelms me. I feel as if he and I are bound as if by chains. I wonder—if we had truly touched, if our hands had met—would we have been able to merge our power and use it against Van Owen?

Instead, Kwame's lightning shrouds me in pain. I cry out and my voice pierces Kwame's mind, echoing through it, hurting him. We grow weak. We let go of Van Owen and topple to the ground, the gun falling soundlessly on the sand. Faint, I turn my head, trying to get my bearings. Kwame is near me—unconscious but breathing. Van Owen stands over us, swaying. He is dazed, but he steadies his feet and pulls himself upright. He shakes off his stupor, breathing deeply as he stares at his hands, staring as if he has never seen them before. Before I pass out, I hear his voice. It seems louder, fuller somehow, though he is still weak from our struggle.

"What," he cries, "have you black witches done to me?"

SIX

"So, I was talking to Coach Dodge," began Jerome. He'd been dreading this conversation, but he couldn't put it off any longer. It needed to happen.

Regina turned away sharply and gazed out the open passenger side window. Two white police officers were trying to pry a Black homeless man off a grate next to an electric company repair truck. The steam from the grate curled around the man, making it look like he was floating in a cloud. Regina leaned out the window, craning her neck to watch. The homeless man was crying as the cops tugged at his arms. Regina leaned out even farther.

"Be careful," Jerome told her as he checked the rearview mirror, but Regina seemed not to hear him. Her eyes were closed.

The homeless man suddenly lurched to his feet, unnaturally spry. He wiped his eyes, gathered his belongings, and trotted off, waving. The two policemen stared at each other and shrugged.

Regina pulled herself back into her seat and stared up at her brother. There were tears in her eyes.

"Why are you crying?" His head shot back and forth from the road to her. "Are you okay?"

She nodded and smiled as she wiped her sleeve across her face and then lowered her arm to let the wind dry any remaining tears.

They drove on for a few more blocks, Jerome eyeing her

periodically. "Gina...look, I know this is hard to talk about, but we all keep avoiding it." He swallowed before going on. "About Coach Dodge...he told me he talked to you."

She glanced at his hands, and Jerome glanced at them as well. They were so massive that the steering wheel looked like a toy in his grip. Their father had bought the used truck because Jerome was too big to fit comfortably in most vehicles. But, he was too large even in the truck. Every time they passed over a bump, his head bounced against the roof. And he had to hunch over the dashboard in order to see the traffic lights.

"His wife's a speech therapist," Jerome went on. "Maybe she can help you with whatever problem you're having. Pop doesn't like when I bring it up, but I see you at school; he doesn't." She didn't react, so he continued. "Gina, I know your grades are really good, but the punks are gonna keep on picking on you. What's gonna happen once I go off to college next year?"

Regina opened the glove compartment and withdrew a pad of paper and a pen. She wrote: "Terry will still be here. He'll watch out for me." She held up the pad for Jerome.

"Terry?" he sighed, scratching his forehead. "Terry can't even watch out for *himself*." He thought about the lunchroom—Akins and his girlfriend. He'd heard that the argument started because the girlfriend had picked on Regina. "If I hadn't been in the lunchroom today, what do you think would have happened?"

Regina scribbled a response and smiled as she flashed the pad at her brother: "You wouldn't have gotten lunch." She laughed without making a sound, her shoulders bouncing up and down like a cartoon animal's.

Jerome fought to keep a straight face, but he finally gave up and laughed out loud. "Yeah, all right. It's funny. You make me laugh. You're always making me laugh. But you can't go through life writing notes on a pad. Whatever it is that's keeping you from talking, we have to deal with it."

"Why?" she wrote back.

"Because you're not..." He had almost said *mute*, but he despised that word, which he had heard students whisper about her. "You used to talk. A lot. And there was nothing wrong with your voice. It's not like you sounded weird or you stuttered or something. Hell, you were the youngest kid in your class, and you still skipped a grade! But then you just stopped talking. And I just...I just don't get it...and I want to help... I..."

Jerome's voice trailed off. Reluctantly, he found himself thinking of the day that she'd stopped speaking. He could still remember the sound of her scream—pain and fear mingled together. He'd raced upstairs and found her crying, kneeling over Terry, shaking him as he lay crumpled on the floor, passed out but with his eyes open and staring upward without any expression.

"What happened?" Jerome had demanded, dropping beside Terry and checking that his brother was breathing. Terry *was* breathing; he was alive, but Regina was so odd, just staring at Terry, saying nothing. Then Terry woke, dazed, explaining—unconvincingly—that he must have slipped and fallen. Two years had passed, and no sound had crossed Regina's lips since.

"I don't get it," Jerome repeated to her in the truck. "You're *not*...mute."

"Well, I can't talk," Regina wrote on the pad. She turned to a fresh page and continued. "So maybe I AM MUTE NOW."

"I don't believe you."

"Terry believes me," she wrote, underlining Terry's name and pointing to it as Jerome read it.

As he stopped at a red light, Jerome turned to the window to hide his annoyed expression. A hansom cab crossed in front of them at the intersection. The horse looked too old, too weak to be pulling the hefty carriage and the two men who rode in it. They were young Black men who looked more like gang members than coach drivers. One of the men pointed at Jerome and snarled his lip as if to say, *What are you looking at?* They seemed familiar to him. Jerome was certain he'd seen one of them before, perhaps with Warren. He thought of the money he'd passed through the fence earlier. *That's the last time,* he promised himself. *The last time.*

It wasn't until he was parking the car in their driveway that he spoke again. "You used to *sing,* too," he told Regina. "I used to love when you'd sing." But she was already unbuckling her seatbelt, already opening the car door and turning to wave goodbye.

"Hey," he called after her as she shut the door, "what time is Terry working till?"

She held up seven fingers and walked toward the front door of the dilapidated two-story townhouse. As she turned the key, Jerome gazed upward to watch the cracked aluminum siding sway in the wind. In a moment, Regina would race upstairs to their grandmother's room, just as she did every day when she arrived home.

He glanced up at Willa's window, wondering what the two women of the household did in all those hours they spent secluded in that room. Sometimes he listened outside the closed bedroom door, but he rarely heard even a sound except for Willa's piano. If he stood there too long, though, Willa would usually announce with a lilt, "Regina, open the door. Let your brother in."

He usually did go in then, just for a few minutes. Willa was good to him. She would ask him to tell her everything that had happened at school or at practice. She was interested and loving and gentle. He always assumed she must be lonely up in her room all day, but she seemed complacent somehow. The room got sunlight and had a private bathroom. There was a telephone beside her bed, but Jerome had never heard her use it. There were books but no television set and no visitors except for her grandchildren. Since she could barely walk and hadn't left the room in years, there was little chance of her making any new acquaintances. He'd tried to encourage any change in her habits—a class at the church, a drive, anything. "Grandma," he would say, "I can put you in the wheelchair and take you for a walk around the neighborhood..."

"Oh, no, child," she would tell him softly as she patted his arm, "I'm fine right here, watching over all of you."

And she did seem fine. She had Regina. She had her piano. She never complained. She never showed any sign of anger at being almost completely bedridden for eleven years. He wished that he could force himself to spend more time with Willa, but there was always something off-putting about her. He could never quite place it. Was she too calm? Was there something hidden behind that calm—something that everyone in the house seemed all too willing to ignore. He thought of the day Regina was born. So much had happened, yet no one ever spoke of it. *Why,* he wondered, *is there so much silence in this family? And so many secrets?*

"Too many damned secrets," he said aloud. He put the truck in reverse and started backing out of the driveway, but he heard the front door creak open and saw Regina coming toward him with a severe expression, as if she'd suddenly remembered a point of contention. As she walked, she scribbled furiously on her pad. Jerome stopped the car just as she slammed her pad hard against the dashboard window. Then he read the message through the pane: "When were you going to tell me?"

"Tell you what?"

She smirked and wrote, "About Warren!"

Jerome's foot nearly jumped from the brake as he rolled down his window, and he managed only a stammered "Uh" in response.

Regina looked hurt as she wrote in her pad, "You've been seeing him!!" As he read, she pointed her finger at each word to give them even more emphasis than the exclamation points had already afforded.

"Yeah," he said, "well...I don't think he wanted anyone to know we'd been in touch. Did Terry tell you?"

She shook her head no and folded her arms across her chest, pouting.

"Gina, you know Pop would be pissed if he found out that Warren was coming around us. It's just..."

But she was already running toward the house and slamming the front door behind her. The bolt slid across. Soon she would be upstairs, and the bedroom door would close, leaving Regina alone with her grandmother again.

Jerome backed the truck out of the driveway, but he couldn't take his mind off Warren. They had been so close when they were young. Warren and their father had been inseparable too—back in the old house in Saratoga—but the seeds of discontent had already been sown. Jerome remembered when he first saw the change in Warren.

Jerome was six. He was in the garage with his father, who was teaching him to box. Carl was holding the heavy punching bag, instructing Jerome how to strike the bag with maximum force.

Warren was fifteen, but when he burst in, sweating and frantic, he already looked much older. He seemed almost to be shaking.

"Pop," Warren pleaded, "I need..."

"I'm busy right now," their father said. "Good, Jerome. Now step into it. Use your weight."

"Pop," Warren tried again, "it's important."

Jerome was extremely large for his age—nearly five feet tall. He grunted as he stepped forward, striking the bag harder.

"Yes, that's it," said Carl. "Warren, did you see that? He's making dents in the bag."

Warren's eyes were shifting back and forth, but their father seemed not to notice. "Yeah, Pop. Jerome's really strong. I've been telling you that for months, but..."

"Yeah, but you didn't say *how strong.* This isn't just strong for a six-year-old. This is strong for *anyone.*"

"I know, Pop," said Warren. "Listen, I need to show you something..."

Jerome threw several punches at the bag, putting all of his body weight into them. The bag resounded with each blow, and Carl, not ready for the force of them, was knocked backward.

"Damn," grunted Carl.

"Sorry, Pop," Jerome apologized. "I guess you weren't ready."

Carl glared up at Warren. "If your brother weren't bugging me, I wouldn't have lost my footing. Now let's try that again."

Warren turned and walked off. "Fine, I'm gone." He climbed onto his bicycle and rode off toward the heart of the city. When he returned several hours later, he was no longer anxious, though his expression seemed oddly tranquil and his eyes seemed not to focus on anything. He entered the house and walked straight up the stairs toward his room.

"Where've you been? We're eating dinner in here," their father called out to him, but Warren just kept on walking. He entered his room and shut the door.

Jerome hadn't thought about that day in years. It surprised him that he could still see it so vividly. But he didn't want to see any more of it, so he averted his thoughts, turning them instead to the issues at hand: work and training.

Jerome knew it would be useless to look for his father at Stilson Stable. It was a Monday, which meant that the Stilsons were still at their house in East Hampton, so Carl Kelly was in charge of the stable. And the only place to look for him at 5:00 in the afternoon would be in Macombs Dam Park with Hippolyta, his favorite.

As the car crossed Macombs Dam Bridge, Jerome tried to spot his father near the running track in the park, but the traffic was thick, and Jerome knew he'd better keep his eyes on the road. Still, he thought it shouldn't be difficult to spot a Black man and a white horse, even when looking down on a dirt track from fifty feet above. He remembered how his father had taught him to drive on this bridge, which stretched across the Harlem River to the Bronx. Jerome had been behind the wheel only a handful of times when his father told him, "All right, kid, you're ready. Drive me to work." Only fourteen at the time, Jerome was in a state of panic. His previous driving had been limited to parking lots and deserted streets. The bridge suddenly seemed narrower than it ever had from the passenger seat; the steel post dividers between the two lanes threatened to sideswipe the truck; the oncoming traffic looked too wide for its lane. But once he'd made it across—without hitting cars or dividers—Jerome sensed in his father a trait that had previously been undetectable: trust. His father trusted him.

Jerome parked the truck on 155th Street, exactly halfway between the stable and the park, and proceeded on foot toward the park entrance. Before he'd even made it down the block, he heard a loud neigh and saw Hippolyta's regal head rising up the hill toward the park entrance, Carl Kelly at her side. At the sight of his son, Carl slapped the horse lightly on her back, spurring her into a slow trot. Carl ran hard to stay with her, keeping one hand on her all the time. The horse wore no saddle and no bridle. Jerome sighed at his father, though he had trouble keeping his eyes off the awesome form of the elegant, white quarter horse.

"Pop," Jerome said as Carl and the horse came to a stop, "you know those cops are gonna give you a ticket again if you keep taking her out unsaddled."

His father grunted, stroked the horse's mane, and turned away. Jerome stared up at Hippolyta. The horse was truly magnificent.

Greg Stilson had purchased her when she was only a year old, ostensibly as a gift for his daughter's birthday, but Stilson had high hopes that Hippolyta could be trained to race. The Stilson family had made a name for itself as a keeper of horses for New York's elite. Most of the horses they tended actually belonged to Westchester families that had purchased horses as trophies to impress their neighbors. Periodically the owners would drop by the stable, bringing friends and relatives to ooh and aah before being offended by the smell and promptly leaving. Sometimes a family would request that their horse be delivered to their home so they could watch it strut uncomfortably in the backyard for a party. There were a few owners who actually took the horses out themselves, but that was rare. Eventually, most of the horses were sold to the Stilsons at a fraction of market value. And then Jerome's father took care of them until Stilson could resell them at a profit.

"Did you take her around the track?" asked Jerome.

Carl's eyes gleamed for a moment. "A few laps."

"How'd she run?"

"Hippolyta doesn't run," Carl winked. "She flies."

Hippolyta was unusually tall for her breed. Too tall. Quarter horses were bred to race short distances. The Stilsons had spent a small fortune on trainers and jockeys for her. They had paid to have Hippolyta boarded and trained in Saratoga for nearly a year, but her running times were never too impressive, so she had returned to the Harlem stable to stand around looking pretty. Jerome's father, though, had always harbored a suspicion that Hippolyta's shortcoming as a racehorse wasn't that she was too slow but that she just wasn't cut out for quarter horse racing; she was meant to be a long-distance racer. Carl had ridden her around the quarter mile track in the park, and she seemed never to find her stride until the second or third lap. He and Jerome sometimes pondered whether—even at four years old—she could still be trained to race.

But they held their tongues. The Kelly family had been horse caretakers for generations—since the slave days. While Carl was an outspoken man, there was one sterling rule that had been passed down: *Don't ever tell the boss he's wrong.*

"No saddle again?" asked Jerome.

"She doesn't like it."

Jerome raised an eyebrow. "Told you that, did she?"

"Yes," said Carl, ending the discussion, "she did."

Jerome loved hearing—and often asked his father to repeat—the story of the day Carl had accepted the job from the Stilsons. Carl Kelly didn't quibble about salary or benefits. He knew it wouldn't make much difference anyway as the Stilsons had a reputation for being cheap. Besides, they were willing to pay him off the books. His only demand of his prospective employer was to "Let me see the stables." It was a sunny afternoon when Greg Stilson led him into the barn. Carl Kelly didn't stop to look at any of the horses. He didn't check the cleanliness of the facility. He didn't inspect the feed or the equipment. These were all things he could improve later. He simply walked to the center of the stable and stared up at the ceiling. Then he turned to Stilson and said, "Good, I'll take the job."

"A horse caretaker cares about only two things," Carl Kelly taught his son. "One, the barn's gotta be large enough, and two, there can't be any electric lighting." Carl was adamant that animals don't respond naturally unless they're treated naturally. It was hard enough on the horses just living in an urban environment. Why make matters worse by confusing a horse's inner clock? Electric lights mimic sunshine, which was horrific enough when used to force chickens to lay eggs several times a day. Even domesticated dogs and cats, though, suffered from minor irregularities such as excess shedding when conned—by unnatural light and heat—into believing that it was always the warm season of the year. A horse was a big animal with a stubborn nervous system—a nervous system too difficult to repair once damaged. Carl's father and his father before him had taught the same lesson: *We don't confuse the horse.*

So the stable was rather dark when Jerome and his father entered. It was late afternoon, and the eleven skylights spread out across the forty-foot high ceiling offered the only light therein.

As they closed the stable door, a hansom cab wheeled by— different from the one Jerome had seen earlier. The horse was younger, and there was only one man at the coach. Again, though, it was a young Black man. He wore gold jewelry over his white t-shirt.

"Why the hell are there so many of those things around here lately?" asked Carl. "Who in this neighborhood is gonna pay twenty-five bucks to ride in a carriage?"

Jerome agreed—he, too, was curious about the carriages—but he had an agenda and wanted to act on it while he had the courage. "Pop, I wasn't going to say anything. Terry probably wouldn't want me to tell you, but something happened at school today."

His father stopped walking but remained with his back to his son. He took his hand from Hippolyta's mane. The horse stood still, her head resting against his shoulder. "What happened?"

"At lunch today, there was a fight..."

"What happened?" The tension in his father's voice was growing.

"No one got hurt."

Carl spun around. "Just tell me what happened."

"Some punk from Terry's class picked a fight with him." He stopped and looked down. "I heard later that the guy and his girlfriend were picking on Regina."

Carl glared. He was livid. "And where were you?"

"I didn't see anything till the dude had already jumped on Terry. I got over there and stopped it."

His father's breathing was still elevated. "Is Regina okay?"

"Yeah," Jerome said. "Nobody touched her." He paused before answering the question his father hadn't asked. "Terry's okay too.

This kid Stephon and his girlfriend were just trying to piss off Terry by making fun of Regina, and Terry got in his face about it.

"So Terry started it?"

Jerome shrugged and nodded. "Look, I didn't want to make a big deal about it. I only told you because it just seems sometimes like you never give Terry credit for anything, and I wanted you to know that he'd do anything to protect Gina."

"Yeah?" mocked Carl. "Well, what difference does that make if in the end he's gonna lose the fight? He'd be better off just walking away and getting his sister to safety, not trying to play hero."

"You know, Pop, maybe you should spend some time with Terry, teach him how to fight. You did it for me. You did it for Warren." Carl said nothing. He just stared at his son, seething. The mention of Warren's name had clearly angered him. "Or if you don't want to," Jerome went on, "I can teach him..."

Carl's voice grew louder. "No, you can't! You don't have the time. And I sure as hell know I don't have the time. Terry's not like you." He paused. "And he's not like Warren either." He riveted his eyes on Jerome's. "I've watched him closely since he was born. He's not a fighter. There's nothing there. I wish there were, but there's not. He and Regina are better off just staying at home with their grandmother and doing their homework."

Jerome tried to keep his tone civil. He didn't want to aggravate his father any further. "Pop, it's not going to get any easier for Terry at school. He's a target. He's weak. He's not...Kids make fun of him because of his eyes." His father flinched. "We could at least teach him how to defend himself. If he could fight..."

"Trust me: he doesn't have it in him. Just look at him. Skinny as a toothpick. The last thing he needs is to think he's strong enough to defend anyone. Would be waste of time."

"A waste of time? That's what you said about Warren, and look what happened to him."

Jerome's father approached him slowly and stopped directly in front of him, looking up at his gargantuan son as if they were equal in height. In deference, Jerome lowered his eyes to the ground. "Now you listen to me, son, 'cause I don't want to have to say this again. *I* didn't abandon *Warren. He* abandoned *us.* He abandoned this family." The words were coming out choppy, sliding between anger and gloom. "I did my best for him. He walked away because he'd rather get high than face up to responsibility." He spit on the ground. "And his mother died for his choices." He stopped and shook his head back and forth as he continued. "Fine. Fine. Go ahead and help Terry. Go ahead and teach him how to fight if he'll let you. But don't you ever mention Warren to me again. He's dead to me." With that, he turned and headed downstairs to his office in the cellar.

After returning Hippolyta to her stall, Jerome patrolled the stable, patting the horses' heads, sneaking them carrots and sugar cubes, and talking to them softly. Since he was a child, Jerome had heard his father speak to the horses. Jerome had always made fun of him for it, so he wasn't quite ready to admit that he'd adopted the same practice himself. He kept his voice hushed.

"When you're done slipping candy to the breeds," his father's voice echoed from the intercom, "you can brush down Hippolyta."

The stable was almost the size of a city block. It housed forty-three horses, each in a twenty-by-twenty stall. The stalls were spread out in a rectangle around the edges, thus creating a huge ring in the middle where the horses were allowed to wander from time to time. Jerome considered letting a few of them stroll there, but his father had given an order. As he brushed Hippolyta with the water and alcohol mixture, he decided it was a good time to broach the subject of Regina—from a safe distance. He remained in Hippolyta's stall and switched on the intercom, opening the channel to his father's office in the cellar.

"Pop, I was talking to Coach Dodge..."

"About your stupid play this morning in practice?" his father quipped.

Jerome stopped stroking the horse and lowered the brush. "What do you...? You saw..." Jerome stared at the intercom on the wall as if it were animate, as if it were his father's face, scowling, accusing, hardened by time and tragedy.

"Yeah, I saw. And I didn't like what I saw, so don't let me see it again. I let you play football because it's important to you, but if you're gonna play, then play..."

Jerome knew that his father sometimes watched practice from afar through a pair of binoculars that he kept in his car. For a moment, Jerome worried that his father had seen what had come afterward—Warren at the fence. But that wasn't possible. Had he seen that interaction, Carl Kelly would have charged into the park and interrupted it. Warren was off-limits in every way. "Pop, I'm just trying not to hurt anybody...You're the one who told me to go easy on the other kids..."

"Don't you talk back to me," his father raised his voice but kept his tone even. "What is it with you today? Since when did you start questioning me?"

Jerome wanted to go on—to point out his father's hypocrisy. After all, Jerome was so much stronger than the other boys. He loved playing football, but he couldn't afford to let loose and actually injure someone. "Fine," he said softly. This isn't even what I wanted to talk about."

Through the intercom, Jerome could hear tools clanging, a lock opening.

"Coach Dodge's wife—" Jerome went on, "she's a speech therapist. I was talking to him about Regina because she's got him for math this year. Coach said she couldn't even bring herself to say 'Here' or 'Present' when he called attendance. She just raised her hand and waited until he saw her." Jerome paused and listened, but his father said nothing. "She's not getting better. It's been two years since she spoke even a word. She's not talking at home *or* at school. Coach Dodge says his wife could meet with Regina—for free—to, you know, try to help her with her problem..."

"What?" his father snapped. The sound of tools stopped.

"Like I said," said Jerome, "Coach Dodge's wife might be able to help out. I mean, it's been a long time since we tried anything new, and Gina's not getting any better." Jerome was surprised at how vocal he was being on this subject. Face to face, he could never bring himself to mention Regina's problem. His father was intent on keeping the family hidden—no doctors, no attention. And Jerome understood why. He'd accepted long ago that if he was going to play football, he could play well enough to win, but not so well that scouts would start noticing. But he still wanted to get help for his sister, and the intercom somehow took away his fear of his father's temper. "Coach says his wife has dealt with stuff like this before. It's usually not a physical problem. It's usually a mental thing—like insecurity." He continued describing the potential therapy, mindful that his father had stopped speaking. He touched on how tough high school would be for Regina as a social outcast. Finally, after making his argument, he stared at the intercom and waited for his father to answer.

There was nothing.

"Pop?" he asked.

Silence.

Jerome dropped the brush into the pail and walked to the intercom. He spun the volume knob to the highest setting. An electronic hiss filled the stall. "Pop, you there?" he called out again. In response, he heard only a short click and then silence again. Even the hiss was gone.

His father had shut off the intercom.

SEVEN

The world is shaking. Swaying back and forth. Around me from all sides, I can hear men's voices. Yet it is the water that has awakened me. It is on my feet and across my chest. It sprays the side of my face. My head throbs—but from the inside, not from a bruise. I know where I am, but I force my eyes open so that I can see the bars of my cage.

Water surrounds the ship, and yet my throat burns from the lack of it. We have traveled so far that I can no longer see my land, my Africa. The water is blue and cold and beautiful and rough, and my cage sits on the deck of the ship. Men walk by me as if I am not even here.

The roof of my cage is covered with some sort of cloth—a black curtain—to shield me from the sun, which still breaks through the bars on the sides. I have slept here for hours—perhaps days even—and my skin feels raw and burned. My face is scraped and coated with dried blood, as are my legs and arms and feet. It is as if I had been dragged across the sand and thrown to the floor of this cell on the deck of Van Owen's ship. He has chosen to keep me alive—barely.

As I force myself up to a sitting position, wrenching the stiffness from my body, the visions return. I see a white horse striding across a bridge, her rider panic-stricken. I see Regina furious because she has never even met her oldest brother. I see Van Owen standing at the bars of my cage—this cage—but it is nighttime then, and he is crying because someone has died. The visions recede, chased away by a loud voice.

"The girl's awake," shouts a man in a tattered uniform. As he walks by my cage, his stench wafts in. The stench of rotted meat. His eyes go to my exposed breasts, and I throw my arms across my chest and pull my knees up to cover myself. That seems suddenly important. He spits on the floor of my cage, missing me by inches. I twist so that my back is to him. Through the bars on the aft side, the sight is the same. Water. Endless water. Nothing more. I long to drink.

"Yeah, she's awake," another man bellows as he trots over from astern and bends in to have a look at me. He manages a rotted, cracked tooth smile, holding up his hat to block the sun so he can get a better view. "What are you covering yourself up for? We've all *seen everything* already."

"Get away from that cage, Harrow," another man calls from behind me. He is on a platform above the main deck. He stands at a wheel, turning it slightly every now and then. He is young. He turns to an older man beside him and asks him to "take over." Then he hops down from the platform and approaches my cage. I have not seen him before. He did not come ashore with the others. He is somehow different in spirit from the rest of them. I know just from looking.

He stares in at me, clutching the bars as if it is he who is imprisoned. His hands are blistered and worn, and he looks fatigued. For a moment, I forget where I am, and I pity the poor man. His eyes are sorrowful, and they meet only my eyes, not traveling down my body. He steps back, turns away, reaches into a barrel, and pulls out a cup with a long handle at the end of it.

"Water," he says to me as he passes the cup through the bars.

"You've been asleep for three days," he mumbles softly, certain that I won't understand him. "Drink it." He motions with the cup as if I am a child who does not know what to do with it. He means no offense, though.

I reach out my hand and learn just how weak I am. When I take the cup, my arm shudders. I gulp the water in one swallow and slip the handle back through the bars. "Thank you," I whisper back to him in a raspy voice. The man stares back at me dumbfounded. Without realizing it, I have spoken to him in English.

"What are you doing there, Roland?" another voice asks. I recognize the man's shadow even before he is near, and I know his voice. My people's conqueror. My father's murderer. Hendrik Van Owen.

Roland takes the cup from me and tries to hide it behind his leg as he turns to face his captain. "Just checking on her, sir."

Van Owen steps into view. He wears a baggy white shirt, white pants, and black boots. His long hair, tied in a ribbon when he was on my shores, is now loose, fluttering in the ocean wind like a spider web, covering one of his blue eyes. His skin is smooth, barely weathered by his days at sea. He is perhaps fifty years old, but he has the look of man who appeared old even when he was young. But I know that Van Owen will never truly be old. Because of me.

As he approaches the cage, his hands rest in his belt, one of them clutching his whip. "Roland," he says in a mock gentle manner, "if I'd wanted you to check on the girl, I would have asked."

"Aye, Captain," says Roland, lowering his eyes to his shoes.

"Return to your post," Van Owen orders as he scans him suspiciously. Before Roland can move away, Van Owen adds, "And give me that cup." Roland hands him the cup and heads back toward the stairs and the wheel. Then Van Owen, still a few feet away, leans toward me, pressing his face against the bars so that his wild hair blows into my cage and his shadow blocks the sun. "So," he intones softly to me, "you've decided to return to the land of the waking then, have you?"

I don't want to give him the joy of seeing my anger, but my hands give me away, clenching into fists around my knees.

He looks out at the ocean, reveling in his belief that I don't know where we are or where we're going. But I do. First we'll dock in Boston. He'll cover my cage completely with the black curtain as his men lead the others—the ones stored below—past me, parading them like cattle. I won't see them, but I'll hear their chains rattle as they pass. I'll shout my mother's name, wondering if she's still alive and among them, wondering why there are some things still hidden from me when I seem to know so much of what is to come. "Mother," I am calling weeks from now. "Mother?" She doesn't answer.

"What are you daydreaming about, little witch?" Van Owen interrupts my vision.

I turn away from him and gaze off. Though we drift in a vast watery emptiness, in my mind I can see my final destination—his plantation in North Carolina. There, I will be forced to call him Master.

"You look strong enough, little witch," he interrupts. "I was beginning to worry, but I think you'll survive the trip after all."

I know I will. I see years and years to come, so many of them filled with pain, both old and new, all of them haunted by the memory of my father's death at his hand. He is pulling the trigger even now, for my visions are of the past as well as the future. The bullet strikes my father over and over, killing him again and again. I cannot stop it—the bullet or the vision.

Van Owen remains at my cage for quite a while, holding vigil, watching me as if I am an oddity. So I give him nothing to watch. I turn my back to him and stare out at the water. He doesn't complain—not even under his breath. When I turn back much later, he has gone, probably returned below deck. A tall cup of water sits at the far end of my cage, though. Beside it is a clump of stale bread. I know that he has left them for me. So that is why he was so angry with Roland—Van Owen wanted to be the one to give me nourishment, to be my savior. I wish that I didn't have to take anything from him, but I have no choice. I swallow the bread and wash it down with the water, trying not to remember that his hands touched them. Trying not to acknowledge that my life is in his hands. That I live only because he allows it.

I hide for several more hours in the shadow of the curtain, constantly shifting away from the sun, from side to side of my cell. My throat is constricted from the heat. I know that I will live through this trip, but that knowledge offers little comfort. I feel as if I am dying. Only days ago, I was a princess about to be married. Now I am a caged beast, forced to accept sustenance from my father's murderer.

With the night, most of the men retire below, so no one is left gawking at me. I curl up in a corner of my cage, huddling for warmth from the cold night sea winds that taunt my wet body. I try to imagine I am back in Africa—or even working in the fields in North Carolina—anything to make me feel warm and unafraid and not so alone.

"Ho, there," a man's voice whispers suddenly. It's Roland. Again he stands beside my cage and looks in on me with pity. Again his hand stretches in, offering me water. I drink it down and return the cup, and he fetches more. "I can't bring you food. Someone might notice if I take anything from the galley. But since the captain's asleep now, I can at least offer you water."

I drink down the third cup and the fourth before I finally whisper back in English, "Thank you."

"So I didn't imagine it earlier," he says. "You do speak English. How do you...? I don't understand..."

"I don't either." My accent, I notice, is Southern, almost like Van Owen's. I speak like a woman from North Carolina.

Roland thinks he has it figured out. "Did you escape from America and go back to Africa?"

"No. I've never left Africa. I...I just know your language."

We both struggle for words, but I am stifled by fatigue and he by shame. Finally, he speaks again. "We've changed course, you know." I stare back as I drink again, listening to him speak. "The Pinnacle—that's the name of this ship—was supposed to land at Cuba. That's the only possible safe destination for this kind of ship. But the captain's taking us straight to America now. He says it's because of you."

"Because of me?"

"Yes, he says that..."

Suddenly Roland drops to his knees on the floorboards beside my cage, his eyes bulging wide. He looks down at his chest, and we both see it at the same time—the sharp tip of a knife protruding from his ribcage. It slides back into the wound, the blade disappearing inside him before exiting his back, and he coughs while blood rushes from his chest.

"You should have obeyed my orders, Roland. That's what a first mate does." Van Owen is speaking slowly, purposefully, but with no emotion whatsoever. "When I was a first mate, I followed orders. Even when my captain beat me for no reason at all, even when he forced me to work for days at a time without rest. No matter what was asked of me, I obeyed my captain's orders. Without question."

Roland's body is twitching. With one hand he grabs hold of one of the bars of my cage. With the other, he tries to cover the wound to slow the blood. I gape in horror, unable to help. He knows he is dying, but he tries to hold on to his last few breaths. Why did I not see this in my visions? Why is this moment new to me? What else is still hidden?

"This is your fault, witch," Van Owen says softly. "You brought me up on deck. Every night, you call to me, drawing me up here just to look at you, don't you?" His eyes are fixed on me, not even noticing the blood that drips from the knife, painting red dots on his bare foot. "What sort of spell is it you're casting on me?"

Ignoring him, I crawl forward and touch Roland's trembling fingers. He is dying because he tried to help me, and I don't want him to die alone. Instantly, Roland grabs my hand, pulling me even closer to him. His eyes meet mine, which are wet with tears. He breathes in sharply, making a horrible gurgling sound as blood stains his teeth. He tries to speak but only sputters crimson.

"I'm sorry," I tell him in a whisper, so that Van Owen cannot hear me speak in English. I look down at our hands touching, and, in a flash of a moment, I see Roland's entire life. He grew up in Boston, the son of a banker. His father lost the family's money in a foolish investment and then committed suicide by stepping in front of a carriage. Roland had been attending a university, but he had to quit after his father's death so that he could learn a trade. His mother suffers from dysentery, yet she continues to work as a cook in a hotel. His sisters scrub floors in the homes of former family friends. Because he loved the sea, Roland found a way to make a living on it. Whenever possible, he worked on fishing boats or cargo ships, but the family was so delinquent in paying the father's debts that Roland took this job with Van Owen, a former business partner of his father's. He had known he would hate serving on a slaving ship. But he could not have known just what sort of man Van Owen is.

The influx of Roland's memories stops abruptly. He slouches forward, his face sliding down the bars of the cage until his shoulder meets the floor and he can fall no farther. His grip on my hand loosens, and he dies without a sound, though the blood continues to flow from his wound and from his mouth.

"Bleed," says Van Owen. "Yes, go on and bleed. What else can you do?"

I look up at him. He is dressed as he was earlier—all in white—but his shirt is loose. His eyes are sleepy, as if he woke suddenly and came up on deck because he imagined me calling to him.

"What a shame," he goes on talking to Roland, "to see you like this now. I didn't take you ashore in Africa because I knew you didn't have the stomach for hunting, but I did think you'd be a good officer here on the ship—that you'd do as instructed." His accent is thicker than mine—more deep Southern. The vowels are long and drawn out. He sounds like a learned gentleman from Kentucky. Consonants are swallowed up by the vowels. His drawl is harsh to the ear. "What story shall I tell your mother then, Roland? Perhaps that you were rocked overboard during a gale? Or maybe that one of these African warriors slit your throat and hurled you into the waves—even as you were trying to feed him. Yes, I like the sound of that one."

I crawl back to a deep corner of the cage as Van Owen rambles on, but I can't take my eyes off of Roland's, which still stare back at me.

"When I was a first mate aboard the Antares," Van Owen continues while kneeling and placing a hand on Roland's shoulder, "Captain Remy—Dayton Boyd Remy—had us moving gems through the Barbary Coast. Now *those* were dangerous trips, Roland." He strokes the dead man's hair as if petting a dog. "Waves thirty feet high. Storms for weeks on end without surcease. This— what we're doing here—this is nothing. This is a holiday. We capture a few hundred barbarians, kill a few for sport. It doesn't take much effort. Even if only a third of them survive the trip, we make a fortune. The Barbary, though, was full of cutthroat pirates—men for whom killing never needed a reason. The sort of men who make me look genteel by comparison. Such were the men who attacked our ship at nightfall, and it was my fault. The captain was asleep down below, so I was in charge. I had the conn. I was so tired, though—nodding off in the fog—that I didn't even see the pirate ship that had ambled up right alongside ours, barely a stone's throw away. Not until their plank came thundering down on our bridge, and their men started running across it, boarding our ship. I rang the bell, and our crew raced up to the deck, but the pirates were upon us in seconds. They knocked me down, dragged me back onto their ship, and threw me into a cage below deck. I could hear the fight even from there. Guns firing. Men screaming. Then, finally, the pirate ship pulled away with seven of us American-born men aboard. Were the rest of my compatriots all dead, I wondered? I assumed not. My new ship seemed to retreat in a hurry. Certainly, the pirates would have taken our ship if they could have, but I didn't know then for sure. All I knew at that moment was that I was a captive of Barbary Corsairs. And I was frightened." His gaze suddenly turns to me. "Probably almost as frightened as you are right now."

The moonlight catches his face, and I notice the tears running down his cheek. I wonder if they are tears of self-pity for his days as a prisoner or if he weeps for Roland. Or for me.

Sighing, he stands slowly and throws his head back in the wind, letting it dry his tears. "Yes," he nods, "I was a slave, just as you are going to be a slave, my little African devil witch. My slave. Mine." He stares hard into my eyes and repeats the word: "Mine."

Against the night sky, his eyes are a spectral white, and he looks far more the devil than I ever could. He doesn't scare me, though. What scares me is the vision I keep seeing of him: it is years from now, more than a century away. He sits in a window, looking the same age as he does right now. He stares out, focusing on nothing, concentrating, almost lost in a trance. Then a smile crosses his face. "Yes," he says softly. "Yes, Dara. I see you now. Weakened with child, are you? I'll be there with you soon."

Dara? I have seen her in other visions. I've seen her children as well—Terry and Regina and the older ones, Warren and Jerome.

For a moment, I wonder if any of this is real—if I'm still in Africa, deep in a nightmare but waking soon to my wedding and a blessed life with Kwame. The visions answer me, though, showing me the ceremony once more, my father falling, always falling. This is a nightmare, but it's also real. It's all real.

I try to keep focus on something solid to root me in the moment—I focus on Roland, his eyes locked forever in a pained gape—but the images won't recede. They flood into my mind with startling succession.

"Mother," I hear myself calling only days in the future. "Mother, are you here?" Chains rattle by me. I hear whips slapping the flesh of my people, but I see none of it. The curtain covers my cage like a shroud. "Mother," I shout, "it's me. It's Amara."

"Amara?" a voice answers. A man's voice. Kwame's voice. He's alive!

EIGHT

Terry often spoke about his after-school job as if he hated it. He didn't, though. Being a delivery boy at Harlem's largest supermarket wasn't fun, but it did offer two perks: money in his pocket and time away from the house—specifically, time away when his father arrived home from work.

When he was younger, Terry had assumed that his father's workday must be awful. Perhaps Carl Kelly loathed his job, and that was why he was so angry all the time. On the day Terry had gotten the job at Greenway Market, he took a bus along the river to Stilson Stables, anxious to tell his father the news of his first job—finally an accomplishment that Carl Kelly might appreciate.

Their father had never allowed Terry or Regina to accompany him to the stables. "Horses are big and smelly and dirty," he'd always told them. "There's nothing there for you to see. You don't want any of that. Besides, they can be dangerous." That was his father's standard excuse for barring Terry and Regina from all sorts of activities: it was dangerous. "Be careful," he would say, whether his children were heading to school or even to the bodega for a half-gallon of milk. Terry couldn't remember, though—had their father been any different before their mother's death, or had Carl Kelly always expected peril at every turn?

At age fourteen, Terry was determined to brave his father's wrath and surprise him at the stable with the news of his first job. He rang the bell on the stable's big double door. It made no sound, but Terry still waited for a time before he circled to the rear of the building and climbed on a dumpster to peer through the window. He stood there for some time, unable to peel himself from the sight. The Carl Kelly that he saw—the one talking to the horses, laughing, smiling, and thoroughly enjoying himself—was a man that Terry didn't know. This man was joyous. This was not the dour presence that came ranting through the front door every night, complaining about every article of clothing that Terry hadn't hung up, about every piece of silverware that was a fraction of an inch out of place in its drawer, about every cupboard door left slightly ajar, about everything that Terry hadn't done or had done wrong. Just thinking about his father's temper caused Terry to flinch. But, this man, the one frolicking with the horses, was content.

Terry didn't interrupt his father's pleasure that day. He walked home. And, as he trudged across the bridge, he tried to make sense of his father's behavior. How could Carl Kelly be so jovial at work and then come home so irritated every night? Had Terry ever seen his father as happy as he was at the stables? Terry tried to remember anytime over the last several years when he'd actually seen Carl smile. He could envision isolated moments when Carl seemed happy—watching Jerome play football; tossing Regina in the air...but that was before Regina stopped speaking. Now Carl Kelly rarely had grins even for her. Mostly, he gave her sad looks, pitying glances, gentle sighs. And he never had kindness for Terry. No words of encouragement. No compliments. No appreciation. No acknowledgement. As far as Terry could tell, his father saw him as did the bullies at school: weak, worthless, effeminate. Terry wasn't powerful and confident like Jerome. He wasn't brilliant and adorable like Regina. He was skinny and plain and frail. Everything Carl Kelly didn't want in a son. Worse, he had his mother's green eyes. *Perhaps,* he wondered that night, *Carl Kelly didn't hate his job or his life. Maybe it was only Terry that he hated. Just Terry.*

It had been more than a year since that trip to the stable, but Terry still thought of it nearly every day as he walked home from work. He thought of it now as he toted two heavy grocery bags along Riverside Drive.

"Where you going with those bags?" Stephon Akins called out, prying Terry from his reminiscence. Akins and Leticia were riding in the back of a hansom cab carriage. The horse was an aged palomino with wobbly legs. The driver was a young Black man who looked familiar to Terry—perhaps a former classmate. The carriage stopped, and the two passengers descended to the street. The hansom cab wheeled away, the horse limping.

"What do you want now?" asked Terry, even as he looked around for a place to run, for a stranger to notice.

"You heard me," said Akins. His hands hung at his sides as if he were an Old West gunslinger waiting for a signal to draw. Leticia stood beside him, her arms folded across her chest. "Where you going with those bags?" asked Akins. "You steal that shit?"

It was Terry's last delivery of the afternoon and the only one he made without a bicycle—the same delivery he made at the end of every Monday afternoon since he'd started working at Greenway. It was the one delivery that Terry always looked forward to—Marco Fenelli's apartment. Marco, an eighty-year old retired criminal who hadn't left his apartment in decades, was Terry's confidant. Terry had often told Marco about the intimidation he endured at school— particularly from Akins. "Stand up to him," Marco had told him. "If you keep running, he'll just keep coming back. Stand up to him once. Even if you lose, he'll respect you for it, and he'll stop coming after you." Marco's advice wasn't panning out.

"I'm working," answered Terry as he tightened his grip on the bags and kept walking. He heard the footsteps behind him. He knew that the couple was following him, but he hoped they'd grow bored after a few blocks. If Regina had been correct about the lunchroom encounter—that Akins had backed off not because Terry had stood up to him but because Jerome had interceded—then Jerome's threat should be enough to keep Akins at bay.

"*You* got a *job?*" mocked Akins. "What kind of fool would hire a faggot like you? You're so skinny that you can't even carry more than two bags."

Leticia smirked as she joined in. "Your little mute bitch sister could probably carry more than you." She grabbed at one of Terry's bags, missing, but her fingers caught onto the delivery tag. The sticker tore in half. She glanced at it before stuffing it in her pocket.

Terry looked down at the bag. Marco's name was on it, but the address was gone. He bit his lip to keep from responding. Marco's apartment was only three bocks away. Perhaps Terry could make it that far without another altercation. "Just leave me alone," he said, but his tone sounded pleading, and he knew it.

"Leave me *alone*," Akins mimicked. "You're always alone. Nobody likes you. Even your brother didn't get up to help you until I had you on the ground like a little girl."

Terry thought of the lunchroom fight, wondering what he could have done differently.

"And I ain't scared of Jerome Kelly," Akins went on. "Yeah, he's big, but he's weak. He just *plays* at hurting people—in a game. And he can only hurt you if you let him get close, and I ain't gonna let that happen again. I can do any shit I want to you, and I don't have to worry about Jerome Kelly. He comes near me, I'll pull my piece and shoot the bitch right in his face."

"Ooh," gasped Leticia. She tried to cover it with a laugh, but even she was surprised at what her boyfriend had said.

Terry kept on walking. It had begun to rain. The water glanced off the plastic bags that Terry was clutching against his chest and poured down his cheeks like tears. Still, he refused to stop and adjust the bags; if he did, he would give his pursuers an opportunity to surround him or grab the bags. He thought of running into traffic. There were still a few cars passing by. Perhaps Akins would be less likely to start a fight in the glare of headlights and onlookers. But stepping into the street or running into a store or calling for help—they were all escapes. Akins would only come back the next day or the next, wouldn't he? Perhaps, Terry thought, his only option was to follow Marco's advice: don't run. So he kept moving at an even pace.

"Jerome Kelly," Akins continued, "I've seen him play. He's got no instinct for blood. He takes people down—he tackles them—but that's it. He don't make anyone hurt. If I hit you now, all Jerome will do is come threaten me again. Then I'll just wait until after practice. I'll wait by his car. And just when he gets in the driver's seat of that red pickup truck, I'll come right up to the window, and I'll stick my gun in his face and..."

"Stop!" Terry bellowed as he spun toward them. The wet grocery bags fell from his arms and flopped onto the sidewalk. Akins watched silently as a pink grapefruit slipped from one bag and rolled toward a grate. "You aren't going near Jerome," Terry went on. "You go near him and I'll be the one at *your* car window."

Akins stood frozen in place. Leticia stared at her boyfriend, who seemed to be gasping to get words from his throat, but nothing came. Terry noticed the boy's silence and felt suddenly empowered.

"I'm not playing around with you anymore!" said Terry. "I've been putting up with your shit for too long. Now both of you just get the hell away from me."

Akins and Leticia started backing away slowly, almost mechanically.

"Get away from me," Terry roared. The boy and girl responded by turning away and moving faster. "Get away!" And they ran.

Terry's throat felt raw. He had the urge to tilt his head back and let the rainwater fall on his tongue. Instead, he remained still, catching his breath as he watched Akins race down the street. Leticia couldn't keep up, but she lingered only a few paces behind. Their footsteps were resounding slaps on the damp pavement, echoing across the Harlem night. The pair ran through red lights, dodging cars and broken bottles and passersby. They just kept running.

NINE

The ship crawls toward America, swaying in the tides of four continents. The days drag on into weeks. Weeks of hot and hotter days of rocking, of watching the adjustment of sails, of listening alone at night to the creak of the boards, of wondering how much worse it is for my people below.

I hear talk of Gibraltar and Cuba. Sometimes when Van Owen is below deck, the men grumble while hauling in fish or mopping water from the boards. They complain about bringing a cargo of slaves directly into a northeastern harbor. They speak of the dangers of the African Squadron, a naval patrol that scours the waters for illegal slave traders, and yet the men never bring their arguments to Van Owen. They're too afraid. Perhaps they keep in their minds the image of Roland's corpse, which Van Owen ordered them to leave on the deck by my cage, rotting, for two days. Only when the albatrosses started picking at Roland's flesh did one older sailor find the courage to plead: "Please, Captain, it'll bring sickness to all of us. The lesson's learned, Captain." At that, Van Owen nodded. Two men dragged Roland by his ankles—his head scuffling against the deck, his eyes still staring back at me, upside-down—to the edge of the boat and sent him tumbling into the waves.

They fly the United States flag from the highest mast and display crates of palm oil across the ship's bridge just in case they are stopped, though Van Owen doesn't appear concerned at all. He seems composed, fully in command of everything and everyone around him. I wonder whom he has bribed for safe passage.

Sometimes I am curious just where we are, what islands we're passing, what waters we sail through. I rarely know. Most of the men will not speak near me. After Roland's death, they eye me with caution and stay far from my cage.

Twice, I've had to endure what the sailors call *Dancing the Slave.* Van Owen leans against the mast, waiting as his men bring five or six of my people from below. "Here," the sailors say, "drink this." And they force the Mkembro and Merlante fisherman and hunters and farmers to drink the foulest of rums. When my people begin to sway from the drink, the sailors bring out the drums they stole from my ceremony. They pound on the instruments, poorly mimicking our rhythms, howling at the air like beasts, crouching as they clap along. And then they crack their whips against the boards and command my people to dance.

I don't want to watch. Hunched in my cage, I hide out of shame—shame for me, shame for my people, shame for the ignorance and cruelty of man. But then I hear the Mkembro voices rising above the sailors' roars. Even as my people dance, drunk and frightened, even then they sing in our native tongue, railing to our gods, calling curses down upon the evil men. The bloodless white devil, they cry as they pass in front of Van Owen, shall crumble and melt to nothingness. They stare at Van Owen, who remains oblivious to their curse, and they call out, *The gods will dissolve him.*

Even as they dance for him, they defy him. I promise myself that I will do no less.

Late each night, long after the moon has risen and most of his men have gone to sleep, Van Owen clears the deck so that he can be alone with me. Sometimes he wanders along the bridge, watching me from different vantage points. Other nights, he sits beside my cage and speaks to me, telling me of his childhood in Kentucky and the Carolinas, of his mother and father and their fierce love for their only child. Sometimes he reads to me from the Bible, telling me of good and evil, explaining sin to me, lecturing me that the Bible holds answers to all questions. Yet even as he reads, I find myself doubting that he believes the things he says. One night, as he tells me the story of Moses, he shuts the book in anger and walks off to stare at the water or up at the stars. "Man shalt not take a wife from the daughters of Canaan," he shouts at the sky, wagging his finger toward me. Most of the time, though, he simply stares at me as if I am a puzzle, as if he can learn my secrets by observing me. So I give him nothing to watch. No movement. No reaction. No emotion. Even as visions stream past my eyes—visions of him and me and my progeny and all the horrors to come—I sit silently, watching him as he watches me, trying to learn what I can use against him one day.

It storms for the next several days—fierce storms—but I welcome them; the whipping wind against my wet body reminds me that I am alive. And the storms keep Van Owen away, for the deck cannot be unmanned in a squall, and he won't visit me when the others are watching. So I am given even less food and water than usual. As it rains, some of the men circle my cage and laugh, as, like an insect, I crawl on my chest, licking the water from the sullied cage floor. With what's left of the rainwater, I wash my hands, for I have used them at night—when no one is watching, and I can empty my bladder in peace—to brush the urine from my cage.

Once a day, they bring the sick or dying prisoners on deck, those who will not fetch a good price even if they survive the trip. So the sailors remove the afflicted from the pens down below before the healthy ones can be infected too. I jump to my feet, wondering if I will see my mother's face. I try to recognize a necklace or a bracelet. Is she still alive? Is she on the ship or still back in Africa? But it's never my mother who emerges from down below, weak and filthy and encrusted with dirt and blood.

The sick have already lost their will to live, so they don't even struggle as the slavers lead them forward. Their chains already removed, they are simply walked to the end of the deck and told to step into the water. Sometimes they turn to see me in my cage before they go overboard. They all know who I am. The chieftain's daughter. The princess. Perhaps, seeing what has become of me makes it easier for them to accept their end. For if even a princess is a caged zoo animal, then what chance had they to fare better? They stagger toward the plank, all hope gone, and when they enter the water, they do not resist its pull. They fall into the surf and vanish forever.

The rebellious ones, though, are dangerous, for they cannot be broken—and so they are feared. They could incite others to rebel. For them, the end is different. As they are tugged toward the edge of the ship, the white men beat them with sticks and slash them with sabers. Still, the strong ones struggle against their shackles and curse their captors. Finally, just before they're thrown overboard, the defiant ones are killed. Van Owen likes to watch them die. He has them stabbed or struck over the head, for bullets are too expensive to waste on them. Then the chains are removed so that they can be reused. Only then are the men tossed into the water.

It's just before dawn when the noise begins from deep below. At first I wonder if there's a commotion of some sort—perhaps an uprising—but these are not African voices that I hear. It is the crew. Someone has looked through a telescope and seen the land we're approaching. As the men stream onto the deck, embracing and slapping backs in cheer, I look toward a dark, shriveled mass in the distance. For a moment, I envision it as it will appear a century from now, the smokestacks and office buildings rising so high that I can see them even from here. In this time, though, I see only gray skies and a pier and a plethora of ships that dot the waters of Boston Harbor.

"Cover her cage," shouts Van Owen from behind me. I spin to see him pointing at me. He seems even cleaner somehow. Whiter. As if he has been up for hours, preparing himself for our arrival. Beside him are two pale young boys of no more than fourteen years each. Scrawny and tired, they wear the tattered remains of once fine clothing. I have not seen them before. They squint at the coming sunlight as if they've been in darkness for weeks. They stare at the shore with yearning. When they turn toward Van Owen, their fear is palpable. Each has burn marks on his arms and wrists. One of them has burns on his face. I wonder how many lashes they wear across their backs for not following the captain's edicts with the requisite alacrity.

"The curtain," Van Owen bellows. "Climb up there and unfurl it now."

The two boys rush to opposite sides of my cell. Hurriedly, they climb the bars and hoist themselves onto the roof of my cage, where sits the black curtain that has offered me some mild cover from the sun these past five weeks. I can see the impression of their feet through the fabric as they try to unroll it.

"Come on, lads," their captain shouts, "we're almost there. We have only an hour at best to unload, and I have no desire to pay off any more Yankee militia than I have to."

The last thing I see before the curtain is lowered over the sides of my cage is the harbor, empty save for a handful of men who stand waving at our ship, unaware that they are about to receive the latest illegal delivery of African souls—perhaps the first to arrive at this port in years. Perhaps the last ever.

When the ship finally docks and the boat grows almost still for the first time in weeks, I can see nothing through the black curtain except a gray morning mist fighting to pierce it. The heat is so intense and there is so little air that I feel close to passing out. Sailors' shadows rush by me, carrying crates and making room for the parade of Africans soon to come.

"Captain Van Owen," a new voice shouts from the dock, "you're at least a week earlier than I expected. But welcome home to the Pinnacle and you and your men." The man sounds older—perhaps sixty—and has a different accent. In his inflection, I hear a sort of arrogance tinged with stupidity and blindness to those of lower stations, traits I know I will find often in men of power in this new land.

"Mr. Steering," says Van Owen, "while I welcome your welcome, let me be clear about one thing: Boston is not my home."

"I suppose so," Steering agrees. "If it were, you'd surely be a more contented man." He says it with a laugh, but he aims to offend.

"I'll be content when I'm back on my farm, smoking my own tobacco fresh from the earth."

"You say that every trip, Mr. Van Owen, and then you're back out at sea within a few months. Perhaps your home doesn't offer you the happiness you say it does."

"My home offers me plenty of happiness. It would seem, though, that this country is set on impinging on my happiness."

Steering pauses before responding in a softer tone. "Captain Van Owen, you're in the *other* Carolina. *Your* state hasn't been grumbling about Lincoln and secession like your sister state."

"Mark my words, Mr. Steering, if that Illinois Whig wins the election, South Carolina might be first to secede, but North Carolina will not be far behind."

"Illinois Whig? Why, I'd heard Lincoln wasn't actually born in Illinois—that he's originally from Kentucky." He pauses for effect. "Say, isn't that where you hail from?"

Van Owen ignores the bait and continues his thought. "We in the South have no need for the laws of the North. It's another nation down there, and if we have to build another union to protect and maintain the sovereignty of that nation, then we will."

"Captain Van Owen, while you know I share some of your political views, I fail to recognize how you—of all men—have been fettered by Union laws. If it's the Union Navy that frightens you, then why not just forego the money you make moving slaves and stay in your beloved South on your beloved farm?"

Van Owen's voice is harsh when he answers, as if he is sneering. "The navy doesn't frighten me, Mr. Steering, and it's been a long time since I transported slaves just to make money. These days, I do it for one reason and one reason alone: to prove that I still can. But I am done with sea travel."

"With a fine slaving schooner like this one? I highly doubt that."

"In the future, you and your partners will have to find another man to captain the Pinnacle. Hear me true, Mr. Steering. I do not jest."

"Tobacco may make you wealthy, Captain Van Owen, but slaving seems to whet your appetite for adventure, no?"

"Adventure?" Van Owen ponders. "I think I've had my fill of adventure for the time being. Be sure to have my take forwarded to me by the end of the week. Good day, Mr. Steering."

Steering's tone shifts. He sounds confused even as he maintains his pretense of joviality. "You won't be sticking around for the hospitality of Massachusetts, then?"

"Hospitality? In Massachusetts? Mr. Steering, I believe they call that a contradiction-in-terms. Besides, I'm feeling a bit impatient. I've brought a little souvenir back from the other continent—

something just for me. And I want to get it back home as soon as possible so I can examine it more closely."

"Jewels, Captain Van Owen? Artifacts?"

"Something vastly more unusual, Mr. Steering." He pats the side of my covered cage as he continues: "A Nubian witch princess."

Steering laughs, certain that Van Owen is joking. "Fine then, Captain. Keep your secrets, but tell me—did you encounter any difficulty in Cuba?"

"Cuba?" says Van Owen, feigning puzzlement. "Oh, yes, we *were* supposed to stop in Cuba, weren't we?" He breathes in deeply. I imagine him relishing his pause, staring at the sky as if he owns it. "I don't much like Cuba. We skipped it altogether and brought the Africans directly here. I thought you'd have figured that out by now."

Steering laughs again, but there is no humor in Van Owen's tone. Although I cannot see their faces, I can sense Steering's pompous smile fading into an expression of bewilderment.

"Good day, Mr. Steering," says Van Owen, enjoying the joke that only he and I are getting.

"But," Steering says, still perplexed, "the...shipment...you did...?" His voice trails off as he begins to understand that he no longer holds the power in the situation.

Van Own answers by displaying his dominion, calling to his men in a voice that echoes across the harbor: "Crew—let's show Mr. Steering some Southern hospitality. How about a little entertainment? Let the pageant begin!"

His men must be baffled, but they follow his order nonetheless. I hear them racing about the bridge, trying to prepare the deck— tugging open the steel traps that seal the human cargo below, turning cranks to peel away the bars. The stench hits my nostrils even before the sound of the shackles reaches my ears. A whip cracks. A man shouts, "Move, you beasts," to two-hundred men and women who don't understand a word of English. Then comes the dull clanging. It is a dissonant song of feet shuffling and rusty chains rattling against bleeding ankles and wrists. I try to focus only on the rhythm—only the cadence of the shackles, only the drumming of blistery feet on splintery boards—to help me forget for a moment that these are my people being led into lives of servitude and degradation.

In our Mkembro myths, there were gods and demons, deities who blessed or cursed us, but all men, regardless of how purely or heinously they lived, could look forward to an afterlife of light and mercy. In our philosophy, there was no hell. Likewise, even for the lowest, life was never mercilessly grim. We had slaves even in Mkembro. It was common when a clan won a battle that it would take some of the vanquished as slaves, but they were not treated as American slaves. Our captives might have been enemies once, but we never forgot that they were men and women, just like us. Eventually, most of them were accepted into the clan as equals.

As I listen to the leaden footsteps of my people and allow myself to hear their moans, I ponder their chances of survival. Some will be dead within days. Some of the survivors will endure conditions even worse than what they have suffered on this sea journey. They will have their identities stripped from them. They will never again see their homeland. Nor will their children. Nor will I.

"What is the meaning of this, Van Owen?" Steering shouts in a coarse whisper. "You've brought slaves *here*—*to Boston*? Are you mad?"

Van Owen doesn't answer. I think of Roland all those weeks ago. On my first waking night, he told me of the original plan—to unload the slaves in Cuba. But then Van Owen diverted the ship so that he could return to America sooner, with me. I wonder what Steering will do with these hundreds of slaves that Van Owen has carted here. Perhaps he will hire another captain to turn the ship back toward Havana. He goes on with his complaints, pleading with the crew to send the slaves back down below, but Van Owen's men obey only Van Owen. The slave parade goes on, snaking around the deck, a perverse procession of hapless ghouls.

I wonder if the Africans even notice my cage, covered as it is. I wonder if they were loaded into the ship before I was. Or was I thrown in this cell and left exposed for all my people to see while they boarded? Were they marched past the daughter of their king while she lay unconscious and caged? Was my mother among them? Did she see me this way—a prize animal for the white demon? Did she wonder if I was to be entertainment for our captors—an African princess to be roasted alive in the sun?

"Mother?" I cry out. Then louder: "Mother, are you here?" But the sound of the whips, the whimpers of my people as they are struck, the shouts of the slavers who herd the prisoners like cattle, the creaking of the boards, and the rolling of the sea—all of these things conspire to drown me out. I call again, even louder this time: "Mother, it's me! It's Amara!"

There is some sort of fracas nearby—the chains grow louder. There is running and smashing, and the whips are even fiercer. Van Owen is cursing at his men. A woman screams as if she is being trampled by the mobs. I swear I hear her bones break against the deck. I hear Mkembran voices. Then two gunshots chime, and everything grows quiet.

Van Owen's voice cuts through the silence. "You see, Steering, even these Negroes put up a better struggle than your Union Army would against Southerners." Steering mumbles unintelligibly. He must be livid, worried that local authorities might have heard the shots. Van Owen laughs and then relents. "All right then, men, it appears Mr. Steering has had enough. Move the savages back down below."

The shuffling starts again. The chains rattle. The Africans march back toward hell.

"Mother?" I call. "Are you here? It's Amara..."

"Amara?" a voice answers. Kwame's voice!

"Kwame?" I stutter through tears.

"Kwame, what is happening—that commotion?" I ask in Mkembran.

"Our people—Merlante and Mkembro—they tried to fight together against the white men." His voice is filled with pride that our people fought as one—even without being united by our marriage.

"Then run—you must join them," I tell him. "Get free while you..."

"The fight is already over. I was below. I heard the sounds, but I could not get past our people to get up here to the battle."

Although the fight is over, the white men must still be in flux, for no one seems to notice that Kwame has stopped beside my cage, that he is whispering through the curtain.

"My mother," I ask, "have you seen her? Is she alive?"

"I don't know," he answers too quickly.

But I do know—even before my mind stirs and I feel my consciousness traveling through the black sheet, I know. I have known all along.

At first, there is only silence between us; I cannot hear the roar of the people or the whips or the shackles. I am no longer here in the cage, though I know I am. Then I feel my perception drifting outward as if pulled elsewhere. Drifting out of me and into Kwame's thoughts, into his memories. I do not question how. I do not fight it. I just watch:

It is weeks ago back in our land. He is asleep—passed out beside me after our struggle with Van Owen. A sharp pain across his back rouses him. He hears a harsh slapping sound, not unlike the sound of a tree branch cracking in half against the wind. The sound comes again and again almost in time with the waves of pain across his back. Finally he jolts to full wakefulness and realizes that the pain and the noise are from the whip that is lashing him again and again. Kwame looks behind him to see Van Owen almost thirty feet away, wielding the leather lash. It swings again, slapping against Kwame's back. He cries out and staggers to his feet, and then he sees the chains. While he slept, his arms and legs were shackled together so that he cannot stand fully upright. The chains are too short, so he is forced to hobble on all fours like an animal. As Kwame lurches forward, he notices me still unconscious on the ground. So he follows Van Owen's dictates—hoping that by appeasing the slaver, he might deter Van Owen from harming me. With scores of his people and mine, he is led down the beach, trotting through the water in chains toward the massive schooner. There are bodies all around—African bodies—some who fell, some who were struck, some who drowned. He passes a female body, facedown in the water. There is something familiar about her garb. As he struggles past her, he nudges the body with his arm. She twists slightly, and her face is partially exposed. It is my mother.

I break from Kwame's memory in time to hear him say, "Goodbye, Amara. I will..."

"Move away from her, savage," Van Owen's voice rings out from the other side of my cage.

"Kwame!" I shout. "Kwame, run!"

I hear more tumult—chains rattling, sticks and whips striking.

"Hit him again," cries Van Owen.

I keep calling Kwame's name, but I hear only the mayhem of the battle.

"No!" Van Owen screams suddenly to his crew. "Don't touch him! I know this one! Don't touch his chains! He's..."

Then there is that sound gain—that odd tone that emanated from my father when he fought the white men—the sound of a violin bow playing music backwards, a sound I haven't yet known. Men cry out in pain. The sailors should have listened to Van Owen, for, in the bowels of this slave ship, Kwame has learned better how to harness his power. Even in Africa, we knew that lightning will travel along anything metal—a spear, a cooking tool, a chain. The men have touched Kwame's chains, and they have been burned by lightning.

Through the curtain—even in the daylight—I can see the surges of light, Kwame silhouetted, lightning flowing from his hands, riding across his chains and burning the flesh of the white men who tug on them. The men let go, and Kwame lets up for a moment. The sparks gone, the curtain goes dark again, and I can see nothing, but I hear the sound of three men toppling to the boards.

"Stop him," shouts Van Owen.

"Damned black beast," says Mr. Steering. "How did he do that? What's he got there in his hand?"

"Amara," Kwame calls from the other side of the schooner, "I will come back for you..."

He's wrong. I will never see him again.

"Don't let him get to the water..." cries Van Owen. But it is too late. I hear the splash. Kwame has gone over the edge. He has gotten free.

There are gunshots. The men are firing at the water.

"I got him," cries a shooter.

Suddenly the curtain is lifted. The sun streams into my eyes, almost blinding me. Van Owen is there, his face only inches from mine. He has lifted the curtain, so that I'm partially exposed, squinting in the light.

"You filthy black witch," he grunts at me. "You caused this disturbance." In defiance, I smile back at him. Then I see the cane in his hands, its end facing me. It passes through the bars, careening toward my head. "Your lover is dead. You won't get the same chance to spread any more disorder." The end of the cane slams into my forehead, and the world goes black.

TEN

Warren tilted his face toward the sky, testing the rain. The sky was almost purple, and there was still some thunder in the distance, but the rain had lessened slightly. He stepped out from under the awning where he had taken shelter when the storm came. He'd thought about returning to his halfway house, but he liked the sound of the rain, the way it built from singular drips into torrents pouring down and cleansing the world. He listened now as the torrents faded into drips, only to be drowned out by thundering, running footsteps.

It was a boy and a girl, and Warren knew the boy. "Akins! Where are you going?"

Akins and the girl slowed to a walk, almost skidding to a stop ten feet beyond Warren. "What's up with you two? Cops chasing you?"

"No," said Akins, severely out of breath. "We... we were... we were back at the... We were... he told us to run, and we...we..."

He's a freak," the girl chimed in. "The whole family—they're *all* freaks. What just happened?" She turned to her boyfriend, walking toward him as if seeking the comfort of an embrace. She put her arms around him, but he didn't raise his. Finally she let go and backed up. Turning to Warren, she asked, "Who are you?"

"That's Warren," Akins answered for him. "He's a customer. From the flophouse on 135th." He smiled, amused at Warren's living situation.

It's not a flophouse. And I'm not your customer anymore," said Warren. "I'm through with that."

"Yeah?" laughed Akins, "since when? I just sold you some shit this afternoon. And if you're through with it all, then why are you standing outside in the dark all alone at night like you're waiting for more?"

"You heard me," Warren said sternly, "I'm through. That was my last high. I'm just standing out here enjoying it till it wears off." Warren removed his baseball cap, shook the rain from its visor, and stuffed it into his back pocket.

Now that Warren's face was visible, the girl gave him a look of surprise. "You old," she told him.

She was right, Warren knew. Most of Akins's clients were probably other high school kids. Warren was only twenty-four, but he looked thirty or more and as tired and worn as his clothes. He caught her scanning him up and down as if he were a vagrant, and he threw a warning at her: "You ought to get out of this business while you can." He straightened his jacket and pulled himself up taller. "And stay away from people like him," he added, gesturing toward Akins, "or you'll end up looking like me."

The girl answered, "I don't need you to tell me what to do."

Akins opened his mouth as if he, too, had a tough comeback for Warren but then thought better of it. What came out was considerably less combative. "People like me? My product's been good enough for you for the last year."

"Well," said Warren as he turned away and ducked back under the awning, "it's not good enough anymore." The rain had started to come down hard again, but the two teenagers stayed in the downpour, still visibly out of sorts.

"Whatever," cried the girl, enunciating the word with a harsh hand gesture toward Warren. "Enough with you." Then back to Akins: "What was that before—some kind of magic trick or something?"

Akins was shaking his head as if trying to remember something. "I don't know. It was like hypnosis or some shit. I felt like his voice was inside my head..."

"I'm *telling* you," she answered. "That whole family. The older one's like this big giant, the girl's a weird little mute freak, and that skinny middle one—he's like a magician or something."

"Yeah," said Akins. "All of them."

"So what are you gonna do about them?" asked the girl.

"Same thing I told him I would. Gonna get my .38 and just wait for him after school. Maybe I'll wait for the whole family—all three of them together. Just pop 'em all." He formed his hand to mimic a gun, the thumb twitching with each sound effect he made with his mouth. "Ptow! Ptow! Ptow! Take out the whole Kelly family with one clip."

Warren turned his head at the sound of the family name. "Who?"

"The Kelly family," said Akins. "They're these strange freaks at school. Skinny Terry and his giant brother and his little mute-freak sister. I'm gonna waste all three of them."

Warren approached with quick strides, his fists clenching. "Kelly," he said, "is my last name too." He grabbed Akins by the lapels of his jacket and walked him backward until Akins collided with the streetlamp that shone down on them. Their faces lit, Akins's eyes grew wide while Warren's eyes felt like slits.

"Don't you mess with me," Akins blustered. "You hurt me and my boss will..."

"I don't give a damn about your boss. You just told me you're gonna kill my brothers and my little sister."

The girl was making odd, frightened sounds, but she didn't move. Akins struggled in Warren's grip. He hurled a punch at Warren's jaw, connecting but doing no damage; Warren barely flinched. He only slid his hands up from Akins's lapels until they fastened on each side of the boy's temples. Instinct was taking over, and Warren was letting it.

"You can take my shit," Akins begged as he struggled in Warren's grip, pushing and kicking to no avail. "You can take the crank and the horse—all of it!"

I told you," said Warren in a monotone. "I'm through with that stuff. And I'm through with you."

"You hurt me, and...they'll kill your whole family," Akins warned. "My boss..."

Warren could feel the blood pumping in his chest, moving faster, rushing toward his hands. He could feel the eyes begin to glow, become iridescent, the way they always did. Akins swung wildly, but his punches had no effect. Then the burning started.

Sparks crackled from Warren's hands, tiny lightning bursts against Akins's forehead. Akins's hair stood on end as Warren's hands began to glow. Warren tried to close his eyes. He wanted to let go, to turn away, but he couldn't. Akins screamed as the crackling lightning rose from Warren's hands, enveloping Akins's head in a red and yellow light.

"Stop it," shouted the girl. "Stop it! You're gonna kill him!"

But Warren couldn't stop. It was too late. It had been this way since he was a teenager. Once started, the current wouldn't break until it was spent. He felt Akins's body shudder, twitching and spasming with each lightning surge. He tried to let the boy go, but his hands felt soldered to Akins's head as the sparks flashed and receded, holding firmly until the tremors slowed and Akins's weight felt heavier and heavier. Then, when Akins's eyes rolled back and smoke began to emanate from his still body, Warren's hands finally opened and released the boy. Akins fell to the street without a sound, a lifeless heap. Even in the rain, the stench of burnt flesh was thick in the air.

"Oh my God," the girl murmured, her hand to her mouth, "oh my God," more rabid with each repetition, "oh my God." She backed up slowly, unable to scream, but she finally found the will to turn and run.

Warren lifted his hands, which were still bathed in a silvery haze. He was breathing hard. He shook out his hands, squeezed them into fists again and again, but the glow wouldn't fade fast enough. "Damn," he mumbled. "Can't..."

He looked down at Akins's unmoving form. He crouched and leaned in toward the dead boy's face. "No," Warren said, his voice so warped that it didn't sound like his own. "No..." His hand brushed against Akins's hand. It was cold though the boy's body still smoldered. Warren did a quick survey of the area. There was no one around. No cars. No people. No one except the girl had seen anything. His high was fading, and the paranoia was starting to set in. He felt his heartbeat quicken as he thought about what he had done. Murder. He had committed murder. He had killed someone.

He could feel the sweat forming all over his face, coming again and again even as the rain washed it away. "No," he repeated. "No..." He glanced again for onlookers. Not a soul. He was about to move away, but then, frantically, he reached into Akins's inside jacket. "Where is it?" he asked, fumbling and shaking. Finally he found the large, clear plastic baggie in a zippered inner pocket. He knew what was in it. He could feel several smaller baggies inside the larger one. Some tiny paper envelopes, too. There were pills in some, marijuana and cocaine and crack in others. And vials of heroin in others. Akins always had the heroin. He called it "horse," a word that lots of street kids used, but Warren never would. He respected horses too much, loved them. He was raised to. He didn't respect heroin, but he did need it.

He snatched three of the smaller envelopes and stuffed them into his own jacket packet, inadvertently spilling some of the pills and powder over Akins's body. Most of the pills rolled down the body and landed on the sidewalk. The powder collected in a small clump over Akins's chest. For a moment, Warren stood there watching as the rain turned the little cocaine hill into a puddle of gray mud. He thought of a day he had spent at the beach once with his parents and his two brothers. Carl Kelly had played tirelessly with his three sons—building sand castles, dunking the boys in the water, throwing a football—while their pregnant mother watched from beneath an umbrella. Warren wondered when things had gone so wrong. He shook his head in sorrow and then turned and stormed off, his footsteps resounding like hooves on the damp pavement, echoing across the Harlem night.

ELEVEN

I may have slept for days. Perhaps only hours. I can't be sure. It's dark again. The curtain surrounds me once more, but it's different somehow—smaller and rounded at the top. I can feel the boat rocking, but the rhythm is choppy and short, as if we're in the midst of a gale. Everything's changed, though. There's the smell of nature here: trees and grass and plants and animals. And animal manure. The sound and scent of the ocean are gone, replaced by a clip-clop song that is lovely, melodic, familiar. I've heard it in my visions.

"Yah," a man's voice calls, accompanied by the snapping of a rope. A horse whinnies in response, and the clopping grows more furious. The boat rocks sharply, but I know that it's not a boat. I'm in a carriage. By the hoof beats, I know that there are at least two horses pulling it. I've seen horses only in visions—this notion of beasts of burden is still unfamiliar to me—but I know I'll come to love them, and I feel safer now, knowing that I'm among them. After all, we have so much in common: we both ran free once, only to be forced to labor at the will of others.

We ride on through the night. The scents of North Carolina are so familiar, so pleasant, though I know they shouldn't be. The fields are rich with the aroma of corn and sesame, almost masking the pungent tobacco fragrance that we're approaching. I almost feel guilty that I love these scents, for they are America's scents. They are not mine to love.

The carriage makes a sharp turn. "Ho," calls the driver. "Whoa." The horses slow and stop, and so do I—finally stationary after so long. No swaying of the oceans, no rocking of the carriage. The driver and another man jump to the ground from the perch. The canopy above me peels back, and the curtains open. I expect to see Van Owen and his men, ready with whips and weapons. I'm mistaken. There are a dozen men there, staring at me. But they're dark-skinned like me. They're clothed like white men—shirts and pants and shoes—but their eyes are filled with both pity and revulsion. Perhaps some of them remember how they looked and felt when they first arrived here. Perhaps some of them were once even my own people. For most of them, however, America is the only home they've ever known, and they've never even seen an African in African dress. They were born in captivity. Born slaves. To them, I probably look like a savage—a reflection of their past.

"You see, witch?" Van Owen says from a distance, though I cannot see him. "You see—I'm smarter than you are." His voice is calm and even and slow. Gone is the bark in his tone when he was the captain of the ship, ordering scores of sailors. Now we're on *his* soil. He steps from the shadows, the only white man among a sea of Africans and African descendants. He's dressed all in white again. I wonder if he was the on the wagon with me, or if he came by some faster method and has been here awaiting my arrival for some time. Are there trains yet? The visions are so confusing. In my head, I see airplanes in the skies. *No, I tell myself, that's another time, another generation.* "You see, Amara," Van Owen goes on, "I'm not going to let you touch me or anybody my color. I've seen firsthand what you can do when you touch someone, but I don't think you're about to hurt one of your own." He tilts his head and smiles coyly, though convinced that I don't understand his words. "Are you?"

The African men—the male slaves—are confused. They see how

I'm dressed—the rags of West African wear, the beads in my hair. They know I must have just arrived in this country, and so they can't comprehend why their master is expending such resources on me— and why he's speaking to me in English. I pretend I'm seeing them for the first time—that I don't know all of their faces and what will happen to them over the years that I'll spend here with them.

Van Owen orders the oldest slave, Harry, to take me to the small shack at the end of the row of slave dwellings. To tie me up and leave me there on the cot. Harry points, and I walk in front of him. I already know the way to my cabin. My legs are stiff from the ride. It hurts to walk, but I don't show it; Harry already feels bad enough about his assignment. He averts his eyes from my naked torso, even as he applies the ropes as his master instructed. Before he closes the door to leave me there alone, he turns back to me, his eyes registering embarrassment more than anything else—as if he's ashamed to be the first African American I have met, ashamed of his powerlessness, ashamed for all of us. His hands are meaty and worn and dry as sand. There's a scar on his forehead that must be decades old. He's an old man who has seen so little joy in his time. He has never seen Africa. He was born a slave in America, and he will die a slave in America. I can see him months from now, swinging from a tree by his neck—his punishment for helping me. Death follows me like a shadow.

The shack is a damp, one-room hut that reeks of mold and tobacco seed. There is one dim light from a failing oil lantern. The floor is the earth itself, with worms and dead grass and hidden crickets chirping. Beside the bed is a musty tan throw rug—a withered hand-me-down from Van Owen's mansion. It's covered in dust. In but a few days, I will have this place livable. I'll find I even enjoy beating the dirt from the rug. Now, though, I wait propped up on the bed, leaning against the wall with my hands tied behind my back. My heart quickens at the sound of footsteps outside. The door rustles as it opens.

"Well," says Van Owen, "I trust you find your new home to your liking."

I don't answer. I stare back into his eyes with a century and a half of hatred.

"What's the matter, witch? Don't you have any African curses to hurl at me?"

I don't even blink. He nods his head back and forth like a scolding schoolteacher and shuts the door behind him as he steps inside. Then he approaches the bed.

"You look mighty pretty there, all tied up, waiting for me the way you are." His voice is as easy and calm as his words are rife with unspoken threats. "You *wanted* me to come in, didn't you? You were *hoping* I'd come."

My visions are like memories—distorted and jumbled. In my mind, I can see him on top of me, his hot breath on my neck. But we're dressed differently. It's daytime in the vision, but now it's night, so perhaps I am safe.

"Oh, don't worry, little witch. I don't think I'll take you tonight." He emphasizes the word *take*, saliva spraying from his mouth as he says it. "I just came to talk to my new girl in her new home." He sits beside me on the bed and crosses one of his legs over the other. Even his boots are white, and so clean, as if the soles of his shoes evade the dirt on the ground. He swims in mire and yet remains unstained.

"You know," he continues while staring at me, his pale eyes boring into mine, "I was thinking how lucky I was to meet you. You and your betrothed. Y'all have given me a gift of sorts. A strange and precious gift, the likes of which no white man since Jesus Christ has been the recipient."

Alone with me, his voice, rich with that odd, aristocratic accent, is softer, yet still grating to my ears, and I find I have to struggle just to make out some of his words, even though I know most of them before he says them.

"Yes, I am a man blessed. Your betrothed—the one who threw himself into the ocean yesterday and got a bullet for his trouble—he gave me this." His gaze goes to his hand, which he holds up between our faces, waving it back and forth as if passing it through water, the fingers trailing slowly behind like the tail of a kite. His head blocks the lantern so that his features and expression are hidden in shadow for a moment. Then I hear that eerie hummingbird sound, and Van Owen's fingertips begin to glow. Soon, his entire hand is covered in crackles of tiny lightning sparks that dance across his knuckles. As quickly as it started, the lightning dims and fades. He exhales and smiles and turns back toward me. "That's what I got from the boy witch. Now let's us see what I got from *you.*"

His hands stretch toward my face, cold fingers gripping me on opposite sides of my head, just like Kwame did to him at the wedding. He closes his eyes. I try to pull back, but there's nowhere to go. Behind me is the wall. Van Owen is in front of me, and to my side, and all around me. I close my eyes, trying to shield my mind from his as he tries to tear into my thoughts. Outside, a blue light flashes, and I open my eyes again. And I scream.

TWELVE

Marco Fenelli was sleeping in his easy chair when he heard the shouting and the pounding.

"Mr. Fenelli? Marco? Open the door..."

Marco bounded to his feet and instinctively reached for his gun, but there was no gun strapped to his shoulder. It hadn't been there for many years.

"Marco," the voice came again. It was Terry. Marco's back was stiff and his walk uneven as he tried to rush to the door. His wrinkled bathrobe, tied around a yellowed tee-shirt and long-out-of-style gray suit pants, felt loose on him. *I'm shrinking,* he thought to himself. *God's punishment.*

"Marco, come on. I can hear the TV. I know you're in there."

"Hold on, kid," said Marco as he undid the four locks and opened the door to the sight of the breathless teenager. Terry burst in and raced through the tiny apartment and into the kitchen to drop his two tattered grocery bags. "Where's the fire?" Marco asked as he checked the hallway before locking the door. He counted the locks aloud as he turned or slid each one.

"You're not gonna *believe* it," said Terry, as he strode toward the center of the room. His hands were shaking. His eyes were wild and intense, bouncing from wall to wall and back to Marco's tired eyes.

As Marco passed the mirror, he stroked the two days' growth of beard on his chin. His skin was a craggy, pale olive color, and he turned quickly from the reflection. He shoved the previous day's clothing from a stiff wooden chair and offered the chair to Terry, but the boy was not ready to sit. "What happened? Did you hear from Warren again?"

Terry nodded yes but held up his palm to deflect questions. "Yeah, Warren's been around—Jerome and I gave him some money—but that's not it. Today was the first day of school, you know. And you remember I told you about Akins?"

"The bully, yeah." Marco sat in a torn, vinyl-upholstered chair and raised a comb to his slicked-back, thinning gray hair. He noticed the almost empty wine bottle he had left at the foot of his chair and thought of trying to conceal it from Terry, but there was no need. His drinking was no secret. Terry, after all, had been delivering Marco's wine for more than a year.

Barely stopping for air, Terry began telling about his day—how Leticia had insulted Regina. Marco chimed in with "Good" when Terry got to the part where he'd told Akins, "Tell your girlfriend not to talk to my sister that way." But Terry was honest. He didn't embellish or hide his humiliation. He described how Akins knocked him to the ground, holding him there until Jerome showed up.

"But I thought there was something weird," Terry went on. He was speaking too fast, but Marco was used to that from him. "I didn't think Akins even saw Jerome. It seemed like Akins was reacting to *me*. 'Cause I had just said, 'Get off me,' and pushed him, and Akins jumped right up. But Regina thought that Akins must have gotten up because Jerome came over to help. I mean...I know you haven't seen him yet, but Jerome's huge..."

"Yeah, you've told me." Marco wasn't following every detail of Terry's narration, but he was gleaning enough to get the big picture. "And then what?"

"Well, he just jumped up off me like he was freaked or something..."

"Well, with a guy Jerome's size standing over him, what do you expect?" Marco laughed.

"No, Marco," Terry scolded, "you're not listening. It was like Akins was...I don't know..."

Marco stared at the boy, betraying no emotion at all. He reached for the bottle at his feet and refilled the filmy glass on the arm of his chair.

"Anyway, tonight," Terry continued, "I was on my way here. It was my last delivery. You know, I always come here last." Marco nodded. "You know," Terry said sheepishly, "'cause it's on the way home." Marco nodded, knowing that the boy made his last stop there every Monday simply so that he could spend extra time with the old man. "So I run into Akins and Leticia again just a block from Greenway..."

"They were probably waiting for you."

"No, they didn't even know I worked there. Akins was probably just dealing there or something."

"He deals? Akins deals?"

"I think so. Everyone says he does."

"In my day," Marco interrupted, "you couldn't even get into that sort of business unless you knew someone or were related to someone." He didn't know why he was going off on this tangent, but he couldn't stop himself. "How'd he get into it?"

"I don't know. It doesn't work like that anymore. Anyone who wants can get into it. People you knew are all dead by now."

Marco wanted to argue that they weren't *all* dead, but instead he found himself reminiscing. He had told Terry bits and shreds about the past—his days as a loan shark—a low-level cog in a Brooklyn crime gang—a life Marco was forced to flee after an affair with the wrong woman. But that was decades ago, and Terry was basically right: Marco didn't know much about the modern criminal world—especially in Harlem. After all, Marco hadn't even left his apartment in years. What had begun as a forced exile had evolved into agoraphobia. Marco couldn't make himself walk outside even if he wanted to. "Go on, kid," he said.

So Terry went on, explaining about Akins and Leticia following him—how they had started insulting him again. "They're trashing Gina and Jerome. Akins calls Jerome a pussy. He says Jerome is strong but not tough..."

"I've heard you say the same thing about Jerome."

"Come on, Marco, will you let me tell the story?"

Marco relented, motioning for Terry to continue.

Terry exhaled with frustration before going on. "So then Akins says he's gonna bring his piece to school and wait for Jerome and sneak up on him and blow him away..."

Marco's neck stiffened and he squinted. "He said that?"

"Yeah."

"Damn it. Well...well we've got to... *you've* got to tell someone..."

"No, Marco. You're not letting me finish. I think I stopped him already. I..." Marco almost did a double-take.

"You hit him?" Terry suddenly looked shy.

"Well, no..." "What'd you do?"

"I...I told him to shut up."

Marco looked him up and down, checking for signs of a lost battle but saw none. "And what'd he do?"

"He shut up. It was weird. He just, like, stopped talking all of a sudden." Even Terry looked puzzled as he recounted the story. "He got really stiff—like he was sleepwalking or something. Both of them did—Akins and Leticia."

Marco stared at the boy, his eyelids twitching. "Uh huh."

When Terry spoke next, his words came slowly and evenly, spilling from his mouth with an upward inflection at the end of each sentence. "And then I told them to get away from me." He looked directly into Marco's eyes. "And they did. They just turned away. It was like a magic act on TV or something, where the magician tells some guy to cluck like a chicken, and the dude just does it. They were like zombies." He sounded more and more perplexed as he went on. "They didn't even look scared or anything. I told them to get away—really loud—and they started moving away. So I yelled, 'Get away,' and they ran, and they just kept going until I couldn't see them anymore."

Marco sipped from his glass and swallowed without expression. He rotated the wine glass and raised it to his mouth again, gulping down the remainder. He stared into the empty glass as if searching for something. When he turned back to Terry, his glance was more sorrowful than anything else. "So they *obeyed* you," he said in a monotone. "Just turned and ran off."

"You don't believe me," said Terry, sounding disappointed.

Suddenly Marco was on his feet, his eyes alert and ready. He clutched Terry by his upper arm and yanked him toward the small kitchen at the rear of the sparse apartment. "Sit down here," he ordered as he placed Terry in a metal chair at the rickety table. For a moment, Marco felt embarrassed as Terry stared down at the stained red and white checked tablecloth. The grime was so set-in that the tablecloth could never be clean. But there was no time to worry about that now. Marco needed to know something for sure.

He rummaged through the cabinet beneath the sink until he found an unopened wine bottle. Within seconds, he had pried out the cork with a corkscrew and snatched a coffee mug from the dish rack and placed the bottle and mug on the table. Then he sat down opposite Terry and stared into the boy's eyes.

"Okay, I want you to do to me what you did to Akins."

Terry started backing his chair away.

"No," insisted Marco, grabbing Terry by the wrist. "Stay put, and do what I tell you."

"Why?"

"Because...just because." He let go of Terry's wrist and put both of his own hands flat on the table. "Now do what you did to Akins and his girlfriend. Make me do something—something simple. Tell me to...pour a drink."

Terry's eyes shifted several times from the bottle to the coffee mug and then back to Marco's creased green eyes. "Go ahead," Marco demanded, "tell me to do it."

Terry rolled his eyes as he said it: "Pour a drink."

Marco just stared at him with a sour expression. "No, *tell* me to do it. Don't just say the words. Order me the same way you ordered Akins to get away."

Terry repeated the words, louder this time and with conviction, but the result was the same. The old man didn't budge.

Marco checked his hands; they were both still firmly on the table. He took a deep breath. He wasn't going to enjoy what he was about to do, but he felt he had no choice. "Damn it, Terry," he snapped as he grabbed the boy's forearms and squeezed hard.

"Hey," Terry stuttered, frightened.

"When I tell you to do something," said the old man, "I expect you to do it. Now tell me to pour the goddamned drink."

Without even thinking, Terry followed the instruction. "Pour the drink," he yelled at the old man. "Pour the goddamned drink!"

Marco's eyes turned glassy. His face lost expression. He released Terry's arms and took up the mug in one hand and the wine bottle in the other. Then he tilted the bottle, filling the mug with wine. Finally, he put the bottle and mug down, placed both hands down on the table, and stared straight ahead.

Terry jumped out of his seat and backed up until he slammed into the cupboard behind him. "Shit," he whispered, "it worked."

Marco could see and hear Terry. He could still feel the room around him—the bottle and mug on the table, the smell of the cheap wine, the sound of Terry's voice—but it was as if he was a spectator, watching from afar with no control over his senses.

Terry approached him slowly and tried to make eye contact, but Marco couldn't control his own gaze.

"Stand up," Terry said sharply, and Marco did, but he did it in is own style. He pushed his chair backward from the stood, rose, brushed away non-existent dust from his pants, and pushed the chair back in.

"Now take the bottle and go to the sink," Terry told him. Marco obeyed. He held the bottle over the sink, staring straight ahead into the dark blinds that covered the window. "Now pour it down the drain."

Marco could feel the bottle turning over. He could hear the liquid exiting the bottle, sloshing through the spout, easing through the ancient pipes. *What a sad, lonely sound,* he thought to himself.

"What the hell?" Terry whispered. Then he moved quickly to the door and shut it hard.

Marco could hear the apartment door close and Terry's footsteps on the stairs, but he couldn't quite understand what any of it meant. It was much longer before he jolted, suddenly aware of his surroundings and in control of his body.

He spun around, remembering that the door had shut and that Terry was gone. He was still holding the empty bottle, the last drops trickling downward onto the linoleum. He almost smiled at the thought of Terry forcing him to dump out the liquor. The boy was looking out for him. "Damn kid," he mumbled as he put the bottle in the sink and ran toward the front door. Opening it, he leaned out and called Terry's name twice. He got no response. He breathed in deeply and stepped into the hallway. His face reddened as he took another step. And another. Soon, he was standing at the top of the stairs that led down to the building's entry foyer, which led to the outside world.

He gripped the handrail and extended one foot over the second step. *Just go*, he told himself. *It's just eleven steps and then you're there. You've counted them enough times.* Then his foot started quivering. His leg picked up the motion. He felt a pain in his stomach. His heart was rushing. He had to place a second hand on the railing just to keep his balance. "Damn it," he called aloud as he backed up toward the open door to his apartment, holding a palm against the wall for support. Once inside, he locked the door and leaned back against it as he caught his breath.

Within a minute, the nausea had passed. He was back inside—in his own home. He was safe. He retrieved the phone and sat in his easy chair, cradling the phone in his lap for nearly a minute before sighing and lifting the receiver. He dialed the number from memory, watching the old rotary phone click and whirr with each number. He waited for the hello on the other end before speaking. "It's me," he said. A pause. "You were wrong. It's not just the women."

THIRTEEN

"Arise and shine," Harry says, gesturing with his hand for me to climb from the bed.

It's my first morning on the plantation. Oddly, I have slept well. I peel away the frayed little blanket that covers me, wondering how it got there. My body creaks as I rise to my feet and try to remind myself that I am sixteen years old; I only *feel* like I'm ninety.

In the daylight, Harry looks more youthful than he did last night when he led me to this shack. He's quite fit for a man in his sixties, perhaps the only benefit of a lifetime of slave labor. When I stand and face him, he stares at my African garb, which covers little. He turns away, embarrassed, and tosses me a pair of pants and a shirt.

"You're a tobacco-farmer now," Harry tells me, "so you better start dressing like one." A gentleman, he keeps his back to me while I change into the musty, gray clothing. "One of the women says that was the outfit of a queen you was wearing." He paused, waiting for me to respond. I don't, so he goes on. "She came off a boat, too, but that was about thirty years back when she was just a child. She says she can barely even remember it now, like a dream." He sighs as if he's amused, but I know he isn't. He doesn't even suspect that I understand any of what he's saying. He's speaking to me to offer human contact of some kind. "She's the only other one here who came off a boat. I don't know from Africa. I was born right here in

North Carolina. But I'll tell you one thing you better learn right now: princess don't mean nothing here. The only royalty here is Mas'r Van Owen. The sooner you accept that, the better. Now let me hear you say it," he tells me, his back still to me as he opens the door, letting in the rising sun. "Let me hear you say 'Mas'r Van Owen'."

"Master Van Owen," I say quickly, and Harry spins back around to look at me, stunned that I have understood and responded so quickly and so clearly. I return his glance as if I have no idea I've done anything special, as if I'm just mimicking.

I don't speak English to the other slaves for some time after that. I don't want to scare them; they wouldn't understand how an African just off the boat can speak English as well as their master does—with a Southern accent no less. So I let them teach me the language. I follow them into the fields, where they train me in skills I already know, such as how to pick tobacco for curing. I pretend that it's new to me, though my visions, like memories, have instructed me in knowledge that I won't have for months or years. I point randomly at objects and stare inquisitively until someone says "tree" or "water" or "chicken." Then I nod as if I've just learned the words, as if I'm collecting them in my mind like tobacco in a barrel.

Kneel. Bend. Reach. Stab. Twist. Snap. Drop.

Repeat.

These are the most essential instructions. I spear row after row of tobacco with a stick, twisting and breaking the leaves at the root of the stem, feeling the calluses form across my palms. I lay the stick into the barrel, take up another one, and start again. Once a barrel is full, Harry or one of the other older men comes along with a donkey to tote or roll it back to the barn, where they spray it with ammonia and hang it. They don't know why, but I do. Ammonia triggers the nicotine, making it more potent, making the smoker more addicted. Sometimes, in my mind, I can see the cigarette vending machines that will sprout up across this country decades from now, spewing out the poison—from plants just like these—that will cause the deaths of millions. For now, though, I find that I actually enjoy the scent of the fresh leaves. The aroma is both acrid and sweet at the same time. It's the scent I associate with America, a pleasant scent masking an insidious danger.

Harry is in charge of all slaves. They rarely just call him Harry, though; he's always "Mister Harry." He spent decades toiling in the field and proving his loyalty to his master, so now he's the head slave. He doles out the work assignments, the food, and even the punishments. One spirited young slave, Sam, who is my age and was born here on the plantation, likes to brag about how well he took a "whupping" from Harry just a few months ago. Sam had pocketed some tobacco leaves and, stupidly, tried to smoke them at night after the plantation had gone to sleep. He stole out of his quarters behind the chicken coop, rolled the tobacco into a ball and stuffed it into a pipe he'd made from an apple core. Then, seated on a hay bale, he leaned back against a tobacco barrel and struck a match. He didn't even have a chance to inhale. The flame illuminated the sealed-off area, revealing the faces of Harry, Van Owen, and two white guardsmen, who stood only yards away.

"You were correct, gentlemen," Van Owen said to one guard. "Sam *was* planning on taking a smoke tonight with my tobacco."

Sam didn't struggle as the white guards led him out to an oak tree behind the horse barn. As he tells the story, Sam makes it sound as if he was cocky, but I can tell he feared they'd kill him. The white men tied him to a tree with his chest facing it.

"Five lashes, Mister Harry," Van Owen commanded. "That should be enough. Wouldn't you agree, Sam?"

"Yes, Mas'r Van Owen," Sam answered. "That'll be enough. I won't do it again."

"No, Sam," Van Owen told him, "next time you'll probably do

worse."

Then Harry counted twenty paces and turned toward his target and followed his master's orders.

"And I didn't cry out once," Sam tells us. "Not even once. Mister Harry was swinging with all his might. You must o' all heard that whip..."

His mother, Norma, always defends Harry, though. After hours of instructing me in the finer points of stripping the leaves from the vines, she stands up from her bucket of tobacco and wags her finger in her son's face: "If Mister Harry had swung with all his might, you'd have been in bed for weeks, not days. Mister Harry may be old now, but he's still the strongest man on this farm."

Van Owen is off conferring somewhere with his Confederate comrades, planning their new union. He might be away for weeks. They say he makes periodic announcements to his slaves, informing them of the political happenings and warning them to behave in his absences. They act as if he cares about them. More than once, Harry tells me what a good master Van Owen is—a churchgoer—and what a good man he is. "Must be six years ago, I got thrown from a horse," Harry says. "Master Van Owen comes running full speed from the house. He was watching from the window, saw the whole thing. Master picks me up in his arms like I'm a baby, carries me to his wagon, and drives me into town himself to see the doctor."

Sure, I think to myself, *he wants his head slave healthy to keep the others in line. He didn't show you any kindness. He was just protecting his investments.* But I don't say a word. I just turn away.

"You'll see," says Harry. "Mas'r Van Owen—he's a good man, a good Christian man." But I know he's trying more to convince himself rather than me.

In the kitchen, I sneak a look at a wrinkled newspaper that the women use as kindling to start a cooking fire. The date reads

October 9, 1860. The news on the pages is irrelevant local chatter. The date is what's important to me. I sift through the random knowledge imprinted in my mind and recall that soon eleven states will secede from the Union and form their Confederate States of America, paving the way for the nation's bloodiest days since it murdered the original Americans. I cringe when I think of the term *Civil War*. How can war ever be *civil*? And what could be less civil than wanton murder? In visions, I have seen Van Owen in his gray uniform. So proud. So certain of his good fortune. And, later, so defeated.

Hundreds of thousands of people will die in the coming battles, but Van Owen will not be among them, a fact that makes me doubt all of my people's stories of higher beings that guide our days on this world. For what sort of god would allow Van Owen to live when so many good people perish?

The weeks roll on. With each one, I ease my charade a bit. Gradually, I move from speaking in the thick African accent—which I lost even before I left Mkembro—to speaking whole sentences in drawled Southern slave English. Every day begins the same way: Harry knocks on my door to announce that the workday has started. Some mornings, I wake confused. I look around my bare cabin—with only its bed and chair and four thatched walls—and I feel certain that something is different. Perhaps the lone chair has been moved slightly. Perhaps the dirt floor is not as it was when I went to sleep. I look for footsteps, but I never find any. Wouldn't I wake, I wonder, if someone had entered? If Van Owen had entered?

Harry always knocks on my door first—for mine is the cabin closest to the main house—and then, through the thin walls, I listen to him make his way down the rows of slave dwellings, knocking and calling until all 150 slaves are awake. I am the only with private quarters. The others are crammed six or seven to a room. The conditions are pleasant, the older slaves tell me, compared to what they experienced on other plantations. But they have all heard worse stories—stories about the cargo holds of slaving ships: weeks of sitting upright, pressed together so tightly that breathing was a chore and air a commodity. I hear tales of cargo hold Africans who strangled the weak and the dying among them just to make more room or more air—or perhaps just out of madness. I am too ashamed to tell them that even in the Middle Passage, I had my own room, albeit a cell on the deck of the ship.

We slaves eat our meals together. We sit on splintery benches and eat tasteless offerings. The food is mostly grain cereals, though sometimes we are treated to small portions of catfish or beef or possum or cornbread. The worst part is the blandness. I long for the rich and richly colored spices of my home. I am so starved for flavor that I find myself imagining how food would taste if it were spiced with tobacco.

Many of the other slaves' faces are scarred from branding or beating. Several men are missing a finger or a hand or several toes, punishments for trying to flee or from simply looking at white women. One man has only half his tongue. One woman has a scar across her throat. Others seem so bruised emotionally that they rarely even lift their eyes from the ground. They bury themselves in their work as if dedication can hinder woe. Yet, sometimes, after meals, there is music. A few of the enslaved break out instruments made from basins and washboards and wood-and-wire, and they play and sing and dance. Often, their songs are religious, evoking stories of Abraham or Moses or Jesus. I wonder if they have ever beheld artists' renderings of these figures—white men, always. White men with white features and white thoughts. My brethren here know nothing of the beliefs that should be their heritage. They have no connection to their past, to their ancestors. Such is the legacy of slavery. It tears us from our past, it tears us from ourselves.

The strangest thing about the plantation is that I see only slaves here. I know that there are armed white men who guard the plantation from afar, but I never see them. Meanwhile, Van Owen's mansion looks large enough to house every slave on the farm, yet I never see anyone but Harry enter or exit it. I hear nothing of Van Owen having friends or a wife or children. One day, when the other slaves are eating, I sneak to the window of his mansion and gaze inside. I can see only his sitting room: a mahogany floor, walls covered with Victorian tapestries and religious paintings. Overhead, a giant crystal chandelier hangs from the ceiling, each dangling glass shard offering a distorted reflection of the entire room. Some of the decorations are so familiar somehow. I feel that I have seen them in visions—but not here. It was the same room, but it was in another place, another time.

Suddenly, I feel a hand on my shoulder. I spin, cursing myself for my curiosity, ready for battle.

"Amara," Harry says to me, nodding his head back and forth, "you know better than that. Mas'r Van Owen will be back anytime now; you best get yourself back with the others." But there's something in his expression that worries me. His words don't feel like a warning at all—more like an expression of fear.

The other slaves sometimes speak of running away. One day during the morning work hours, Norma—Sam's mother, who does most of the cooking—sees me staring off when I should be picking tobacco. With my bucket in my lap and my arms hanging limp at my sides, I must appear as if I'm sleeping with my eyes open. I'm lost in a vision, watching Regina do her homework while Terry sits near her reading a book. Norma shakes me from my reverie and points to the surrounding fields, warning me, "They're watching. They're *always* watching."

There is nothing there, though, but rows and rows of tobacco plants and trees and fields.

"They're watching," she repeats, nodding, "so *you* watch *yourself.*"

I don't see *them* until my sixth week, when an altercation breaks out between two slaves. A young man has taken improper liberties with another slave's wife, and the two men begin brawling in the horse barn at twilight. The tumult is such that I hear other slaves racing toward the barn to intervene. Before I can even make it out of my bed, Harry's voice resounds through my closed door.

"Stay put," he calls to all of us as he trots off toward the barn with his whip in hand. I crack the door slightly and watch him closing in on the barn, but he's too late. The white men get there first. Four of them, half-clothed, come tearing across the tobacco fields, rifles in hand. One of them has two dogs on a lengthy leash, snarling and barking as they gallop toward the barn. Barely able to hold them back, the man finally drops the leash, and the dogs continue on their own, trained as they are to hunt Black men. And then I hear sounds that will stay with me for all of my days—the screams of two men being eaten alive by dogs, as four white men look on, laughing. Harry stops running. He stares toward the barn for a time, his hands shaking. Then he turns back toward the slave housing and ambles home, head hung low. As a woman's voice cries out in horror, I think of Norma's words: *They're watching. They're always watching.* They are.

After the melee, I lie awake all night, trying to induce the visions—trying to complete the pictures that I see. I long to understand why I've seen so much of the future and yet so much is still hidden from me. I lie in the darkness, emptying my mind of all thought, beseeching the visions to come, but they don't.

The next morning, I am ready for first meal even before Harry knocks. Instead of moving on to the next house, though, he enters mine. I'm seated cross-legged on the ground. He walks toward me and kneels, facing me in that strange crouched position that tobacco-planters find comfortable and comforting: both feet flat, back hunched slightly forward, rear-end hovering inches from the ground so that all weight is on the feet. He rocks easily forward and back, shifting his weight from his heels to the balls of his feet, and I wonder just how many decades he spent in the fields in this position for it to come so naturally.

"I hope," he says with a slight stutter, "you weren't too scared by what happened last night."

"It was...sad."

"I came to check on you 'cuz I was worried 'bout you."

"Why?"

"'Cuz Mas'r Van Owen told me to watch out for you."

"He did? I haven't even seen him here since my first night."

"He comes and goes." Harry looks down. "He says all kinds of things 'bout you. Crazy talk that you're some sort of witch princess, that you're dangerous. Other things, too."

"Do you believe him?"

He breathes in, tries to offer a denial that he can't quite muster. "Well, I don't know what you are, but I've never seen anyone learn English as fast as you."

"And that makes me a witch?"

He smiles a bit, and, for a moment, I can picture him as a young man—handsome, strong, and yet never free, always a slave. He has never lived anywhere but this plantation. He has always been someone's property. I try to imagine how I'd view the world if I'd never seen Africa, never experienced free will. But then I wonder if it's better to know freedom only to lose it—or never to know it at all.

"I saw the mas'r come visit you on your first night," Harry

confides.

I don't answer.

He moves his head back and forth and speaks slowly, painfully. "I heard you screaming. I wanted to come help you, but..."

"It's okay, Harry." What could he have done to help me? Any intervention would have meant his death.

It takes him three tries to get the next questions out: "Did Mas'r Van Owen... did he *touch* you? Did he hurt you...?'"

"No, Harry. He just wanted to scare me." I think about that night—Van Owen's hands on my head as he tried to wrench his way into my thoughts. I screamed. And I resisted. I kept him out by focusing on Mkembro, by thinking of the colors of the foliage and the taste of the fruit paint. Even as Van Owen pressed harder, I thought of the sounds of the birds, of the way the ocean howled as it struck our sands, and I smiled. And then, just outside, a blue glow lit up the horizon. *Lightning?* I wondered. Van Owen spun, his expression curious. His gaze went first to the gap in the wall—to the blue light spilling in through it and then receding—and then back to me, his eyes tracing my body hungrily. And then he stormed from my hut. Finally, I abandoned my façade of strength, and I passed out.

"When you screamed," says Harry, "I thought..."

"No. He didn't hurt me. And he was distracted by lightning outside."

Harry's tired, old eyes met mine and then shifted away.

"Yes," he said, "I remember that flash. It wasn't lightning, though."

There is something in his voice—something he wants to tell me. He opens his mouth as if he will tell me, but then he stops himself and turns the topic back to Van Owen. "He ain't going to stop, Amara." His tone is dire. "I ain't never seen him like this with a woman before, not any woman. The way he watches you."

"The way he *watches* me?"

"All the time, Amara—from his window, through the curtains. He stares at you, and then he turns away like he feels guilty or something. When he left for his Confederate meetings, he said not to let you get too comfortable—just put you through the motions— and I started thinking maybe... maybe... he's gonna hurt you or something..."

"Maybe he just plans on sending me elsewhere," I tell him, confident that I will live. After all, the visions have shown my four generations of descendants. I've seen myself old and stooped. This plantation is not my last stop in this life.

"Amara, the way he looks at you—the way he grits his teeth when he talks about you—I think he don't trust himself around you." Harry's mouth turns downward, his lip almost quivering.

"I don't think it's safe for you here."

I finally realize then that Harry doesn't mean that Van Owen is going to kill me. He is concerned instead that Van Owen is becoming obsessed with me, that his obsession may drive him to a different sort of violence against me.

He is risking a great deal telling me these things, betraying Van Owen's trust. "Harry, you shouldn't be here. If Van Owen learns that you warned me...They say he'll be back from Charleston soon..."

He shakes his head no, his puffy eyes looking strangely intense. "Amara, Mas'r Van Owen's been back a lot since you've come. He comes for a night or so and then he goes again. He just don't let himself be seen. He been back from Charleston three days already. I bring him his meals. I bring him newspapers and letters and wine and other things. Sometimes he come out at night when everyone asleep. Sometimes he come in here to see you." Our eyes meet. Suddenly, I share his fear. "I saw him once. He was just sitting there in that chair by the bed, watching you sleep. I heard a noise at night, so I peeked in your window hole and I saw him."

So Van Owen *had* been in the room with me. The chair *had* been moved.

"I think you should leave. Tonight. I can help you..."

I remember my vision of Harry—the one I had when I first arrived—the one of him hanging from a tree. I hadn't thought of it since that first night, but now I know for certain: I am the cause of it. He will die because of me, because of this conversation we're having right now. I stare into his sad, sad eyes and try to make a connection. Perhaps my visions are not definite. Perhaps I can change the reality they show. Maybe Harry can live. "Harry, if I leave, you must come with me..."

"Oh no, Amara," he almost laughs, his voice proud as he shoots down my offer. "I'm in charge here. I've got responsibilities, people to look after. I can't leave here. This is my home."

How then can I convince him, I wonder? Harry is old and set in his ways. Even more so, he is right—he does have people to look after, people who are safer because he's here.

"Harry, what if I told you that I am a witch, and that I can see the future—and that it's dangerous for you to stay here?"

He stands quickly and straightens his pants as he if were wearing an expensive suit instead of stained overalls. "I don't want to hear no more talk o' witchcraft. That other one talks about witchcraft too."

"What other one?"

He stares at me. "The other one who asks about you." Suddenly, he looks embarrassed. "But I promised..."

He wants to tell me more, but I can see he won't—not because he's scared but because he won't break a promise. He's not talking about Van Owen. But who else? I think about entering his mind and taking the truth from him, but he is such a simple man. How can I betray him—invade his mind as Van Owen tried to do to mine?

Before I can decide, he starts shuffling backward, speaking too quickly, desperate to end the conversation. "He's brown as you and me, Amara. You got nothing to fear from him." All I came to say is the guards play poker every Thursday night startin' at midnight. So, if somebody wanted to leave the farm, that would be the time to do it. That's all I came to say."

Before I can argue, he's out the door, continuing with his morning wake-up routine and leaving me to contemplate where one can run in a foreign land, with only waking dreams as guideposts.

The day slides by. I keep watching Van Owen's mansion, looking for some sign of life or movement. I wonder if he's in there, watching me with his telescope—the same one he pointed toward my homeland all those months ago. I keep trying to bring on some vision of a runaway attempt, but there is none to find. I have no foresight about fleeing here. And the visions come only when they wish to, not when I entreat them.

By midnight, I begin to grow certain that I'm not supposed to go anywhere—that it's best for Harry and me and everyone else if I remain where I am. Perhaps I'm supposed to stay here until Lincoln sets us all free. Then, as I prepare to retire for the night, my door creaks open. I'm ready to turn and face Van Owen. I'm strong and rested now. I feel that if he were to challenge me now, I could infiltrate his mind and destroy it from within. The door whines. I take a deep breath and spin—and I see Sam, the boisterous, young slave whom Harry punished weeks ago.

"Are you ready?" he asks, holding tight to the doorframe, his eyes wild.

"Ready for what?"

"Mister Harry sent me. He said you needed an *ess-cort*—that you don't know your way around here. I'm supposed to get you to the edge of town. He 'spects me to come back after I lead you out, but I'm gone. I ain't comin' back."

I already know what Harry's punishment will be if I run. What retribution would there be then for Sam?

"Sam, you must go back to your cabin now. It's too dangerous. You don't know what might..."

"I can't go back, Amara. I had to sneak past the poker cabin to get here. There's a guard outside there with two of them hounds. I was lucky to get by them the first time. I'd never make it back without them seeing me. We've got to go. Come on."

I have no choice. He can't go back, and he won't go on without me. The damage has already been done. Harry has already broken Van Owen's trust; Sam has already escaped his cabin. I must go with him.

I stay close behind Sam as we scuttle across the tobacco fields. We rush breathlessly through the crops, and the scent is intoxicating. I want to fall on my back and roll in the leaves, to drink in their fragrance, to cover myself in their aroma. I resist the temptation.

Sam turns back every now and then, and, in the moonlight, his eyes show such fierce intent that I have no choice but to be pulled along by his fervor. Like Harry, he has never known freedom. How can I tell him that if he waits but a few more years—for Lincoln's proclamation—we will *all* be free? I would never be able to convince him, and it's too late to turn back anyway. So we run. For what feels like hours we run until finally we meet a narrow stream shaded by a row of elms extending for miles.

I think about the blue light that distracted Van Owen and about Harry's words about that other one. Who was it? Harry said that the man spoke of me and witchcraft. What can it mean? If I leave now, I'll never know. But Sam brings me back to the moment.

"Mister Harry says we should wash off our feet in the water,"

Sam tells me, "to keep the dogs from tracking us."

We step into the stream, but the instant my feet hit the chill water, my head goes light, and a vision comes, so vivid that I lose all sense of the present. All I can do is watch.

Van Owen is seated on the edge of a mammoth oak desk in a long, narrow room with a glass wall on one end. He wears a black outfit—a suit unlike any from this era. A chandelier hangs overhead, illuminating the red mahogany floor. The room is almost identical to his mansion sitting room, but I know it's not the same room. The glass wall, the clothing, the texture of the place—everything says that it's more than a century ahead.

A steel door opens and two dark-skinned young men enter. They wear gold chains and dark jackets. With them is a young dark-skinned girl. They lead her across the room to Van Owen, who berates them for entering without knocking. They tell him that the girl is the companion of one of their associates, Akins.

"He's the kid at HCS," says one of them. "He does good business for you." He pauses. "This girl says he's dead."

"Dead?" says Van Owen.

"How did he die?"

The girl stutters as she speaks. She's frightened. The room frightens her. Van Owen's gaunt face and ghost skin frighten her. Even more, she's frightened by something she's seen. "This guy—Warren—he killed him. H-h-he burned him. He just touched him and burned him up..."

Van Owen's interest is piqued. He practically springs from his chair. "How did he burn him?"

"With his hands. He touched him, and Stephon...he just burned up... with like electric shocks or something..."

The two Black men turn toward each other with incredulous looks, but Van Owen orders them to be still. "Did it look like lightning?" he asks.

"Yeah, like little sparks of lightning coming from his hands." She seems comforted somehow that Van Owen is interested, that perhaps he believes her, as if it confirms for her that she has not gone mad. *"How did he do it?"*

He ignores her question and tries to calm her so that she will be more helpful. *"What's your name, child?"*

"Leticia. Leticia Mark."

"Well, Leticia Mark, I can't be letting people go around killing my employees. This has to stop, so why don't you just tell me everything that happened."

She speaks of Terry Kelly, the Terry of my visions, the soft one—sensitive, hurt, harangued by his father, who thinks him weak. Leticia explains how she and Akins confronted Terry, taunting him, until Terry lashed out, commanded them to run, forced them to do as he said, just by speaking. So he is not weak, then. He is like Berantu, Kwame's father, who could make others obey his spoken commands—even when he didn't speak their language. Berantu, who was felled, like my father, by a bullet from Van Owen's gun. But how could Terry...

Leticia goes on explaining that she and Akins ran until they met Warren, who revealed himself to be Terry's brother. When Akins threatened Warren's family, Warren lashed out, electrocuting Akins.

"Then what?"

"I ran away," says Leticia as she starts to cry. *"I didn't want him to do to me what he did to Stephon."*

"Stephon Akins," Van Owen says, his tone like that of a minister delivering a eulogy.*"* She nods as he says the name again before going on.*"Well, I'm going to see to it that Stephon Akins is avenged, that this Warren is stopped. Now I need you to tell me more about this Kelly family. Don't leave out anything."*

Through tears, Leticia speaks about Jerome and Terry and

Regina. She describes what Terry was wearing earlier and where she last saw him. Finally relaxing, she starts rambling on about her hatred for little Regina, who can't even speak to defend herself.

Van Owen laughs. "Watered-down blood will do that. Fourth generation watered-down blood. No power left for the littlest one. Apparently, only two of the four children got the family inheritance from their mother. I was surprised that there were boys born to that family at all. Amara and her offspring had birthed only girls previously." He pauses for a moment. "And those girls certainly had voices!"

Leticia mumbles, "Regina can talk. She just stopped doing it."

Van Owen's interest is piqued. "What did you say?"

"She used to talk. Now she just stares at you and pretends she can't talk."

The slaver's eyes widen, and I feel a chill. He remembers how I did the same thing when I arrived at the plantation. I had to hide the fact that my voice had changed so drastically—that I spoke with my older voice even as a teenager. My West African accent had vanished, supplanted by the North Carolina voice that emerged with the foresight. And then, later, I sometimes stayed silent because I didn't know the extent of the power he had taken from me. I worried that he could hear me every time I spoke, no matter where he was—that using my power or even speaking would allow him entry into my thoughts.

"Regina," he says and then repeats the name twice more, stretching out the vowels like he is tasting a wine. He closes his eyes and cocks his head as if he is listening for her. "Think about Regina," he tells Leticia. "Picture her in your mind."

The girl frowns, but Van Owen repeats the request more forcefully, and Leticia complies. She thinks of Regina at school, sitting in the classroom, entering the cafeteria, her braids swinging as she walks. And even I can see her. In the same instant, Van Owen and I see the resemblance: Regina looks exactly like me as a child.

Van Owen's eyes spring open. His mouth curls almost into a smile, and he speaks with hunger, his chest rising and falling. "Amara..."

"What?" Leticia asks, confused.

Van Owen's eyes are locked on Leticia's, but he's not looking at her. She is beneath his notice. He is thinking only of Regina and of me. Finally, he responds, his voice more urgent, nearly breathless. "Are you sure you don't know where Terry might have been heading?"

Her eyes light up. She thrusts her hand into her pocket and comes out with a small, torn piece of paper and hands it to him.

"An address? It looks like it's from a delivery tag."

"Yeah, he's a delivery boy at a supermarket."

Van Owen hands the scrap to his underlings. He tells them to bring his automobile to the front of the building. "Bring duct tape," he adds. "And masking tape too." As he turns, I see through the glass window that his sanctum is in a stable. How fitting—Van Owen lives in a stable like an animal. He's recreated his North Carolina drawing room in the rear of a stable, relegated to pretending he's still an aristocrat even as he hides away in a barn.

Finally, when the two men have left, Van Owen turns to the girl and walks toward her. "So, this Terry Kelly—he just spoke, and you had to obey?"

"Yeah. It was like magic."

"Not magic—witchcraft. African witchcraft. It's a subject with which I have some experience." Suddenly Van Owen looks all around him as if he feels he is being watched, as if he senses something—someone. Me. His eyes dart back and forth, and then a slight smile crosses his face, and he settles down. "How strange. For an instant there, I felt a familiar pair of eyes on me."

Leticia looks confused. "I should get home..." she starts to say.

I feel that I must be screaming aloud, telling the girl to run, to get out of that room before it's too late. But it's already too late. It was too late the moment she stepped in there.

"No, Leticia," says Van Owen, "you're coming with us."

"Amara!" Sam's voice breaks through the walls of my vision. "Amara, what's wrong with you?" We're standing nearly waist-deep in the stream, and Sam is shaking me. "Come on, Amara, we've gotta keep moving."

I look into his naïve, young eyes, suddenly feeling a century older than he though we are the same age, and I know what I must do. "Van Owen is going to find me," I tell him. "So whatever direction I go, you've got to go the opposite way."

"But Mister Harry told me to stay with you until..."

"It doesn't matter what Mister Harry told you." Without meaning to, I grab onto his upper arms, trying to shake him—to force him to pay attention. But I, too, am young and inexperienced. This magic—this *African witchcraft*—is not yet second nature to me. As soon as my hands touch Sam's bare skin, I find myself swimming in his thoughts. They bubble to the surface as if they are my own memories. I feel Harry's whip on his back all those weeks ago; I feel his boyish—and not so boyish—attraction to me; I feel his restless urge to know what freedom feels like. I release my grip on him, but I keep my mind in control of his body. I face him due north and start him running—running toward freedom. And I plant one thought in his head: *Amara is fine. Amara is safe. I must run north.* When I release his mind, he keeps on running.

I may learn to use this power yet.

As I step out of the stream and head back toward the plantation, I wonder how Van Owen felt me watching him all those years from now. Can he always sense where I am? Since he stole some of his abilities from me, perhaps he shares some innate connection with me. When I touched him back in Mkembro, I entered his mind;

perhaps a bond was formed then—one that I can never break. Perhaps this is why he is forever linked to me and to my family, why he feels the need to hunt us. Perhaps he is as haunted by me as I am by him.

My trek back toward the farm is much slower than was my escape. Without Sam goading me on, it takes almost three hours to creep back through the tobacco field on my hands and knees. At times, I'm almost certain I hear voices or see light at the edge of the field, but they always fade, so I assume it's just my fear playing tricks on me. I wonder how far Sam has gotten and if he'll make it to safety. I comfort myself with the belief that pushing him on without me has perhaps saved both Sam and even Harry, but as I near the edge of the field and skulk onto the dirt road that leads toward the slave housing, I know that I have guessed wrong.

The voices of the guards and the lights of their torches await me. Seven white men stand just a few yards from me. In front of them, squatting on the ground, lighting a match against a stone, is Van Owen. He raises the flame to his pipe and looks toward me with a smile, and I understand: we *do* have a connection, one I can never escape. My mind is not completely linked to his—he can't read my thoughts—but we are bound nevertheless. And when I use my power, he can feel it. When I touched Sam—when I took control of Sam's mind—I sent up a sort of flare that Van Owen could hear. And he knew exactly where both of us were.

"Ah," says Van Owen says with all the calm in the world, "our final guest. I told you she'd be along soon enough." He stands, displaying his pristine Confederate uniform. He inhales from his pipe and blows a huge smoke ring. The circular loop lingers like a white target against the cobalt sky. The tobacco scent is sweet. My heart jumps when he tells his men, "Bring the boy."

Two white men step from the shadows, tugging Sam forward. The boy's eyes are bulged wide. His mouth is covered with a piece of white cloth tied in a knot at the back of his head. The men throw him to his knees in front of Van Owen. Sam stares into my eyes, pleading silently.

"Do you see what happens when you try to leave me, Amara?" asks Van Owen. "I didn't want to hurt this boy. Hell, when he stole my tobacco a few months back, he got only a lashing. I love my little Africans. You're all like children to me. I want you all to be happy here. There's just one thing and one thing only that I need you all to accept: you *belong* to me. You're all *mine*."

He draws a pistol from his belt, and I know what I must do. I am the reason Sam is going to die; he deserves this gift from me. I close my eyes and—without touching him this time—I join with Sam's mind once again. I open my eyes and I see through his: I am standing in front of him. Van Owen is raising the gun, pointing it toward Sam's head. I don't want Sam to see this. Even if it's just for one moment, I want him to know what I know: what it means to be free. So I create a different scene for Sam to watch—a different reality, a different world. The world he should have known.

It's morning. From your hut of dried mud, roofed with branches from the sumac tree, you hear the mandrill calling to his family. In the distance, the tide rolls softly upon the shore, the ocean breeze carrying the scent of juniper and sedge. You rise and stretch and step into summer. The sun beats down, sweltering and yet inviting. Comfortable. This is home.

Around you, children run and climb and play. Some of the adults head to the fields to tend to their crops. Others venture to the water to catch fish. The fruit of their labor belongs to them and them alone. Nobody makes them work. They do so for the good of their families and their people and their land. Their Africa. Your Africa.

You look closely at the people. Everyone has brown skin. There are no interlopers here. No masters. You are your own master. You breathe in deeply, reeling in the pleasure of freedom and...

Van Owen pulls the trigger, and Sam falls face forward into the dirt.

"That was a nice little picture you gave the boy, Amara." He winks. "Yes, I saw it. Don't you know by now that you can't use your power without me feeling it too? It's too bad you couldn't do the same for Mister Harry. I didn't bother waiting for you for that one."

I walk past Van Owen without looking at him, without looking at the guards, without looking at Sam's dead body on the ground. I walk past the rows of slave houses. Inside her cabin, Norma is wailing, the others warning her to stay quiet. As I approach my shack, I already know what I will find. I walk past the tree but don't turn to look at it until I am in front of the closed door to my cabin. Then I can wait no more. I turn and let my back fall against the door, sliding down until I am seated on the ground, staring up at the branch, staring at Harry spinning and swinging by his neck, his scaled hands tied behind his back, his mouth contorted in pain, his sad, sad eyes empty, gazing into nothing.

In the morning, the guards will come and cut the rope. They'll take the body behind the barn and burn it, the stench of scorched flesh shrouding even the pervasive redolence of the tobacco. For tonight, though, I'll remain here with Mister Harry, watching him sway in the autumn wind. I'll stay with him all night, forcing myself to learn what has somehow eluded me until now: that no African born in America can ever truly know freedom.

FOURTEEN

Warren crouched beneath the stairwell, trying to keep his eyes on the second floor window across the street. The sound of his breathing distracted him. The feel of his sweat seeping through his shirt distracted him. The headache was coming soon—he knew it—and that distracted him, too.

At least he was comfortable there beneath the stoop of the abandoned building. He knew it well. He'd been there many times before, staring up at the second story window across the street as he waited for Terry.

Warren wasn't permitted to go home—his father had decreed years ago that Warren must never come back. So he found a job. And an apartment. He even promised himself that he would go back to school. There had been so many promises made and so few kept. He never did return to school. The first job and many others after it were lost. Several landlords had evicted him for unpaid rent. He lived now in a derelict rooming house, and his moments with his brothers were brief and stolen—watching Jerome at football practice, walking Terry home (or close to home) after Terry's last grocery delivery. But Warren tried not to take advantage of his brothers. He tried to ask for money only when he could not afford to eat—and he used it for drugs only when the craving was unbearable. His promise to his father—to stay away—had been kept fully in only one regard: Warren never went near his family's home or near his sister. He never even allowed himself to see her. It would have hurt him too much. She had almost died because of him.

He leaned out from beneath the stoop and stared up at Marco Fenelli's window across the street. The light was still on. There were two shadows moving about. Terry was still in there with the old man, the recluse that Terry had spoken of. Initially, Warren had been suspicious of Terry's friendship with Marco—*what did this old man want with a teenage boy?* But Marco had proven to be harmless: a broken down mobster, hidden away for decades. Just a lonely hermit who needed company. Perhaps, Warren reasoned, Terry had found in Marco the fatherly guidance that their father couldn't offer.

Warren's head was pounding. The headache was so intense that he felt as if someone were inside his brain pushing to get out. His temples throbbed, the pain pulsating. He looked down at his hands. It had been almost twenty minutes since the confrontation, and the glow was finally fading. A passerby might think only that Warren had spilled fluorescent paint on himself, though the veins on the backs of his hands were still swollen and trembling, the blood still pumping too fast. He closed his eyes and took several deep breaths in and out. He thought of his words to Jerome just that morning by the football field: *It's all gonna be better.* He thought of the declaration he had made to Stephon Akins only minutes before murdering him: *I'm through with that stuff.* He had meant both pledges. He was going to create a better life for himself—without drugs. He could get by without them, he was certain of it. He tried not to think about the headache or of Akins's smoldering body. He concentrated on breathing. He focused on the circular pattern of the air traveling in and out of his lungs. He listened to the breath flowing into him, draining out of him. After several minutes, his heartbeat began to slow, his respiration became more shallow and relaxed, his headache started to recede. In a moment, the headache and the glow would both be gone. He took in one last, long breath and opened his eyes.

Immediately the headache returned, roaring through his brain. "Damn it!" he whispered, pounding his fists on the underside of the concrete stoop. "Why? Why now?" He resolved to concentrate on something else besides his own predicament. He looked up again at Marco's window—no change—and then at the building entrance. He wondered if Terry might be up there for a while, perhaps sharing with Marco the story of Terry's altercation with Akins. Warren wondered how he could tell Terry that Akins would never bother him again—without also revealing Warren's involvement in Akins's death.

He thought about what Akins and his girlfriend had said about Terry. They had both used the word "magic." If Terry did have some power, then maybe, like Warren, he also needed time to *come down* after using it. Perhaps Terry might stay upstairs with Marco for a while longer. There was time then. Time for one more high—one *last* high, and then never again. Just enough to ease the pain. To slow his heart. To diminish the glow. "Never again," he said to himself. "One last time."

He rolled up his jacket sleeve, revealing his bare forearm, which was dotted with red scabs and pinpricks. He opened the largest bag he had taken from Akins. The tiny plastic vial rolled onto the ground, tinkling like glass. He reached inside his jacket and withdrew a tiny metal spoon. He rubbed it along the ground until it held a few raindrops. His hand shaking lightly, he emptied the vial's contents—a brown, tar-like substance—onto the spoon. Then he produced from his pants pocket a black cigarette lighter, which he held beneath the spoon. The brown substance intermingled with the raindrops until it was smoother and thinner. Next from his jacket pocket came the syringe and the worn rubber hose, creased and flaking. The street lamp above the building was broken, but Warren didn't need light. He had performed this act so many times before. He could find a vein blindfolded. He dipped the needle into the spoon and tugged on the plunger until he could feel the liquid filling the barrel. Once the spoon was empty, he tossed it deep under the stoop. "Never again," he said. Then he wrapped the hose around his arm so that the veins rose up like routes on a roadmap. He tapped the plunger, spraying the first dash of dark liquid into the air, eliminating the air bubble. He grunted, breathing harder as he traced the tip of the needle along the veins. He could barely wait for the relief. The sensation reminded him of when he was a child, watching his mother baking. She had always let him spy on the cookies through the oven window, his mouth yearning for that first taste.

Finally, he found a spot that felt right, a vein that wasn't too compromised. He drove the point down, the skin resisting for just a moment before breaking as the needle slid in. Warren barely felt it. "Never again," he repeated. He pressed on the plunger, releasing the heroin from the barrel, sending it coursing through the needle and into the vein, into his blood. He thought of that first time, so many years ago, when he'd gone to his father for help, but Carl was too busy teaching Jerome to fight, too busy to listen. It was only marijuana then—just a joint or two to bring him down. Later, when pot and hashish and Quaaludes no longer worked, he finally turned to heroin. Warren knew it immediately, even that first time: heroin would always work for him.

The rush came almost immediately, a wave traveling through him, the wake coating his body like a frothy tide breaking on a dry shore. The swell made him reel, knocking him from his crouch, dropping him to his knees. He rocked unsteadily and then rolled onto his back, staring upward at his hands silhouetted against the storm-cloud evening sky. The glow was gone. His hands looked normal again. The headache had dissipated. "Yes," he whispered. "Yes."

He lay there for some time; he didn't know how long. He watched the clouds rolling by, the sky shifting from gray to black and then back to gray. The street was quiet, so he listened to the sound of his own breathing and imagined that he was the one making the clouds move, that he was blowing them away.

Then he heard a door shut, and he swung his gaze back to Marco's building. Someone was coming out—Terry!

The boy moved quickly down the gray stone front steps. He stopped and looked both ways, and even listened for a moment, as if making sure that nobody was hunting him anymore. *They're not,* Warren wanted to call out, but he started to feel sick again at the thought of what he had done.

Terry reached the bottom of the steps and turned toward Seventh Avenue and the path home. He looked almost happy, energized. Was he smiling even?

"Terry...." Warren heard himself saying, but the word wasn't coming out right. His tongue felt heavy and numb, and he sounded like he was moaning, not speaking.

Nevertheless, Terry heard something and stopped for a moment. Seeing nothing, he moved on.

Then, a car door opened, and a young girl's voice rang out. "Yeah, that's him! That's Terry Kelly!"

A Black man in a leather jacket leapt from the front seat. With two quick steps, he was upon Terry. He grabbed the boy from behind. With both hands, he covered Terry's mouth. When he withdrew his hands, Terry's mouth was covered by what looked like gray duct tape.

Akins's girlfriend leaned out from the passenger window and cackled again, "That's him!"

Why is she here, Warren wondered, and *who's she talking to?* He tried to jump to his feet, to call out, to do something, but his body felt like melted wax, like he was dissolving, decomposing all over the sidewalk.

Next, the man wrapped one arm around Terry's midsection, pinning Terry's arms to his sides. With the other hand, he reached into his jacket pocket and came out with a cloth. He covered Terry's nose with it. Within seconds, Terry went limp.

Finally, with tremendous effort, Warren staggered to his feet and stepped out from beneath the stoop. "What's going on?" he mumbled.

The rear passenger door was open. There was someone inside, but Warren could see only a shadow. In the front seat, the driver, a Black man, rolled down his window and eyed Warren up and down.

"That's him," Leticia whined, "the one who killed Stephon!"

The man in the back seat bent forward, but Warren couldn't see his face.

The first man was wrapping more duct tape around Terry's wrists, binding them together behind his back. He slung the boy over his shoulder and carried him toward the car.

Warren tried to move forward, but his legs were so weak. Everything was so weak. He felt himself swaying, barely able to hold himself upright, but he tried his best to sound strong "Get away from my brother!"

The man in the backseat leaned out into the moonlight. His face was gaunt and pale, the skin almost translucent.

Warren felt cold suddenly.

And then Hendrik Van Owen climbed from the back seat of the vehicle and stood tall and erect, his eyes focused on Warren Kelly.

The pale man smiled, cocking his head to one said as if pondering something interesting yet insignificant, and started walking toward him. "So, you're Warren Kelly. I've been hearing some interesting stories about you and your family."

Warren's tone was hushed again. He stuttered as he spoke. "You're...you're him. You're..."

Van Owen held a cane in his left hand, though he seemed not to need it. His right hand began to glow. "Yes," he said, "I am he."

Warren planted his feet and raised both his hands, pointing them at Van Owen. His legs were wobbly, his stance unsure, but his teeth were gritted. "You're dead. You're a dead man!"

All at once, though, his expression fell. He shook his hands, clenched them into fists, shook them again—the same way he had when trying earlier to diffuse the glow. This time, though, he was trying to bring it back, but it wouldn't come.

"Not fast enough, boy," said Van Owen as sparks hailed from his right hand, and lightning shot out from his fingertips.

Warren dove behind the steps, back into his hiding place under the stoop. The lightning blast struck the bottom step, and the concrete exploded into rocks and dust.

"Come out of there and I'll let you live," Van Owen chirped as he advanced toward his prey. "I might even give you some of that brown goo you love so much."

Beneath the stoop, Warren laid both his hands against the stone wall that connected the building to the one beside it.

"Come on," he whispered. "Come on." He closed his eyes and groaned like a weightlifter. This time, his voice carried.

"Come on!"

There was a loud hum, a blue flash, and then Warren was gone.

FIFTEEN

I'm not trusted here, not since Harry and Sam were killed. The other slaves eye me strangely, as if I'm not one of them, as if I'm their enemy. I never tell them the whole story—that it was Harry who told me to run away, that I had no choice but to join Sam in the escape attempt, that I didn't want to run at all. Excuses will not help. Two men are dead because of me; that is all they know. Though they all understand the longing for freedom and what it can drive a slave to do, they want nothing to do with me. I work alone. I eat alone. I am a pariah.

The part of me that was once the daughter of a chieftain wants to berate them for chastising me. Who are they to question me or my motives? Who are they to judge me? But I haven't walked in their shoes. I haven't lived my life in captivity as they have. They're scared and beaten down; they live daily without hope of something I always took for granted—freedom. They know that Van Owen is the real enemy, but hating their master will serve no purpose. They cannot challenge him. Blaming me gives them purpose and helps them cope. And I can't fault them for it.

Almost three months after my escape attempt, Van Owen has all of us meet in front of his mansion. The white guards line us up in neat rows like headstones on a dirt graveyard. They position themselves on all sides of us, rifles in their hands, dogs at their sides.

Then, as if part of a choreographed stage play, the mansion door opens, and Van Owen strides out, dressed in white. At his side is a minister, a white man, bald, perhaps sixty years old, wearing simple black clothing and a white collar. His nose is too large for his face, and his eyes are sunk deep, making him appear somber and plain and almost kindly. Van Owen's voice is imposing but not quite as autocratic as usual.

"This is Father Jamison. He will be tending to your souls, for, as he tells me, they do need tending to. Perhaps a little God in your lives will make you appreciate how good you have it here." His head turns sharply, his eyes fixing on me. "Though some of you don't seem to think so."

I try to listen, but I am not interested in the foolishness he wants to sell us. He rambles on about a pinewood church that we are to build right on the ground where we stand. The men are to do the hard labor—the actual construction—while the women are to sand and polish the wood and line the pews daily with flowers. Van Owen calls it "a family venture inspired by the light of the Lord."

I think of another light, a blue light I saw recently. Where was that? I cannot recall. But my mind is taken over by a vision of another blue light. I focus on it.

The light is so bright, bursting out from a crawlspace at the foot of a building. Someone is in there—Warren Kelly. The broken son. His hands are pressed against stone. He is covering the stone with blue light.

Van Owen is approaching him, a cane in his hand. He walks so confidently, a hunter closing in on his prey. There is a hum and a flash from beneath the shattered steps. Van Owen recoils for a moment, bracing for an assault, but the light fades. Van Owen moves quickly toward the building. He ducks beneath the stoop. Beneath his feet, metal and glass crumble into shards. Warren's syringe. Van Owen searches the tiny crawlspace, but no one is there.

Warren has found some other way out.

Van Owen climbs the steps and walks to a car. Leticia is inside.

"What was that you shot at him?" she asks. "Was that the same thing he used on Stephon? Was it like some kind of taser?"

Van Owen says nothing, though his face is twisted with confusion. He clambers into the back seat, avoiding Terry, who lays sprawled across the car floor.

"Did you get him?" Leticia asks louder. "Did you?"

"Take us back to the stable," Van Owen orders the driver.

Leticia will not relent. "Just tell me—did you get him? Did you...?"

"Enough," Van Owen says softly. He closes his eyes, and Leticia's face loses all expression. She stares straight ahead as if lost in a dream. Her head bobs from side to side with the movement of the car.

And then I am back at the plantation, where Van Owen is still talking. Some of the other slaves seem pleased with his words. Many of them already call themselves Christians, which pains me. They know nothing of their people's beliefs. They yearn instead for platitudes about the meek inheriting the earth.

"The Lord," he goes on, "watches over all of us. He is my shepherd, just as I am yours. He keeps me in line, just as I keep you in line." He gestures with both hands to the vast, fertile plantation grounds. "He provides for me, just as I provide for you. He rewards me for taking care of you, just as you will be rewarded someday for all your hard work."

I cringe as I listen, wondering if he truly believes this drivel. There is no God. How can there be when Van Owen has been rewarded so richly for so many evil deeds? What sort of god would permit the empty promise that meekness and toil shall be rewarded with prosperity?

"On to your work now," he orders. We begin to move toward

the tobacco fields. "Amara, stay here a moment, won't you?" I stop and turn toward him. "Come here." He introduces me to the minister, who shakes my hand and smiles insipidly. His hand is soft and damp, like a sponge. His eyes travel up and down my body in a manner that I hadn't expected. He reminds me of the ranker sailors from Van Owen's vessel. "Amara is one of the newest workers here," Van Owen goes on. Father Jamison nods. "She's descended from royalty. Daughter of a chieftain. She's really rather...unusual."

I find myself thinking of a vision I had once: Carl Kelly is introducing his fiancée to his father. *This is Dara*, he says. His father smiles and nods his head, staring approvingly, with joy, with innocence.

"A chieftain's daughter?" says the minister, speaking slowly, as if to a child. "Tell me, Amara, in your land, did you have gods that you prayed to?"

Van Owen tries to interrupt, to clarify that I don't yet speak their tongue. I prove him wrong.

"We did not pray," I tell Father Jamison. "We honored our gods with our songs and our deeds. We lived our lives in such a way that we praised the deities simply by living justly."

The minister stares at me strangely, stunned by my mastery of the language. Van Owen's mouth gapes. It is the first time he has heard me speak. He knew I could understand English, but he had no idea I could speak it so well—with a Southern accent even. He bites his lip to keep himself from scolding me and turns to Jamison with a forced grin, pretending he's proud of me.

Jamison eyes me with a curious expression. "You didn't pray? Surely, though, since you've arrived in America, you've heard the others praying. Captain Van Owen tells me of the joyous songs you all sing in the fields. I so look forward to hearing them. Surely you've been moved and wanted to join in the singing."

I think of the songs of my people. I think of my wedding day, of the joy in the faces of the Mkembro and the Merlante as they sang *Dji mi sarro ti kee la ti na-arro.*

My face is stone as I answer the minister. "I don't sing here."

"You see," Van Owen chimes in quickly. "You were right, Father Jamison. You *are* needed here. Amara needs you to cleanse her soul and bring joy to her life. She needs you to make her sing. You may return to your work now, Amara."

They turn and begin to walk back to the house. It is Jamison who speaks first. "Hendrik, I still feel this is but folly. These Negroes have no right to petition the Lord with prayer. They are beasts of burden. The Lord put them on Earth to labor, not to be blessed or forgiven or rewarded for their piety."

Van Owen's tone is serious, as if his word is the last word. "Father Jamison, I like a clean house. The heathens' conversion to the Lord's way will serve to make my house cleaner, will it not? And surely your ministry has benefited amply enough from my patronage that I have earned your presence here once each week, has it not?"

They drift toward the house, so I don't hear the minister's response. I feel soiled. I walk off toward my place in the tobacco field, anxious to plunge my hands in the dirt to cleanse the skin that the minister touched. I turn back to scan the spot where we will build the church. Three years from now, I will burn it to the ground.

SIXTEEN

Regina waited patiently throughout the phone call. She wanted to enter her grandmother's thoughts and listen in, but she'd made a deal with Terry and another one with Willa as well—no eavesdropping without permission. Still, Regina wondered who could be phoning her grandmother.

The old woman wasn't doing much of the talking. Mostly, she was listening to the male voice at the other end, her face rife with questions. Finally, she told him, "Always," and hung up. And then she remained almost motionless for nearly a minute before saying, "He's like Berantu." The phone was still in her lap, her hand still holding down the receiver. "Terry's like Berantu. I don't know how he could have that ability, though. Berantu wasn't in our family." She shook her head back and forth. "Yet Terry has his power. He can make people do things just by telling them to."

Regina sat on the edge of the bed, staring at her grandmother. "*What are you talking about?*" she asked telepathically. "*Who was that?*"

"So you really weren't listening?" she asked with a smile. "Good girl. That was Marco. Apparently, Terry was right about the fight in the lunchroom. Akins didn't jump off of Terry because he was afraid of Jerome. He jumped because Terry told him to jump. That's how the story went about Berantu also. He just told the slavers to stop in their tracks, and they did—even though he was speaking another language altogether."

Regina looked up at the ceiling, straining to remember the tale of Berantu. Then she turned back again to her grandmother. Even in moments of confusion, it was always such a relief to be in this room, where nothing was hidden. Regina could communicate silently with Terry—they had their secret—but there was so much he didn't know, so much that she couldn't tell him. So much that only Grandma Willa knew. *"Tell me about Berantu again?"* Regina asked.

"Child, you already know everything I know about him." With a flat voice and a bored expression, Willa recited the words she had been taught to memorize and pass down. "Berantu was the leader of the Merlante. He was Kwame's father. If the marriage of the two bloodlines—the Merlante and the Mkembro—had gone forward, if Kwame and Amara had married, then their offspring might have had even more remarkable power, passed down not just to the girls but the boys in the bloodline as well..." Then she broke from the legend and offered her own commentary. "But the Merlante are all gone now, and Berantu's bloodline died out when Kwame was killed trying to escape Van Owen's ship. And you and I are all that's left of the Mkembro now."

"But what did Marco tell you?"

Grandma Willa told her—that Terry had made Akins and Leticia run away, that he'd forced Marco to pour a drink and then empty an entire bottle. Throughout, Regina's lips were slightly parted, her eyes slightly scrunched, the way a child might look when she refuses to believe what she's hearing. *"How? How could Terry have this ability without my knowing? And I doubted him today in the lunchroom. I feel terrible..."*

"When Terry gets home tonight, we'll talk to him together. And we can both apologize for keeping everything from him. He should be back from work soon. You'll need to get him upstairs before your father gets home. I don't want Carl finding out about Terry fighting. The last thing we need is for Terry to start telling his father about controlling people with his voice. The less your father knows, the better. He wouldn't understand any of this."

Regina took the phone and returned it to the bedside table. Then she walked to the window, trying to catch sight of Terry, but the streets were empty. She closed the curtains and turned back to Willa. The old woman looked fine, but Regina went to sit down beside her.

In a casual tone, Willa said, "Regina, I'm okay up here by myself. Why don't you go downstairs and wait for Terry?" Regina nodded, and she was halfway to the door when her grandmother added, "Would you mind closing the curtains, though?"

"*I just did,*" Regina said. She turned to the window—to the curtains that she had just closed—and saw that they were spread open again. She spun back toward her grandmother, greeting Willa's mischievous grin with one of her own.

"Go on downstairs," Willa told her with a smile. "You know I can close them myself if I need to." As Regina exited the room, the curtains slid closed again. Then the piano started playing a blues ballad. Regina scurried back to watch the show. The piano keys were moving up and down. The pedals were rising and falling. The ragtime dance number soared through the apartment. From her bed, Willa winked. "Go on downstairs, dear. Let Grandma practice."

Regina finished her homework on the living room couch, watching the clock and springing up every time she heard even the slightest sound from outside. Her father and Jerome were due soon from the stable, so she hoped Terry would make it home before them. She had begun to worry when a knock came at the front door. Knowing that Terry never forgot his keys, Regina walked toward the door with an unsure gait. She stood on her tiptoes and peered through the peephole. The face she saw was familiar somehow. The man was tall, dark-skinned, perhaps thirty years old. Rain dripped from the baseball cap he wore.

The knock came again, a bit louder. "Pop?" the man called in a raspy voice. "Open up. It's important."

Regina wanted to ask him who he was, but she felt sure she already knew. And Grandma Willa's voice from upstairs confirmed it.

"Oh my goodness," she called, "I know that voice." Regina turned back, her lips trembling as she opened them to speak, but her grandmother shouted, "No, child. Don't speak."

Regina stepped back from the door, quivering. *"But, Grandma..."* she said.

"I know, dear. But you can't," said Willa, her voice nearby. Regina spun around and saw her at the top of the staircase. Regina had known that her grandmother could stand and walk—she was able to care for herself upstairs after all—but Willa rarely allowed anyone to see her struggle. She didn't want the children to know her as a weak, hobbled, old woman. But Willa could never look weak. There was too much fire in her. "Don't speak, Regina," Willa repeated. Clutching the banister with one hand, she waved her other hand toward the door, and the deadbolt unlocked. "Open the door. Let your brother in." The words sounded odd to Regina, but she didn't know why.

Her fingers shaking, Regina turned the handle and pulled the door open. Windblown rain misted in, so Regina was squinting as she looked for the first time into her oldest brother's eyes.

Warren stepped into the doorway, frozen at the sight of her. "Regina...?"

She nodded slowly.

He was soaking wet and trembling. His eyes were bloodshot and tired. "I'm sorry," he whispered; it was all that he could think to say. "I'm so sorry." At first, she thought he was apologizing for old mistakes, but then he looked up toward his grandmother and went on. "It's Terry. He got him. He got Terry."

SEVENTEEN

The war comes, as I knew it would. Upon Lincoln's inauguration, the South secedes and takes Fort Sumter, but little changes for us here. Van Owen—now Captain Van Owen again—goes off to fight with his Confederate Army. The white guards who don't join the war yet have a new responsibility: keeping Union soldiers out of the farm as well as keeping slaves in.

Van Owen rarely comes home. Sometimes, when I'm certain he is away, I practice using my powers. I don't want to violate the other slaves—I've done enough harm to them already just by being here—so I enter the minds of the guards. I remain quiet; I don't take over their minds. I just listen. I need to practice for the day when I have to defend myself against him. That day is coming soon.

The other slaves still keep their distance from me, so I keep my distance from them, an outcast among those who should be my family. I pick tobacco. I stay in my cabin.

Occasionally, when I wake in the mornings, I still find the chair out of place in my room. I wonder, *How does he do it? How does he come in so quietly that I don't hear him? How long does he remain? What goes through his mind as he watches me sleep? Is he able to see my dreams? Would I know it if he tried?*

Then, for the next few nights, I lie awake almost all night, waiting for him to return and spy on me. It is on an evening in April 1863, after the fields have thawed from a harsh winter, that I finally see him again. He opens the door to find me sitting up in my bed, waiting. His uniform is spotless, the tails of his coat flared from the tight gold belt, his polished sword hanging from it. He remains still for a moment, stunned that I have been expecting him, and then he approaches me, pulls up the chair, and sits down facing me.

"The war goes well for us, Amara. I suppose you've heard."

I keep all emotion from my voice. "You lie, or you are blind. It goes poorly. You will lose."

"Did you see that in one of your visions then?" I jolt a bit, and he nods. I've been inside that head of yours, Amara. I confess: I don't know how to unlock *everything* in there yet, but I will. I've got all the time in the world."

"If you knew everything, you'd know that your war is folly."

"Sometimes a man has to fight for his country no matter the cost."

"Oh, is that what you're fighting for?"

"The state of North Carolina and its people have earned the right to live the life we have built for ourselves, free of Union rules and Union philosophies."

"Even if your Confederate philosophies run against the laws of gods and humanity?"

He glares at me, his nostrils quivering at the plural, *gods.* He breathes in sharply, exhales, and smiles. "No, Amara, you won't bait me. I came here to sit peacefully with my favorite possession." He almost spits that last word, laboring over it.

"And that's what I'll do."

I raise my rhetoric. "I suppose it must be hard for you to accept it, Captain, that you're going to lose the war bitterly, that the North will be victorious, that slavery will be abolished and written into history as a blight."

"You're delusional, girl," he snaps, rising to his feet, the chair toppling backward to the dirt. "There will always be slaves. Once you've been in chains, you're never free. You know that." He strides toward the door. "And no matter what happens, I'll be back for you. You'll always be mine."

He is right about that. He will be back for me. I've seen it:

It's almost two years from now. March 1865. General Sherman's army is spread throughout the Carolinas, and Confederate General Johnston stages his final offensive against Sherman at Bentonville. Van Owen fights at Johnston's side, trying in vain to turn back the Union army. Nearly one thousand Confederate soldiers are killed, and almost double that number are wounded. As Johnston surrenders to the Union Army, signifying the fall of the Carolinas, Van Owen steals away on a horse to make his way home to the plantation. He's already received word that his guards have run off—and so have his slaves. He knows that his plantation will be forfeited to the Union. Still, he rides on, hiding in muddy forests, sleeping in trestles, fleeing from the occupying forces. It takes him three days to make it here, but he will not be denied. As I feel his approach, I rise from my bed and enter the main house. I stare up at the chandelier crystals glittering in the light of a kerosene lamp. The lamp fits easily in my hand. I enjoy the warmth of the polished glass against my skin. I savor each step as I exit his house and approach his church. I exhale as I toss the lamp through the window and set the church ablaze. Then I return to my cabin to watch the flames cleanse the ground where Father Jamison spoke of heaven while condoning hell on Earth.

When Van Owen arrives at my door, he is filthy, ravaged by battle and fatigue, and his stench enters the room before he does.

"The church?" he asks. "Your doing?"

I smile in response but say nothing.

He pretends he isn't angry, but I can feel it emanating from him.

"I'm surprised to find you're still here, Amara. After all, I told you I'd be coming back for you."

I stand to face him, showing no fear. "Just as I told you that you'd lose the war."

He turns and checks behind him before shutting the door. He peers out the window, looking for Union soldiers. Then he pulls the curtains shut. "Why did you stay when all the other slaves left?"

No hesitation whatsoever. "To kill you."

With that, he seems to relax. "Now, Amara, we both know I don't die today. You've seen me in your visions—decades from now, more than a century even. Why, I was stabbed and shot and musketed in battle, and I didn't die. Since we first touched back in Mkembro, I don't believe I've been sick even a day. I feel stronger than I've been since I was a teenager. I may well be immortal." He unbuttons his shirt and opens the collar to reveal several scarlet wounds across his chest. They appear more like burn marks from fire or branding than gashes from bullets or blades. His hand brushes over them and he winces for a moment. "Electrical fire, Amara," he says in response. "It cauterizes wounds." He smiles. "As the poet Percy Shelley wrote, 'I change, but I cannot die.'"

He's right. He will survive for generations, never aging. I don't kill him here, today, and we both know it. He sees through my bluff. I haven't remained on the plantation to kill him. I've remained here for the same reason that he hunted slaves long after he needed the money or trappings that the quests brought him—to prove that I can. I must face him for the same reason that he went off to fight a war he knew he would lose: because sometimes one must fight for one's country, even when one has no country left to fight for. Though I am loath to admit it, I have remained here because of the lessons he taught me. Van Owen has taught me to face my fears.

"So what is it," he asks, "that you think you can do to me?"

"This," I speak softly, closing my eyes. With only a thought, I show him what I have learned. I project my consciousness into his. To my dismay, he stands there and allows it. He throws up no defenses. He opens himself to me. I can still feel my own body. I can still see with my own eyes. At the same time, though, I am also swimming in his thoughts, in his memories, as if they are my own.

"Go ahead, witch," he taunts me. "Do your worst." I test my control of his appendages, forcing him to reach for his sword. As soon as his hand touches the hilt, he surrenders even more, opens his thoughts to me even more fully, bares his soul to me. Slowly, I force him to draw the sword.

In an instant, I know what he knows: that as much as he claims hatred for my "African witchcraft," he glories in these occasions when our minds are one—for he has never opened his heart or mind to another human being—except me. He reels with pleasure while I am sickened by my discovery. And in that moment, he takes his advantage.

Effortlessly, he defies my control over him and returns the sword to its sheath. "Now *I've* got something to show *you*, Amara."

Suddenly I find myself lost in a vision of his making, ensnared in a net of his memories: *I am walking along a beach in the summer. The sun is bright and hot. The water is clear and blue; I look down to find I am ankle deep in the ocean, but my feet—what are these strange boots? They are men's boots. And in my gloved hand—a revolver? For some reason, I am laughing. My heart is beating wildly. Around me, slaves are running, screaming. No, not slaves— I've been in North Carolina too long—they're not slaves; they're Africans. In the distance, Van Owen's ship looms, huge, dark, waiting. I am home on the shores of Mkembro. But I am not Amara. I am he—I am Van Owen. I am living his memory.*

"Move, heathens," I shout, raising my pistol, pointing it at a woman who has not kept up with the others. "You are too slow, old woman," I bark at her. As she turns to face me, I pull the trigger,

and I see my mother's face. The bullet explodes into her chest, and she sails backward into the water. I move on, already forgetting her. She is nothing to me. An animal. A thing.

The world grows dim and silent, and then I'm back in the cabin with Van Owen, out of his thoughts, back with my own, watching him approach me. He shoves me backward onto the bed, but my mind is locked on the vision of my mother.

He killed her.

I feel his hands tearing at my clothes, peeling them away. How strange, I think, that I feel shame because my body is exposed. Not so long ago, I wore almost nothing and yet walked freely among men.

He murdered my mother.

I feel his face on mine, his beard scraping against my neck, his fingers grabbing at me, his mouth against mine.

"No," I plead. "No... please..." I kick and scratch, but I can't push him away. I am weak, too weak to fight with my mind. The vision of my mother has weakened me, drained me. I keep seeing it. He killed her. He killed my mother. He killed my father and my mother.

"You should be proud, little witch. You faced up to me. You tried. Sometimes, that's all we can do." He is on top of me, reaching, prying, pressing against me.

For a moment, I remember my vision of the boy, Terry. Generations from now, Terry has pale eyes like Van Owen's. Is this, then, where the blood is tainted? Is Van Owen the father of my progeny?

We stay like this for a time, struggling. I hear him breathing harder in odd grunts and gasps. Then, finally, he bounds to his feet and begins fastening his garments. He's still panting.

Was that it, then, I wonder? Did he take me? I felt no pain below, where I should have. I sit up and pull my frock closed to cover my body. And then I see his face. It's flushed and wrinkled into a scowl. He's incensed. He has failed.

"You can't..." I say. "You can't take me. You're not capable of it, are you?"

"Filthy, black witch." I see his hand swinging long before it connects with my face. The slap sends me careening backward onto the bed. My head slams hard into the wall, but I barely feel it. "This is your fault," he roars. "This is the legacy of this power you gave me." He struggles for what to do next.

"You're impotent," I say, enjoying the sound of the word, elongating the vowels, enunciating each consonant. "You stole your power from a woman, and now you can't perform as a man."

He reaches for his sword but doesn't know what to do with it. Then we hear the horses. He runs to the window. They've arrived; the Union army has found him. He throws the door open but turns back to issue his farewell. "You'll never be free of me, Amara. Never." He is calm, assured even, for we both know the threat isn't idle. "You are mine and you *always* will be mine."

He races outside. I stand in the doorway, watching as he springs onto his horse and rides south toward the mountains, seven soldiers in blue uniforms close at his heels.

And I laugh full-throated and loud until tears stream from my eyes. Yes, he has wounded me again and again, and our war is far from over. This time, though, I won the battle. He runs from this cabin a hunted vagabond stripped of his virility. I leave here a free woman.

EIGHTEEN

"What do you mean *he* got Terry?" Willa cried, still leaning on the banister. "*Who* got Terry?"

Warren ran his sleeve over his face to wipe away the rain and the tears. He glanced up at his grandmother for just a moment and then looked down again. She was so much older than when he'd seen her last—on the day Regina was born. He knew that she rarely left her room these days, and he blamed himself for that. He could still hear his father's voice: *Look at what's happened because of you. Your mother's dead because of you!* He could still feel the sting. *Don't ever come near this family again!* Warren wouldn't have come back now, but he had no choice. This was bigger than old wrongs and old warnings; his father could understand that, couldn't he?

"I need to see Pop. Where's Pop?"

"He's at the stable," said Willa.

Warren turned toward the door. "Then I'm going there."

Regina was still beside him. She gazed up at him and began to speak, but her lips did not move. His eyes widened as he heard the voice in his mind, the words resounding as if echoing in a cave: *"Warren, tell us what happened to Terry."* The tone was not that of the trembling young girl he saw in front of him. It was the voice of a Southern woman—older, mature, strong.

"Regina?" Warren asked, cocking his head to the side, "are you doing that? How...?"

"It doesn't matter how," said Willa. She could hear the voice too. "Tell us what happened."

He wanted to explain everything—how Akins had threatened the family, how Warren had lost control and murdered him in the street, burned him alive—but he couldn't allow them to know about his heinous act. He could tell them only of the aftermath: "I know where Terry makes his last delivery every Monday. Sometimes I meet him there and walk him home. I got there tonight and...there was this car...Some guys grabbed him...I tried to stop them, but I couldn't do anything..."

"Was there a pale man?" asked Willa. Warren could only stare. "A pale white man?" she asked again.

Warren nodded, perplexed that Willa could know. He looked from her to Regina, still mystified that Regina had some sort of odd power. "I couldn't do anything. They took him. They took Terry into their car..."

"Who took Terry?" came a booming voice from outside.

Warren spun to see his father just outside the doorway. He, too, looked older, smaller somehow, but his anger was as vivid as ever. He grabbed his son by the collar of his coat. "What have you done?"

"I didn't do anything, Pop. It wasn't my fault..." He struggled in his father's grip.

"Regina," Carl ordered, "help your grandmother back to her room. I need to talk to...this man alone." Regina obeyed, racing up the stairs and taking Willa by her arm.

Once they were out of view, Carl shoved Warren out of the house, sending his eldest son stumbling to the wet concrete. "What have you done?" he barked over the sound of the pelting rain, his hands trembling.

"I didn't mean to do it. I just didn't want him to hurt Jerome or any of them. He said he was gonna shoot them."

"Who did?"

"Akins." Warren lowered his head. "He's a dealer."

His father scowled. "I *knew* you must still be using. That's why I didn't want you ever coming around here, polluting your brothers, dragging them down with you. Now tell me what happened to Terry?"

Warren described his altercation with Akins. He pulled himself up to his knees as he spoke but kept his eyes to the ground. "I lost control. He said he was gonna hurt Jerome and Terry and Regina. I didn't mean to kill him. I just couldn't stop..."

Carl gritted his teeth and shook his head back and forth.

"You killed him? You killed a boy?"

Warren nodded, crying.

"And then what?"

Warren recounted what had happened outside Marco's apartment: the car, the men, Van Owen climbing from the back seat.

"Dear God," said his father. His arms dropped to his sides.

"I couldn't fight him," Warren went on. "I was all worn out from Akins," he lied, avoiding mention of the drug he had injected to calm himself, the drug that had left him weak and unable to fight. He thought of the blue light, of hiding under the stairs and then suddenly finding himself blocks away. Had he imagined it? Had the heroin high fooled him? But there was no time to dwell on it now. "I had to run. The punks with him, though—I've seen them before. They work for this guy named Dominus. They work out of this hansom cab stable on Thirty-seventh and Eleventh. That's who Akins worked for, too." He started to say more, but he couldn't force the words out.

"What aren't you telling me?" his father demanded.

Warren took closed his eyes and took a breathed. "I think that

Dominus and Van Owen might be the same person."

Carl glared at him, his eyes widening. When he finally spoke, his voice was so full of anger that Warren thought his father might burst. "So you've been buying your drugs from Hendrik Van Owen?"

"I didn't know," Warren cried, his throat aching. "I swear I didn't know. All I knew is Akins and some others worked for some pale white dude named Dominus. I'd never seen him before tonight. I didn't know..."

"And now you've led Van Owen right to your brother, who can't protect himself..."

"No! I wanted to do something, but I couldn't..."

His father seemed not to hear him. He was lost in thought, bobbing his head from side to side. "But why does Van Owen want *Terry?*"

"I don't know—that's what I keep trying to figure out—but we can go after him together. "I can help..."

"You want to go *with* me? Why? Haven't you already caused enough damage to this family?"

"I can help, Pop!"

"How?" Carl's voice was even louder now. "How? You're probably so stoned that you can't even control yourself. Everything bad that ever happened to this family is because of you. Your mother's dead. Your brother's taken. What else is there left for you to destroy?"

Warren shuddered. "You've got to let me help..."

Carl hesitated. "Tell me one thing. Are you high now?"

Warren grew silent.

"Look me in the eye, and tell me you're not high."

Warren raised his eyes and tried to open his mouth. Then he returned his gaze to the ground. "It doesn't matter what I am. I can still fight. I can..."

"Go! Just go, and don't ever come back. Don't ever come near this family again! We're not your family anymore."

His limbs heavy, Warren pulled himself up and staggered off. Once he was sure that his father wasn't watching, he ducked behind a parked car and turned back to watch.

His father hadn't moved. His arms were tense at his sides, his hands molded into fists. He lifted his head to the night sky as if looking for inspiration. Then he seemed to catch sight of the light in Willa's window. Warren looked there too. The window was wide open.

Warren knew that Willa and Regina must have heard the argument below. But how much, he wondered, could they possibly understand about preternatural powers and an enemy who lives forever? Such matters had always been kept secret by the men in the family. Then he heard his father's voice.

"I'm coming, Terry," Carl Kelly said to himself as he moved toward his car. "I'm coming for you, son." And with each step he took, the wind swirled around his feet.

PART II

The Convergence

NINETEEN

An elevator door opened onto a carpeted hotel hallway. The walls were painted silver gray; the doors were a dark gray; the rugs were a deeper gray. Even the scene itself seemed gray, as if from an old movie. From the elevator, a lean, olive-skinned man in his thirties craned his head out into the hallway. "Okay," he whispered, still scanning for onlookers, "I think it's clear. Come on."

An attractive dark-skinned woman, younger than he, glided from the elevator, laughing. She wore a light-colored dress with a matching scarf around her neck. "You're so suspicious. You're worse than my grandmother. Nobody followed us here."

The man caught up and made sure to stay one pace in front of her. He was only slightly taller than she, but his pinstripe charcoal suit elongated his slender form. Under his left arm, he carried a black hat with a gray band around it. In his right hand was a small suitcase.

"What's our room number?" the woman asked.

"Here," he said, unlocking Room 714. He flipped on the light and led her in before angling his neck out to check the hallway once more. Seeing no one, he set the Do Not Disturb sign on the handle and locked the door.

Immediately, the woman turned out the light and draped herself around his neck, almost hanging from him. "You see?" she laughed.

"Nobody followed us. Nobody cares."

"They care. Trust me, they care."

She kissed him hard, pressing him against the door. He held her tightly, and she wrapped her legs around his waist as he carried her to the bed. He tried to lower her down gently, but she pulled him on top of her, giggling.

"After eleven months," she said, *"I can't even believe we're actually alone."*

The man seemed to relax. He rolled onto his back and put his hands behind his head, his suit jacket opening to reveal a large handgun in a shoulder holster.

"My god," she gasped. *"Every time I see that, I want to scream. I wish you didn't have to wear it all the time."*

"Maybe soon I won't have to." He stood and removed his jacket. The Times Square neon flashed in the window, dimly lighting the room, and she watched him in silhouette as he unstrapped the holster and placed it in the bedside drawer next to the Bible and slid the drawer closed. He unbuttoned his shirt, revealing a white, tank top undershirt. He was thin, but his muscles were taut and defined. There was an easy grace to his movement, almost catlike. He slipped through the room like a lightweight boxer.

He stopped and looked at her staring up at him from the bed, and he smiled. *"You are so beautiful."*

"I'm not," she said, suddenly shy.

He sat beside her and stroked her face with the back of his hand. *"You are."*

"Then why aren't you kissing me, Marco?"

He leaned in toward her. *"I love you, Willa."*

The telephone rang, pulling Willa from her reminiscence. She stared at the bedside phone for a moment, listening to it ring a second time, a third time, before lifting the receiver.

"Hello? Yes. That's right—we're going to Thirty-seventh and

Eleventh. Please hurry." She hung up the phone and looked over to see Regina standing in the doorway of the bedroom. "That was the taxi service. The car will be here in seven minutes." Regina nodded but kept her eyes to the ground; she looked uncomfortable. "You were watching the memory, weren't you, Regina? You saw what I was thinking about."

Regina raised her eyes and then lowered them again. Her expression didn't change, but her response was clear: she had broken the rule. She had been looking inside Willa's mind. She had seen the memory.

"It's okay, dear. You *should* see it. I knew you might. I've been guarding my thoughts around you for too long." Regina still didn't look up. "It's all ancient history now. I should have told you about Marco a long time ago. I should have told all of you. He's your grandfather after all."

Regina seemed to have already figured that out. "*Why didn't you tell us?*" she asked, her thick Southern voice rolling telepathically through Willa's mind. Regina had been speaking with Amara's voice for two years now, but Willa still hadn't grown accustomed to it. She knew that voice so well—Amara had raised Willa after all—so Willa knew the cadence, the pace, the tone, the accent. It was a voice from another time. It was antebellum. There was no one else alive who spoke with that accent. No, Willa remembered, there was one other. And she would see him again this night.

She thought of how difficult these last two years must have been for Regina—forced to silence her voice, to endure ridicule at school, to worry her family—all because Willa had told her to avoid being noticed. What a thing to do to a child. But how would the world have reacted to a little girl from Upstate New York who overnight started speaking like an older Southern woman?

Perhaps just as bad, Willa had pressed Regina to use her ability sparingly—not to reach out with her mind. But she *had* to make

161

Regina hide her ability. For decades, Van Owen had been able to track Amara—to find her—whenever Amara used her ability too forcefully. And Regina's ability and now her voice were the same as Amara's.

Willa felt the guilt closing in on herself. So many secrets. So many lies. So many half-truths. So much hidden. She thought of Terry. Regina and Terry had such a fierce connection. He knew about Regina's ability. The two children were linked in so many ways. Their love and trust for one another was palpable. But Willa had forced Regina not to tell Terry anything about the family's past. Secrets and buried pasts had become a way of life.

And now Regina wanted to know why Willa hadn't told her about Marco being her grandfather. "Why didn't I tell you?" she finally answered. "Why did I tell everyone that your grandfather was a musician who left me? A million reasons, none of which seems worth anything right now. Sometimes, once you keep a secret long enough—or tell a lie long enough—it just gets harder and harder to let go of it." She sighed. "Terry has known Marco for more than a year now. There were times I wished that Marco would just break down and tell Terry everything, or that Terry would just figure it out on his own. Just put it all out in the open. But it's too late now to..."

Regina's voice was severe now in Willa's mind. *I want to know more. Show me more. Show me the rest of it.* Willa closed her eyes.

The room was dark. Neon flashed through the hotel window, lighting the room in staccato bursts. It was an hour before dawn, and even midtown Manhattan was quiet. Then the silence was broken by a loud thump.

"Marco, what's that?" asked Willa.

A second noise followed, this one even louder. Marco turned on the light and flew from the bed, fastening his belt as he raced across the room. "Get your clothes on," he whispered. His body was tense and ready. His green eyes were alert and active. He was already preparing for a dozen scenarios.

"Get down," he told Willa.

The lock shattered, and the door fluttered open, and two men in dark suits stumbled in, guns drawn, but Marco was already upon them. He was waiting just behind the door, and, as soon as the men entered, Marco sprung at the smaller of the two, knocked the gun from the man's hand, and pressed the barrel of his own gun against the man's jaw. "Don't make me do it," Marco hissed. "Don't make me do it."

The second assailant didn't seem fazed. He raised his gun fearlessly, but it dropped from his hand as if pulled to the floor by a magnet. All eyes went to the gun as it struck the carpet. The man almost dove for it, but Marco shoved the smaller man at him, and the two intruders fell to the floor in a heap.

Marco flipped the door shut. "Don't even think about moving," he told them, his gun pointed at them. "Who are you, and why are you here?"

The men glanced at each other and then back at Marco. Behind him, Willa was pulling on her clothes. One of the men turned to watch.

"Don't look at her," said Marco. "I've got the gun. Look at me." He tipped the table lamp toward them. He didn't recognize the larger man, but he knew the other one. He was in his mid-twenties with the hairless, smooth skin of a boy. "I know you. You're Leo, Jr.—Leo Moretti's kid. Why are you here?"

"It's just a job," said Leo Moretti, Jr. "It's nothing personal."

"That's not what I asked. Why are you here? What does your father want with me?"

"My father doesn't want anything. Your father does. He didn't want to send his own guys after you, so he asked my father to do it for him."

Marco squinted his eyes. "My father sent you after me?"

"Not after you," said the larger man, who hadn't spoken yet. The message was clear to everyone in the room. The men were there for Willa.

Marco trained the gun on the man and almost stuttered as he asked "Why?"

"You know why," said Moretti. "You're a capo's son. You can't run around with...with someone like her."

"Say it," said Marco. "With someone like what? Say it."

"With a Negro."

Marco gazed at Willa, who was livid, her arms crossed over her chest as if she were fighting off a chill. "I want to have a word with these boys," he told her. "Will you go in the bathroom for a bit, honey?"

"No," she said, her voice flat as she lowered her hands to her sides. I want to hear this."

Marco knew it was useless to argue with her. He turned back to the men. "So my father sent you here to kill my girl?"

"Not to kill her," said Moretti. "We're supposed to take her somewhere."

Marco stared for a time, waiting for the man to elaborate. Finally he murmured "Where?"

"To Dominus," said Moretti.

Marco stared, confused. "Dominus? Why?"

"I don't know. That's just what I was told to do. Dominus wants her; that's all I know. He's the one who told your father that you were dating a colored girl."

Marco kept the gun pointed at the two men, but nobody moved for some time until Marco finally spoke. "I'm gonna do you a favor, Moretti—I'm not going to kill you or your friend here." The two men began to rise. "No, I didn't say you could leave. I'm not done talking. As I said, I'm gonna do you a favor. I'm gonna let you live, *but that's a big favor, so you're going to owe me one in return." He eyed the second man. What's your name?"*

"Jimmy Falcone."

"Well, Jimmy Falcone—first, you and Leo, Jr. are going back to Daddy Moretti and telling him you found me but that she wasn't with me." He stopped for a moment and then turned to look at Willa and then back at the two men. "No, scratch that. You're going to tell him you caught up with us too late—that we were already leaving the hotel, that you saw me take her to Penn Station, that you saw me put her on a train. You're gonna say that she got on a train heading...to...Minnesota... and that she was crying. And I got on another one heading west. You're gonna say that you followed me onto the train and roughed me up to find out where I was going. I told you California—Los Angeles—and that I wasn't ever coming back here."

"Your pop's not gonna believe any of that," said Moretti. "He's not gonna take my word...he'll know I'm lying..."

"No," Marco told him, "nobody's gonna be a liar—because everything I just said is gonna happen just like I said it."

"No," interrupted Willa. "I'm not leaving you..."

Marco turned to her. He kept his eyes on her even as he continued speaking to Moretti and Falcone. "The two of you are gonna go outside now and wait in your car. In about ten minutes, Willa and I are gonna leave this hotel and get in a cab. You're gonna follow us to Penn Station, and it's all gonna happen just like I said. So nobody's gonna be a liar." He turned back to the men. "And you've got no reason to double-cross me because you won't have blown anything. You just got the job too late."

The men waited for Marco to nod that it was okay for them to rise, to bend down to retrieve their guns, and then to head for the door.

They exited, the door closed, and Willa exploded. "I am not leaving you..." She threw herself against him. "You promised we'd be together. You promised..."

"I know," he kept repeating, but she couldn't hear him over her outburst.

"It's 1955. Negroes have been free for nearly a century! Who says that you and I can't be together?"

"Everybody says it, Willa! Everybody says it. You know I want to be with you. There's nothing I want more, but we can't be together here. Not now." He was buttoning his shirt, pulling on his jacket.

"Those were guns they had out."

"Well, I took care of one of the guns," she interrupted, cockier than she felt.

"Yeah, I saw. But it's not safe for you here. You heard what they said. They weren't coming after me. They were coming after you." Willa opened her mouth to speak but said nothing. "I don't know what Dominus wants with you," Marco went on, "but I'm not gonna be the cause of something happening to you. If we both leave New York, maybe they'll leave us both alone, and then we can meet up soon somewhere."

"No," her stern voice rang out, "I'm not running away." She pulled herself from his grip but remained facing him. "I've spent my whole life hiding because that's what my family is supposed to do. We hide. We cower. We run. Well, I've done enough running..."

"Are you listening to me? I love you, Willa. I love you. But I can't let them get you. This guy Dominus is a sick bastard. They say he's the grandson of a slaveholder from down South somewhere— that he's always talking about how Negroes should still be slaves. Lord knows what he wants with you. My father does business with him because it's profitable, but nobody likes the guy, and nobody trusts the guy. There's something...off about him..."

Willa's expression changed from angry to curious. She just stared at him for a time. And when she finally spoke, her tone was odd, as *if she already knew the answer to the question she was asking.* "What does he look like?"

"Pale. White hair. Light eyes. Real thin."

Willa's face went numb. "Van Owen," *she said in a monotone, her eyes glassy.* "Hendrik Van Owen."

"You see," said Willa as she dropped Regina's hand and closed off the memory, "there's still a lot you don't know."

Regina blinked several times and shook her head as she freed herself from her grandmother's mind. *"Why did you keep all of this from me?"*

"I didn't want you to dwell on anything that might bring Van Owen to you—anything that might help him sense you and find you. He met Marco only once, but he was able to see me in Marco's thoughts—to know about my abilities. Even Amara couldn't keep him from finding her. He could feel her from thousands of miles away when she used her ability intensely or when she was in pain." Willa groaned as she tried to stretch her legs, which shook with the effort. "But it's too late to worry now. Van Owen has found us. He must want his revenge for what I did. He must have known that if he took Terry, I'd go after him." She stopped for a moment and seemed lost in thought. "I just don't understand how Carl and Warren know about Van Owen. Dara never told Carl anything about our abilities or our history..." Her thoughts trailed off only to be supplanted by Regina's.

"Maybe it doesn't matter how they know," Regina explained. *"I just know that we need to get to Van Owen before they do. And you need to tell me now what else you've kept from me."*

Willa's eyes welled with tears. "I've been so blind." She felt the irony of declaring blindness to a girl who spoke with Amara's voice. "And I can't let you be blind too. You need to know, to *see*, everything—from the beginning."

Willa found her way back to the bed and sat again. Then she

closed her eyes and opened her mind, allowing Regina to watch the play of memories as they shifted to an endless white sand beach surrounded by blue water. In the distance, the trees were deep green. The vista was freer and more expansive than anything Regina had ever imagined.

"What you're seeing now," said Willa, "are not *my* memories—they're ones that were shown to me by Amara. These memories are hers. And this is where we came from. This is Mkembro on the shores of West Africa. Before the slavers came."

TWENTY

At Lincoln's command, Africans in America are free, though many of us never truly learn what that word means. We don't have money or land or social skills or the right skin color to fit into American society. Most whites don't accept us; some never will. Still, I try to mimic the euphoria of my brethren with tireless talk of forty acres, mules, and equality. Some of them head out west, seeking land and new frontiers. Some veer to the North, chasing rumors of prosperity that won't play out for decades. Most of them stay in the South, on the plantations, and become sharecroppers, only to get cheated by the plantation owners. They work all season and then line up to be paid, only to be told that the cotton or tobacco—whatever crop it is they grow—fetched bad prices this year. No matter how abundant their harvest, most sharecroppers finish every year breaking even or in debt. I'm through with plantations, but I have no illusions that new surroundings will offer me any greater happiness, so I, too, stay in the South.

Knowing what comes next for me, I follow my visions to the door of the Jasper family in Whelan, Tennessee. For nearly two years, I live in the tiny room down the hall from their daughter Cecily, working as maid and nanny. Although Cecily is only three, I take it upon myself to teach her to read and write. We keep it a secret from her parents until she is five. Once they discover how advanced she is in her studies, they promptly hire a college-educated tutor for their "genius daughter." Of course, I don't tell them that Cecily is not so remarkable—that she has simply benefited from my ability to teach her from inside her mind. Sometimes, as she sleeps, I fill her thoughts with letters and words and pictures, training her how to decipher them. There are moments when I fear that Van Owen is out there somewhere, listening for me—waiting for me to use my mind in this way so that he can locate me—so I use my abilities only in short bursts. It occurs to me that he could have returned to a life at sea or moved across the country or to another continent even, but I know I can't allow myself to be careless. I enter Cecily's mind, I do my teaching, and then I exit before I can be traced. Once the Jaspers limit my duties solely to cleaning their mansion, I leave Whelan. I leave it, though, with two newfound loves—teaching and children.

For some time, I find similar work with families across the South. I always begin my tenure as maid, but, within a few weeks, I take on the mantle of educator and then nanny. Within a year or two, I move on, before anyone notices how quickly their children are progressing, before they can tell all of their friends about the miracle worker of a nanny they've employed; I don't need that sort of attention. Still, I always leave with a reference for my next job. It pains me sometimes to know that I'll never hold a job as a real teacher—in a school—but I must keep myself hidden, tucked away within the homes of others until I know that I'm strong enough to defend myself against Van Owen. For the visions are never clear enough to inform me exactly when our next meeting will be.

I rarely venture into public, though the only people who might know my face are other former slaves and plantation guards. "Don't you ever go out, Amara? Isn't there a man in your life?" the mothers of my charges sometimes ask. "There was a man once," I tell them, "but he died." I leave it at that. I don't speak of my days in

Mkembro, or of the tobacco fields of the plantation, or of the sound of Kwame's body hitting the water as the bullets hailed from the deck. He was beautiful. I barely knew him. He's gone. That's all that need be said.

They must wonder why I sometimes wake screaming or why they find me sitting on the porch at twilight, staring into nothing, remembering terrors past and to come. There are still so many visions that I cannot understand. Some I have seen only once, such as the scene of the girl, Leticia, with Van Owen. Others keep replaying. I've seen my father die at least a hundred times. I've seen Van Owen storm into my wedding ceremony just as often. I've seen my descendants—Terry and Jerome and Willa and others—in various contexts, dangerous and benign, but I've seen so little of my own future. It is as if fate has chosen to show me only what has already passed or else what is so far ahead that I cannot affect it. I've seen again and again Van Owen's attempt to rape me. With each viewing, I gaze more intently, trying to glean something new from it. Sometimes I just revel in the outcome—his leaving unsated and emasculated. Sometimes I focus on how he used his mind to subdue me. I try to dissect his methods so that I can mimic them. Sometimes I spend hours trying to understand how Kwame and I managed to pass our powers on to Van Owen. It should have been possible only through lineage—the way Kwame and I inherited ours from our fathers—but Van Owen gained his powers from through our touching him. There is still so little I know of these abilities I was born with and which my descendants shall inherit. My father, who might have taught me our history—where these powers came from, why we have them—is gone. I am the oldest of my line. I have seen the panoply of the African American future unfold. Just as many of us lost our parents and families when we were herded into slaving ships or sold on the slaving block, so too shall generations of Africans in America go through life never knowing their parents. In particular, so many children will never know their fathers. It was ingrained in us in plantation life—families split up by slave trades or broken apart because so many of us never had a community to teach the necessity of the family structure. Will we ever break the cycle? Will we ever find unity?

Sometimes, I still see my father in combat with Van Owen. Did he, I wonder, have the gift of foresight as I do? Did he believe me, I wonder, when I came to him before my wedding and told him of my visions? Had he already seen himself? Did he know that a battle was coming but that he had no choice but to face it? Did he know that this prescience allows one only to *see* the future but not to *change* it? Or did it even occur to him that I might share in the family birthright of unnatural power? Did he think it was limited only to the males? Did he tell me to run because he couldn't dream that I could have the strength to face his murderer in battle?

The bullet flies again and again. And my father falls each time. His blood flows like water. I think of Van Owen's wounds—the ones he showed me when he came to rape me—they were like scorched holes in his chest. He claimed that he had been shot and stabbed in the war but that he had repaired the wounds. "I change," he said, "but I cannot die." He was boasting, trying to impress me with his invulnerability. And yet he bled. Just as my father did.

And anything that bleeds can die.

TWENTY-ONE

Even unconscious and dreaming, Terry could still see the face of the man in the back seat of the car. The hollow, haunted, sapphire eyes, the ghostly white skin, the ravenous mouth. It was the face of death, but it had a name. Terry knew it from somewhere. Even unconscious and dreaming, he knew the name: Van Owen.

The memories coursed through his mind, pulling him from era to era, across five generations. A beach, tranquil and untouched. A farm with scents so soothing but with an undercurrent so brutal. A dozen cities across the South, transient homes for a princess forced to live like a refugee—a woman named Amara, pursued always by the pale man named Hendrik Van Owen.

He could feel the tape covering his mouth, covering his eyes, wrapped around his wrists and ankles, binding him like a prisoner. Like a slave. He knew that he was dreaming, that he shouldn't be able to feel the tape or recognize what it was, and yet he could. Somehow, he was both awake and asleep at the same time.

He thought of Regina; he wished that she could see these dreams. *Regina would understand,* he was certain. In spite of their four-year age difference, Terry and his sister were connected like twins. They understood each other; they could read each other— ever since that day when she stopped speaking and started communicating without words.

That day seemed decades ago. It was evening. He and Regina were playing cards when her eyes went glassy. Terry thought she was pretending to be in a trance, something a playful little girl would do. He reached out for her, to shake her. His fingertips brushed against her bare arm, and it started: images flooded his mind—death, pain, blood, lust. And that face. That man's face. It had been there two years ago in those images—the pale man, the man from the car! Van Owen. A man determined to hate and kill and dominate. It had been too much for Terry then; the nightmare was too real. He couldn't bear it. He tried to close his eyes, his ears, his mind, to shut away those harsh memories that weren't his, bury them far from everything, where he'd never have to see them. And that's what he'd done—sealed them away, forgotten everything but their effect.

Even so, he wondered sometimes if there were answers in those visions—something to explain why Regina's voice had changed, why she could now communicate telepathically. But whenever Terry thought about the images, he would instinctively compel himself to think about anything else.

But why, he wondered now, *was the pale man there in those visions two years ago? Who is he? What does he want with me? I need to know. I need to understand.*

The dream stopped. Terry woke fully and became aware that the tape was indeed real—fastening him to a chair, wrapped around his wrists, his ankles, his eyes. The tape tugged on his skin, tearing at his eyelids as he struggled against it. So he sat still and thought of that man with the white hair. He concentrated on that face—its rigidity, its cruelty, its hardness. And, for the first time, Terry didn't retreat from the face or from the memories. He let them come. First, there was only a trickle. Van Owen on a ship, Africans in a field, chains. But, as Terry opened his mind more and started to delve, the memories came flooding back.

It was all so familiar, as if the memories were his, and all he had to do was watch them, experience them, live them. From the beginning.

So there he sat, a captive physically and mentally, watching the waves crash on the shores of Mkembro in West Africa, and in the distance, the shadow of a slave ship darkening the horizon.

TWENTY-TWO

In visions, I've seen Dara with Carl. I've seen Willa with Marco. I've seen Rolanda with William. They laugh and argue and cry and love and collapse against each other as if their arms could fit around no one else. But as my first labor pains double me over until I am crumpling into Ray Franklin's arms, I try to feel what my descendants will feel. I allow Ray to scoop me up tight against his chest, to support me and the child within me, but I know that all I feel for Ray is appreciation, a natural response to the love *he* shows *me*. I appreciate him. I respect him. I care about him. I trust him. But I do not *love* him the way he loves me. I'll never know that manner of love. Perhaps I've seen too much hate.

"We've got to get you to the hospital," he tells me, cradling me toward the front door of our Atlanta apartment.

"No. No hospital. I told you it's not safe. Take me to my room." My right arm is curled around his shoulder. In my hand, I can still feel the first page of the newspaper, the sight of which triggered the first contractions of childbirth five weeks too soon.

"Not safe?" Ray stutters, "It's a hospital, Amara." In his mind, though, I can hear the doctor's words from six months ago: *"Your wife is forty-six years old, Mr. Franklin. This won't be an easy pregnancy, especially since it's her first. She's got to stay off her feet. You have to bring her in every month for an examination and keep me notified of any changes in her health..."*

"It doesn't matter how old I am," I tell Ray, accidentally responding aloud to my memory of the doctor's words. "The child will be fine. I've seen her."

But Ray keeps leading me toward the door until finally I realize I have no choice. I reach into his mind with mine and make the decision for him: *We will stay here; we will have the baby at home.*

He stops short, his hand on the doorknob. He lets it go and turns around. "Yes, I think we should have the baby at home."

I haven't used my power like this in years. I've tried to stay silent, tried to keep myself and my abilities hidden, tried to be vigilant always, but I can't afford to be careful now. I also can't afford to let Ray take me to a hospital—a public place—when I'm this weak.

He carries me to our room and lays me upon the bed. He sits in the chair beside me, stoking my hair, cooling my forehead with a wet cloth. Ray is such a good, gentle man. I do wish I could return what he feels for me. Instead, I dwell on the guilt I feel for lying so much about my past, for never confiding in him about who I am, where I came from, what I'm capable of. And now I'm doing far worse: I'm taking away his free will, just as mine was taken from me so long ago.

The contractions come again and again, pain shooting up my spine until my head snaps backward. I scream, but the sound emanates not from my mouth but from Ray's. I want to release him; I don't know if I can keep control over him when the contractions peak. What if I pass out? Will Ray be able to deliver the baby on his own? As I told him, I know that the baby will live, that she'll be born healthy, that I will call her Rolanda, named for Roland, the first American man who showed me kindness, bringing me water and then dying for it.

I steal another glance at the newspaper headline and the accompanying picture: *National Tobacco Corp. Names New*

Chairman. The face is unmistakable. It hasn't changed one iota. The skin is as pale as it was thirty years ago, the eyes as vacant, the smile as subtly contemptible. He hasn't aged a day. Beneath the photograph, the caption reads *Donald Van Owen, son of noted Confederate Captain, Hendrik Van Owen.* So he is posing as his own son. The article details his rise within the company, how he introduced new techniques for treating the tobacco, new guidelines for shipping cigarette products across the ocean, and how he has recently moved to Atlanta from Montgomery, Alabama. He is here in Atlanta with me. I curse my poor judgment for staying in the South, but I know that he would have found me eventually no matter where I went.

The contractions grow more intense. The pain is unimaginable, like a force within me is pressing outward me from the inside. I can see Ray twitching, trying to climb out of his daze. For a moment, he begins to exert control.

"Amara, we've got to...," he says, trying to stand.

But I grab hold again. I will not go to a public place—a hospital—and be so exposed in this condition. I tell myself that as soon as the child is born, I will convince Ray that we must move elsewhere. We will leave Atlanta, even if I have to force my will upon him to make it so.

As if in response, Ray announces, "We can't stay here." I can't discern whether these are my thoughts about Atlanta or his about my birthing the child here in our tiny apartment above the hardware store where he works. I can't think straight with the labor pains tearing me apart. Trying to give myself a moment's peace, I decide to put a calming thought in Ray's mind. I show him a fabricated image of the three of us—him, me, and baby Rolanda—walking by a lake. The water is clear and reflects a perfect blue sky. The fields are combed with flowers; birds chirp a melancholy song.

Then another contraction comes, closer than the previous. Ray and I scream together. It jolts me up almost into a sitting position. I try to maintain the fantasy image for Ray, but then my constructed world shudders, the ground quaking at the sound of Van Owen's voice.

"Amara," his voice erupts in my head, *"what is this trite charade?"*

He's found me. My eyes glance everywhere, searching the bedroom, searching the vision, but only his voice is here. Somehow, in the weakness of labor, in the struggle to use my power to control my husband, I have let down my guard. Van Owen has *heard* me. From somewhere in Atlanta, he has sensed me, and he has latched onto my thoughts as a beacon. While I hid and became complacent, too afraid to use my ability for fear that he might sense me, he has grown more and more powerful. And he has found me.

"There is no lake, Amara. This is an illusion. Who are those people with you?" Then his tone turns angry, accusing. Jealous. *"Who is that man at your side?"*

I maintain the vision of the lake and the countryside, but I remove Ray and Rolanda. At my side now, instead of a husband and a daughter, is a rifle. I hold it up at shoulder level and shout, "Show yourself, coward."

"Oh, I will," Van Owen says softly, *"but first, why don't you go to sleep."*

Above me, in the vision, the sky turns dark. Violent clouds roll like factory smoke across my perfect sky. Lightning explodes in jagged bolts, striking the water near me. My feet are bare and wet, so the electric shock jolts through my body. I know that the lake is only a fantasy—my own creation, infiltrated by Van Owen—but the pain is real. The lightning currents burn and jar me at the same time. The next bolt comes, lighting up the sky in a brilliant, burning white that doesn't dissipate. All I can see is whiteness, filling the sky, spreading outward, spilling all over me. It burns my eyes; they feel like they're melting. I keep waiting for the light to fade—for my lakeside scene to return—but everything stays white. I try to leave the fantasy, but it won't end. Consciousness begins to creep away, its flight offering an escape from the pain of the contractions and the pain of the blinding light. The baby will be here soon; I must stay awake. If I pass out, I won't be able to protect her. But the contractions are mounting, successively closer, and I don't know what happens next—I haven't seen it yet. *Who will protect my baby?*

Van Owen answers me: *"I will, Amara. I'll protect her. You just sleep. Sleep and dream. I'll see you soon. All's forgiven, my dear."*

"Ray," I stammer aloud, just before I slip away, "wake up. I need you."

TWENTY-THREE

"Who the hell are you?" Marco asked in his toughest voice. He'd opened the door only because he thought it must be Terry knocking, but this Black man in the doorway was older and a stranger, though there was something familiar about him.

Rainwater dripped from the man's face and clothes, creating a widening puddle at his feet. From the doorway, he stared Marco up and down. He removed his baseball cap as if in respect, revealing eyes reddened with fatigue and perhaps something more. "I'm Warren Kelly, Terry's brother," said the man, his voice hoarse and raspy.

Marco gaped for a few moments before nodding. "Yeah, I've seen you. I should have recognized you."

"Where've you seen me? I heard you don't go outside."

"I've seen you. Sometimes I look out the window after Terry leaves, and I see you waiting for him across the street."

"Oh." He took a breath before blurting out what he'd come to say. "Some guys got him. They got Terry."

Marco's voice grew loud. "*Got* him? What do you mean they *got* him? Is he..."

Warren's voice was flat. "They took him. In a car. I saw them, but I couldn't stop them. They had..."

Marco was agitated. "What guys? Was it what's-his-name...Akins?"

Warren turned away, glancing around the room as he spoke. "No, but they work for the same dude Akins worked for—guy named Dominus."

Marco's expression turned from distress to despair. "Van Owen. Akins works for Van Owen? That's why Akins has been bullying Terry all this time?"

"No." Warren stepped inside. His eyes darting about, taking in the meager apartment, before settling back on Marco. "Terry says you used to be a gangster." He paused. "The real kind."

Marco sighed before mumbling, "That was a long time ago."

"I'm going after Terry." He wiped the rain from his forehead. "You coming with me?"

Marco felt his heart rate jump. His breathing became erratic. In only seconds, sweat formed at his temples. "I don't know what I can do...I'm old...I can't..."

Warren's tone turned to disgust. "I should have known." He started moving quickly toward the door. "Terry thought you were all that—like you were something back in the day. This was a waste of time. You're just some broken down old man." Marco stood in the doorway as Warren stomped down the stairs, muttering under his breath, "I'm not wasting any more time on you." He opened the front door to the building. "I shouldn't even have come..."

Marco stormed out of his apartment in time to look down the stairwell and see the building door close. He peered down at his feet. He gripped the banister with shaking hands, his face hot, his breaths coming in tiny gasps. He felt as if he'd been tossed under a harsh wave that was pitching him about violently. *Vertigo*, a doctor had told him years ago, but Marco had known it was something much worse: fear. And fear could be conquered only by something stronger than fear: resolve.

The wave pulled him forward, step by shaky step, down the stairs one at a time, each step measured, in a lumbering line toward the building door, which seemed so far away. His hands clung to the banister, his knuckles white from the force of his grip. But by the time he reached the ground floor, he almost felt balanced. He was moving more quickly. He was still breathing hard, and he could feel the dampness on his face, but his heart was thumping not with fear but with anticipation. It had been so long.

The brass door handle was cool against his palm. He groaned as he turned it and opened the door and propelled himself onto the landing, into the wet, cool night air. Into the world outside.

"Warren," he shouted down the block, his voice thicker than before. "I'm not just some old man. I'm your grandfather. And I'm going with you."

By the time Warren made it back into the building and up the stairs, Marco was already in his bedroom, pulling a white dress-shirt over his tank-top undershirt.

As Marco turned toward him, Warren finally looked straight at him. "You've got green eyes," said Warren. "So does Terry." He opened his own swollen eyes wide. "So do I... when they're not red."

"My best feature," Marco smirked. "That's what Willa said. Glad I could pass them on."

Warren watched as the old man prepared himself. "Terry says you haven't left this apartment in like forty years."

"Yeah."

"How come?"

"'Cause I forgot how."

"That's no answer."

Marco held back a smile. He could imagine Willa saying that same phrase. "Well, I don't have any other answer. At first I *had* to stay in hiding. There were people who didn't want your grandma and me together, for obvious reasons. It was 1955. Nobody liked it when a white man dated a Black woman. Especially my family. And Van Owen has always had this thing for your family. He was chasing Willa. I figured if he found me, he could use me to lead him to your family. I couldn't do that to Willa or your mother or to any of you. So I hid." He turned away for a moment. He wanted to tell his grandson about the all-consuming fear that Van Owen imbedded in him, but he wasn't ready to talk about such things, so he continued with a half-truth. "And once you hide away long enough, it only gets harder to change. That's something *you* should understand."

Warren shifted his weight, squirming as he changed the subject. "I stopped at my family's house before coming here. I wanted my Pop to come with me...but he wouldn't take me. He's going after Van Owen himself."

"Damn," Marco snapped. "He's gonna get himself killed."

Warren wanted to say that his father could take care of himself, but he was thinking of something else he'd seen at home. He stuttered, trying to get out the next words. "I saw Regina. First time ever."

Marco nodded and then asked, "Did you see Willa?"

Warren nodded.

"You didn't tell Willa about Van Owen, did you?"

"Yeah, I did. Seemed like she already knew who he was, too. How do *you* know about him?"

"Long story." Marco opened a dresser drawer and retrieved a shoulder holster and a Smith & Wesson K-22 Masterpiece pistol. He had held it from time to time over the years, taken it out to clean it and admire it, but it had always felt foreign to him, a relic, something that belonged to a younger, stronger man. He marveled now that it felt natural. He tried not to admit to himself that it even felt good in his hands. He loaded the chamber and filled a suit jacket pocket with extra bullets. His movements were smooth. He spun the barrel and returned the gun to the holster, fastening it over his shoulder with agility. Warren watched intently. "That's an old gun."

"So am I," said Marco with a smirk as he pulled on the gray pinstripe suit jacket. "We both still work." He retreated into his closet and returned with a tie around his neck. He stopped near the door and checked his image in the mirror.

"Dressing up nice for your funeral?" Warren asked him.

"My funeral? Nah, that's long overdue anyway. I just want to look nice for your grandma."

"Grandma Willa? She's not gonna be where we're going."

Marco nodded yes. "Willa will be there. No way in hell she'd miss this. Seems like everybody's gonna be there." He thought of something and smiled. "*Four generations will come together to fight as one.* That's what Amara told me fifty years ago. My guess is she was talking about today." He donned a faded gray fedora and tilted it forward so that it almost concealed one eye. "It's gonna be a big family reunion."

As he headed out the door, he turned back to survey the empty apartment.

"What's wrong?" asked Warren.

"Nothing," said Marco. "I just wanted to look at the place one last time." Then he shut the door.

TWENTY-FOUR

It's raining outside. I can hear it beating against the window. It's dark. It must be nighttime. A baby is crying.

A door opens and closes. Rubber shoes squeak across a polished floor. Someone lifts my wrist, squeezes softly for a time and then lets go.

A man's voice, familiar: "How is she?"

Another man: "Her pulse is much stronger. Her temperature's back to normal. She should be fine. Just call me or one of the nurses when she wakes up."

It's still so dark. Why don't they turn on the lights? How can they see in the dark, these men? Why can't I? Are my eyes closed? I can feel my eyelids fluttering. My other senses are returning. I can smell the soap and alcohol in the air. My fingers are moving; I can feel the bed sheets, crisp and rough against my hands. The bed is soft. Too soft. The baby keeps crying. I lift my hand to my face. Why am I so weak? My belly burns. Everything burns. Why does that baby keep crying?

"Amara?" The familiar voice—Ray's voice. "Amara, everything's okay. You're going to be fine."

"The baby?" I ask him.

"The baby's fine. She's beautiful. Do you want to hold her?"

Without waiting for an answer, he lays her next to my right

186

shoulder. She stops crying, but I can feel her wriggling about. I brush my fingers against her smooth, smooth skin. I roll my palm over the tiny tufts of hair on her head.

"Ray, it's so dark in here. Can you turn on the light?"

He pauses before answering. "It's daytime. It's bright in here."

I can hear the fear in his voice. I raise my hand, waving it over my face, over my eyes. Gently, I lower my fingers toward my eyes. I can feel my eyelashes twitching, my eyelids opening and closing. I can't see. I'm blind.

"I'm going to get the doctor," Ray tells me.

Suddenly, I feel a chill.

"No," says another familiar voice, "don't get the doctor, Ray. Stay here with us, Ray."

I try to sit up, but I'm too weak. I pull Rolanda against my chest. "Ray, run! Get help..."

"Who are you?" Ray asks, confused.

"Who am I?" asks Van Owen, playful but indignant. "I'm Amara's owner. I'm the man who found her and brought her here to this new land where she wouldn't have to live out her life as a savage. I'm the man who rescued her from primitivity and gave her civilization. And how do you reward me, Amara? You run off and marry without even asking my permission."

"Nobody owns anybody anymore," Ray seethes. "Now you leave this room before I send you out on your back."

I reach out with my mind, trying to find Van Owen's, but it's so difficult sightless. I've spent decades growing accustomed to seeing my targets, looking them in the eye before infiltrating their minds. Now I'm a blind woman groping in the dark.

"Ray, go...please... get help..."

I hear a struggle, bodies shoving, pushing, a fist colliding with bone.

"Ignorant cur," Van Owen thunders. "How dare you strike me?"

"No, Van Owen, don't hurt him...please. He doesn't know... he doesn't..."

"I don't care what he knows. He shouldn't have touched my property."

Ray is wheezing, his breaths coming in choked clips. What's happening? Has Van Owen entered Ray's mind; is he holding Ray in thrall while strangling him?

The baby is wailing. I squeeze her against me and try to sit up, but the pain across my middle is searing. I kick and swing with my free arm, trying to do anything to distract Van Owen.

"Please stop... please don't hurt Ray..."

I hear the terror in my voice, and I know that I've been wrong for so long—in spite of all I've seen and done and known, I've clung for decades to my adolescent belief that Kwame was the only man I could ever love. Yes, he was beautiful and heroic, but I didn't know him. I've clung to an imagined future, to a promise never realized. Kwame and I were strangers. Ray is my husband, the father of our child, the man I have made a life with, the man who is dying for me now. And I love him. And so, desperate, I finally say it for the first time: "Please, Master Van Owen...please...I'll go with you..." But my epiphany comes too late.

There's a thud, a body hitting the floor. Then Van Owen speaks again.

"There. It's done. And just like Roland and Harry and Sam—and any other man who dares to put himself between me and my property—his death is on you."

"No..." My voice is so weak and distant. "Ray...," I say through tears.

"You brought this on yourself, Amara. I didn't come here for him or even for you. I came for the child."

"What? You can't take my baby..."

"Yes, I can and I will. The child is mine, just as much as you are.

You owe me. Everything that is yours is mine and ever shall be. You took something from me when you gave me this power. You took away my ability to impregnate a woman. I won't have any children of my own. I won't get to pass my gifts on to my offspring, but I can make sure that no one else is raised to challenge me." He stops speaking for a moment, as if he's just staring at me. Then his voice changes to an inquisitive tone. "Why are you staring off that way, Amara?"

I don't want him to know that I cannot see. "Because I don't want to look at you. And because I'm conserving my strength..."

"You *have* no strength, Amara. I had the nurse show me your chart just before I forced her to lead me to your room. You were unconscious for hours, and they had to cut you open just to get the baby out. They call it a caesarean section. You're so weak you probably can't even muster the force to stand up, let alone fight me. Somehow you're blocking me from getting at your thoughts. But I can tell just by looking at you that you've got nothing left to use against me."

I can hear him moving closer.

"Now I'm going to take the child and..."

The baby screams, and I hear Van Owen exhale strangely, as if stunned by something.

"How did you do that?" he asks through labored breaths. He grunts as if he's struggling against something, as if he's unable to get any closer to my child and me. "What are you doing? How are you putting up this...this wall, this invisible wall? Tell me how!"

I wonder if he's gone mad, if his own guilt is somehow keeping him locked in place, unable to get to the baby. I hear that strange high-pitched hum. He's going to use his—Kwame's—lightning. In my arms, Rolanda twists and shrieks. I can imagine the terror of seeing this hideous man with electricity crackling from his fingers. I feel an odd vibration as if I'm leaning against a motor of some sort. I wonder if my senses are so skewed that I can't even feel Van Owen's lightning coursing through me. He mutters incoherently like a weightlifter striving to use every last vestige of his might to raise an object that's simply too heavy. He's still trying to get to me—to us—but somehow he can't. Then I remember my father, who could wave his hand and hold off an army. Against my chest, Rolanda twitches as if she's struggling too. Her little body shakes. And then I'm certain. The wall is real. And Rolanda has erected it. It is she who is defending us against Van Owen. She has been born with an ability. Even fresh from the womb, her first instinct is to protect herself against Van Owen. From the floor, I hear a moan. Ray is still alive!

"Let go of me," Van Owen cries. Ray has grabbed him. I hear a dull sound as Van Owen is pulled to the floor.

"Help us," I shout. "Someone please..."

The lightning hums. The baby screams. Ray howls in agony. The smell of burning flesh fills the room. Then the door bursts open.

The doctor is the first one to speak. "Oh my God..."

I can only imagine what he sees—my husband burned and smoldering on the floor, Van Owen shooting electricity from his hands, and a baby shrieking in its mother's arms.

A nurse screams. There are footsteps outside, lots of them. People are running to my room.

"Get out of my way," Van Owen yells. I hear a commotion—people shoved, equipment knocked aside as he races out the door. The woman keeps screaming, but the baby is cooing quietly. I rock her softly, trying to block out the smell of death in the air, the weakness that pervades my body, the fear that makes me quiver. I focus on nothing but Rolanda's tiny noises.

I can hear the doctors trying to find Ray's pulse. They won't. I'm reaching out for him with my mind but finding nothing.

Soon the police will be here to investigate Ray's death. They'll ask who the murderer was. I'll tell them to fetch today's newspaper, to look at the picture on the front page. The doctors and nurses will corroborate. They all saw his face. The murderer was Donald Van Owen, newly appointed chairman of the National Tobacco Corporation. In the coming years, there will be many more newspaper and magazine articles speculating as to why a white business leader stormed a hospital room to murder an unimportant Negro man, and to try to kidnap a newborn Negro girl.

Van Owen will return, I know, perhaps with a new name or title, and he will live for generations. In this era, though—in this identity, which he clearly worked so hard to establish—he's finished. He will not be a leader or a famous or celebrated man. He will be a known criminal, forced into hiding, relegated to anonymity. And, blind or not, I will be ready for his next lunge at infamy, and so will my daughter.

TWENTY-FIVE

Carl Kelly slammed his cell phone down on the dashboard. Jerome was still not answering. "Where the hell are you, son?" he shouted to himself.

As he raced his car across Macombs Dam Bridge and toward the stable to find Jerome, he eyed the return traffic—two lanes packed solid—and wondered how he would make it back to Manhattan. Then he remembered that there had been a Yankee game that afternoon. The team was in a pennant race and was playing its chief rival, the Boston Red Sox. He thought of how his father would react to his son's apathy about baseball. Barton Kelly had been a man of many passions: baseball, horses, his wife, and, most of all, training his only son to be ready to face Hendrik Van Owen someday.

Carl thought of the stories his father had told him—stories that Carl had told to his sons Warren and Jerome. The legends had been passed down through five generations of male descendants, each one trying to maintain the original tale, reciting it word for word while adding his own story at the end. Carl suspected that much of it must be myth, but it was the only family history he knew.

First there was Tongra, chieftain of the T'mikra clan. They were a peaceful people. There was harmony until the three white men came. They called themselves explorers. They said they had no desire to conquer the T'mikra; they wanted only to study the tribe and how they lived. *Tongra allowed the three men to live among the T'mikra for one day only. He shared food and drink with them, allowed them to partake in the T'mikra rituals—even to smoke of the tribal pipe. Then, at night, after the rest of the clan had gone to sleep, the three white men shared with Tongra their own smoking pipe. In the morning, when the white men departed, Tongra was altered. Overnight, he had changed. His mind was addled. His thoughts were jumbled. Over the next several years, he seemed to age decades. Believing that his death was near, he knew that he must name a successor. So he sent his twin sons Merlante and Mkembro on a quest into the wilderness, declaring that the one who returned first with the fabled Keema root would be declared leader upon the chieftain's death. The Keema root grew only in the depths of the haunted cave atop the region's highest mountain. The root was imbued with ancient power, power that Tongra had discovered decades earlier.*

Mkembro and Merlante were sent on different paths for the weeklong journey, but they arrived at the mountain at the same time. Defying their father, they refused to race against each other to determine who would reach the Keema root first. Instead, the brothers decided that they would seek it together and decide later which one would return with it. So they scaled the mountain and entered the cave together. They descended into its caverns for two days, defeating serpents and dark spirits and wild beasts. Then they came upon the Keema, a blue-leafed root growing from the cave floor. It was surrounded by a ring of blue fire that rose from the ground and flared nearly to their shoulders. Each brother tried to pass through the flames but could not. The flames did not burn them but instead formed a sort of shield—a barrier that prevented the two from crossing. So the brothers came up with a plan: they would traverse the barrier together. From opposite sides of the ring of fire, they stepped toward it as one and passed through the flames unscathed.

Together they knelt to tear the Keema from the ground but quickly discovered that the root was not a root at all for it was not planted. It simply rested on the ground. The Keema was not in fact a plant but instead a living, pulsating blue flame that swirled in arcs, forming leaves of lightning in the air. The flame was always in motion, always changing. As the brothers moved and spoke, the flame veered and the lightning sparked in response. But when each brother knelt to touch it, the flame vanished, only to return when once the brother moved away. So they tried the same approach that had worked on the blue flame barrier. Together they knelt. Together they touched the Keema. And together they felt lightning course through their bodies.

Instantly, their minds were filled with confusing visions—dreams that lasted years but played out in mere moments, showing them different possible futures. In some visions, Mkembro ruled the T'mikra tribe; in others, Merlante did. Each stream, though, was marked with discord and strife between the brothers. In one where Merlante ruled, Mkembro was so envious that he murdered his brother and took over the village. In another, Mkembro ruled but had such desire for Merlante's wife that he banished his brother and took the wife for himself. In another, Merlante raised a great and brutal army that pillaged its way across the continent. In others, their rivalry, always fueled by jealousy or envy, was so intense that they killed each other or were driven mad with hunger for power. But in the last vision, the sons ruled together, and only then was there serenity.

Finally, the visions stopped, and the brothers let go of the Keema and were tossed backward out of the fire ring. At once, Mkembro and Merlante could feel the first embers of the strange power that they had been given. Mkembro could move objects with his thoughts and cause the winds to blow with the wave of his hand.

Merlante could enter the minds of others, even animals, and he could not be harmed by anything physical. And they both could cast lightning from their fingertips. They gloried in their newfound strengths, and, throughout the long journey back to T'mikra, they tested their powers and expounded on the myriad ways they could use their abilities to help their people. They accepted the wisdom of the visions—that their plan could flourish only if they ruled T'mikra together. They spoke of the kingdom they would build—a magnificent, tranquil land where there would be no fear, for its leaders would be united.

However, when they returned home to their father without the Keema root, and they recounted their plan to rule together, Tongra grew enraged. He called them cowards, declaring that it would have been better had they died fighting each other for the mantle of leadership rather than return with foolish dreams of sharing power. He demanded that they fight then and there for the right to rule. They refused, and so Tongra banished them from the village, commanding that they go off in opposite directions, cursing them that if they were ever to unite, they would bring a great scourge on all their people. Again, the brothers refused.

Before the entire village, Mkembro and Merlante renounced their father, declaring him mad and unfit to rule. They told of their newfound powers and described their plan for the tribe. Tongra became livid. He spread his arms wide, calling down the winds to beat his sons into submission. But Mkembro held his father at bay with his own mastery of the wind. Furious, Tongra declared that his sons were unworthy of their powers and that they must die. He rained lightning from his fingertips, trying to murder them. As the village watched, Merlante and Mkembro released their lightning as well. They tried only to deflect their father's attack, but they were young and inexperienced with their powers. When they attacked in unison, their lightning was fierce—too fierce. It struck their father and burned him to death.

The T'mikra people were terrified. They trusted in Tongra's curse. "You see," they said, "when you united, you murdered your own father!" The people declared that they would not live in a village ruled by both men—that Merlante and Mkembro must separate forever in order that the T'mikra people could be safe from the curse. So the two brothers followed the wishes of their people and separated. Half of the village went with Merlante, half with Mkembro. They left T'mikra forever to find new lands on which to build their own villages.

So it remained for ages. The Merlante and the Mkembro peoples stayed apart from one another, each flourishing in its own smaller village far from the other. Eventually, the history was forgotten by most. After many generations, most of the Merlante and Mkembro peoples believed that the two clans had always been enemies and were forbidden to fraternize with one another. Only the elders and the chieftain families themselves knew that the two peoples had once been one.

After a time, stories began to circulate that white men were catching and taking Africans from all clans. But the Merlante chieftains were wise. Every three seasons, they would uproot their people and move their village to safer lands. One Merlante chieftain named Ifenoke had the power to hide the village entirely. When the white men would pass nearby in search of captures, they saw only what Ifenoke wanted them to see—an abandoned village. Meanwhile the Mkembro were wise as well; they, too, found ways to hide. Sometimes they would vanish for decades but then return just as suddenly, their people looking no older.

But then Glele, a tyrant leader of an enemy tribe, made a pact with a white slaver named Van Owen from the land called America. In return for jewels and the safety of his own people, Glele led the white slavers to other African clans—small, hidden clans. For years,

Glele helped the slavers pick away at the Merlante and Mkembro and others. Afeard that their people were vanishing, some of the tribes formed pacts of protection with one another. Communication began even between the Merlante and the Mkembro. The Merlante leader, Berantu, sent a message to the Mkembaro leader, Warrendi, suggesting that they join together to fight Glele. He proposed that, as a sign of trust, his son Kwame would marry Warrendi's daughter Amara. Warrendi agreed, and the wedding ceremony was planned. The two peoples came together at Mkembro. The people marveled that their rituals, their languages, their songs were eerily similar. A glorious unity was in the making. But as the ceremony began, Van Owen arrived with his army of slavers, for Glele had met them on the shore and led them to the wedding. The tribes were unprepared for battle and could not defend against the interlopers' guns. Berantu and Warrendi were killed, but their offspring rose to avenge their fathers. Just as Merlante and Mkembro had pierced the ring of fire together generations earlier, Kwame and Amara charged at Van Owen together. When the two betrotheds touched Van Owen, their powers were kindled, and Tongra's curse was fulfilled once again. Kwame and Amara had never used their powers before and could not control them. Their attacks flowed through Van Owen and struck each other, weakening Kwame and Amara but empowering the slaver. The two collapsed, beaten, and Van Owen stood triumphant, having gained the abilities of both Kwame and Amara.

Van Owen slaughtered and captured the rest of the two tribes, taking many of them aboard his ship. Amara was placed in a cage on the deck; Kwame was thrown below with the rest of the prisoners. But when the ship docked in Boston, there was a revolt, and Kwame broke free and dove into the water. He swam and ran for 12 days. Fatigued, he was captured in West Virginia and brought further South, where he was forced to be a slave at the Dunwoody horse farm in Mildred, Tennessee. On that farm, he was given a new name, Charles. And a man named Kelly taught him the skills of blacksmithing and horse rearing. When Kwame escaped and headed north during the Civil War, he took the name Kelly as his surname, calling himself Reginald Kelly.

After the war, he searched the South for any sign of Amara. He traveled to the Van Owen plantation but found that it had been taken by the Union army and converted into a military training base. Amara was nowhere to be found.

Kwame remained in the South, working as a blacksmith on several farms. Eventually he married and raised a son, Graydon Kelly. Graydon, like his father, was born with the power of lightning. He, too, worked with horses. One day in Memphis in the late 1890s, when Graydon was still a teenager, he was walking home late at night. He saw two thieves attacking a white aristocrat. Graydon was about to intercede to help the man—but the man rose up and knocked them back seemingly just by staring at them. The man looked around to make sure that no one was watching. Seeing only Graydon—a Black youth—the man turned his attention back to his two attackers. Grinning with delight, he released lightning from his fingers, incinerating the two assailants. Then he approached Graydon. The aristocrat was tall, gaunt, pale. All sinew and vein. His eyes were piercing blue. Graydon recognized him in an instant from the stories his father had told him: it was Hendrik Van Owen, but somehow—though decades had passed—he had not aged. While Kwame had died young, Van Owen was still the same age he was when Kwame and Amara passed their powers on to him. Somehow, the joining of their abilities had not only empowered Van Owen, but it seemed also to have made him immortal.

As Van Owen approached him, Graydon was frightened, but he readied himself for battle, even as he knew he was too young and inexperienced to challenge the slaver.

"You look familiar," Van Owen said, perhaps noticing unconsciously how closely Graydon resembled Kwame. *"Do I know you?"*

Graydon could feel Van Owen trying to read his thoughts, so he focused his thoughts only on horses and nothing else, and he shook his head no.

"Do you like living?" Van Owen asked him.

Graydon nodded yes.

"Then do it somewhere else," Van Owen told him and walked away.

So Graydon left the South. He traveled all the way to New York, to Saratoga, where he took a job as a horse trainer. Eventually, he bought a small plot of land in the town of Hamlin. He was urged by many to start his own business, but he preferred to stay in the shadow of others and live his life unnoticed—to keep his name off all public records. He married and had a son, Cameron. He passed on to Cameron the stories that had been told to him by his father, and he passed on his lightning power as well. He raised Cameron to stay hidden but taught him how to use his power. After the horses were tended to, Graydon and Cameron would spend hours training, in case they should one day cross paths with Van Owen.

Cameron married and raised a son, Barton, who also wielded the lightning, and Cameron prepared Barton for the day when he might have to use it against Van Owen.

That was where the story had stopped, for Barton was Carl's father, and he had died when Carl was only a teenager, when Carl's powers were just beginning to surface. So Carl had taught himself. And he tacked his own name to the end of the story when he told it to Warren and Jerome. He had not shared the tale with Terry or Regina. How could he? Terry was physically weak and had never exhibited any sign of special abilities, and Regina was a girl—the first ever in the Merlante line—and she was frail like Terry. She had even lost the power to speak.

As Carl thought of his two endowed children, he wondered whether he had been rash in sending Warren off when a conflict was brewing—especially when Jerome couldn't be part of this fight. He was needed elsewhere.

"Wake up," Carl shouted as he tugged on Jerome's shoulder.

Jerome rolled over in the pile of hay and sat up. "What time is it?"

"Van Owen is here in New York. He's taken Terry. I'm going after him..."

"What?!" Jerome jumped to his feet. Beside him, Hippolyta stirred and rose up as well. "How? Where are they?"

Carl related the story that Warren had told him—how Van Owen had taken Terry into a car and was holding him at a Hell's Kitchen stable—adding at the end, "But you're not going with me. No one's home watching Willa and Regina. I kept trying your phone, but you didn't answer. So I had to come here to get you."

"Damn! I had my phone off for school and then forgot..."

"I know. Now go home and watch over your family."

"No. *You* go watch them," Jerome argued. "I'm younger than you. I'm stronger than you. He can't hurt me. You've spent years training me. Nothing hurts me, you know that. Let me go. I can take him."

"No, you can't. I've prepared you to face him in a physical fight because that's the only thing I *can* prepare you for, but that's not how he's going to come at you. Once he sees that he can't hurt you with strength, he'll come at your mind, and you won't be able to stop him. Now get in the car and go protect your family. *That's* your responsibility now." He put his hand on his son's shoulder. "Van Owen wants *me*. First, he came at me through my wife; now he's taken my son. He's gone after two people who couldn't defend themselves against him, two people who didn't have any power to fight him. I've got to end this now. Your sister and your grandmother need you."

"Pop..."

"You heard me. If I don't come back," he said more softly, "you take the family and leave. Go somewhere far away. Just fade away, change your names, and don't do anything to attract attention to yourself. That's what the Merlante did. And that's what our family has done in this country, and that's why we're still around. Take the pickup. Macomb is packed solid because of the game, so take the 145th Street Bridge."

Jerome lowered his head. He was done arguing. "Be strong, Pop," he said as he embraced his father.

The hug was uncomfortable for Carl. He'd had so little human contact for so long. Nevertheless, he raised his arms and patted Jerome's back awkwardly, marveling at how much larger the boy was than the last time he'd held him. "Go on now," he said. "We've lost enough time already."

Jerome stepped away, nodding, and then he ran outside and jumped in the pickup truck. Carl watched with pride as his son peeled out and headed home to guard the family.

Then Carl ran back to his own car. But as he reached for the door handle, his mind immediately returned to the traffic. *How would he make it to Manhattan?* "No," he said aloud, "there's a way to get there."

TWENTY-SIX

The first days and months of motherhood are so very hard. I was blessed with both foresight and eyesight, but now that I have lost the latter, the former has fled as well. The visions are gone. Sometimes over the years, I treated them as a curse, but now I yearn for them. There are times when I wish I could see even my most recurrent one—my wedding—even though I would have to watch my father die yet again. Without the visions, I feel I have lost my connection with my past and my future. My link to my family. Is this how it feels then to be human?

I try not to allow myself to fall into self-pity, though. I have a daughter to raise. Ray gave his life to protect us, and I must honor that sacrifice.

Refusing to live in the dark, I find a way to see again. I learn to use my daughter Rolanda's eyes as my own. When she is only two, I discover that if I listen to her voice and focus hard enough, I can join with her mind and see—through her eyes. The sensation is strange—going from complete darkness to sight again—and the world looks different from how I remember it. The colors seem brighter somehow, less ominous, making me wonder how the horrors I've seen have colored everything about how I view the world.

For much of her youth, I rarely leave Rolanda's side. Where I go, she goes. This trick makes daily life easier in the short-term, for it is almost as if I'm not blind at all. I have her eyes. But then Rolanda goes to sleep, and once again I can barely make my way through our tiny St. Louis apartment without stumbling into something. Still, I refuse to show my vulnerability by asking anyone for help—or by going to a school for the blind. I must maintain minimal contact with others, for Van Owen could be anywhere. I need money to live on, though, so once Ray's savings run out, I finally reenter society at large. I train myself to walk with a white stick like any other blind person. And I make a living selling tapestries and quilts that I create myself. Sewing, like so many things, comes easy for me, as if I've always known how to do it. I could almost do it blind, but Rolanda's eyes are always there to assist me. My work is so good that I'm sometimes able to convince tailor shops to send me seamstress work when they have too much on their plates.

I support us like this for years. I even save money. We move often just to be careful—multiple cities in Missouri, West Virginia, Alabama, Louisiana—always using different last names. Rolanda seems content most of the time. She should resent me for sheltering her so, schooling her myself, keeping her home with me perpetually. But she understands about Van Owen. She doesn't remember him in the hospital room, but she trusts me that he is a threat, that he will return, that he will come after us again. And her trust is enough to keep her at my side.

She trains with me, strengthening her powers, learning how to expand her shield so that it doesn't cover only her or only us—as it did in the hospital room—but a much larger area, even an entire house. Her power isn't like mine. It's not invasive. It doesn't involve using her mind in the way that I use mine. Still, I worry that Van Owen will sense her if she uses her power too often or too grandly.

By the time she's in her twenties and has relegated herself to a life as a seamstress at her mother's side, I finally realize what a disservice I've done her. Yes, I've kept her safe by sheltering her at home with her old, blind mother, but I've also secluded her far too much from the world. Alone with me, she talks a blue streak, but in public, she is silent. I wonder if I've been blinder than I realize, if I've hidden her so much from life that she doesn't know how to have one.

I try to convince her to learn another trade, for she isn't handicapped like I am; she can do more than sew; she need not sit at home with needles and threads and her mother.

"But I like sewing," she tells me, "and I like being home with you."

"There's more to discover, Rolanda."

"I don't need more."

It goes like this for many years. We move, we change our names, we find new buyers for our quilts, new tailors to give us work, and then we move again. Never more than a few years in the same city. Never enough time to let anyone know us too well. Never long enough to leave an impression anywhere.

The Great War comes. I already know how it will end for Americans—hollers of victory even as they stand over scores of graves. I also know it won't be the last war.

I can feel that odd mixture of fear and euphoria that permeates the minds of men at wartime. I lived through it once already. For Rolanda, though, it is difficult to bear. She has trouble comprehending this senseless urge for battle that puts into question the lofty evolution that man believes he has attained. To combat Rolanda's sadness, I try anew to convince her to build a life apart from me.

"You should find somebody. A partner." The words ring hollow, so reminiscent of what my employers told me during the years that I wandered alone across the South.

"I don't need a partner, Mother." Her tone is serene, confident even. "You don't have a partner, and you're doing fine."

"I had my partner. I'm an old woman now. You're still young. You shouldn't spend your life alone."

"I'm not alone. I have you."

"You need more than me. You need to live." *How can I get through to her?* "Mother, let me show you what I've learned from you."

"What do you mean?"

"Let me show you what I've gained by staying with you." She closes her eyes for a moment and then opens them again, her expression strangely empty. "Tell me what I'm thinking."

I reach out to her mind. Nothing. I take a step toward her. Still nothing. I hold out my hand and take hers. I can feel her palm, her fingers, her warmth, but nothing else. I can't hear her thoughts. I can't join my mind to hers.

"Rolanda, how are you doing this? How are you blocking me out?"

"By willing myself to do it. By willing myself to be strong." There is a giddiness in her voice. "You're right, mother—you *are* getting old. Soon you may not be able to protect yourself against him if he comes again." She doesn't say his name. She doesn't need to. "So I'm making myself stronger. I'm going to be so strong that we can go anywhere we want, be anything we want, use our powers any way we want, and he won't even be able to sense us."

I want to tell her that she's wrong. I want to tell her what I know from visions I saw years ago, but I don't. She needs to live unencumbered by what I know, unencumbered by the knowledge that no matter how hard she trains, no matter how strong she becomes, it won't be enough.

A few months before her thirtieth birthday, Rolanda makes me promise that we will celebrate by going anywhere she wants. I promise, not guessing what she has in mind. But, as our train heads southward, I know we are headed even before the conductor announces our destination. I want to deny her, but Rolanda has asked so many times about about Van Owen, about the plantation, about slavery. She deserves to see it. Of course, I don't realize that she has brought us here not for her but for me.

The train ride is interminable. The colored car is hot and packed and airless. I find myself thinking of my people piled linke cargo into Van Owen's ship, but I don't tell Rolanda. We don't speak much during the ride. My thoughts dwell not on what is before us but what happened so long ago. Finally, we reach Raleigh and board a carriage to the coastline—to a town called Cresswell, the closest one I remember. That takes almost another seven hours. Another scorching ride, this time outside, for we have to sit with the coachman. I hold Rolanda's hand and watch through her eyes as we pass by fields that have become roads, outposts that have become towns, until I see a faded path and I call for the coachman to stop. I can imagine the astonishment on his face, as Rolanda assures him that this is our destination. Then it's a two-mile walk across lands dry and marsh-like until we are standing in front of what used to be the Van Owen plantation. After the North's victory in the Civil War, it became a Union army base for a time. It's a paint factory now, surrounded by a fence, so we can't even get close. The fields have been paved over with cement, but I can still smell the remnants of what was there once. Perhaps just a sense memory, the sweet aroma of the tobacco leaves wafts through the Southern summer air, bewitching me, and I think about all of it: myself at sixteen years old climbing half-naked from the carriage, Sam on his knees with Van Owen's gun pressed to his temple, Harry swinging from the oak tree, his old, swollen hands tied in supplication behind his back.

Then I get careless. I forget that while I am connected to Rolanda's mind, using her eyes to see, my mind is open to her. My memories are unguarded, free for her to see them. I think of that day at the end of the war: *Outside, the church is aflame. In the distance, the Union Army is approaching. Inside, Van Owen is on top of me, tearing at my clothing, struggling desperately to take me, to rape me, but failing, forever failing. My victory.*

Rolanda gasps. I feel her recoil, breaking her link with me. I stand there, one hand on the hard steel fence, the other on my white stick. Blind again.

"That's why," Rolanda says. "That's why he came after me when I was born. That's why he'll keep hunting this family, especially the children."

I tell her I don't understand.

"In the hospital, he told you he was angry because he can't make a woman pregnant. He told you he came after me because he doesn't want anyone born who's strong enough to challenge him." She breathes in sharply as if she has just gleaned something new. "I think there's more. You gave him this amazing gift—this ability to see into other people's minds, to make them listen to him, to make them do whatever he wants them to. He needs to tell himself that he despises you. You're a savage, after all. But I think he *loves* you for what you gave him." I am nodding no, opening my mouth to protest, but Rolanda goes on. "He *wanted* you, Mother. He *craved* you. He wanted to possess you...to have you—in every way. I could see it in that memory. It was more than desire or lust. It was a hunger." She pauses, and I hope she's done, but she isn't. "I think he *hates* you for it too, though. I think it tears him up inside that a woman—an African woman—was the one who gave him his power. I think he wants to hurt you because he can't stand feeling indebted to you. He wants to take and hurt everything that is yours and everything you've created."

We hardly say another word for the remainder of the trip. As she leads me in a circle around the gate, we face due north, and I remember my first carriage ride here along the un-hewed roads, me in the back discovering the scent of the tobacco crop, climbing from the carriage in the tattered garb of a chieftain's daughter on her wedding day, staring for the first time into the faces of African-Americans.

It's not until Rolanda is forty-one years old that I sense a change in her. It's 1930, and I'm eighty-seven years old. We have returned to Georgia so I can show her the apartment where we lived and her father's store and the hospital where she was born—and where her father died. She likes it here, so we settle down in a small house just outside of Atlanta. We make the rounds to the local tailors to drum up business. For a while, things go on as they always have. We spend most of our time at home alone. We do our sewing; Rolanda delivers our work to the tailor shops. Then it happens finally—she starts spending more time away from the house. I don't mention that I notice. I pretend that nothing has changed, but I can feel it in her manner: she is lighter, more energetic, more content, elated even. When she tells me, I have to struggle to contain my knowing smile.

"I've met someone. His name is William. He's the tailor at the shop on James Street..."

William. A fine man. I remember him from the visions. "You haven't told him, have you? About us...about what we can do?"

She doesn't answer. She hasn't told him. How could she? Rolanda has spent most of her life cooped up alone with her mother. Now that she has finally fallen in love, why would she take the chance of telling this decent man about our cursed history and our unnatural talents?

Rolanda and William marry at his parents' home in Savannah in July 1931. I don't see the ceremony, but I listen. When she says, "I do," her voice breaks. She cries, and I cry with her. For a moment, a vision comes to me—my first one since the blindness. I feel as if I'll crumble to the ground, so I clutch the armrests of my chair as I watch: *I am in a cabin in the mountains somewhere. Rolanda is pregnant, lying on the bed, writhing in pain. She shouldn't be hurting this much. Something is wrong.*

"Mother," Rolanda says in the present, her hand on my shoulder. "Would you like to dance with your son-in-law?"

"I won't take no for an answer," says William.

His arms are strong, and I have grown smaller. He practically carries me across the dance floor like a child. He's talking, but I can't hear him over the vision, which plays again and again in my mind.

Rolanda is seven months pregnant when the news comes. I grab her hand as she goes for the door. I have already read the thoughts of the policeman who stands on the other side. "Are you Rolanda Harris?" he asks. She tells him yes. "I'm sorry," he says, "I have bad news for you. Your husband, William Harris, was killed earlier this evening. He was struck by a delivery wagon on his way home..."

Rolanda doesn't make a sound, but I can feel that she is no longer standing beside me. She is on the floor. When I kneel to her, she is on her side, shaking, rocking, trying to speak.

I lie down beside her. I hold her. I place her head on my lap and stroke it for hours without saying a word. And I hope that she won't ask the question. Finally, of course, she does.

"Did you...did you...?" She doesn't finish, but I know what she was trying to ask: *Did you know?*

I don't answer. She doesn't need me to. She knows the answer.

She also knows that her child will endure what she did—growing up without ever knowing her father. And Rolanda will endure what I did—growing old without a partner. Somehow this shared loss allows her to recover her senses. Her breathing grows steadier. The tears stop coming. And she asks, "Where do we go next?"

We don't sleep that night. We begin packing. We will stay in Atlanta for the funeral, but not another day afterward. We won't live in this place where we lost our husbands. I convince her to let us go somewhere secluded, somewhere that the child can be born safely. We choose South Carolina. We rent a one-room cabin in a town called Shady, far from civilization, near the state's southern border. On the road there, in William's Model-T, Rolanda, who has taken care never to ask me about the future, finishes the question. "How much did you know?"

I think carefully before I respond, as I don't want my answer to lead to more questions, ones that I will not answer. "I suspected it. I had seen things. At your wedding, I had a vision of your child being born, but William wasn't there. Knowing how much he loved you, I knew he wouldn't have missed that moment for anything."

"The baby? Will everything be okay?"

"The baby will be fine," I tell her, not lying. "I've seen her. She's beautiful."

"Her? It's a girl?" I nod. "Then I'd like to name her after William. She'll be Willa."

"Yes, that's a lovely name." A name I've known for some time.

"Where was she? In your vision, where was she?"

"I was holding her, feeding her from a bottle. It was sunny outside. A beautiful day."

She waits for a moment. "Was I there?"

I've said too much. "I don't know. It was brief. I'm sure you were there somewhere."

"Yes," she says softly, "I'm sure I was."

In her third hour of labor, when the contractions are becoming unbearable, I tell Rolanda to squeeze my hand every time she feels pain. I stand above her as she writhes in the bed, sweating, fighting to bring Willa into the world. Her body jolts. She clenches my hand lightly. "It's okay," I tell her, "I'm here." Less than a minute later, it happens again, and she squeezes harder. This goes on for some time. Eventually, she is clutching my hand so hard that it hurts. I can't help thinking about Atlanta, about Rolanda's birth. How did Van Owen know I was in labor? How did he sense it from wherever he was, in some other part of the city? What prescience—what inseverable link between us—allowed him to enter my mind at that moment when my contractions started in our Atlanta apartment? How did he find that hospital? My power has never been that strong, that precise. Or was it power at all? He has always had some sort of connection to me. Perhaps he has cultivated some ability to sense me not only when I use my power, but also when I am weak or scared or suffering.

"Squeeze my hand with the pain," I repeat. "It'll help."

She moans with the next contraction, but her hand is limp.

"Rolanda?"

Another contraction comes. Her body tenses, then releases. Her breathing gets more hurried, then it slows, but, again, she doesn't squeeze my hand. "Rolanda, are you all right?" No response. "Rolanda?"

"*She's busy*," says a man's voice. It echoes in my thoughts exactly as I remembered it.

"Where are you?" I ask Van Owen, spinning my head as if I can still see, as if he is standing here in the room with us.

"*I'll ask the questions," he says. Where are you?*"

I think about how long I have had these gifts but how few times I have had to use them in battle. Meanwhile conflict and battle have been his passions. "You won't find me," I tell him.

"Oh, I will, Amara. I'll find you. I sensed your daughter's fragility weeks ago. I sensed you worrying about her. I felt you moving, traveling. Somehow you're keeping me in the dark. Somehow I can't see what you see. That's a new trick you've developed. I'll have to work on that too. I'm not sure how you're doing it, but I'll figure it out."

He still doesn't know I'm blind. It was he who caused my blindness—by casting that flash of lightning into my vision during my own labor—but he doesn't realize it. So I taunt him. "You won't figure out this trick. And I've got all sorts of new tricks. You come near us, and I'll show them to you."

"I'm already near you, Amara."

"Rolanda," I ask aloud, "can you hear me?"

"Yes." Her voice is soft, as if she's struggling with more than the labor pains.

"Can you hear him, too?"

"Yes, Mother," she winces. "I've been hearing him for several hours, ever since the contractions started." She squeezes my hand to deflect the pain of another contraction. "I have walls up. He can't get inside my thoughts—he can't hear me—but I can still hear him. He won't stop. I think he's getting closer, Mother." Her whole body stiffens, and she screams with the next contraction, only seconds since the last one. The baby is almost here. "But I won't let him in this house. My walls are too strong even for him. I'm sure of it."

Even as a baby, Rolanda was able to protect us—to keep Van Owen from being able to touch us—but I wonder how long she can maintain her barrier around the house, around us, around her mind as she's trying to birth a child. I want to leave her side, go out in front of the house and wait for him. But without Rolanda's eyes to see through, I wouldn't see him coming. There are other ways to challenge him, though. "I'm going for him," I tell her.

"No. I need you here."

"I'm not leaving." I start to reach out with my mind. If he can find my mind even here—if I can hear his voice in my head—then I can find *him*, too. I can find his mind and attack it, just as he is attacking ours. I send my thoughts beyond the walls of the cabin, past the dirt road and the trees and the pond. I feel the life teeming all around us. Farmers and children and fisherman, and others. I hear their thoughts, but I pass them by. My target is a much darker presence; that's what I focus on—darkness. I follow its scent across miles of the thoughts and emotions of others until I hear him. "*Your mother can't protect you*," he is telling Rolanda. "*I'm taking your child.*"

"No," I tell him. "Her mother *will* protect her, Van Owen. I've already seen the child grow into a woman, and she's not with you."

Using his voice as a beacon, I trace its source. I descend upon him and send my consciousness descending into his. I feel woozy as I enter his thoughts. They are as dark as ever. Dark and dank. Filthy desires. Unmitigated anger. And then I am seeing through his eyes. Through a car window that looks out upon the narrow road rushing by. We're passing a store: Shady Bait and Tackle. We're in Shady. He's found us. He's almost here!

The sensation is so odd, being with Van Owen a mile away and yet here with Rolanda at the same time. She is grabbing my wrist, squeezing. "No, Mother, stay away from him. I need you here."

He turns a corner, taking his car down the path along a pond. The path that leads to our cabin. With the next twist in the road, he should see a little white bridge that veers left over the pond, but I concentrate and alter his sight, painting him a different scene with my thoughts. Like an artist, I complete the foreground and the background, making the image whole. I show him a path that veers right. I fill out the picture with precise detail: it's a dirt road but the woods that surround it are bright and lush and dotted with cherry blossoms. Chickadees and wrens soar overhead. Two possums dig a hole near the base of a century-old oak tree. I wonder if I have overdone it—made it too obvious—but he falls for the charade and takes my imaginary road. And he steers his car down a grassy embankment and directly into Shady Pond. The car belly-flops into the pond. The freezing water flows into the car. He tugs at the door handle, pushing it open and throwing himself into the murky water.

"Damn you, Amara," he hisses, realizing what I've done.

Rolanda screams. She yanks my wrist. "The baby."

"I need to fight him," I tell her.

"No," Rolanda shouts. I feel suddenly as if someone has struck me across my skull. Van Owen yowls in pain and falls backward into the water. My consciousness is whisked from his body and thrown back into my own, into a different kind of darkness—one I know well. Rolanda has thrown up a shield around me, dragging my mind back to the cabin and into my own body. She has become even more powerful than I knew.

She tugs on my arm, pulling me toward her. "I can't let you fight him. I need you here."

"I can beat him, Rolanda. Let me go."

"No, Mother, you have to live, to raise Willa."

"What are you saying?"

"You know you don't kill Van Owen now. You've seen him in the future." I know what she is about to say, and I try to interrupt, but she is too smart. She has known all along. "But you haven't seen *me* in the future, mother, have you? You saw yourself with Willa, holding her, taking care of her, but I wasn't there. You said it yourself."

I stutter as I lie to her. "I meant only that you weren't there in that one vision. That doesn't mean that you're not alive..."

"Mother, he already took my father. I won't let him take my

child as well. I can hold him off, but I can't push the baby out while I'm holding him back, while I'm keeping my walls up around the house."

"*Filthy black witches,*" Van Owen shouts in both our minds. I can hear him sloshing through the pond, trudging toward the shore.

"Then let the walls down," I tell her. "Let me fight him."

"No. That's not what's supposed to happen. You have to raise Willa."

"I'm old," I plead with her. "I can't raise another child. I'll be dead soon..."

"Then will yourself to live," she says, as if telling me something obvious. "Will yourself to be strong, just as *he* has. Your power is natural. You were born into it. He wasn't. He stole it from you and Kwame. Yet, somehow, he doesn't age. Fueled by hate, he wills himself to stay alive. Do the same, Mother, but do it for something good. Will yourself to live for me and for Willa."

I hear a pounding. I wonder if Van Owen is already here, so I listen harder. It is Van Owen, but he is not at our door yet. He's pounding at Rolanda's mental barrier so he can find our cabin.

"*Let me in,*" he cries.

"You have to take the baby out," Rolanda tells me.

"How?"

"You have to cut her out of me."

"I can't..."

"It's the only way. Don't you understand? I can't relax my body enough to push her out while I'm keeping Van Owen away from us."

"I won't..."

"You have to."

I think of Rolanda as a baby, there in the hospital with me in Atlanta. Her first act was to protect us from Van Owen. She has remained at my side through her entire life, acting as my eyes, my lifeline to the world. She's my child. She's all I have. How can I cut into her?

"Do it, Mother. Take the baby out of me..." She squeezes my hand, and I find myself pulled inside her thoughts, staring out through her eyes again—one last time. I watch her other hand as it reaches beneath her mattress and withdraws a knife. She holds it out to me. She knew he was coming. She knew we might need the knife. She planted it there. She had this plan all along. "Take it, Mother."

I can see Van Owen in her mind. He has created an image to frighten us, a manifestation of himself to distract us as he makes his way here. He's dressed in his Civil War grays, wielding an axe, swinging it at Rolanda's invisible wall again and again. It's only a construct, I know—no more real than the false road that I forged—but it feels real even to me. With each blow, the wall becomes more and more visible and more penetrable, gossamer-thin cracks forming all over it. It's beginning to crumble.

"Do it now," Rolanda cries again. Finally, she sees that I cannot stab her, so she lifts the knife herself and thrusts it into her belly, just above the baby. She flinches but doesn't scream. "Now," she whispers, "barely able to speak as the blood pools across the blade's dark hilt, "you have no choice. I'm dying anyway. Finish it or you'll lose both of us."

She's right. I've known it all along. I've always known that Rolanda doesn't survive childbirth—that I raise Willa on my own. I've always known what's going to happen.

I take the knife. I feel its weight and the weight of what I know I must do. I tell myself it has already happened—it has after all. The knife moves swiftly, easily, slicing shallow along my daughter's abdomen. The crimson black blood wells around the incision, but Rolanda keeps her eyes open, allowing me to see. She winces, but I don't stop. She screams, but I don't stop. I feel my own tears fall on my hand—the one holding the knife—but I don't stop. I have no choice. Finally, done cutting, I put the knife down on the bed beside her and use my hands to draw back her skin, imagining it as a garment she wears to cover herself. I have sewn so many garments, weaved so many tapestries. I pretend I am looking at one of them now—something inanimate, something unreal, not my own daughter's flesh. I plunge my hands inside her, reaching through her, pulling, ripping, grabbing for the baby. My hands envelop its tiny, wriggling body. Rolanda howls as I pull the child out of her. She closes her eyes, almost passing out from the pain, and, for a moment, all I can see is Van Owen's manufactured image beating its axe against the shattering barrier.

Rolanda opens her eyes. Her voice is weak. "Let me see Willa." I hold the child toward her. Willa is tiny, bald, covered in her mother's blood and fluids. I place her against her mother's face. Rolanda kisses the baby's cheek. "Yes," she says, "my child, my baby, newborn princess of Mkembro. And what power shall *you* wield, little one?"

With each swing of Van Owen's imaginary axe, Rolanda shudders, as if she's about to pass out. She can't last much longer. I take up the knife again and cut the umbilical cord before drawing the blanket over Rolanda's ragged torso. Willa is making cooing baby sounds, but she isn't crying. Willa is too strong to cry.

"Thank you, Mother," Rolanda whispers, barely audible. My vision has become dim, which means hers has too. She is almost gone. Her breathing is labored. There's nothing anyone can do for her now. There never was. "You have to go now," she tells me. "I'll hold him back. Once I'm gone, I don't think he'll be able to track you. It was my labor pains that drew him to us."

"I love you, Rolanda. I..."

"I love you, Mother. Tell Willa how much I loved her. Go..."

I squeeze her hand. I press my lips against her palm, my tears dripping onto it. Then I let it go, and I run toward the door holding the baby in one hand and the knife in the other.

"You want me, Van Owen?" Rolanda shrieks behind me, "then take me!"

I throw the door open and turn down the corridor, and suddenly everything is black. I am blind again. What will I do? Van Owen howls suddenly, strangely. I pull Willa tight against my chest, and my sight returns. The world is gray and blurry, but I can make out light and shapes. Instinctively—without even meaning to—I have linked with Willa's mind, and I'm using her newborn eyes to see.

My first sight is Van Owen pressed up against the cabin wall, his arms pinned to it, a fly wrapped in an invisible web. He throws his head back and yelps. It's Rolanda's last act. She is leaving the world the same way she came into it—defending me against Van Owen, holding him at bay with her power. From within the cabin, I hear her scream. Her last gasp. And she's gone. My daughter is gone.

I have only one chance before Van Owen recovers from Rolanda's attack. I charge at him, raising the knife—still coated in her blood—and plant it in his chest.

He wails, his voice octaves too high, and collapses in a heap on the ground, the knife protruding from his sternum like a handle on a factory machine. Blood seeps from the wound. He seems too disoriented to counterattack. I think about invading his mind or withdrawing the knife and stabbing at him again, but I don't. Rolanda was right: I don't kill Van Owen now. Willa is my first priority. I must get her to safety.

William's secondhand Model-T starts with a rumble. I pull Willa's tiny body on my lap, propping her up so I can see the road. I press on the gas and head north, saying a silent goodbye to my daughter and to the South, neither of which I will see again.

TWENTY-SEVEN

Marco breathed in deeply as Warren and he descended the steps outside the apartment building. The rain was still falling hard. The air was cool and wet, crisp even, like winter high up in the mountains. "Where's your car?" he asked.

Warren was several feet ahead, examining each car parked along the narrow street. "Don't have one," he said. He stopped in front of a dated gray sports car. "This one looks good, though. BMW."

"Whatever. Cars today all look like toys. Break the window."

"It might have an alarm," said Warren.

"Oh, give me a break," Marco sighed. "We'll be out of here in twenty seconds." He scanned the ground for a heavy object but then turned back toward his stoop. On the end of the banister, screwed into the stone, was a steel fixture that resembled a small globe. Marco twisted it, unscrewed it, and lifted it from its perch. "Huh," he laughed, "this thing was loose forty years ago, and no one's ever fixed it." He took several quick steps toward the BMW and then smashed the globe into the driver-side window. The window shattered. There was no alarm, only the sound of glass shards falling to the concrete like a thousand tiny bells.

With his hat, Marco brushed the fragments from the front seat and was about to sit but then thought better of it. "I don't know these streets anymore. You drive."

Marco sat in the passenger seat and drew a switchblade knife from his pocket. He poked it at the ignition, but Warren, behind the wheel, held up a hand to stop him.

"You got us in," said Warren. "I'll do the next step." He touched his index finger to the key slot. A tiny spark emitted from his finger, and the car gurgled to life.

Marco offered not even a hint of surprise. He turned to the road and watched it rush under their feet. Warren seemed perturbed at the non-reaction. In response, he plowed through two red lights and a stop sign on the way to the Westside Highway entrance.

"So, you've got it too?" Marco asked finally.

"Got what?"

"You have...abilities," Marco said, "like your mother and your grandmother."

Warren frowned. "My mother? What are you talking about?"

"That thing you just did...whatever you call it. You got it from your mother and from Willa. And before that, from Rolanda and from Amara. You don't have to pretend. Willa told me everything. I know your whole family history."

Warren cast an odd look at the old man. "You're confused. The power comes from my father's side. We're the last descendants of the Merlante clan of West Africa." He said it with pride, as if he'd been waiting all his life to reveal the secret to someone.

"The Merlante? No," said Marco. That was the *other* family. You've got it mixed up. Your family comes from the Mkembro tribe. Amara's father was Warrendi, the leader of the Mkembro. That's who you were named for. Willa told me all this."

Warren shook his head no as if correcting a child. "How could Grandma Willa know any of this? My father is the direct descendant of Kwame, heir of the Merlante. Kwame escaped from Captain Hendrik Van Owen's slave ship in Boston Harbor in 1859, and Van Owen has been hunting our family ever since. My father started telling me our family's history the first time he saw me start a fire with my hands when I was eight years old." For effect, he snapped his fingers, and a small electrical flame shot upward from his thumb, lighting the inside of the car in an eerie blue glow. He closed his palm and the glow vanished just as quickly as it had appeared, leaving no marks on his hand. "Pop made me learn the whole family history, made me recite the stories over and over."

"Dear God," said Marco, "you don't know. None of you know. Your mother—my daughter, Dara—she never wanted your father to know about *her* power. She thought he'd be safer if he didn't know anything, so she kept it from him." He was working it out in his head as he spoke, his head bobbing as if he couldn't quite believe what he was saying. "And, all that time, Carl must have been thinking the same thing: he was afraid to tell *her* about *himself.* Somehow, those two found each other, Dara and Carl—the Mkembro and the Merlante—it's almost too crazy to be a coincidence. But they kept everything secret from each other." He paused. "What about Jerome? Is he...?"

Warren was beginning to understand. "Jerome's got it too. He's strong. And nothing hurts him."

"And your father?"

"Similar to me." He paused. "But I can do more." He was defiant as he spoke. "He doesn't even know half of what I can do."

The Westside Highway was packed, but traffic was moving. Warren weaved the BMW between the two faster lanes, passing every car he could.

Marco was mumbling, still dwelling on his discovery. "Your father and your mother..."

Warren shot back, "You've been hiding away all these years. Did you ever even meet my mother?"

Marco's voice got softer. He was ashamed, but he answered directly: "I saw her at the beginning—the day she was born, the first few days after that, but never again." He kept his eyes on the road. "I couldn't...Van Owen knew me. I couldn't take a chance that he might find me again—that I might lead him to Dara or Willa or any of you, so Dara and I only spoke on the phone. She always thought that eventually I'd come outside again. But I couldn't...." His voice trailed off as he thought about his self-imposed exile.

"Why'd you stop going outside?"

Marco retorted flatly, "Why'd you start using drugs?"

"What do you care? You ain't been around my whole life. You don't know me or what I've been through."

Marco was insistent. "I'm not scolding you. I know I don't have the right. I just want to understand why you've done this to yourself—why you get high."

Warren was silent for almost a minute. He stared ahead, watching the traffic lights flicker in the rain. When he finally spoke, his voice was distant. "Sometimes, I feel like...it's like I pass through a doorway into some other place. And no one can see me there. No one can hurt me. No one can be disappointed by me." A pause. "But no one can help me either. It's like I block out everything and forget everything. I'm lost...out of view for a while."

"And drugs are the only way you can get there?"

Warren shook his head. "Sometimes. And sometimes drugs are the only thing that helps me get *back* from there. Sometimes, especially after I use my power too much, I get so lost I almost don't know how to come down. I feel like I'll just drift away. Vanish. The drugs bring me back down. They make me feel human again."

Marco said nothing. He just sat staring at the road, nodding.

"So why'd you stop going outside?" Warren asked again.

Marco didn't hesitate this time. "Because of what Van Owen did to me."

"What did he do?"

"Van Owen was there when your mother was born. He's been

there almost every time a child was born in your mother's family. Rolanda, Willa, Dara, Regina." He paused, not giving Warren time to reflect, but he saw the boy flinch. "We never really understood why. Maybe he wanted to get to the child as early as possible—take it, corrupt it somehow. Or maybe try to steal more power from your family than he had already stolen."

"What happened when my mom was born?"

Marco looked out the window. They were at 103rd Street. They'd be nearing Hell's Kitchen soon. "Our ride's not long enough."

"I need to know. I might not get another chance."

Marco removed his hat and rolled the visor up and down as he spoke, staring at the hat instead of looking at Warren. "I was third generation Italian—Sicilian. We were connected, if you know what I mean..."

"You were mafia. I know."

"It's a dumb word. Nobody I knew ever used it. But...yeah, I was mafia. I met Willa when she was playing jazz piano in this club in Brooklyn. We started sneaking around, seeing each other after midnight in secluded parts of the city. Black and white didn't really mix back then, so I was worried for Willa—and for me—if my family found out about us. So I decided to quit the family business. Willa and I packed our things. And we met up in Manhattan, planning to leave on a train the next day."

There was a fender-bender on Eighty-sixth Street. Traffic was stalled as two police officers sorted out the conflict. Warren tried desperately to pull the car toward an exit, but there was no chance. They were stuck until the accident could be cleared. Warren pounded his hand on the steering wheel. He was frustrated but still engrossed in the story.

"Back then," Marco went on, "the families—the mafia—didn't really do business with outsiders, but somehow this guy from outside—Peter Dominus—he started getting in good with the families. He was a high-class cocaine dealer, and this was back before cocaine was being sold on street corners. His stuff was so high quality—and he was bringing in so much money—that the families couldn't say no to him. The deal was too good."

"So you dealt? You *dealt* cocaine, and you're asking *me* about using drugs? At least I never sold it, never got anyone else to use it!"

"I didn't deal," Marco told him. But then he paused. "Not directly." He exhaled, wanting to keep lying to himself, but there was no use anymore. "But I was part of the business. I was young and stupid. It was all I knew—to do what my family did."

Warren nodded.

"But you're right," the old man went on. "My hands are just as dirty as if I sold cocaine myself." He breathed in and out. "Anyway, Willa and I tried to skip town, but somehow Dominus found out about me and her—I don't know how. He told my family about us, and they sent these two goons after us. That's when Willa realized that Dominus and Van Owen must be the same person. So we ran away separately—Willa went to Minnesota, and I went to California—and we met up a few weeks later in New Mexico...and she told me she was pregnant." Marco smiled. "Her grandmother Amara was with her. She was blind and—more than a hundred years old, and she looked it—but she was still strong and feisty. She got around so well you'd never know she was blind. I found out later she had this trick: she could connect with other people's minds and look out through their eyes." He spun the fedora on his finger. "She was an amazing lady. She talked in this old Southern aristocrat accent."

"Just like Regina," Warren interjected, shaking his head back and forth.

Marco didn't understand, but he didn't belabor the point. The traffic was starting to move again. The accident lane had opened up.

"We don't have much time," said Warren.

"Right. So at first I'm thinking, as soon as Amara finds out I'm a gangster, she's going to send me packing. Plus, she climbed out of slavery, and here I am, a white man who got her granddaughter pregnant out of wedlock! But she never gives my color a second thought. First time she hears my voice, she says, 'Oh, it's you,' as if she already knows me. Weird. Anyway, she says we have to go far away for the birth of the child. So the three of us take off. We travel for a while, town to town across the west coast, never staying in the same place too long. I learn all about your family—Amara's family. I see the two of them practice their tricks."

Warren looked perplexed but said nothing.

"Amara...she was something. She knew the future, but she wouldn't tell us anything. She said it was safer if we didn't know. Then, out of the blue one day, she announces that we have to go to Maine. We ask why, and she just says that's where Willa's supposed to have the baby. So I buy us cross-country rail tickets to Maine—to this cabin in the mountains where my family used to hide people. Amara works out this plan for the day of the birth. I wait out in back by the woodshed, near the edge of the mountain. It was pretty scary—no rail or fence or anything—just this big cliff and then nothing, like if you took one step back, you'd just go over the edge. And it's early March, deep winter. There's snow everywhere, and I'm freezing my ass off. Amara and Willa are in the house. Willa's in labor—I can hear her screaming. I want to be in there with her, but I do what Amara says—I stay by the woodshed." He fumbled with his hat and coughed, though it sounded like a laugh. "Amara had told me that Willa and our daughter were gonna be fine. She said to me 'Don't worry, you're going to make it too. I know how you die. It's not here, and it's not for a long, long time.'"

She told you how you're gonna die?"

"Not many of the details. She said she didn't know all of it anyway." He paused. "At first it was strange to know that no matter what I did, I was going to be around for a while. But it kind of takes the pressure off things." Marco wanted to stop, but he knew he shouldn't. "So I'm there hiding in the snow, and, just like Amara said, Dominus—Van Owen—pulls up in this green DeSoto. He climbs out of his car, and I hear Amara's voice in my head: *Shoot him. Shoot him now.* In all my days in the mob, I never shot anybody. I roughed people up. I waved my gun around, made a lot of threats, but I swear I never shot anybody. But I knew what Van Owen was, and I knew he was there to take my daughter and to hurt Willa, so I didn't have any choice. Van Owen steps out of that car, and I fire—BLAM BLAM—two hits right into his chest. He staggers back like he's hurt, but the guy should be dead, you know, taking a load like that in the chest. He looks at me. I'm about to fire again, but then I see his eyes just drilling into me. I feel this strange chill, and I realize he's there in my head with me, reading my mind, listening to my thoughts, taking control of my body. I look down, and suddenly my gun's lying there in the snow. He made me drop it. I'm trying to reach down and get it, but I can't move. I'm just standing there like I'm frozen. His hand comes out from inside his coat. I figure he's pulling a gun, but then I see blood dripping from it—and there's a light coming from his hand. Amara had told me he might do this, but I didn't believe her. How could it be real? But she was right—his hand was glowing, just like yours does. He's got blood all over his chest from the bullet, but he starts pressing his hands against his chest—cauterizing the wounds...with electricity from his hand."

"Yeah," Warren agreed. "I do that too when I get hurt. I got shot once in my shoulder, and I pulled the bullet out with sparks—used it like electricity, like a magnet—and then I sealed the wound. Hurt like hell for a few days, but it healed." He stretched his shirt collar downward, displaying a jagged burn mark running along the right side of his chest. "This one's from a knife wound, he added, pointing to another scar. "The doctor at the hospital told me it was going to take like sixty stitches. Hell with that. I fixed it myself."

Finally, the traffic was flowing again, and Warren found an opening. He took the exit at Fifty-sixth Street and headed east toward Ninth Avenue.

"So," Marco went on, "Van Owen fixes his wounds. Then he smiles and starts walking toward me. I try to move, but I can't. It's like my body's not mine anymore. Van Owen's getting closer, and I'm thinking Amara's wrong—I'm gonna die *right now*, before I even get to see my daughter born. But Van Owen calls out, 'No, Marco, I'm not going to let you off that easy. I want you to stay alive so you can suffer.' I hear this weird hum, and these images start appearing in my head, like I'm watching a movie or I'm dreaming, having nightmares. I see myself shooting Willa...shooting my own mother. Shooting little children and priests and strangers. I see myself murdering my whole family. They're all bleeding. There's blood everywhere. I can feel it on my hands and running down my face. It's like I'm swimming in it..."

Marco thought about explaining that the fear and the blood sensation stayed with him for months—especially every time he tried to leave his apartment. That by the time the images stopped coming, agoraphobia had become a way of life. He *couldn't leave.* He looked down at the hat in his hands. He had crumpled it. The visor was bent irreparably. "Damn," he muttered. "I wanted to look good for Willa."

"What happened next?"

"I passed out. When I woke up, Willa was standing above me holding the baby. She told me she threw Van Owen off a cliff... and that Amara's dead. Amara's lying there in the snow not too far from me." He paused. He pressed the brim of his hat against his knee, flattening it as best he could, and then returned the hat to his head.

"I buried her under a tree behind the house, overlooking the ocean. Facing southeast, toward West Africa."

They passed Forty-Second Street and continued down Ninth Avenue. Without warning, Warren suddenly veered the car toward the curb near Port Authority, almost smashing into a parked taxi as he stopped. "You're not what I thought you were gonna be," said Warren as he opened the car door. "I came to you because I thought you could help. And I thought: this guy's old anyway; it doesn't matter if he gets killed if he can help me save Terry. But I'm not getting my grandfather killed tonight." He put his finger to the ignition and sent lightning into the key slot. The dashboard sparked and crackled, and the engine shut down. "I'll see you, old man," he said as he climbed from the car and took off in a sprint down Ninth Avenue.

"Hey," Marco shouted after his grandson. "Warren...come back here." But he was gone.

Marco clambered out, his legs stiff and slow—too slow to run to the stable. So he trotted to the first parked car he saw. It was a huge, run-down silver Thunderbird. *Now this is a car*, he said to himself. He reached inside his jacket and withdrew his gun. He glanced around—the street was full, but no one seemed to notice him. He spun the gun in his palm so that he was clutching the barrel. It took him two swings before the butt of the revolver sent spider-thin cracks along the driver-side window. The third hit created a jagged hole big enough for Marco to reach in and open the door. Once seated, he pressed his jackknife into the ignition and twisted until the engine roared to life. "Sorry, Warren," he said aloud though his grandson was long gone, "Amara told me years ago that I would die in New York City defending my family, and I'm not about to prove her wrong."

TWENTY-EIGHT

Raising Willa isn't easy. Rolanda was demure and obedient and focused. Willa is wayward and stubborn and reckless. She defies me constantly. She refuses to stay hidden. She's loud. She insists on playing piano in nightclubs where gangsters hang out. She runs off with her boyfriend—a white man—and gets pregnant! It's enough to drive an old woman mad.

Still, her childhood can't have been easy for her either. My youth was ravaged by my parents' murders, by Van Owen destroying my people and tearing me away from my home—but at least I knew my mother and father. I grew up as a chieftain's daughter. Willa was raised by her grandmother, ninety-one years old and blind when Willa was born. Rolanda was content staying home with me, conversing without speaking. Willa can barely sit down—except when she's playing piano. She learns from a neighbor in our apartment building in Boston. From the beginning, music just flows from her fingers—classical, jazz, and especially that syncopated ragtime she loves so dearly.

I don't tell Willa about the visions I had years ago—images of her hobbled, confined to her bedroom, barely able to walk. At least she'll live to be old, which is more than I could manage for her mother.

Maine is beautiful, majestic, peaceful, like nowhere I've ever been. Here, I feel removed from the rest of the world. When I stand outside, I can hear the wind roll through trees even older than I am, feel gentle snowflakes stroke my face, smell true winter for the first time. Willa lets me see through her eyes. Giant trees greener than anything I've known since Mkembro line the snow-covered back roads behind the house. The white snow dotted with pine needles stretches on endlessly. Winter is cold and yet welcoming. Why did I spend so many years in the South?

Marco and Willa are so good together. Yes, he's a gangster—and he has much to atone for—but we can't all help what we were born into. He has left that world, and that's enough for Willa and for me. And he loves her. I wonder if it was right for me to tell him about his death, but I need him to be calm for what's coming. I need him focused and unafraid.

Van Owen will be here soon. He's followed us across the country. I had hoped to keep us hidden longer, but he's still attuned to our pregnancies. I don't know how. Does he instinctively know when the women in my family are weak? Does he have some premonition when a new Mkembro child will be born—a new threat to challenge him? A new source from which to steal new powers?

I've grown far more powerful in the years since Rolanda died. The visions still elude me, but I've learned to reach out with my mind the way Rolanda did—even to people very far away. I've learned how to block people from seeing or hearing things. Van Owen can't sense me—I'm sure of it—perhaps he thinks I'm dead by now. But I know that he *can sense* Willa.

It's so unjust that every birth in this family must be marred by his presence. No one comes into this family without Van Owen ensuring that one of us leaves it. This birth—Willa's only child, Dara—will be no different. I saw glimpses of it years ago, before the visions stopped coming. I don't know all of the details, but I know how it ends. I like how it ends.

Even as the contractions become severe, Willa keeps asking me if I can feel Van Owen nearby. I lie to her, telling her that I can't sense him anywhere. I can't have her trying to play the hero like Rolanda did. I made a mistake back then: I tried to keep Van Owen *away*. That's not what I'm after anymore. We can't keep him from coming. And I want him *near* me, just not until after the baby is born.

"Push harder," I tell Willa. I can feel the baby crowning, forcing its way toward this tragic world, toward my family's tragic curse. I touch the baby's tiny head with both hands, tugging slightly, knowing she will be the last one I deliver.

Willa screams, but I block it all from Van Owen. I don't want him to know that the child is already here. I can feel him edging his car up the mountain, getting closer; I revel in his frustration as his tires spin against the unforgiving snow, whining on every turn.

"Again," I tell Willa. "Harder this time."

With a roar, Willa pushes, and the child enters the world squinting and crying, green eyes large and ethereal. I hold her softly and cut the cord and clean her off while Willa tries to catch her breath. I place the newborn in her arms. Dara wriggles and coos. My mind goes back to the last birth I administered. I can still feel my knife slicing through my daughter, killing her. Outside, I can hear the car approaching. He's here. So I leave the memories behind.

"I need you to stay here," I tell Willa. "No matter what you hear, stay inside." Of course, I know she won't. Willa never does what she's told.

"What? Is he here?" She clutches the baby tightly against her, but, at the same time, she tries to stand. "Is Van Owen here?"

"Everything's going to be fine, dear."

"But... you're...you're old, Grandma. He's still young... he doesn't age..."

I squeeze her hand. "Willa, don't ever forget: no matter what, he's blood and bone, just like us. And he might not show it, but he's even older than I am." I touch the baby's silky cheek and kiss Willa's forehead. "Not another word now. Stay here. Dara needs you."

"Dara?" she asks. "Is that her name?"

A gunshot rings out. A second one. Willa gasps. "Marco?"

"It's all right. He's all right. I love you, dear. Goodbye."

"Grandma...."

Once I leave the tiny room—where Willa's eyes allowed me to see—I am blind again, and I have to feel my way to the front door of the cabin. I hear Marco cry out. Van Owen is torturing him with horrific visions of realities that never existed and never will. As always, Van Owen is taking pleasure in giving pain. I step outside, letting the door slam behind me so he can hear it.

"That's enough," I shout in their direction. Van Owen loses his concentration, and Marco falls into the snow, unconscious. I wish I could stay alive long enough to help him—to heal what Van Owen did to him. All things heal in time, though, and Marco will find his strength and his fearlessness again when he needs them most.

I saw this scene years ago. And so I rely on my memory as my eyes. Van Owen steps away from the car, turning toward me, his back facing the edge of the cliff.

"Amara?" he says with an odd tone of wonder, almost as if he's pleased to see me. He masks his joy immediately, though, with cruelty. He almost laughs as he sneers, "How old you've become, Amara. Old and stooped. You were almost attractive once. Now you're just a withered old African witch."

"Yes," I nod, "I am a witch. And I'm just full of spells."

His voice is so calm, so assured, his accent as thick as ever. "But your spells are never enough, are they, Amara?" I keep walking toward him. As long as he's talking, I can find him. "All the spells in the world aren't enough to help you, Amara. You've always been weak while I was born to be powerful."

I let him rant. His words are meaningless. I walk on, closer, closer. I will need his eyes for what comes next. I concentrate, relying on the lasting nature of his connection to me; he's never been able to block me from entering his mind. Today is no exception. I reach out with my thoughts, seeking and grasping until I find his. This time, though, I don't stop there. I don't just hover and watch and listen to his thoughts. I send him a surprise, one I've been practicing for years just for this occasion. I open my mind and concentrate, pulling at his consciousness and drawing it into my body, into my mind. His eyes into my eyes. In an instant, I am looking at the world through his eyes, and he is looking out through mine. And now he is the blind one.

"What have you done, witch?" he shouts, waving his arms. "Why is it so dark?"

I can feel him struggling against me, trying to resist, trying to withdraw from my brain and regain his eyesight. He tries to walk toward me, but his footing is shaky. He's never been blind before. He staggers back a bit—closer to the precipice. The wind whips over the snow bank at the edge of the mountain. Although he cannot see, he's still in control of his body, as I am in control of mine. Each of us is simply seeing with the other's eyes. I watch my old woman's body, weak and gaunt and aged as it moves toward him. I'll need to be as close as possible for my next trick.

"Dear God," he whispers, a sudden awareness in his tone. "These are your eyes, aren't they, Amara. Is that why everything is dark, Amara? Are you blind?"

"No, Hendrik, I see better than I ever have. Let me show you."

With that, I let him see again. I let him see what I would be able to see if I still could. I let him see a vision of my creation. I let him see himself as I see him, and so the Van Owen that approaches him as he looks out through my eyes is not wearing the stylish trench coat and suede boots he wears now. He wears the garb of Captain Van Owen, nineteenth century slaver. He carries a saber in one hand and a whip in the other. The whip scrapes the snow as he slithers forward.

"Illusions, Amara," he scoffs. "Illusions can't hurt me." Yet his voice is shaky. If he's not scared, at least he's unsteady. And he's close enough now—only twenty feet away.

I think about the other times I faced him—how I was intent not only to defeat him but to kill him as well. But I was a fool. Van Owen lives for years to come. He'll be alive to face Dara's offspring; I've seen it. Killing him isn't an option, but hurting him is. And I so want to hurt him.

I shout the next words almost ecstatically. "I don't need illusions, Van Owen. I have magic." I reach into my coat and draw my newest weapon, a Smith & Wesson K-22 Masterpiece revolver lent to me by Marco. I look out through Van Owen's eyes and watch my old woman's body adjust my arm until the revolver points directly at him. "Do you remember, Hendrik, when I was too weak to fight you: in the cage on your ship, in my hospital bed after giving birth, in my cabin right after arriving on your plantation—too weak even to raise my arms or my mind in defense. Look at me now, Van Owen. I'm not weak anymore."

With that, I return his sight to him. What he sees is me, pointing the pistol at him. "No," he screams, but I'm already firing.

As I leave his mind and return to my own, I swear I can feel the bullet. Part of my mind is still trapped inside his, and I feel the bullet cutting into him, slicing him apart from the inside, just as I had to do to Rolanda. I hear the humming start. He wants to fire back at me with his lightning. I think of Ray, my beautiful husband, and I fire again. I think of Sam and Harry—my African American friends whom Van Owen murdered—and I fire again. I think of my Rolanda, who sacrificed herself to save her child, and I fire again. I think of my mother and father, the first of my family to fall victim to his hatred, and I fire again. Blind and unable to aim, I fire again anyway, every bullet finding its target. Van Owen howls. I hear him toppling backward, falling into the snow, wheezing as he traces his hands along the wounds, magnetizing the bullets and ripping them from his chest, cauterizing the gashes as fast as he can before his blood can drain away.

"You evil witch," he moans. I can't see him now, but I saw it all in visions years ago. I saw him in the snow, bleeding, scared. The humming grows louder.

I close my eyes and wait for the lightning. I have no defense for it—I am too old and too slow—so I wait. I focus on the chill of the Northern wind against my cheek, the scent of pine in the air, the sound of Van Owen in pain. Then, for the second time in my life, I feel the power that Van Owen stole from my betrothed. The lightning jolt races through me. It blasts my sternum, but the shock spreads everywhere at once. It should hurt—it should feel like fire—but instead it feels cold. Even as I smell my own flesh burning and my heart threatens to stop beating and I fall to the ground, there is no pain. I lie here facedown in the snow, not making a sound, listening to Van Owen panting, coughing, bleeding. I hear him pull himself up to his knees before he falls back down again, unconscious. And I smile. I've won. I've beaten him in mortal combat. Now I can die.

TWENTY-NINE

Terry was weeping. Bound to the chair, unable to move, feeling the tears run from his eyes, leak from the masking tape blindfold, and slide down his face. He was crying for Amara, a great-great-grandmother he had never known, though he felt now as if he had known her all his life. *Get up,* he wanted to shout to her where she lay in the snow, but there was nothing he could do to help her. She had died decades ago.

Finally, he understood the source of the strange images that had infiltrated his mind two years earlier—images that had rendered him catatonic then. He had thought them nightmares, something to bury and forget. But they were memories. And now, after finally allowing himself to experience them, he finally understood whose memories they were—Amara's. *But how,* he wondered? *How did Amara's memories get into my mind?*

He tried to move his hands, but the tape was still firm. His shoulders were sore from struggling, wrenched as they were with his hands tied behind his back. He pushed with his tongue against the tape that covered his mouth. Still nothing. He could hear his breath coming in through his nose in loud stabs. *How long will they keep me like this?* he asked himself again and again. He hated the sensation. Bound. Imprisoned. Un-free. *How did Amara survive so long?*

He wished he could speak to Regina. After everything he had seen—Van Owen and his men storming the wedding in Mkembro, Amara transplanted to the plantation, the coming of the war, Rolanda's birth and death, Willa's days with Marco, the birth of Terry's own mother, and all of the strange powers that had been handed down from generation to generation—he wanted to tell all of it to somebody, and it was Regina with whom he had always shared everything. He was her protector as much as he was her older brother. That Regina communicated telepathically only with him made their connection stronger. He especially enjoyed knowing that their father knew nothing of their silent conversations. Of late, though, he had begun to wonder: had Regina told Willa about her ability? The only women in the house spent so much time together after all, and Regina had never known her own mother. It would only make sense that she would want to share her secrets with Willa. *And if Willa knew about Regina's telepathy, wouldn't Willa have told Regina about the entire family history?* The more he considered it, the more certain he was about it. Regina had been keeping secrets from him! Willa had surely told Regina everything. But Regina hadn't told Terry because she had thought him powerless—she thought it was safer if he remained unaware.

It was making more and more sense: Willa and Regina thought that the men in the family were the powerless ones. As far as Willa and Regina knew, abilities were passed to the women only. Until the current generation, there had *been* only women in the bloodline.

There was no time to dwell on these matters, though. Terry had more memories to explore. He was afraid of what was to come, but he forced himself to watch—to remember—anyway. He opened his mind to Amara's memories, and they came.

THIRTY

Soon Willa will come from the cabin. By then I'll be dead. She'll find me lying here in the snow. My death will enrage her so fervently that she'll wave her hand and send Van Owen over the edge of the cliff. In the winter wind, he'll drift like a loosed scarecrow, careening off the mountainside before landing in a snow bank to rot alive at the bottom of a ravine. I wish I could be there to watch, but I've seen it already. It's an image that has helped me through darker times.

As the chill sets in, I make the oddest discovery—I am losing all sense of my body. How strange. For so long, I protected my earthly body, convinced that it was all that stood between Van Owen and the safety of my family. Yet here, at the end, as my body dies, I finally understand that I am so much more than this mere shell. I don't feel weak. I don't feel powerless or crippled or even blind. I feel *everything*. I feel the snow beneath me and around me. I feel the afternoon sky above me. I feel the trees and the cabin and Marco and Willa and Dara, my newborn great-granddaughter. This form that housed my spirit for these one hundred thirteen years is nothing. It is not me. It is only a container while I am so much more. I am the Mkembro people of the shores of West Africa. I am the tobacco-farming slaves of the plantations of the South. I am the Black migrant workers, scurrying from town to town, in search of safe havens for their families. I am my father and my mother—chieftain and chieftess. I am West Africa, fractured and pilfered and bloodied yet still majestic, still wondrous, still lush, still wild. Still free.

I long to feel the wind against my face one last time. I raise my head, lifting it from the snow. Against my damp cheek, the air is cool, rich with winter frost. The wind seems to whisper to me, urging me to open my eyes. So I open them, and, for the first time in decades, I can see with them.

At first, the world is dim. I see only dim light. But then the light comes into focus. The sun is hidden. Snow is drifting down toward me. I look upward through the ring of evergreens that surround the hillside cabin, trying to remember if one can actually see snow as it leaves the clouds. The sky is deep blue like the ocean near Mkembro. A lonely ibis circles the sky, seeming to evade the snow, its attention riveted to the ground near me, to the stench of blood in the air. I look over and see what has drawn the bird's notice: Van Owen.

He is unconscious, entrenched in the snow as I am. The blood from his bullet wounds has formed an outline around his upper body, painting the snow crimson. For a moment I am disgusted with myself, for I take pleasure in his suffering. I took a gamble by choosing a gun as my final weapon against him, but it paid off. I guessed right. Losing blood is the only thing that can truly hurt or threaten him. This is why he has always been so quick to cauterize his wounds with his lightning. He can survive falls and blows and even bullets, but he cannot survive the loss of too much blood. This is the answer that I have sought for most of my life—how to end Hendrik Van Owen's life—an answer that will die with me here on this mountaintop. Is that the final lesson for me to learn, that the strange powers of the Mkembro and Merlante leaders—telepathy and wind and lightning—are all too gentle, too grounded in the natural world, that in the end, the willingness to draw blood is the only weapon that can win a war against evil? Am I to die knowing the final solution but, like Cassandra, unable to pass on my knowledge?

As if in response, the snow and the winter air and the Maine cabin fold back as if they are nothing more than elements on a painted backdrop. The present is peeled away like an artist's canvas, and I am a seer once more. The future reveals itself in a vision clearer than any I have ever had. And I know what's going to happen. I watch it all—decades of future history—in a moment:

I lie face down in the snow, smoldering yet freezing. Willa throws open the door to the cabin, the baby Dara in her arms, wrapped in a blanket. She runs to my side, kneels beside me in the snow to check for a pulse. There is none. I am dead.

Nearby, Van Owen begins to stir. With great effort, he pulls himself up to one knee. His white shirt, exposed beneath his trench coat, is coated in blood.

"You bastard," Willa hisses. "You killed her."

Van Owen stares at my lifeless body. For just an instant, he almost looks sad. His lips curl down. His eyes squint. Then he remembers himself. He stands slowly, painfully, and begins inching toward Willa, his eyes fixed on the baby in her arms. "Yes," he whispers weakly, "I killed her. She was mine to kill as I pleased. She belonged to me. It was all that was left for me to do with her. Now give me the child or I'll kill *you* as well."

"Go to hell," says Willa. She closes her eyes and raises her arm, her palm facing upwards, her fingertips pointing toward him. Slowly, Van Owen begins to rise into the air. Stunned, he looks down at the snow, farther and farther below him. He hovers flat on his back, twelve feet, fifteen feet, twenty feet above the snow. His arms hang limp. His legs dangle like a puppet's. Blood drips from his shirt and trickles soundlessly onto the white snow like red rain. He winces and spits blood, but he keeps his eyes focused on Willa's. He is trying to steal his way into her mind. "No," she tells him, "I won't let you defile me." Like a queen dismissing a subject, she waves her hand, and Van Owen sails backward over the precipice, screaming all the way down.

Willa tries to look over the cliff after him—to see him bloody and crippled at the bottom of the ravine—but the snow at the edge is not safe. She cannot take a chance. Besides, she knows he survives the fall. She knows she will face him again years from now. I told her that much.

Later, Marco digs through the snow and the frozen ground to honor me with a proper burial. His arms ache from the exertion, but he never falters. Willa stands at the window watching, crying, cursing herself for every time she defied me. I wish I could tell her that I wouldn't have wanted her to be any other way than she is— strong, independent, relentless. Her family needs her that way.

They stand over my grave in silence before Marco leads them to the car and drives Willa and Dara south to New York—but not to the city. He helps them find an apartment in Saratoga before he flees to seclusion in Harlem. He is shaking and twitching throughout the ride, his hands gripping the steering wheel as if he's afraid to let it go. He is frightened, unsure, not himself. Van Owen has done something to him, something that I'm not there to fix. Only Marco can make himself whole again, and he will when Warren comes to him years later.

Abruptly, the scene changes. The images accelerate. Dara is older now—nineteen, bringing Carl Kelly home to introduce him to her mother.

"You're a horse trainer?" Willa quizzes him, enjoying her vantage point as the disapproving mother-in-law. "You think it's all right then to keep horses locked up in barns and raised for the sole purpose of wining money and being trophies for rich white men?"

Carl is young and handsome. The tension is there in his brow, but he lacks the veneer of anger and sadness that will hang from him in his later years. "No, Ma'am, I don't. Too many horses are treated terribly. That's why they need me—to protect them, to help them grow up strong, to keep them comfortable, to make their lives better." Willa smiles, and the scene shifts again.

There are snippets of the wedding. Dara is beautiful, a princess in a delicate white dress. Carl is ecstatic. I marvel as he twirls Willa around the dance floor, even as she keeps her eye on the door, always vigilant, always waiting, just like I was.

Then Warren is born—finally a birth unmarred by Van Owen, who must still be healing somewhere. How many years will it be before he is strong enough again to hunt my family?

Father and son are inseparable; Warren follows Carl everywhere. They are alike in looks and behavior and disposition. Then comes Jerome, big and strong and athletic, even as a child. Warren and Jerome are fast friends, but as Jerome grows, their father pays less and less attention to Warren. Eventually, Warren is left to fend for himself more and more—becoming solitary and sad. Then the third child is born—Terry. He is a weak and sickly baby. Dara stays with him around the clock, keeping up hope even when the doctors warn that he might not survive.

The scene shifts again. Warren is fifteen. He walks through the front door of their Saratoga home, attempting to stand upright and steady, but there's something wrong with him. He's sweating; his eyes are bloodshot.

Carl rises from the sofa. "Where's Terry?"

Warren is confused. "What?"

"Your brother. You were supposed to pick him up from school." Carl begins to look alarmed.

"Oh, damn," Warren says, rubbing his head, his voice faraway and odd. "I kept *thinking* I forgot something."

"*Forgot something?*" his father bellows. "He's four years old! You were supposed to pick him up an hour ago. God damn it! What's wrong with you?"

"Nothing..."

Carl seizes Warren by the shoulders. "Look at your eyes. You're high, aren't you?"

Warren almost lies, but then he seems to take pride in delivering the news. "Yeah, I'm high. So? What do *you* care? I told you I wanted to talk. I needed your help, but you wouldn't listen. I needed..."

Willa appears at the top of the stairs. She is older now but still vigorous, a commanding presence. Dara is beside her, huge in her gray maternity dress; she is nearly due. Still, she glides down the stairs like a dancer. "What's all the yelling?" she asks, trying to lighten the mood.

"Look at his eyes," Carl groans, still gripping his son's shoulders. "He was supposed to pick Terry up from school, and he shows up here high instead. His eyes are so red I can barely see them..."

"Let go of me," Warren shouts, pulling away. "When was the last time you ever cared where *I* was after school or what time *I* got home? And since when did you ever care where Terry is before? You don't pay attention to either of us..."

Carl is incensed. "How dare you raise your voice to me!" He looks as if he might actually strike Warren.

Finally, Dara steps between them. "That's enough! What good is this doing anybody? I'm calling the school to see about Terry."

As she goes for the phone, Carl storms about the room as if he could tear the furniture to pieces. "How long has this been going on?" he demands of Warren.

"What?"

"The drugs!"

Warren stutters as he answers. "A while. I've tried to tell you

243

before, but you never have the time to listen. I...need them sometimes. It's like everything gets to be too much, and I just..."

"You just what? You need to get high?"

"No! Don't you notice anything anymore? I've been trying to tell you about this...but it's like I don't even exist. You don't even realize what I can do now."

Carl lowers his voice. "This isn't the time to..."

"He's not at school," Dara interrupts as she hangs up the phone. "Terry's not at school. They don't know where he is. They think he left a while ago." She looks frightened.

"You see what you've done, Warren," Carl thunders.

"Please stop," Dara shouts, approaching them with one hand on her belly. "Do you have to do this now, Carl? Please..."

"Yes, everybody, calm down," Willa adds.

"If anything happens to Terry," Carl rails at Warren, "it's your fault..."

"No, Pop, it's *your* fault...you set the tone here. Everybody's always on edge because of you... everyone's got to jump at your command..."

"Please stop," Dara cries again, louder but weaker.

"That's right," Carl shouts at Warren, so close that their faces are almost touching, "everyone *should* jump. Life isn't a game..."

Dara gasps and stumbles forward, grabbing onto the couch for support. Carl takes her arm and lowers her onto the cushion.

"It's the baby," says Willa.

"No," says Dara, "The contractions are still far apart. There's time..." Then she cringes again. Another contraction. The baby is indeed coming.

"You see what you've done," Carl tells Warren.

"We should get her to a hospital," says Warren.

"No hospital," Willa and Carl say in unison, each avoiding the other's glance.

"We birth at home in this family," says Willa, feigning calmness. "You know that. Now let's get Dara back upstairs," she adds, helping her daughter up from the couch.

"Carl," Dara begs, "please stop fighting. Just go find Terry."

"*I'll* go find him," Warren offers, starting for the door.

"You'll do nothing," Carl orders. "You'll go to your room and you'll sit there and wait until I get back."

Warren grits his teeth. "You don't get it. You can't tell me what to do anymore." And he races out the door.

"Get back here..." Carl shouts, but Warren is already gone.

"Is he going after Terry?" Dara calls as she climbs the staircase.

"I don't know where he's going," answers Carl.

"Well, then *you've* got to go find Terry."

Carl follows them into the bedroom and kneels by his wife, who lies uncomfortably on the bed. "Somebody has to stay here with you..."

"My mother's here with me. Go after Terry."

"But... you might...need me here...I've always been here when the babies came..."

Dara's voice is gentle, reassuring. "And my mother is the one who delivers the babies. What I need now is for you to find Terry."

Carl kisses her, telling her he will be back as soon as he can. Then he is gone.

Back in her room, Dara looks concerned about more than just the baby. "Terry should be here," she tells Willa. He *has* to be here. That's what Amara told you."

"Maybe I didn't remember it quite right," Willa offers.

Dara shakes her head. "Tell me again what she said. What was in her vision?"

"I don't remember," Willa lies poorly. "It was forty years ago...and she could have been wrong."

"Amara was never wrong; you told me that yourself. So tell me what she..."

"All Amara said was that Terry would be here when Regina is born, that he would keep Regina safe. I can't imagine how, though. Amara didn't know either."

Indeed, that was all I told Willa, for it was all I knew then. In earlier visions, I had seen only Terry holding the baby, keeping her safe from Van Owen. I didn't know then how he would do it, but I feel I will soon.

Dara clenches her jaw with each contraction, never crying out though she is clearly in pain. Willa mops Dara's forehead, soothing her.

The contractions come in waves, but Dara rides them stoically, her focus shifting from window to door to Willa. Finally, Willa announces, "I can see the baby."

"Well, she'd better hurry," Dara says weakly. "He's almost here."

"Who," asks Willa, "Terry?"

"No. Van Owen." She jolts with pain. "I can feel him."

"No...not now," Willa says. "Push, Dara...push...!"

"He knows, Mother. He knows about the baby. That's why he's here. He knows it's a girl. I don't think he could sense the boys...but he knows about the girl..."

"Can you hear him? Is he talking to you?"

"He's *been* talking to me—in my mind—for the last hour, even before Warren came home. That's why I made Carl leave. I didn't want to scare you. Listen..." Dara closes her eyes. "I'll let you hear him." She opens her mind to Willa, but I can hear too.

The voice is raspy. It echoes as if resounding off the walls of a tomb, but the tone is unmistakable. It's Van Owen. "*Do you know how long it took,*" he drones, "*before they found me in that chasm where your mother dropped me? Twenty-three days. My spine was fractured. My neck was broken. Internal bleeding throughout. No food. Only snow to drink for nourishment. Twenty-three days of watching the silhouette of the sun rising and falling. Twenty-three days of near-darkness, near-freezing. The doctors couldn't understand how I was alive. And yet I did live—I willed myself to live. I spent four years in that hospital, learning to walk again, trying to relearn how to use these gifts that fate gave me."*

"You mean the gifts you stole from Amara and Kwame," Dara corrects him telepathically.

"No, Dara," he says. *"You lie to yourself. I was given these gifts because I was meant to have them. It was God's will. Power like this wasn't meant for primitive creatures like you and your kind. By the time I made that last voyage to West Africa, slavery had been outlawed for years. I was a wealthy man, done with expeditions and slave-hunting. Yet I was drawn to take that trip. I was meant to take that trip. This power was meant for a man of my ilk. It's taken me decades to regain mastery over these abilities, but it's all come back. And more. Because this is nature's plan for me."*

"Then you should be happy and just go and leave us alone," Dara answers him.

"How can I? How can I do that when your family owes me so much? Your progenitrix, Amara, belonged to me. She was my property, and, thus, so are her offspring and their offspring. The landscape of this nation may have changed, but natural law cannot be altered. I rescued your family from savagery, from an aboriginal existence, and brought you to this land of modernity and opportunity..."

"Rescued us? You were a slaver and a murderer..."

He laughs his reply with the tone of a parent teaching an infant child. *"You don't know what I am, little girl..."*

"Then tell me what you are—tell me what you want from us."

"That should be obvious. I want your child."

"You can't have her." Dara trembles with pain, but she continues communicating with Van Owen. "If you come near me or my baby, and I'll put you right back in a hospital."

"*Idle threats. If you could stop me, you would have done it already. Your ability might be similar to hers, but clearly you're just a pale facsimile of Amara.*"

"Don't listen to him," says Willa. "Push."

Dara groans as she clutches the bed sheets.

"Almost," Willa urges, "almost...push..."

"*Yes, Dara,*" Van Owen goads her, "*push... deliver that child. I'll be there soon to collect her.*"

The front door opens and then closes again. Willa nearly jumps.

"No," says Dara, "it's not Van Owen."

Terry's voice rises from downstairs, cheerful, full of energy and innocence. "Mom, Pop...I did it...I did it...I walked home by myself!"

"We're upstairs," Willa calls out.

"Grandma," the four-year-old Terry shouts as he drops his book bag and runs up the stairs, "Warren wasn't there to meet me. I waited for a while, and then I walked home on my own...I wasn't scared. I found my way on my own!" He bursts into his parents' bedroom just as Willa pulls the newborn baby into the world. Terry stares in wonder at his sister—so small but with huge eyes that seem to stare out at Terry.

"She's not crying. Is she okay?" Dara asks breathlessly.

Willa pats the baby's bottom, and she begins to weep softly.

"Let me see her," says Dara.

Willa wipes the child with a soft, wet cloth. She cuts and ties the umbilical cord, just as she watched me do all those years ago. She lays Regina across Dara's chest. "Yes," Dara whispers as she gently rocks the child, "you go on and cry. Terry, this is your sister, Regina. It's going to be your job to look out for her." Terry is so awestruck that he cannot speak, but he nods yes. "Mother," Dara says, turning to Willa, "he's almost here."

"Then it's time for me to go." Willa's expression is blank, but her voice is strong. She kisses Dara's forehead, before heading toward the door. As she leaves, she echoes my own words from decades earlier: "I love you, dear. Goodbye."

"No," says Dara, grabbing Willa by the wrist. She breathes in sharply, her eyes glazing over as if she's entering a trance. "The baby's out. I'm stronger now. I can fight him."

"No," shouts Willa as she pulls away and runs from the room. "Terry, stay here with your mother."

There is a flash of light, and the front door to the house cracks down the middle into two pieces—two wooden shards that fall inward to the floor. Willa stops on the stairs and prepares herself. There in the doorway stands Hendrik Van Owen, not a day older than when she last saw him. He wears a tight black leather jacket and white pants tucked into black boots. His hair still hangs to his shoulders. He holds a cane in his left hand.

"You," he rumbles, pointing at Willa on the stairs. "I remember you." He opens his hand, and it begins to glow. "This is for throwing me off that cliff, you sow."

"No," Willa growls. She raises her arm, and Van Owen flies out the door and backward thirty feet, careening into his car, which he has parked on the sidewalk in front of the house. While in the air, though, Van Owen issues his own attack. The lightning flies from his fingertips, missing Willa but striking the staircase on which she stands. The entire house quakes from the impact. The lower stair column shatters, and the upper stairs collapse downward, Willa with them.

"Mother!" Dara calls from the bedroom as she comforts the baby. Willa does not answer. Dara is beginning to panic. "Terry, I need you to be strong now. Come here." She holds the baby out to him. "I need you to take Regina and hide somewhere...anywhere... the closet...the attic... just take her and go..."

Without hesitation, Terry takes the child, but he's too frightened to move. He stands there beside the bed, holding Regina, who stares soundlessly up at him. She reaches up and touches his face. "Mom," Terry stutters, "I...I can't..."

"Protect her, Terry. I know you can. I have to go now. There's a bad man who wants to hurt us and take Regina away from us. I can't allow that. I have to stop him." She is weak as she tries to stand, almost stumbling to her feet.

A car screeches to a halt outside. "You shouldn't have come here," Carl Kelly shouts as he steps from behind the driver's seat.

"Oh, no," Dara says, "not now." She can hear the humming in the air, a buzz-saw sound that almost tickles her ear. Then her face goes blank even as her eyes keep darting back and forth.

"Mom?" says Terry. "Mom?"

"I'm joining your father now," she tells him. "I need to help him." She's reaching out with her mind, trying to enter Carl's, trying to take over his will so that she can protect him—make him run away to safety. But as she invades his mind, she reads his thoughts, and she begins to discover what he has hidden from her—and so do I. *What a fool I've been. What fools we've all been.*

Terry runs to the window, clutching the baby against his shoulder. Outside, Van Owen is on his knees, recovering from Willa's attack, but he is standing to face Terry's father.

"I didn't know," says Dara softly as she reads his mind and knows his secrets. "Oh, Carl..."

Outside, Carl's eyes are empty as if he is sleepwalking. He looks down at his hands, which are shimmering vaguely. His expression suggests surprise as he holds his hands up and stares at them. But it is not *his* surprise that I see on his face—it is Dara's, for it is she who is in control of his mind and body.

"He didn't need me to protect him," whispers Dara from upstairs, her voice strained. "Carl...let me go... let me out, please...God, no...I can't get out of his mind...!"

I can hear her thoughts; I can feel her struggle as she tries to wrench herself free from him, but Carl is lost in a dream world. All he knows is that Dara is there with him—connected to him—and he doesn't ever want to let her out.

"Can't break free..." she whispers. "Too weak. He thinks he's dreaming. And I don't know how to use his power..." The shimmer on his hands fades.

"No," says Carl, but it's Dara speaking the word.

Van Owen is oblivious to the struggle going on in Carl's mind. "Why can't I read your thoughts?" he asks Carl.

The response comes from both Dara's lips upstairs and Carl's lips outside at the same time: "Because I'm not letting you."

Lightning erupts from Van Owen's hands, striking Carl in his chest and knocking him to the ground. Dara screams in pain, but Carl does not. His skin smolders, and his shirt fumes, the tatters burning. But there isn't a mark on his skin. His eyes, though, are still glassy, for Dara is still in control, and Carl is somewhere far away, lost in a fantasy.

"Please, Carl," Dara pleads from her room, "wake up. I don't know how to..."

"How did you survive that?" asks Van Owen. "You're Dara's husband, aren't you? And she's protecting you somehow—throwing some sort of shield around you?" He looks up toward the window from which young Terry is watching. "You're up there, aren't you, Dara? Up there controlling your powerless husband like a puppet, protecting him. It won't help you, Dara. I'll be up there soon to retrieve the girl. She will be mine."

"No!" Dara shouts. Van Owen is right—Carl is like a puppet. Dara is controlling his body as if holding the strings of a marionette, but Van Owen is wrong about one thing: Carl is not powerless. Dara can see into her husband's mind, read his thoughts, see his

251

memories. After sixteen years together, she finally knows who her husband is, and so do I: the direct descendant of Kwame, heir to the Merlante clan.

I've lived longer than anyone has a right to. I had the power of foresight. I saw things that few have ever seen. But I could never put together what was so obvious—Kwame survived his leap from the ship. And Carl is his great-great-grandson, blessed with Kwame's abilities.

But Dara doesn't know how to use those abilities. And Carl is lost in a dream and won't wake from it. So Dara decides that if she can't make Carl fight with lightning, then she will make him fight with his hands. She concentrates and forces Carl up to his feet, makes him run directly at Van Owen, wrap his hands around Van Owen's throat. The two tumble backward, falling to the sidewalk, with Carl on top.

Van Owen's hands begin to glow again. He puts them to both sides of Carl's head. Electrical flames flare from Van Owen's palms, lighting Carl's head in a sickly fire. Carl doesn't even wince, but from her bed, Dara cries out in pain. Her body bobs and writhes as if she's being electrocuted. Her heart shudders. In Terry's arms, the baby wails. He folds her under one arm and runs to his mother's side. He grabs her hand, saying, "Mommy...Mommy..."

"Why won't you die?" Van Owen rages outside at Carl, electric sparks still shooting from his fingers.

Terry pleads to his mother, "Mommy, make it stop."

Suddenly, Dara stops moving. Her head drops back onto the pillow. Her breathing becomes shallow. Tears drip from her eyes. "Terry?" she says weakly.

The boy squeezes her hand. "Mom?"

"Your father...?"

Terry releases her hand and runs back to the window. Carl is lying face down on the pavement. Van Owen is gone. "I don't know,

Mommy. He's not moving. The white man's gone."

Dara lies still, her glassy eyes staring up at the ceiling.

"Mom?"

No response.

"Mom?" Terry asks again as he returns to the bed and shakes his mother's arm.

"She's gone," comes a voice from the bedroom doorway.

Terry turns and sees the tall, pale stranger. His white blond hair is stringy and matted now, his hands dirty and scraped from climbing up the broken staircase. His blue eyes are sunk deep in his head, but they sparkle with joy as he speaks. "Now give me that baby."

Terry presses Regina against his chest, both of his arms wrapped around her as if she is the most precious thing in the world. She has stopped crying but is making an odd, rhythmic, moaning sound, almost like a song. Terry backs up toward the window. He looks down at the pavement, hoping that his father has risen, but Carl is still motionless.

"I told you to give me the girl. Do as I say, boy."

Terry doesn't flinch. "No. I'm protecting her. Mommy told me to."

"Ignorant cur," Van Owen hisses as he steps closer, holding out his hands. He raises his voice: "Get away from that window and give me the girl. Now!"

Terry is frightened, but he glares back at the stranger and tells him flatly, "No."

Van Owen grabs for Regina. Terry tries to maneuver away but Van Owen catches the baby under the shoulders and pulls at her.

"No," shouts Terry, his voice filling the room. He shuts his eyes as he shouts again, his voice booming. "Let go of her. Get away from us! Get out of this house!"

Abruptly, Van Owen releases the baby, and his hands fall to his sides. Terry falls backward and tumbles to the floor, Regina still safe against his chest. He checks that she is unharmed. Then he sits up, his eyes darting around the room. The white man is gone.

Trancelike, Van Owen walks through the creaking house. He jumps from the second floor landing to the bottom of the shattered staircase and exits through the smoky doorway.

Downstairs, Willa is waking. "Dara?" she calls out in a weary, pained voice.

"Grandma," Terry stutters, "we're up here."

"Where's Van Owen?"

"Who?"

"The white man..."

"He left." Terry clambers up and peeks out the window. Van Owen is walking slowly across the lawn, past his car, into the street. "He's outside."

"I see him," Willa says softly. She groans as she extricates herself from the splintered staircase. Her body is bruised, her legs fractured and twisted beneath her. She cannot stand, so she drags herself along the sawdust-covered carpet toward the front door, her arms straining with every yard, a trail of blood behind her. She stares out through the demolished entrance to the house. "There he is," she whispers. "There he is."

Van Owen stops walking. He just stands in the middle of the street, gazing straight ahead, mesmerized. A car honks as it veers around him. Another one passes, its driver eyeing the odd, pale man in his path.

"Too small," says Willa, watching each passing vehicle. "I need something bigger."

A newspaper delivery truck turns the corner. Suddenly Van Owen's eyes lose their glaze. He turns back toward the sidewalk where Carl lies, still unconscious. Van Owen seems confused, as if he doesn't remember where he is or why he's there. Then, his glance shoots upward to the window. A scowl crosses his face. He's aware again.

"How did you do that, Dara?" he asks. "How did you make me leave the house? Aren't you dead yet?"

"You bastard," cries Willa. She's crawling, pulling herself outside on her stomach, her legs scraping along the concrete. She looks toward the delivery truck. The driver is honking his horn at Van Owen. "Big enough," says Willa. Van Owen spins to see the truck and starts moving toward the curb. "No," Willa whispers. She waves her hand at the truck, and it picks up speed, racing toward Van Owen, tires squealing as the driver tries to brake.

"No," Van Owen shouts, his eyes meeting with the driver's.

The driver tries to spin the steering wheel, but Willa balls her hands into fists, and the wheel remains rigid. There is a hollow thump as the truck slams into Van Owen, knocking him backward before slamming into him a second time, crushing him against his own car. His head slumps forward across the truck's hood, his lips parted, blood dripping from his mouth.

Police cars appear. An ambulance carts the unconscious Van Owen away. Paramedics surround Carl, trying to revive him. Finally he wakes, dazed, unaware of what has happened. He fingers his singed shirt. He staggers to his feet, shrugging off any help. He notices Willa on the ground near the doorway. She tries to wave off the ambulance workers as well, insisting that she needs to go upstairs though she clearly cannot even stand.

"Willa, what happened?" Carl cries. "What happened?"

"I...I don't know..." she lies. "I think there was...a gas explosion of some sort. Go check on Dara...upstairs..."

Carl races inside. He climbs up the rubble staircase and bursts into the bedroom. Terry is standing by the window, staring out. He's still holding Regina, rocking her gently. As his father enters, Terry spins to see him.

"Dara?" Carl asks as he inches toward the bed. His hands are shaking.

"She left," Terry says with a distant expression. "She went to help you. She said you wouldn't let her out."

"Dara,...no..." Carl pleads, hugging her against him, pulling her face to his. "Please don't leave me."

"She said she had to help you," says Terry.

Carl seems not to hear. He lowers Dara back to the bed, covers her with the sheet but leaves her face exposed. He finally notices the baby in Terry's arms. "Terry...? What happened? The baby..."

Terry seems barely awake. "Mommy said to protect her."

Carl staggers toward them and holds out his hands for Regina, who is sleeping. "Give her to me, son."

"No," shouts Terry, suddenly furious. "I have to protect her."

"From what?"

"From the evil man."

Carl's eyes open wide. "What evil man?"

"The one you and Mommy were fighting. He wants to take Regina."

"The one Mommy and I were fighting? I don't understand. Tell me what happened."

Terry is shaking, shivering. "The evil man...he wants Regina..."

Carl looks around, his eyes wild. "Terry...was there someone here? A white man? With white hair?"

"Yes...don't you remember, Pop? You were fighting him...you and Mommy..."

"No...I don't..." Carl's face is all pain. He's breathing quickly, almost as if the air is too thin to support his lungs.

Suddenly, Terry bursts into tears, shaking uncontrollably as if all of the restrained anguish has finally broken through and overwhelmed him. Carl can barely look at him.

There are more voices outside and then footsteps downstairs, someone climbing up the rubble. "Mom?" comes Warren's voice. "Mom?" he shouts as he plows into the room and stops in the doorway.

"She's dead," says his father, his voice flat. Warren walks to the bed, his footsteps soft and slow. Dara lies on her back with her eyes still open, her expression almost complacent.

Warren kneels beside her and lays his head on her shoulder.

"You see," Carl goes on, his voice still a monotone, "this is why I was always so careful—why I trained you so hard and made you watch out for your brothers, why I wanted you home all the time. This is why." His head starts shaking back and forth. "*You* did this. *You* caused this." Tears roll down Warren's face. He is shattered even before Carl speaks again. "Look at what's happened because of you. Your mother's dead. Because of you."

"Pop," Warren pleads, standing, "I..."

Carl's voice is so weak I can barely hear him. He doesn't even sound angry anymore. Just empty. "Get out. Get out and don't ever come near this family again. Don't ever come back."

Why? I ask myself. *Why am I shown this vision now—when it's too late?*

All this time, I thought Kwame died when he dove from Van Owen's ship. But he lived, he married, he had descendants. Terry and Warren and Jerome and Regina are descended from *both* of us. The Mkembro and Merlante peoples both survived and finally united through the union of Dara and Carl.

Why? I ask again. *Why only now?*

No answer comes. Instead, the visions jump forward in time. Terry is tied to a chair. And he's remembering something. He's crying as his own memories mix with the ones he watches in his mind. It's all coming back to him. He's remembering what he has kept quarantined in his brain for years. He remembers what I have just seen—the day Regina was born, the day he used his power for the first time, to protect Regina from Van Owen.

He dwells on what comes next, and I watch it with him: his father blaming Warren for everything, Warren running away, Carl moving the family to Harlem, hoping they'll blend in there, invisible in a community of African Americans.

Terry thinks of Regina and wishes she were there with him. He thinks of a night two years earlier. In their Harlem apartment. Upstairs in his room. Regina is nine. Terry is thirteen. He has spent years forgetting the way his mother died, burying the memory of the pale stranger who came to his house in Saratoga. Regina has grown up without a mother at all, nurtured only by her grandmother. Miraculously, though, she is a happy child. Terry and Regina sit there playing, laughing, blissfully ignorant of the horrors that have come before and those still to come.

They are playing the card game War. Regina has won three games in a row, so Terry tries to cheat. Instead of drawing the top card on his pile as he should, he searches his stack for a higher card one than the jack that Regina has just discarded.

"You can't do that," Regina shouts at him, still speaking in her own childlike voice.

"It's only fair," Terry replies, laughing. "Come on. My cards suck. Let me win one round."

Regina folds her arms across her chest. "No. Stop cheating."

Terry laughs as he draws his next card—the queen of diamonds—from the bottom of the deck.

I wish I were a younger woman. I wish I could live long enough to know them, to pass my knowledge to them. To tell them of their history. To tell them who they are. To tell them of Africa.

Then it occurs to me: maybe I can. I've seen Regina in later visions; her powers will be like mine—she'll use her mind, communicating without words. Perhaps, through this vision, I can communicate with her somehow. I don't know how to speak to her from here, but perhaps I can send her a message—or at least a vision—to assist her. Eventually, she will have to face Van Owen; they all will. Perhaps if they know what I know, they can find an advantage.

"Not fair," Regina howls at Terry. "You're still cheating. You pulled that from the bottom of the deck."

"Did not," he snickers, not even trying to hide his deception.

"I saw you!" With a quick grab, she snatches his stack of cards from his hand. "Let's see what your next card should have been."

Regina is laughing. She is comfortable and calm, her mind open. Perhaps this is the right moment. I reach out across time, across generations, across births and deaths and wars, across Dara's and Rolanda's sacrifices, across Warren's drug habit and Carl's anger— until I find Regina. I feel the apartment, the room, the floor, the playing cards, all of them as real to me as if I were sitting there on the floor with my two youngest descendants.

I simply want to tell Regina what it took me more than a century to learn: *Van Owen must bleed.* I focus on the blood, on Van Owen lying in the snow, weak from the bullet wounds that I inflicted, weak from loss of blood. I mold the memory, I make it as real and harsh and detailed as I can, I cast it like a fishing line across the chasm of years. And then I release it into her mind.

In just an instant, I know I have erred. Regina doesn't yet know about our history or about her ability. She doesn't know how to accept what I'm sending her.

Her body tenses. Her senses go numb. The gore of the image— Van Owen, his ghostly white skin riddled with bullet marks, blood oozing from them—is too much for her. She has never beheld such a thing. What was I thinking? What have I done?

Suddenly she lets go of the cards. Terry watches them spill to the floor. Regina is sitting upright, staring straight in front of her, her expression bare. She is frozen, unable to break free from me or from the grisly image. She begins shaking, moaning.

"Oh, very funny," Terry laughs. "What—you're in shock that I cheated? I always cheat at cards. You know that." Regina still doesn't respond. Her eyes start to roll back into her head. "Regina?" Terry says, frightened, as he grabs her by her shoulders. "Gina?"

I try to withdraw my connection, to retreat, but I'm too slow. Regina starts to fall backward, and Terry catches her head before it strikes the floor. And his entire body stiffens. His hands and arms begin to tremble as the currents of time race through them, climbing up his torso, flowing into his neck, through his head, into his brain. The vision drains from her and flows directly into him. Regina slides to the floor, unconscious, but Terry remains lost in my past, linked to it. But then he does something worse—he begins exploring it. Instead of being repulsed by the gore, as his sister was, he becomes curious. His mind latches on to mine, hungry for answers, trying to draw them from me. It is all so fast that I have no time to stop him. He doesn't take only the message that I was trying to send. He takes *everything*. All of my memories rush from my mind and pour into his. He sees all of it: my wedding in Mkembro, my cage on the deck of the ship, my years on the tobacco plantation, the murders of my husband and daughter. A century of hunting and hatred, the denigration of slavery, the horror of the entire African-American existence, and the dark shadow of Hendrik Van Owen that follows our family across time.

For me, here in the snow, only seconds go by. For Terry, it is as if he is living all of it, decades of subservience and scorn and fear and violence and death—every moment in an instant. His hands and arms shake as if he has touched an electrified fence. "No," he moans softly, over and over. "No..."

Regina wakes. She rises from the floor, not sure what's happening. She grabs Terry by the wrist. "Terry," she cries, her voice loud and odd somehow. The tone is lower than it should be, the cadence Southern. "Terry, wake up? What's wrong with you?"

"Regina?" Willa's voice comes from her bedroom. "Was that you? You don't sound like yourself. Your voice sounded just like..."

"Terry!" Regina shouts. She takes him by his shoulders and shakes him, staring into his distant face, trying to find some spark of consciousness. "Wake up!"

His eyes shoot open, but then they shut immediately. And he crumbles to the floor in a heap. Regina screams, her cry echoing through the house.

From down the hall, Willa groans as she forces herself to stand. Slowly, she makes her way out of her bedroom. "Regina," she says in a stunned tone, "I can hear your voice in my mind...just like..."

Jerome has heard the screams too, and he races to Terry's room, making it there before Willa. "What's wrong?" he asks as he bursts in. Regina is kneeling over Terry, but he isn't moving. "Terry?" Jerome shouts.

Regina stops screaming, but she continues to speak without opening her mouth. Jerome doesn't hear her, but Willa does. And so do I.

"Terry, wake up," says Regina without moving her lips. "Please wake up."

I recognize Regina's voice now. Somehow, by connecting with her mind, I have changed her, passed something of myself to her. She is speaking with my tone, my inflection—*my voice.*

Jerome drops to the floor and throws his ear against Terry's chest, listening for a heartbeat. "He's alive. He's okay."

Terry begins to rouse. He looks around, confused—but not frightened. He seems unchanged, unaware of what has happened. His mind, instinctively protecting itself, has treated the images as nightmares. The visions—my memories—that he saw have been buried deep in his unconscious. Just like his memory of his first encounter with Van Owen. The poor boy is a walking history book of horrors and secrets.

Finally, Willa makes it to the room. Leaning against her cane, she stands in the doorway, her face etched with concern. "Regina," she whispers, hoping that Jerome is too busy with Terry to listen, "I heard your voice, but you sounded just like my grandmother, Amara."

As Jerome attends to Terry, Regina opens her mouth, but Willa holds up her hand and whispers, "No, child. Don't speak. I can hear you"—she points to her head and whispers—"in here."

Willa is being cautious. If Regina were to speak—at home or anywhere—no one would understand why she suddenly has a Southern accent. Even more frightening, she may not be able to control her power. Her words might resound in others' minds. So *this* is why the child stops speaking. Willa teaches her not to bring attention to herself. Willa doesn't want Van Owen to hear her. Which means the poor child must pose as mute.

But even as Regina follows her grandmother's instruction and remains silent, Terry rises from the floor. He stares at his sister, and she stares back, and he senses something.

"Are you okay?" Regina asks him, her voice speaking into his thoughts.

And Terry's eyes widen. So, the bond between them—which I have seen in other visions—is formed here. By me. I can change the future even from here. I can communicate with my descendants.

But I have so little time left.

I return to the memory, watching Terry stand, dazed, leaning on Jerome for support. But then the scene abruptly ends, and I am drawn back to Terry's present.

"What are you thinking about?" a voice bellows, a voice I know so well.

Hands rip at Terry's face, tearing away a tape blindfold, and

Terry's eyes strain at the dim light, unable to focus.

"What are you thinking about? " Van Owen asks him again. "You were shaking like you were watching something in your mind—a dream or a vision of some sort—but I couldn't see it. Let me see what you saw."

Terry's eyes start to adjust to the light. He can make out the tall figure in front of him, framed in silhouette by the light of a chandelier that hangs overhead, identical to the one I saw in Van Owen's mansion more than a century ago.

"What," asks Van Owen, "were you watching, boy?" He swings his left arm, slapping Terry across the face with the back of his hand.

Terry's mouth is still covered, so he can't respond, except to moan with the impact. And he can barely hear the questions, drowned out as they are by a very old song that plays in his head. He doesn't understand the words that repeat over and over, but I do:

Dji mi sarro ti kee la ti na-arro.
Dji mi sarro ti kee la ti na-arro.
Dji mi sarro ti kee la ti na-arro.

THIRTY-ONE

Hippolyta glided through the clamorous streets, through the pelting rain. As Carl Kelly rode her bareback along the median between the stalled Eleventh Avenue evening traffic, he looked down at the city rushing beneath him and felt for a moment like an Olympian god astride a mythical horse. He felt like he was flying.

Hippolyta had never even walked through such traffic before—and there had been no time to mask her to keep her from seeing the madness of New York City—and yet she simply raced through gridlock as gracefully as she ran around an empty dirt track. *She's fearless*, Carl thought to himself. As he neared the stable address that Warren had given him, Carl knew that he would have to be just as fearless as Hippolyta this night. *But what is Van Owen trying to achieve by kidnapping Terry—that our confrontation takes place on his turf?* Carl was certain of one thing: an ambush awaited him.

He steered the mare through Hell's Kitchen, past the Intrepid Museum, past the Lincoln Tunnel entrance. He leaned low, his arms almost hugging her neck, ignoring the strangers who stared up at the Black man storming through Manhattan on an unsaddled white horse.

Finally, he saw the street sign that read 37th Street, and he slowed Hippolyta to a walk. She shook her head side to side and whinnied, the rain spraying off her mane in all directions. As he turned west, the street was dark and narrowed by the parked cars that lined both sides. Just past the middle of the block, on the left side, the massive double doors to the stable loomed between two aging, wrought iron gas lamps, their fires dimly burning. A dispirited spotted gray horse exited the wide entry ramp, pulling a hansom cab. The driver, a young Black man, looked like anything but a caretaker of horses. He wore a leather jacket and dark glasses in the evening rain. He steered the carriage westward, not even noticing Carl, who was barely fifty feet behind him. At the end of the block, the carriage made a right turn and headed uptown toward Harlem. Carl realized then why these horse carriages had become so prevalent in Harlem. They weren't offering rides; the hansom cabs were Hendrik Van Owen's business vehicles. He used conveyances from *his era*— carriages—to peddle his filth. More than a century ago, the slaver had taken his pleasure from capturing and transporting and killing and enslaving Black people, but he made his living then from the whites who bought his tobacco. In this new era, it was newer drugs like heroin and cocaine and crack that kept Van Owen wealthy. He had found a vocation through which he could both hurt Blacks *and* make money from them at the same time—by corrupting Harlem with his drugs, trying to ensure that this era's African descendants would be just as downtrodden and defeated as the African-Americans of his time. Carl lowered his head and rode Hippolyta up the driveway and through the dark stable entrance.

At first glance, the stable was hardly distinct from many that Carl had seen or worked in—high ceilings, wooden beams, haylofts. But the smell was rank. Horse stalls flanked the left and right walls. They were tiny, dirty chambers unfit for any animal, let alone broken, ancient carriage horses desperately in need of comfort and care. Carl was sickened by the smell, by the repellant conditions the horses were forced to endure, by the fluorescent lights that hung from the ceiling. Yet he saw no horses. And there was only one hansom cab carriage remaining—an inoperable one, missing a wheel, which lay abandoned near the center of the stable. The facility appeared to be empty, but then a man's voice rang out from the rear of the stable.

"That's a mighty fine filly you got there."

Carl spun his head to see the speaker, who was standing in shadow near a glass room that ran across the width of the rear stable wall. Dark curtains had been drawn, concealing what was inside. The man opened the steel door at the center of the glass wall, pulling something behind him. He wore a sleek black suit and shiny leather shoes and walked with the slightest limp. As he passed under the dim overhead lighting and stopped about forty feet away, Carl saw the stringy, white-blond hair, the skeletal face. There was no doubt—it was Hendrik Van Owen, and behind his back he was dragging something, a chair. Bound to the chair, his mouth gagged, was Carl's son Terry.

Carl swung both his legs to one side of Hippolyta and slid down her rib cage until he landed on his feet. He patted her on the nose, whispering, "You run along now, girl. Wait outside." She obeyed, trotting out through the doors and stopping by the curb.

"Let my son go," said Carl calmly, but he could feel the anger brimming inside him. Around his feet, the dirt and hay began to swirl.

Van Owen seemed not to notice the wind, though. He smirked. "Oh, *this* thing? Is it yours?" He swung the chair in front of him and stood it upright on the ground beside him. Terry's head bobbed from the motion, and he squirmed against the duct tape that held him. Van Owen smiled at Carl and nodded as he spoke. "I remember you. From Saratoga. I recognized you on the security camera as soon as you rode in."

Carl didn't answer. He just moved slowly toward the pale man.

"You know I searched for you and your family for some time—

researched every Kelly I could find—to no avail. You're apparently quite good at keeping yourself hidden."

"I'm not hiding now," said Carl. "I'm right in front of you."

"But you *are* way out of your element. Your wife's not here to protect you this time. Now you're just like any other nigger, aren't you?" His hand began to glow.

"But you are way out of your element. Your wife's not here to protect you this time. Now you're just like any *other* nigger, aren't you?" His hand began to glow.

Carl couldn't understand what Van Owen was referring to—*wife not here to protect him?*—but he had no time to dwell on it. He saw the glow forming around Van Owen's hand, sparks crackling, and he readied himself for the fight he had anticipated for years.

"You were like a little puppet to Dara, weren't you?" Van Owen taunted him. "Tell me, was it demeaning that she was the one with the strength? That she had to fight and die for you? That you were nothing?" His hand grew brighter. He raised it, pointing it at Carl. Electric currents formed in a semicircle around his wrist and extended toward Carl—slowly, as if passing through water. He was showing off his mastery over his power. "Don't bother answering. Those are rhetorical questions. Let me explain..."

"I think you're a little confused," Carl interrupted. "Let *me* explain." He held his right hand in front of him, the fingers pointed toward Van Owen. Instantaneously, Carl's entire hand was covered in a greenish glow. Lightning crackled, rotating around his fingertips like a fishing line before surging forward to meet Van Owen's current in mid-flight. For a moment, the two opposing lightning branches fluttered in the air, intermingling and undulating like competing sine waves. Then Carl closed his hand into a fist. His current enveloped Van Owen's, and the two electrical streams dissipated in the air above them and vanished. "You don't want any of this," Carl told him. "Now step away from my son."

Van Owen contorted his face like an angry child. Before him was another man—a Black man—who wielded the same power that Van Owen did. But Carl was even more adept. Infuriated, Van Owen riveted his attention on Carl, his blue eyes boring into Carl's thoughts.

Carl was ready for this tack, though. He could feel the tendrils of his enemy reaching into his mind. He had no defense for it except a variation on his offense. He closed his eyes and lifted his left hand. The dirt began to dance more vigorously, swirling around his legs like a miniature cyclone. Just as he could feel Van Owen's gaze beginning to penetrate his mind, Carl held his hand out in front of him, folding it into a fist. The cyclone traveled up his body, growing more intense as it climbed. It curled about his chest like a twister, the tiny spirals advancing in ever widening circles around his shoulder, his arm, his hand. Then he opened his fist, and all of the spirals seemed to collect in his palm and rise outward—all of this in just seconds.

At first, Van Owen felt only a breeze, a tickle against his face, but then it grew. The wind struck the walls of the stable, bouncing off, growing stronger, whistling. Van Owen tried to plant his feet. He even reached for Terry's chair to anchor himself, but it was too late. Carl motioned with his arm, and the wind slammed into Van Owen, knocking him backward into the glass wall at the rear of the stable.

Terry, his mouth still covered, struggled in vain against his bindings. For a moment, his eyes met his father's, and Terry nodded with excitement.

Yes, son, Carl wanted to tell him. *This is what your father can do.* He didn't want his son to see this fight, to see his father kill a man, but he had no choice. Van Owen had to die.

The slaver's lips coiled into a sneer as he spoke without a trace of fear in his voice. "I see the resemblance now. I never forget a face. You're the image of that slave boy who dove from my ship all those years ago. You're right. I *don't* want any of this. I don't want to sully my hands with the likes of you." He pulled himself to his feet and strode toward the entrance to the glass room. "I can already sense the girl. She's so very like Amara. I can't hear her thoughts yet or her voice. But I can feel her getting closer. I'm going to keep her. You can have the boy. You can have him dead." He looked up toward the second level loft, which was filled with hay bales and wooden crates. "Kill them both," he shouted.

As Carl looked upward, Van Owen tramped through the steel doorway to his sanctum, shut the door, and slid the bolts across.

From above, from all sides, Carl could hear rustling sounds. A slew of men aimed their guns. He had been right; it *was* an ambush.

THIRTY-TWO

I see a white horse in the darkness. She is beautiful, regal, a magnificent creature. If this is my ride to Valhalla, where are the horse's wings?

Weak and dying, I force myself to focus—remind myself I'm watching a vision. I concentrate on the horse, certain that I've seen her before. Yes, her name is Hippolyta. Carl's favorite. She mills about in front of a stable on a dark Manhattan street, waiting for him. Everything is familiar now. This is Van Owen's stable, the place from which he distributes his drugs to pollute my people. How fitting that it's situated in a place called Hell's Kitchen.

I've seen this stable before—in a vision many years ago; it's the place where everyone comes together. Terry, Carl, Jerome, Warren, Regina, Willa. Even Marco. I told Marco about this day. But I knew so little then. The visions were rarely as forthcoming as those I'm seeing now as I lay dying. Perhaps today, then, I will finally know how it all ends.

Terry is in the chair still, his mouth still covered, but he is watching something glorious. He knows of his father's abilities—he just regained those memories—but seeing the power so close up is something entirely different. Finally, he understands the terrible burden that Carl carries—that it isn't only the loss of his wife that has damaged Carl so, rendering him so withdrawn, so isolated from the world. Carl's instability stems from something just as terrifying—he is both blessed and stricken with godlike powers over the elements. And what man could remain sane and whole with powers like these?

"Warren...come back..." Marco's voice interrupts, and the vision shifts.

Ninth Avenue. Warren can hear the old man shouting in the distance, but he doesn't look back. Marco isn't the worthless rat that Warren had always assumed him to be. Willa had told him once that his grandfather "...was a good man... he just couldn't stay with me. It wasn't his fault." She had told them little else, so Warren had created an image in his mind of a cold man, angrier and sullener even than his father. Someone to hate. Someone to blame. But Warren understands now: Marco *is* a good man, just a flawed one. And Warren knows all about flaws, and he won't lead the old, flawed man to his death.

He runs down Ninth Avenue to Thirty-Seventh Street and turns right. Rows of warehouse buildings and former sweatshops line the dark street. He passes two junkies huddled for shelter in a doorway. *It's good,* he thinks to himself, *that this is ending today, or I'd probably end up like them. I'd rather die fighting.*

The stable is west of Eleventh Avenue, Warren knows. He's been there once before—to buy heroin. It was where he met Akins for the first time. That day, the stable was full of hansom cabs and dealers spilling through the double doors with the day's spoils. Tonight, the block is too quiet. As he nears the stable, though, he sees a large, white shape, eight feet high, moving about slowly by the entrance. Warren's first thought is that Van Owen has invaded his thoughts and implanted the image—a vision of a beast of some sort. He slows to a walk, angling closer to the creature. It faces the door as if waiting for someone inside, but then its head bobs up and down in a stiff, shuddering motion that Warren recognizes. Hippolyta!

Warren has seen his father riding her through Macombs Dam Park many times, though he has never let his father see him watching.

Hippolyta jolts at his approach, but Warren has been raised around horses. He holds up both of his hands in an unthreatening manner, and she lowers her head submissively, pressing her nose against his palms. Nearby, tires squeal. Warren spins as the red pickup truck pulls to a stop, parks across from the stable, and Jerome climbs from it.

Warren is surprised at how big his brother looks. He knew that Jerome always hung his head and hunched his shoulders in his older brother's presence—he'd done it from the day he'd outgrown Warren at age 11—but tonight Jerome is standing at full height and with his shoulders back, and he is massive. Warren pauses a moment just to admire him. "Damn," he says.

"Warren?" Jerome asks. "What are you doing here?"

"Same thing as you, I guess."

"Yeah," nods Jerome. "Pop told me to go to the house to look after Regina and Grandma Willa, but they weren't there, so I came here." He looks up again at the horse. "You brought Hippolyta?"

"No," says Warren. He smirks at his brother and sees that Jerome understands: their father has reached the stable first, and he's already inside.

They began moving toward the stable entrance, but then a hansom cab makes the turn from Eleventh Avenue and heads toward the stable. Another one follows, and two more behind that one, each one with a young Black man at the reins.

"Those are his people," says Warren. He slaps Hippolyta on her rear, sending her running up the block, away from the action.

"Carriages?" Jerome asks.

"That's how he moves his supply around the city. That's his army. If we go in, they're gonna follow right behind us."

"No," says Jerome. "They're not going in. I'm not letting them."

He steps away from the stable, planting himself in the middle of the street, directly in the path of traffic.

A large, beat-up car, a silver Thunderbird, turns at the same corner. The driver honks the horn, trying desperately to maneuver past the carriages.

"Damn it," says Warren, "that's Marco."

"Marco? Terry's friend Marco?"

"Yeah, Terry's friend. And our grandfather. Don't let him get hurt."

A whooshing sound comes from the stable. Fragments of hay and dust blow from the entrance as if cast by a great wind. Warren knows exactly what sort of wind might be blowing inside. "I've got to help Pop," he says as he runs toward the stable entrance. "I'm going in. Don't let anyone get past you."

"Not a chance," Jerome tells him as he readies himself at the offensive line. "Not a chance."

I watch as the Black boys climb down from their drug carriages, their faces stained with spite, their emotions deadened by drugs and money. Were they already like this when Van Owen found them—corrupted, lost, convinced that dealing drugs is the only path to freedom—or did he bring them to this state? Did he poison their minds with twisted ideals, or were they already damaged—like so many African Americans—by the legacy of slavery, parentless, penniless, bitter, and hopeless?

They leave their wagons in the street and race toward the stable on foot. Jerome stands firmly in their path. "You're not going in there," he tells them, "so you might as well just turn around and leave."

One of the men starts reaching inside his coat for a weapon, but another one warns him, "Captain says no guns in public."

There are nine of them altogether facing Jerome. He stands only twenty feet from the stable entrance, preparing himself the same way he would when protecting his quarterback. *They're not getting past me*, he tells himself, eyeing them, trying to draw them in close so that they can't slip around him. Then, as Jerome turns to get a glimpse of Marco—his first sight of his grandfather—the men make their move. Three of them rush at Jerome. He scoops up the first one and hurls him like a sack of animal feed at the other two. All three fall to the street.

The others take their cue. Two of them run for the door, but Jerome is too fast. He tackles them both, jumping up immediately to ready himself for the next set of attackers.

The others take their cue. Two of them run for the door, but Jerome is too fast. He tackles them both, jumping up immediately to ready himself for the next set of attackers.

Meanwhile, Marco moves toward the door, intent on fulfilling my prophecy. He stops to have a look at Jerome. He wants to assist, but the foes are young men. Marco has no means to fight them except with a gun. In that moment, another car—a gypsy cab—pulls up behind the other vehicles. The left rear door swings open. Regina climbs from the cab. Suddenly, her head turns sharply at the sight of something moving nearby. She looks down and notices someone hidden beneath the parked car beside her. She kneels down for a better look. There, huddled on the ground, is Leticia March. The girl is shivering, her eyes vacant. Gently, Regina stretches out her hand and touches Leticia's hand. Leticia's eyes snap open, her mind her own again. She stares for a second, understanding that Regina has helped her somehow. She slides out from under the car and stands. She doesn't nod or speak; she simply gazes at Regina in wonder before backing up slowly. Then she turns and runs off into the night.

As Regina races to the other side of the car and takes Willa's arm to ease her out, Jerome looks on, bewildered. He is the only one of the children who still doesn't know the truth about his family—that each of them is blessed in some way, not just the men, that they are all descendants of Merlante and Mkembro wizards. He tries to quicken the pace of the fight, hoping to end it sooner. The women are still nearly sixty feet from the stable. It will be a long, slow walk—especially for Willa. Jerome is confident that he has time to finish the fight and intercept the two women before they can reach the door. But he can't help but think to himself, *What on earth are they doing here?*

As they shuffle forward, Regina tugs on her grandmother's arm and points at the old man in the pinstripe suit and fedora. For the first time in nearly fifty years, Willa and Marco see each other. Marco removes his hat, runs his hand through his grayed hair to comb it back neatly. He winks at Regina. He nods his head at Willa and flashes her a sad smile. She smiles back at him, tears forming in her eyes. Then Marco draws his Masterpiece pistol, the same one I used to wound Van Owen all those years ago, and he moves through the doorway and into the stable.

Willa tells Regina to pull her forward. Regina moves faster, stunned to find that Willa is keeping pace with her. Regina turns back and sees that her grandmother is hovering above the ground, using her power to lift herself in the air. Regina looks as if she is guiding a parade float.

As Jerome struggles against the pack, Willa and Regina skirt by him and into the stable. Terrified for them, Jerome grabs one of his fallen opponents by the ankle. Grunting, he lifts the youth and begins to spin, whirling the boy like a plane propeller, slapping him into the last of the army before finally releasing the boy, sending him hurling into a car, unconscious but alive. Jerome checks the area one last time. There is no one left to fight. Forbidden to pull their weapons, physically drained, those still conscious hobble away. Finally, Jerome races through the stable doors.

And then we are all together, the whole family—all of us here with Van Owen. And the gunfire begins.

THIRTY-THREE

Carl spun in a circle, eyeing the second-floor landing. He ducked behind a pillar to eye where the shots were coming from. Then he extended his hand toward the rafters, and a whirlwind rode along his arm. He stepped from behind the pillar and shook his arm, and the whirlwind flew up toward the stalkers. Carl could see no one, but he could hear the voices of young men struggling to hold their positions against the wind.

Behind the glass walls at the rear of the stable, two brown velvet curtains parted, revealing the office and Van Owen looking out through the floor-to-ceiling window. From a distance, he resembled a fish in an aquarium, but the aquarium was decorated as a Nineteenth Century drawing room—polished mahogany floors, walls covered with tapestries and paintings and sconces and antique mirrors. Overhead, a giant chandelier hung from the thirty-foot ceiling.

For just a moment, Carl grew distracted by the opulence of the office, by Van Owen standing in the window, watching the spectacle, and he lost his concentration. His wind slowed, and a shot rang out from above. Immediately, his thoughts went to Terry, who was still bound to the chair, still out in the open.

"Terry, get down," Warren shouted from the doorway. Carl turned to see him entering the stable, racing to his father and standing back to back with him, a strategy they had practiced a decade ago. "I've got your back, Pop."

For a moment, Carl had a notion that he should be furious at Warren—*send him away*, he thought—but there was no time for blame or delay or old angers. Now *two* of his sons were in danger. He pressed his back against Warren's and repeated Warren's words: "Terry, get down!"

Terry twisted in his chair, tipping it back and forth before finally knocking it to the ground on its side. His head struck the floor hard, but he remained conscious. He pushed with his feet, inching the chair along the cement floor, trying to make it to the front door, which was more than forty feet away.

Several more shots sounded. Carl checked his sons. No one had been hit yet. He wanted to run to Terry, but he couldn't take a chance of drawing the gunfire toward his son. Warren was right. Fighting was the only option—fighting back-to-back, just like he had trained his eldest son. "Now," he shouted. Together, Carl's and Warren's hands began to glow. Currents crackled from their fingertips and flew upward into the loft. The lightning branched out, randomly striking hay bales and wooden boards. Two men howled in pain. One tumbled from the loft, falling with a thump to the stable floor. Carl glanced at him quickly. It was a boy, perhaps only sixteen. Black. Van Owen was using children against him. "Try not to kill them," Carl whispered, "They're just kids."

A sudden movement near the door caught Carl's attention. He spun, ready to confront a new attacker. An old white man was dashing in, his gun drawn. "Who the hell...?"

"He's okay," Warren told him. That's Marco...he's...he's with us."

"Who is he?"

"He's Mom's father."

THIRTY-FOUR

So Carl knows now. He looks as if he wants to turn and question what Warren has told him, but there's no time. He watches the old man maneuver through the room fearlessly, zigzagging as he runs, keeping his path unpredictable, even as he keeps his eyes glued on Terry.

I am elated to see Marco strong again, but I grieve that he is yet another parent in this family who was unable to watch his child grow up.

Twice, he fires his gun straight above his head, pointed at no one, using the gunfire only as a distraction. Finally, he reaches his youngest grandson. "Hang in there, Terry," he says. Bending down, he grasps Terry's overturned chair by one leg and drags it behind him, heading for the entrance. "I've got you."

Carl and Warren know they must provide cover for Marco and Terry, so they double their lightning attacks, spraying currents as rapidly as they can. Another man screams. His cohorts, all of them still hidden, begin firing their guns again. Marco aims his gun at the ceiling again, and pulls the trigger until his pistol is empty. But the shots from above don't abate. Two of the attackers even make themselves visible, leaning out from behind a crate in the rafters, eyeing the scene below, trying to draw a bead on the white man.

Marco spots them and knows that his chances are slim. He might make it the door without being shot, but Terry is an even easier target. Then Marco spots the abandoned hansom cab, tilted on its side in the middle of the stable, and he moves toward it, dragging Terry's chair with him.

From behind the glass wall, Van Owen watches with a satisfied smile. He recognizes Marco—the man who shot him near the Maine cabin, the man whose mind Van Owen riddled with guilt and self-doubt. *Perhaps,* Van Owen ponders, *this old man needs another bout with fear.* He closes his eyes and speaks into Marco's mind. *"You're going to die, old man. You're going to suffer and bleed and die, just like you deserve."*

Marco hears the voice in his head. He recognizes the tone, for it has haunted him for years. But Marco has nothing left to fear; he has come here to die. He grits his teeth and plows forward toward the carriage, running in full view of the two exposed gunmen. He looks up and sees their teenage faces, their frightened yet rabid eyes, their guns pointing, aiming. "Yeah, Van Owen, I'm gonna die," he says aloud, "and I'm not afraid—not afraid of dying and not afraid of you." He feels the first bullet as it enters his chest beneath his right shoulder. He staggers for a moment but continues on. The second bullet is harsher, like a dagger piercing his back on the left side and exploding through his chest, taking blood and meat and bone with it. But he doesn't stop, even as the air becomes thinner and he can barely breathe. He tucks the chair safely behind the hansom cab and tumbles to the ground beside it. "Terry, are you all right?" he asks, coughing for air.

Terry nods and mumbles *yes* through the duct tape. He doesn't know that Marco has been hit. The old man drops his empty gun and reaches inside his jacket for his switchblade. The hand comes out coated with blood. He wipes it off on his jacket and snaps the blade open. Leaning in toward Terry, he slices through the tape that binds the boy's ankles. He is reaching toward Terry's wrists when

Carl calls out, "No!"

So Regina and Willa have arrived. The child is still holding on to her grandmother's hand, running just a step in front of her. They come through the stable entrance, moving directly toward the glass office. Van Owen's mouth opens in anticipation. He is hungry to strangle the old woman who hurt him so, but he is even hungrier to reach out and touch the little girl. "Regina," he whispers.

But it's Carl who draws my attention most. The poor man cannot comprehend why Willa and Regina are there, what they hope to accomplish. Ignoring the shooters above, he waves frantically at Willa and Regina, shouting, "No! Get out!"

"Carl," Willa declares with an air of impatience as she raises her free hand, her palm extended as if she is holding up an invisible wall, "watch out for yourself, not us."

Carl looks up at the balcony—too late. A gun is aimed directly at him. He wants to dive for cover, but the trigger is already pulled. He can see the shooter's eyes. He can see the barrel jolt as the bullet leaves it. He can almost see the bullet fly. In that fraction of a second, he feels all the mistakes of his life, all the missed opportunities, all the ways he let down his wife and his children. But the moment extends too long. The bullet hangs suspended in midair only inches from his face, so close that Carl can almost read the insignia on the side, almost trace the tiny grooves that were etched into its sides as it left the gun. The shooter gets off one more round. Carl twitches with the sound of the gunpowder eruption, but this bullet also stops in front of him, hovering beside the first one. The air near Carl seems to pulsate as the two bullets float in space. Then Willa waves her hand, and the two bullets drops to the floor at Carl's feet.

Carl looks all around him, wondering how this has happened. The air continues to vibrate above and around Carl and Warren, an invisible barrier protecting them. Carl stares, stupefied.

"No need to thank me, Carl," says Willa.

"I don't...I don't understand..." he stutters, but Willa interrupts.

"Warren," she calls out, "Regina says you can get us into that office."

"Yes, Grandma Willa," says Warren, understanding instantly that Regina has looked into his mind and seen what he is capable of. "I can do that."

"Well," she says, "now would be a good time."

Warren closes his eyes and points both palms toward the door to Van Owen's office. "Watch this, Pop." An odd hum rumbles through the stable, deep and raspy, like distortion from a guitar amplifier. Warren's hands begin to gleam with an odd intensity. There is no crackle of electricity, no lightning branches, only a smooth blue sheen like colored glass that stretches out from Warren's fingers, reaching slowly across the stable like a theatrical spotlight. It shines on the steel door to Van Owen's office, pouring over it like liquid, covering it, illuminating it in the same eerie blue glow. For a moment, the gunfire stops as all onlookers simply gaze at the light. The entire stable is silent. Behind the glass wall, even Van Owen is slack-jawed. "Okay," says Warren softly, his voice strangely calm, "you can go in now."

"Thank you, dear," says Willa. She is still holding Regina's hand, but she is standing now, not floating. She stretches out her free hand, her fingers stroking what should be the door to Van Owen's office. Her hand flows through the glowing steel as if it is only a projection of a door.

"Warren...how are you doing this...?" asks a stunned Carl.

"I don't know, Pop," Warren answers. "I just do it."

"Come on, Regina," Willa whispers, "he's waiting for us."

Regina turns back to take one last look at her oldest brother, and then she speaks aloud for the first time in two years. "Thank you, Warren." She gives him a sad, frightened smile. Then she and Willa step through the bluish door as if it is not even there.

Carl's eyes and mouth gape open. He looks as if he can barely breathe. He starts walking toward the transparent office door, but then Jerome charges through the stable entrance, running at full speed. "Warren, hold the door," he shouts as he tears past his father.

"No," cries Carl as he tries to catch up.

"It's not your fight anymore," says Jerome. "It's ours." He runs through the blue light, through the door, and comes out on the other side.

Carl is only steps behind, but the blue light fades to gray and then to silver and then dissipates entirely, and Carl collides with the door, which has regained its solid steel form. He falls to the ground. Immediately, he is on his feet, pounding on the door. He presses his hands against it, trying to electrify it as Warren did but to no avail. "Make it do that again, Warren! Make it do that again!"

"I can't, Pop," Warren answers in a faint voice. "I'm too...I'm..." He drops to his knees, spent. His hands still glow blue, the shimmer permeating his arms. "Damn," he whispers, "not again."

Carl moves to the glass window, pounding on it, but it is several inches thick. Inside, Van Owen doesn't even pay attention to the rapping at the window. Jerome, Willa, and Regina are inside with him.

From above, the shots begin again. One strikes the glass near Carl and ricochets off.

"Pop," Warren begs, "you're out in the open." Too weak to stand, Warren stumbles over to the overturned carriage where Terry and Marco are hiding. He finds Marco lying on his side, the switchblade still in his hand. His chest is a sheet of blood. His eyes are half-closed. Warren rolls him onto his back and pries the knife from his hand. He rips Marco's shirt open to examine the wounds. There is so much blood, though, that the wounds are barely visible.

For a moment, Warren considers trying to extract the bullets and cauterize—but it is too late, the damage too severe, the old man almost gone.

Terry's legs are free, and he manages to twist the chair around so that he is facing Marco. He drags himself closer to Warren, who uses the knife to slice through the duct tape around Terry's wrists, finally extricating him from the chair. Terry climbs to his knees beside Marco. He tears the tape from his mouth and spits. Then he leans in to Marco. The old man is wheezing, barely able to breathe, but he stretches his arm upward and places a hand on Terry's shoulder. His mouth twitches as he tries to speak, but no sound comes out.

"I know," Terry tells him through tears. "I know who you are. I know everything."

The old man nods and closes his eyes.

I want to send Marco a message as he departs, but then I remember that I'm not there in the stable with them. I'm watching from very far away. This vision, though, is so vivid. My ability to read the thoughts of everyone in the room is so profound.

Inside the office, Willa stands ready. She is the only one who has caused Van Owen lasting injury and pain, the one who has beaten him twice in battle. But Van Owen is the first one to speak, and he says exactly what I'm thinking: "So, the whole family's here." He smiles that same overconfident smile that I've seen across so many lifetimes.

Jerome doesn't wait. For once, he is the aggressor, charging forward to attack first. That odd humming sound returns, and Van Owen's hands begin to glow again with the power he took from Kwame a century and a half ago. He waits until Jerome is only a few feet away, and then he raises his hands and lets loose his lightning barrage.

For just a moment, Jerome slows down; he lowers his head to

look at the electrical stream beating against his chest, charring away his shirt. Then he looks up and begins moving forward again, not a mark on his body. Through the window, Carl watches, elated when he sees Van Owen's awestruck expression.

"Why won't you fall, you lumbering brute?" shouts Van Owen.

Jerome doesn't respond. He doesn't explain that he has spent years learning how to withstand lightning attacks—years being singed and burned and struck by his father, all in preparation for this day. He just keeps his forward momentum, the lightning currents scoring his clothing and slowing his progress but only barely hurting him.

Then I see the thought come to life in Van Owen's eyes. He has realized that Jerome can't be harmed physically. He maintains his lightning attack but begins to reach into Jerome's mind, reading his memories. Almost immediately, he finds a weakness.

"You're worried about Willa and Terry, aren't you?" asks Van Owen, speaking without moving his lips.

Jerome narrows his eyes and tries to close off his mind, to create a mental wall, just as his father trained him to do. However, Carl had no mental powers—no way to prepare Jerome for such an attack.

"Well," Van Owen goes on needling the boy, "you needn't worry about them. They're in no danger from me. You and I both know where the real danger lies."

Jerome's anger rises. He pushes doubly hard against the lightning, taking three great strides.

"All those years of training—your father bullying you, burning you, beating you—did you think it was all in your best interest? Did you ever consider that maybe none of it was about training you at all? Did you ever consider that your father beat you simply because he took pleasure in beating you?"

"Shut up," Jerome bellows, but he is wavering, weakening to the slaver's mental attack, allowing Van Owen in, giving him fodder to press harder.

"Look at how he treated Warren," Van Owen goes on. "That poor boy just needed a little guidance and fathering but could get none from his father, so he descended into the world of narcotics. Look at how Carl treats poor, defenseless Terry. How much longer do you think Terry will last under the same roof with such a monster? Soon your father will drive Terry away, just as he did Warren."

Warren groans in response, "Stop filling my head with lies..."

"Soon you'll leave, too, and your father will have just what he wants—to be alone in the house—with Regina."

"Stop it..."

Van Owen's voice is smoother with each sentence. He has practiced such manipulation for generations. "Yes, that's it. That's what Carl has wanted all along—to be alone with his little girl." The suggestion is revolting and absurd, but Van Owen presses on. "Alone with the silent girl who looks just like her mother. Can you possibly imagine what Carl Kelly might want from her?"

I see it happen then: Jerome begins to let up. Whether it is the lightning or the needling or the telepathic coercion, Van Owen's assault seems to take its toll on Jerome. He doesn't believe Van Owen's words—I'm certain of it—yet he looks undermined by their viciousness, and he begins to falter. But Willa is raising her hand, preparing to mount her attack.

"Yes," Van Owen continues, "your father has told you lies all your life, Jerome. He's prepared you for an epic battle with me, taught you that I'm some sort of scourge against your family. It's simply not true. None of it. It's all backward. It's your father who's the serpent, not I. In 1859, I rescued Amara and Kwame from a savage land. I endowed them with powers that had been in my family for generations. And was there any appreciation? No—only hatred and loathing and resentment and threats. Only fear of the unknown. Only mistrust that a white man might be trying to raise them up above the rest of humanity's dregs. But isn't that the way it always is? Man betrays his maker. Man is so envious that he defies the one who shows him kindness."

Abruptly, Van Owen's lightning stops flowing, and he lowers his hands. Jerome can rush him now, but he doesn't. Instead, he barely trudges forward at all. "I... I don't understand," says Jerome, his face expressionless.

"No, of course you don't," Van Owen says aloud. "How could you? You've spent seventeen years under the same roof with a madman, being indoctrinated into his mad delusions. It'll take you some time to accept the truth, but eventually you'll see that I'm not your enemy. I didn't bring Terry here so that I could hurt him. I brought him here so I could help him, so I could raise him myself, guide him, teach him. You and your family stormed my stable and attacked my students and me. I'm the one who's been wronged here. These men—these young Black men here—they come to me to be taught, to learn how to lift themselves from the mire. Yet you rage in here and inflict violence upon them, trying to tear them back down. I think you owe me an apology."

Jerome's eyes look glassy. He's only a few feet from Van Owen, but he appears hypnotized, bewitched by Van Owen's lies. "I...I'm sorry...I..."

"Yes," Van Owen nods as he pats Jerome's shoulder. "Of course you are. Now, that wasn't so hard, was it?"

"No," says Jerome, "it wasn't hard at all." His eyes glint. The dim expression fades. He grits his teeth almost into a half-smile. He was pretending. Van Owen's bile wasn't affecting him at all. Jerome was far too smart to believe a word. And now he lifts his hand to strike.

For all of the extraordinary powers that I've seen used against Van Owen, I don't believe I've ever been as contented as when I see him suffer the indignity of the backhanded slap across the face, rendered by Jerome. Van Owen's head turns from the force of the blow, and his face flushes red with anger as he staggers backward. He focuses his eyes on Jerome, trying to find a way back into the boy's mind. Jerome doesn't give him one. He strikes again, punching, slapping, elbowing. Blood trickles from the slaver's nose. Van Owen tries to speak, tries to raise a hand in defense, but Jerome punches him again, square in the mouth. Van Owen falls to the floor on his back, his teeth bloodied.

Jerome jumps atop him. "No more," he shouts. "You took my mother." A punch to the jaw. "You kidnapped my brother." Another punch to the nose breaks it with a sickening crack. "Now you've got my sister and my grandmother here, too? No more!" Again and again, he strikes Van Owen until the slaver's face is purple from the clotting. Then, as Van Owen hovers somewhere just above unconsciousness, Jerome raises both hands, clasping them together in a double fist above his head, preparing for one final blow. Van Owen wheezes as he tries to speak. He spits out a tooth. Jerome lifts his hands higher, clenching his jaw for the final blow. Then he waits, and he waits, and he waits. Finally, he looks down with pity at Van Owen, and he lowers his hands. He has the enemy down, beaten, ready to be finished, but Jerome can't escape who he is. Carl's concerns, Coach Dodge's criticism, even Akins's derision—they all pointed to the same Achilles heel that Jerome has known for years: he lacks a killer instinct. He cannot deliver a fatal blow. Jerome realizes it and drops his hands to his sides. And in that moment, he is lost.

Van Owen's glowing hands shoot upward and wrap around Jerome's neck like electric eels. Electricity crackles from them as he twists and presses and finally makes Jerome feel pain. "Barbarian," Van Owen seethes, drool and blood spilling from the corner of his mouth. He looks like a rabid dog.

Carl pounds on the window while Van Owen squeezes tighter,

pulling himself up, pushing Jerome back against the ground, strangling and electrocuting at the same time. Jerome's eyes shut, consciousness gone. Then, suddenly, they snap open again. He is awake, yet he appears asleep at the same time, almost as if he's entranced. His fist seems to rise from twenty feet behind him, the punch colliding with Van Owen's head and knocking the slaver backward into the glass wall. Van Owen shrieks as blood drips from a new head wound at the rear of his skull.

"Good girl," Willa says as she watches Regina dictate Jerome's movements. She is practicing the same trick that her mother did on the day Regina was born. She is the puppeteer and Jerome her marionette. The little girl shuffles her feet, and Jerome stands. She mimes with her hands, and Jerome raises his, grabbing Van Owen by his lapels and throwing him into the adjacent wall. A priceless nineteenth century painting falls to the floor.

"I've seen this game before," Van Owen hisses. He looks toward Willa. "How are you doing this? You don't have that power. But if it's not you, then who...?"

Regina shifts her feet again and Jerome races forward. Again he lifts Van Owen up and throws him, but this time, even as the slaver strikes into a desk, sliding across it and slamming into the wall, Van Owen keeps his eyes on Regina. He watches her mime each of Jerome's movements and understands that it is she who has taken control of Jerome's body.

"So, it's you, is it, little one?" Van Owen groans through bloody teeth. "Yes, it *would* be. You have Amara's eyes. You *would* be the most vicious of all." He offers a sympathetic expression. "I don't want to hurt you, child—you're the reason we're all here—but I won't tolerate this insolence." He waves his hand toward her, making almost a throwing gesture, and sparks fly from his palm like electrified daggers and fizzle out on the floor near Regina's feet. In that instant, I know that he's telling the truth: he isn't trying to kill her. *She* is the reason for all of this. He *does* want her alive—as a replacement for me. He couldn't locate Dara when the boys were born, but he sensed Regina's birth; he knew that a female descendant had come into the world. He wants Regina.

The lightning whizzes by Regina, missing her, forging tiny holes in the wall behind her. But she jolts and loses her control of Jerome, who crumbles to the ground. Regina gasps as Jerome lands in a heap. She recoils, suddenly a child again. Van Owen takes a step toward her.

"No," says Willa, who has walked so slowly across the floor that she has gone unnoticed. She's only a few feet from Van Owen now. "No!" She waves her hand at Van Owen, and he rises into the air, higher, higher. He looks down at the floor, grimacing furiously. His face is already healing from Jerome's attack.

Willa moves her arm back and forth, and Van Owen's body complies. With each of her gesticulations, Van Owen's body shifts in the air, careening into the near wall, the far wall, the steel door, the glass window. He howls with each contact. "Stop it, you filthy witch!" he cries.

She smashes him into a mirror, shattering it. She beckons again with her hand, and he begins to rise again, but he raises a glowing hand and fires off his lightning. It flies upward, seemingly erratically, but the current strikes the cable that supports the grotesque crystal chandelier. The cable rips in two. The chandelier falls downward. Willa doesn't make a sound, even as the chandelier lands atop her back, knocking her down, pinning her to the ground. Crystals shatter and roll across the floor.

But Willa doesn't cry out. She manages only a weak whisper: "Run, Regina, run..."

THIRTY-FIVE

"No," Carl shouted at the glass window.

He could barely breathe. Jerome looked unconscious. Willa looked dead. There was no blood, but the chandelier was tremendous. Its weight had crushed the old woman against the wooden floor.

Carl tried to make sense of what he had seen. *How had Willa performed these feats—stopping bullets in the air, lifting Van Owen off the ground with the wave of her arm?* But there was no time for these questions. Van Owen was back on his feet again, moving toward Regina. Carl had to save his little girl.

He pressed his palms against the glass, trying to electrify the window as Warren had done with the door. He pressed harder, but his lightning just rolled over the glass, offering only a fireworks show.

Then, the gunfire erupted again from above, and one bullet grazed his shoulder. Carl moaned but didn't fall.

"Pop!" called Terry, prying himself away from his fallen grandfather. He tried to jump up, but Warren shoved him back down. Warren forced himself to standing and raced out from behind the carriage. Carl was still focused on the window, still coating the glass in electric fire, but it was having no effect. He was favoring his right side, where the bullet had connected, but he wasn't giving up on getting into that room.

Above, the remaining shooters grew bolder. They made themselves more visible—crouching now at the lip of the loft, four young Black men fired their guns. Another bullet struck Carl. He grabbed at his thigh and crumpled to the ground, weak, his lightning ceasing. Warren ran to his father and knelt beside him.

"Get back," Carl shouted through the pain, trying to push Warren away, but Warren wouldn't relent.

"No, Pop. I won't." He scooped Carl up in his arms, cradling him like a child. He scanned the stable. Then he turned his back to the shooters and began backing up toward the carriage.

"What are you doing?" Carl shouted.

"Saving your life," said Warren as he continued moving backward. Even as the gunfire came, he kept moving. Even as the bullets ripped across his back, he kept moving until he reached the carriage. Finally safe behind it, Warren fell to the ground, and Carl rolled from his arms and landed beside Terry.

"You should have left me there," Carl said. "You could have gotten hit."

Carl looked down at his leg. The bullet had traveled straight through his femur. Seeing the blood, Carl suddenly became aware of the pain. He followed the trail of blood from his leg to where it mixed with another trail—one that came from Warren. "Warren?" he asked.

Warren's breathing was shallow. His voice was soft. Blood was spreading beneath him. "You okay, Pop?"

Carl grabbed his arm. He opened Warren's jacket to check for wounds but saw none. "Where were you hit?"

"In my back."

"Turn over. We can draw the bullet out. We can cauterize. Let me..."

As Warren spoke, blood dripped from his mouth and hung from his lip. "It's not one bullet. It's many. And there's no time."

Carl reached underneath to Warren's back and traced his hands along the wounds. His hand lit up, and Warren groaned as five blood-soaked slugs eased out from his back and fell onto the hay. "You're gonna be ok, Warren," Carl said. "You're gonna make it."

"It's too late, Pop," Warren said, his voice weak.

Carl took Warren's hand in his and spoke with pride. "Terry, did you see? Did you see what Warren did? Do you remember your brother Warren? This is Warren..." Carl was crying. "This is Warren..."

"I know," Terry said, his hand on his brother's shoulder.

Warren coughed. His breathing was labored. "How'd you like that thing with the door, Pop? Pretty cool, huh?"

"It was...it was amazing, Warren," said Carl. "How...?"

"I don't know... I just imagine something's not there, and I can make a passage through it..." The bullets were starting again. The boys in the rafters had reloaded. "But wait till you see this trick. You better cover Terry up, though."

There was a piercing, high-pitched hum. Warren's hands started to glow. Then the light spread. It traveled up his wrists, up his arms, across his chest. He smiled, as if the sensation was almost pleasant, even as the light coated his head. His entire body gleamed as he looked at Carl and Terry and said, "Goodbye." The glow enveloped him, obscuring his features, his clothing, his entire form. He exhaled one last, loud breath, howling as the electricity exploded from him. There was no lightning, no current, no sound even—just a burst of light that seemed to emanate from every part of his body, as if he had taken all of the suffering and disappointment and pain he'd ever experienced and drawn them into a power source at his core and then expelled them all at once. Blue light streamed upward and outward, filling the room. Carl crouched over Terry, shielding him. The light danced across Carl's back, but he was immune to its effect. Above, Van Owen's men screamed as the light buffeted them.

Suddenly, the humming sound returned. Much louder, almost deafening. There was a brilliant flash of blue light emanating from Warren's glowing form. It exploded through the stable, ripping a hole in the wooden rooftop. As the rain poured in, much of the roof fell with it, collapsing onto the loft, burying Van Owen's men in rubble.

As quickly as it had come, the light vanished and the stable was silent. Carl pulled himself off of Terry and rolled onto his back. The pain in his leg was so intense that he could barely move. "Terry, are you okay?"

"Yeah. I think so." He looked around. Where's Warren?"

Carl checked the spot where his eldest son had been. There was nothing there but ash.

THIRTY-SIX

Van Owen averts his eyes from Warren's light explosion. Regina stares into it. The roof caves, crushing Van Owen's men—those poor, corrupted African-American boys all unconscious or dead. The light envelops the stable, and then it departs, taking Warren with it. And Carl and Terry are left combing their hands through a pile of dust.

As I watch Carl weep and Regina cower as Van Owen approaches her, I yearn to comprehend all of the torment that Van Owen has caused. What is it that drives such a man? Why, after all these years, does he still chase us? Why—after a lifespan three times that of most men, and myriad victories—why does he still find the urge to press on, to hunt, to strive, to live? Our magic— Kwame's and mine—gave him his power. But I can recall no Mkembro legend of anyone who lived for eons without aging. What is it that makes Van Owen immortal? Is there something in the rage burning within him that fuels him, compelling him to fight against his mortality, against nature, against time itself? Or is it something else—some lesson taught to him by his father and his father before him, telling him to despise all those who look different from him, drilling it into him that his only goal should be to rise by climbing over those weaker or gentler or more innocent or darker skinned than he?

When I watch Carl, I can sense the maxim that guides him: *By any means necessary.* For Carl, these are words of inspiration from his youth, the words of Malcolm X, who was able to put voice to the day-to-day struggles of Africans in America. This credo represents the depths Carl will go to, the forces he will face, the energy he will expend to keep his children safe. Can it be, I wonder, that Van Owen lives by a similar credo but that he applies it differently—to self-centered ends?

All creatures are driven to live, to stay alive. If we could, we would all cauterize our wounds with lightning and seal our blood inside us so that it can never trickle away. How much of ourselves, though, would the rest of us be willing to sacrifice in order to go on living? What piece of our souls would we sell? How many lives would we be willing to destroy to extend our own?

Most of us are repulsed by such questions while others like Van Owen never consider asking them.

As much as the internal currents of Kwame's and my power keep Van Owen alive, I know there's something more: Van Owen yearns to conquer, to take, to own, and—most of all—to force his will upon others. It is these deeds that feed him, the lust for new conquests that drives him. It is only when those things that he feels *belong* to him are taken from him that he is weakened. He feels pain at the thought that he no longer possesses me. He feels rage that he can't own my children and their children as he once owned me. He's whole only when he's stealing freedom from others, inflicting slavery on them or polluting them with drugs. And he feels fear only at the thought of losing his *own* freedom, as he confided to me when he first spoke to me on his ship. Perhaps it's time, then, that he remembers how it feels to lose what was once his. And, like Van Owen, I will myself the power to make it so. By any means necessary.

"Run, Regina, run," Willa whispers.

In his glass room, Van Owen is still dazed from the light. He staggers, trying to find his footing. And Regina looks so frightened, so young—younger even than I when I faced the madman for the first time. She turns toward the door and then to Jerome's unconscious body and then to Willa's broken one. Her lips tremble.

"Run," Willa repeats. "Now, while he's dazed."

But Regina remains calm. "No," she says.

Van Owen turns, his interest piqued at the sound—the tone—of her voice. Suddenly, his expression takes on that hungry affect it had when he came to my cabin to rape me.

"You must go now...please..." Willa pleads, her voice weak and fading.

"No," Regina repeats. Her saucer-like eyes drill into Van Owen's as she raises her voice louder, speaking in my Carolina accent. It isn't the voice of a Harlem child. It's the voice of a West African princess who has seen her parents killed, her village destroyed, her life and her people ravaged, her descendants hunted. It's the voice of resilience, of righteous indignation, of vengeance. It's my voice. "I'm not leaving. Amara will help me."

"Amara?" Van Owen laughs. "She's been dead for fifty years."

"No," she tells him calmly, "she's right here with me. Aren't you, Amara?"

So she senses me. Somehow, she knows I'm watching. But what can I do—here from decades previous, dying on a snowdrift in 1956? She's facing Hendrik Van Owen half a century away, and yet she seems absent of fear. Why? Does she know something that I don't? Has she had a vision of her own? Does she know that I can do something to aid her in some way?

What is it, Regina? What can I give you? Tell me...

She blinks. She tilts her head to the side. She hears me. And she answers. "Amara, you know what to give me—what you tried to give me once before, but I was too young to understand. Your history. *Our* history."

My history? Was *that* it then—was *that* the purpose? Was *that* the reason I was given the power of prophecy all those years ago on the day of my wedding? Were the visions not meant only as portents? Was I not meant simply to watch the visions so that I could plan ahead and try to avoid tragedy? Am I not simply an African Cassandra, doomed to know the future but powerless to affect it?

"*No,*" Regina answers me.

She's right. I will *not* be Cassandra. I *refuse* to be Cassandra. Cassandra was a pawn of the gods. I am Amara, princess of the Mkembro clan, and I am no one's pawn.

With one word, Regina has told me what I couldn't learn in all these years. The visions weren't portents; they were portals. For those brief moments when I saw them, I was granted connections to my future and to my past. I was being allowed to communicate with my descendants—to teach them, to show them what had come before, to help them learn from the past. To give them a connection to their heritage. I just didn't understand. I watched the future play out, thinking it untouchable. It isn't.

I feel the numbing snow and remember where I am—dying on a mountain. The cold spreads over me, but I *will myself* to hold off death for just a few more moments. I *will myself* to live and remember what has gone before:

I see my father and Kwame's father at the mouth of the cave, making the nuptial pact. I see my mother preparing me for the ceremony, coating my face with the fruit paint—I can taste its sweetness even now. I see my father leading me through the village. I see Kwame coming toward me, young and strong and beautiful. I see Van Owen tearing through our jungle with his machete, killing my father and my mother, slaughtering my people, taking us. I see my cage on the ship. I see Kwame escape. I see North Carolina, with its wondrous fields and scents, all marred by hatred and slavery and hanging trees. I see decades of struggle, of my people—the Africans and the African-Americans—fighting for survival, for self-respect, for life. I see Van Owen pursuing me, hunting me, hunting my family. I see him injured and bleeding. I see him running. I see him murdering my daughter. I see him hating, always hating, always fighting to hold us back, to keep us from living with dignity, to keep us apart from one another, to keep us from learning from one another, to keep us from being a family, to keep us from passing on what we have learned—our stories, our knowledge, our past.

I see. I see it all. I hold all of it in my mind for an instant, remembering it, cherishing it, cleaving to it.

And then I let it go.

I send it all to Regina. I show her everything. I give her all I have and all I am. I give her what she asked for: our history.

The girl's eyes shut for just a trice as her mind fills with my memories. Her head rocks back as she struggles to grasp the stream of knowledge that flows into her. Van Owen jumps on the moment and strides toward her, but Willa is ready. Pinned down and dying, the old woman draws on her last bit of strength. She waves her fractured arm toward the hundreds of shattered chandelier crystals, raising them from the floor and sending them flying toward him like knives. The crystals tear at him, scraping and lacerating and puncturing. Blood streams from him in a hundred new places.

Immediately, he shuts his eyes and begins to radiate lightning from his hands. He touches the sparks to his skin, sealing the wounds—cauterizing them—one by one.

"Hendrik," Regina shouts at him in my voice, "you don't have time for that now. You need to run. The pirates are here."

"What?"

"Don't you see them?" she asks. "Are you blind?"

With only a thought, she infiltrates his mind with visions. She has reached into one of my earliest memories—on Van Owen's ship, when he came to my cage and told me of the Barbary pirates who kidnapped him when he was a young man, the one time in his life when he knew the fear of slavery, the horror of captivity—and she has thrown it back at him.

Van Owen reels. The wounds begin to drip again. In his mind, he's a young man. The room has become the vessel Antares. The pirate ship has pulled alongside it. The Barbary corsairs have stormed the ship; they're beating him, taking him, locking him in a cell, chaining him to a galley oar, forcing him to live as a slave.

In the present, he rocks backward, weak, but doesn't fall. His eyes dart around the room as he lives out his most harrowing memory, his darkest moment, his greatest fear.

He struggles to catch his breath, whispering, "I know what you're doing, Amara, but visions can't hurt me." He takes one step forward, then another, and then he stares out, cognizant again, the visions spirited away. He glances down at Willa and speaks in a guttural tone: "Your grandma's dead, little girl."

"Grandma?" Regina cries out, her concentration broken like shattered crystal. She is a child again, small and frail. She looks down and sees that Willa is indeed dead, and it breaks her. She falls backward against the steel office door. For all of her wisdom and poise and strength, Regina is still just a motherless child, and I have failed her. Everyone has failed her. Van Owen has killed her mother, her grandmother, and all the women in the family line before her. He has beaten her brothers and her father. She is all alone in the world now, and I am decades away.

Van Owen draws a white handkerchief and wipes the blood from his face. "You speak like Amara. You look like Amara. You lash out at me with lies just as she did. You're just like her—a little African girl who needs to be taught who her master is."

He begins moving toward her again, but Regina doesn't look frightened. A thought has entered her mind—a vision, in fact. She stares into his eyes, looking confident somehow.

"Why are you smiling, child?" he asks her.

"Because," she says, "I know what's going to happen."

And then she begins to sing:

Mai Wa kmaro

Mai Wa kmaro

Dji mi sarro ti kee la ti na-arro

"What is that, child?" he asks her, "some African prayer?"

She doesn't answer. She just keeps singing, repeating the last line of the song again and again.

Dji mi sarro ti kee la ti na-arro

Dji mi sarro ti kee la ti na-arro

Dji mi sarro ti kee la ti na-arro

It's the song from my wedding day. I can remember walking to my ceremony with my father, hearing both clans—the Merlante and the Mkembro—singing it together, attesting that the two tribes had once been one, affirming that they were destined to be one again, that they *must* be one again in order to face the direst of threats.

I have little life left in me, but I finally understand. I have finally played my role and passed on what our people have always lacked: our history, our past. And now Regina knows what *has* happened and what *must* happen—she knows what I must tell her even before I know it. And she waits now only to hear me tell her what she already knows she must do.

I give my last thought—my last words—to you, daughter of my daughters. I call to you across five generations: "Open the door, Regina. Let your brother in."

THIRTY-SEVEN

Open the door, Regina. Let your brother in.

Terry heard Amara's words echoing in his mind, just as his sister did. Regina spun on her heels and pulled the three bolts across, unlocking the door. She turned the handle, and the office door slid open. Terry watched it sweep outward, and he sprang to his feet. He could see Regina in the doorway. He could hear Van Owen threatening her, ordering her to shut the door.

"Regina!" Carl shouted. He forced himself up to one knee, but his bloody leg gave out, and he dropped down again. "Terry, help me get over there."

Terry didn't answer. He was moving too quickly toward the door.

"Terry," his father called, dragging himself across the floor after his son. "No, Terry! Don't...you can't..."

"Yes, Pop," Terry said, "I can."

Even before he reached the door, Terry could hear Van Owen's voice. "Are you trying to run away, little girl?"

"No," Regina told him. "I don't need to run away." And she went back to her singing. *Dji mi sarro ti kee la ti na-arro.*

Van Owen's face sank at the sight of Terry entering the room, the gag removed, his voice no longer fettered. The boy stepped in front of his sister, and Van Owen pointed a glowing hand at the two children, preparing to strike.

"No," Terry ordered. "Lower your hand."

Van Owen's hand fell to his side. He opened his mouth to speak, to threaten.

"No," Terry told him calmly. "Don't speak." He paused for a moment to dwell on the vision that Amara had passed on to him two years ago. He'd tried to lock it away, but the image had returned to him in nightmares so many times: that ghostly white man, blood spilling from his chest, electricity crackling from his hands. Fifty years ago, in the snows of Maine, Amara had shot Van Owen again and again. He had lain there in the snow, bleeding, weakening, nearly dead. Terry had been so confused by the image. *Who was this man? What does this nightmare mean?* But he understood it now. And he knew how to end it. His memories of Regina's birth no longer buried, he remembered the pale man who came to his mother's bedroom to steal Regina away. Terry had beaten Van Owen then, sent the villain away simply with the power of his voice—by speaking up, by telling Van Owen to leave. As a four-year-old child, Terry had defeated Van Owen with only a few words. This day, he would need only one. He stared into Van Owen's twitching eyes and gave the order: "Bleed."

Van Owen stood completely still for a moment. Then his body began to tremble. He looked down at his hands and tried to scream, but no sound came from his throat. He could only watch as the blood started to trickle from his cuts. Even the cauterized wounds began to burst, blood bubbling to the surface and dripping in slow streams. It fell from his hands, his arms, his mouth, his eyes. It oozed down his shirt, his pants, into his shoes—filling them until it spilled out again. He shut his eyes, trying to concentrate, trying to will the blood to stop. When he opened his eyes again, though, the blood was gushing even more. His shoulders slumped. He began to collapse. He tried to clutch the wall, the door—anything—as his body shook violently, the blood draining faster and faster, covering the floor around him in an inky, bilious puddle.

The sight was horrific, but neither Terry nor Regina turned from it. Through Amara's memories, each had seen what Van Owen had done to their family. This was a fitting fate.

Finally, Van Owen plummeted to his knees. The veins on his forehead swelled and ruptured. His white hair, wet with blood, fell from his head and slapped against the floor in wet clumps. He opened his mouth, trying to let loose one final threat, but there was no strength left to push the words out. Exhaling a serpentine gasp, he collapsed forward into a lake of his blood. But it still kept streaming from him, spreading out over the floor of the office, pouring through the floorboards, dripping away. As the last ounces of sustenance left his veins, his skin began to collapse inward, his aged bones began to crumble. Soon, all that was left was crimson ash and blood-stained clothes.

"Terry?" Carl asked, his eyes wide as he crawled through the doorway and saw what was left of the slaver. "*You* did this? But *you*..."

"*We* did it, Pop. We all did it."

The police were easily misled. When they seemed skeptical, Regina made them feel calm. She didn't speak. As Terry and she had planned, she gave them visions, showing them what she needed them to see: a kidnapping, a rescue attempt by the family, a building full of drugs, full of dead and unconscious criminals. No more explanation was needed. None of it would ever make complete sense—the detectives and the press would wrestle with it for weeks, ever eager to link the narcotics operation to Warren, the drug-addicted older brother who seemed to have escaped before the police arrived. In the end, though, the rest of the Kelly family would emerge unscathed, Regina promised Terry. "Trust me," she told him, speaking aloud. "I know."

Terry and Regina watched the medical examiners as they wheeled Willa's and Marco's bodies out of the stable and into the ambulance, side by side. As the driver tried to shut the door, Regina stepped in front of him. She reached under the sheet and touched her grandmother's hand. It was stiff and cold and lifeless.

"It's not her anymore," Terry told her.

Regina seemed not to hear him. She leaned in close to Willa's ear and whispered, "Goodbye, Grandma."

Jerome was awake but still dazed, insisting he didn't need medical attention. When the ambulance team argued that he'd been unconscious for twenty minutes, he suggested that they instead tend to his father. There were already several paramedics working on Carl, most of them perplexed by the odd scar tissue that had already formed over his wounds.

"He heals fast," Jerome told them, but his eyes were staring off, locked on the pile of ash where Warren had been. Jerome knelt and ran his hand over it.

"Your father's leg looks bad," a paramedic interrupted him. "Damage to the muscle, probably. Might have to stay in the hospital."

"Where's Hippolyta?" Carl called out suddenly.

"She's fine, Pop," Terry told him. "I already checked her out. The police are taking her back to your stable."

Jerome helped carry Carl's stretcher to the ambulance, and then he climbed in after them. Carl tried to push him away, though. "You should stay with Terry and Regina. They need you to protect..."

Jerome shook his head. "They're going to ride behind us in the police car. Besides, there's nothing to protect them *from* anymore, Pop. And you should know by now that Terry and Regina can take care of themselves."

Just before Jerome shut the ambulance door, Regina leaned in and Carl looked up at her, tears in his eyes. Terry appeared next to him and patted his father's shoulder. "It's over, Pop. It's okay."

"But he's gone," said Carl. "Warren's gone.... It was my fault... I should have..."

"It's not your fault," Terry told him. "Warren couldn't stay. He knew that a long time ago. I think he stuck around only because he was waiting for this day."

Carl clutched Terry's arm and squeezed.

Regina knelt close enough so that only her family could hear her. "Amara told me," she said softly, "about our people—the Mkembro and the Merlante." Carl marveled at the sound of his daughter's voice, the maturity of it, the richness of her North Carolina accent giving it the timbre of experience. "There are words that our people sang at all of our ceremonies—in moments of celebration and tragedy: *Dji mi sarro ti kee la ti na-arro.*"

"What does it mean?" asked Carl.

"In unity," she said, "we shall find strength."

EPILOGUE

Harry wanted to believe what his master had told him. He needed to believe that Captain Van Owen was a good man—that he wouldn't hurt the new girl. But why, Harry wondered, would Captain Van Owen make him tie up Amara and leave her alone in the cabin?

"Well," Captain Van Owen said to her as he entered, "I trust you find your new home to your liking."

Harry couldn't allow himself to hear more. He quickened his pace back to his own cabin. He lifted the broom and swept at the floorboards, trying to drown out Van Owen's voice. Swoosh, swoosh, went the broom. Then the word "witch "broke through the din, causing Harry to pause for a moment, confused. Until he began to sweep even more vigorously, more loudly, until the master's words were faint against the backdrop chirps of the crickets and cicadas that inhabited the tobacco fields.

Finally, when the words seemed to have subsided, Harry stopped his sweeping motion, only to give way again to Van Owen's voice.

"...Now let's us see what I got from you," he barked at the girl. "Let me see inside that filthy, primitive mind, Amara!"

Harry looked at the broom in his hand, wanting to rush to the girl's aid, but then a brilliant light flashed outside, filling the cabin and the tobacco field. The girl screamed.

Harry's head spun, and he watched the blue aura fade soundlessly to the north. He dropped the broom and strode from his cabin, unsure where he was going—to help the girl or to investigate the blue light? Only a few steps from the cabin, he heard the moaning. A man's voice behind Harry's own cabin. He ran toward it.

There on the ground was a Black man. He wore a tattered jacket and blue dungarees. He was young, perhaps in his twenties, barely more than a boy. Across his forehead and matted hair was an odd hat with a broad bill. The white lettering almost glowed in the moonlight.

As Harry neared the figure, he knew one thing for certain: this was not one of Van Owen's slaves. Harry had heard there were free Black men somewhere in America. He had never seen one, but he wondered if this was how they dressed.

Then he saw the blood. There were bullet holes across the back of the boy's jacket, red streaks extending from each. Blood dripped from the boy's mouth as well, but he was still breathing.

Harry looked around. He couldn't hear Van Owen or the girl. Whatever was happening in that cabin, it would have to wait. This boy was dying.

Harry knelt and placed his hands under the boy's shoulders and started dragging him, into the grass, along the edge of the tobacco fields, down to the old toolshed that only Harry used these days.

As he pushed the door open and lowered the boy onto the splintery floor, Harry finally asked, "What's your name?"

The boy's voice was faint, weak. "Warren," he said. "Warren Kelly."

ACKNOWLEDGEMENTS

When Shirley Ariker read an early draft of this novel, she told me that I hadn't yet lived enough with the characters. She was right. I've now spent so many years with them that they've grown weary of me and are eager to live on their own on these pages. Thank you, Shirley, for your wisdom, guidance, and support. Thank you also to Karen Sylander, who gave me confidence early on when I needed it; to Thelma Mariano, who gave me the insight to rework the structure; and to Tom Adelman, who gave me the courage to spend hours on each sentence.

This is a work of historical fantasy, so I had some leeway to play with history. Even so, I did considerable research to ensure that I knew the history and that I didn't stray irrevocably far from it. To that end, I must thank the late Dr. Clark Everling, who recommended sources to help me comprehend the barbarism of the Middle Passage, the people who justified the ownership of human beings, and the mindsets that drove both of those atrocities.

Finally, I thank the two who give me reason and strength every day.

ABOUT THE AUTHOR

R.B. Woodstone is a writer, educator, and musician living in Brooklyn, New York, with his wife, their child, and two nutty animals.

R.B. is fascinated by stories that blend fantasy and history. He is white and respects that some people are uncomfortable with white authors writing Black characters, but he believes that white Americans must explore and address the ramifications of slavery, one of America's original sins. He is drawn to write these stories, some of which are seen best through the eyes of Black characters. To that end, R.B. labors to create Black protagonists who exist for their own sake and not as machinery to facilitate the emergence of white protagonists.

Half of the proceeds from this novel will be donated to Equal Justice Initiative.

R.B. is currently working on several novels including *Time in Chains*, the first sequel to *Chains of Time*. He is also writing a rock musical based on Dante's *Inferno*.

Made in the USA
Las Vegas, NV
02 May 2024

89435146R00187